CHAMPION *of*
FATE

ALSO BY KENDARE BLAKE

CHAMPION

of

FATE

KENDARE BLAKE

Quill Tree Books
An Imprint of HarperCollinsPublishers

This book is dedicated to Mia Togle,
One of my very first readers,
And to my horse, Lassie,
Who both passed away in 2020

These ageless warriors and immortal horses are for you.

ONE

THE FOUNDLING

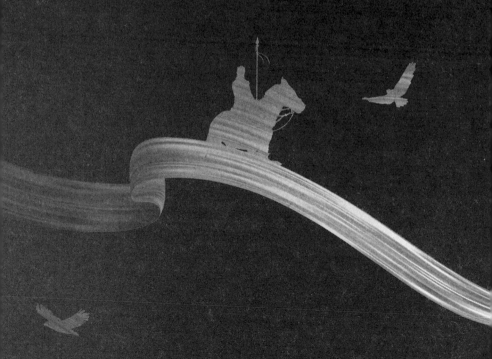

1.

THE SETTLEMENT

The rice balls in the basket looked wrong. It didn't matter which way she stacked them or how carefully she and Mama had rolled and rerolled them into perfect shapes, stuffing each with sweetened paste made from the fruit that grew so plentifully around the new settlement. New fruit, tangy and soft, with a texture somewhere between bread and a root vegetable. Fruit that Reed had never seen before they came, not even in the large marketplace by the pier, where nearly anything could be found.

"Enough fussing with those balls," Mama said. She had changed into her finest shift: soft linen dyed a dark crimson. "They will taste no better, and you're likely to dent them. Pick up the basket. Let's go."

She sounded not cross but distracted, like she was giving the order to herself rather than to Reed. Today they went to see Orna, the Wise Woman. And Mama was no more excited about it than Reed was.

"She won't even eat them if she knows I touched them," Reed said. And to make the point she reached out a finger and touched one again.

"That isn't true," Mama said. But she used her thumbs to wipe spots of dirt from her daughter's face and tugged her shoulders straight before they marched out of the lodge.

Reed didn't like the new settlement. A new settlement for a new beginning, Papa said, but it was a jungle—hot and wild, the air too wet, and everything seemed to fight them: branches snapped back and hit her in the nose. Long grasses tangled around her slim, tan ankles to keep her from getting where she was going. Reed missed the port city where she'd grown up. Stone-paved roads and strong buildings, horses and ships and merchants who spoke many tongues.

"Why does it matter if Orna likes me or not?" Reed asked as she and her mother walked. "She can't do anything to me."

"It matters because it is unlucky. And because eventually it will make others . . . It will change the way others look at you." Mama paused and reached down to smooth Reed's long, dark hair. "Besides, she does like you. She was only irritable because of the seasickness and then the travel."

Orna was on the last boat to arrive in the port from their home country. It was her arrival as much as their readiness that signaled it was time to depart for the settlement. Papa and Mama said she was a great mystic and a great healer who bent the ear of the gods. And she had hated little Reed the moment she set her old eyes on her.

"Mater Orna," Mama said when they reached the door of the lodge. She used the honorary 'mater' to signify that they came to her as family. Had they come for healing or blessings, Mama would have called her "Healer Orna" or "Wise Orna," as the case allowed.

"Come in."

They stepped through the door—which was not much of a door but a flap made from woven reeds and plant fibers, the same fibers that comprised the basket that Reed held—and found Orna seated on the floor, on silk pillows and a thick wool rug. Reed had heard

Mama whisper that the pillows wouldn't last long in the heat and wetness before they started to grow mold. Killy, the oldest daughter of the family who shared space with the Wise Woman, came forward to greet them from where she sat in the far corner, tending three toddlers. But when Orna saw them she simply said, "Oh, it's you," and went back to playing a solitary game with colored stones that Reed didn't know how to play.

Mama nudged her, and Reed stepped forward to offer the basket of rice balls.

"For you, Mater Orna," Reed said, and lowered her head. She and Mama waited in the silence. Long silence. Until Mama lost her temper.

"You don't really mean to ignore her when she is right in front of you!"

"When who is right in front of me?" Orna asked.

Mama's lips drew into a thin, grim line, an expression that Reed knew well. But Orna didn't seem afraid, despite Mama's great height and her strong arms, muscled from pulling fish from the sea and the river. The men of their people worked the earth. Papa knew how to make brick from mud and clay, how to sow seed and build lodges, but one day, Reed would work the water like her mother, strong enough to wade into the current and pull up the traps of crab and crayfish, strong enough to battle the fish who bit their lines. Even the flat ones, who hugged the silt and sand at the bottom.

"Reed is a good girl and a hard worker. I don't care who you are; I won't let you treat her like she is cursed!"

Reed's chest warmed as Mama pulled her to her waist. No one was as fierce as Mama was. Not Papa. Not Auntie Lira. And certainly not mean Orna, who sat on legs like thin sticks and had cheeks like empty cloth.

"I never said she was cursed," Orna said. "Nor did I say she was bad. I only said she was not ours." At last, she looked at Reed, and Reed wished she hadn't. The emptiness in that look made her feel even more invisible than before. "Not ours," Orna said again. "Not mine and not yours, plain for anyone to see. So why get attached?"

"Orna," Mama said, and tried once more. "Wise Orna, what does that mean?"

Orna's eyes dropped to the basket of rice balls and for a moment Reed thought they had won, that she would take them and the unpleasant errand would be over.

"Take those out of here," Orna said. "And let the girl have them. Give her something sweet. I do not think she will be with us for much longer."

"What does that old hag know?"

Mama was irate as they walked through the settlement, past other lodges and the communal hearth, past the site of the future church—now just a square of large smooth stones.

"Mama," Reed said, and tugged on her shift. They were passing the enclosure where they kept the goats and sheep and the many donkeys who had helped them carry their belongings through the wet, wooded country. Reed would have liked to stop and feed them a few rice balls, but Mama brushed her hand away and stalked on. She didn't stop until they reached their lodge, and burst through the flap so quickly that it swung back and hit Reed in the face.

"Wise Orna," Mama sneered to herself as she tore out of her good crimson dress and pulled on a white work dress yellowed with water stains. "More like Foolish Orna. Wicked Orna." She wrapped her dark hair in brown fabric and secured it with a rough length of cord.

Mama looked at Reed, and Reed heard Orna's words. *She is not ours. Not mine, not yours.*

"What a lot of nonsense."

Reed peered into the basket of rice balls, and Mama's foul mood eased: she cracked a rueful smile and laughed, which made Reed laugh, too.

"Go ahead," she said. She reached in for a rice ball and took a big bite. "We can have a treat before going to the river. We deserve it, I'd say."

Reed took two rice balls before going to change out of her good shift. By the river they dressed for the heat, with dark fabric over their shoulders to protect from the sun and white linens for easy wading into the shallows. River work should have been cooling, but where the water stagnated in the bend, it was sometimes as warm as a bath.

She walked with Mama out of the settlement to the river, eating a rice ball in tiny bites to make it last. She tucked the other one into a pouch around her neck, too high for the water to reach. She thought about offering it to Mama. But instead she decided to save it for Grey Anders, her favorite donkey.

That night, Reed lay by herself, tired after hours in the sun and mud, stretched out in the shadows while the rest of the lodge talked; gathered families trading the stories of the day. Papa sat on the only chair with two of the smaller children on his knees. He had his shirt off and laid across his lap. Mama snatched it from him and flicked him with it.

"Dress before dinner," she said, smiling. "You're starting to look like an Orillian."

"And so I am," he said, but he took the shirt back and pulled it over his head. "So are we all, now that Orillia is our home. In this new place we can leave our old things behind: no more leathers and woven cloaks. No more armor." He placed the children on the floor and stood to take Mama's face in his hands. "Or your jeweled pins. This place demands new ways."

"And what about what we were? Does that have no value?" Mama didn't often speak of their lives before the port, but Reed had heard her say that in their home country, Papa was a rich man and a great soldier. Stories like that made Reed wonder why they ever left. But Papa spoke of the settlement as a great adventure.

Reed didn't see the adventure in biting flies and digging for clams. She didn't feel it in the hard ground under her sleeping mat. But she loved her father. Everything would be fine, as long as he and Mama said it would be, and Reed let her eyes drift shut.

The raiders came while the fires burned low and bowls from evening meals still rested in drowsy laps. They wove themselves into the settlement on silent feet, first one, then two, then many more, armed with short swords and spears and sharp knives strapped to their belts. They looped through the families in loose coils, like a lazy noose tossed around the head of an unwitting animal.

And then they pulled it taut.

Reed was asleep when the attack began, her head resting on her arm, thrown up toward the cooking fire as if waiting for someone to place a bowl of stew in her hand. She didn't see her parents' faces freeze when the raiders stepped into the light, their cheeks marked with a blue paste. She didn't see her father stand and hold out his hands, nor hear him say, "We have nothing." So she didn't see the raider swing his sword and cut him down.

It was her mother's scream that finally ripped her from sleep, and in the end, it was also what saved her. Mama charged their attacker and held his arms high, pushing him through the lodge like an ox. She meant to shove him right out through the door flap, but instead he pivoted and they slammed into the lodge wall, which had been built for peace from long sticks, plant fibers, and dried clay. The entire side of the lodge came down, right onto Reed, and she pulled her knees up tight as it knocked the breath from her lungs. Scrambling, she clawed at the ground, afraid she would be trampled and crushed into the dirt. All through the settlement came screams and wails and the sounds of running, stomping feet. The air smelled of smoke.

"Mama!" Reed pushed herself toward what she hoped was the way out. Rough bark and sharp grasses cut into her shoulders and legs. She had to help Mama. She would fight, and then they would run and hide by the river in the tall grass. When the sun came up they would find Papa and the others.

She pushed forward toward an orange-red glow, more light than the cook fire usually gave off. *The lodge is burning*, she thought, and then her mother's body hit the ground in front of her.

Mama lay on the dirt floor, head rolling from side to side as blood ran from her chest to pool in the hollows of her collarbone. Reed froze.

"Mama!"

Mama looked at her. She saw her, huddled in the wreckage. *"Stay,"* she mouthed.

"I can't," Reed whispered. But she did as she was told. She remained still and quiet as fewer and fewer screams cut through the night, and the fire set to the lodge burned itself out. She stayed through the dark of night and into the morning, when the sun came up and showed her that her mother was dead.

2.

THE WARRIORS BY THE RIVER

The two riders had been on the road a long time and looked the worse for it; the light hemp of their shirts had pulled thin to holes, and they were spattered with mud to the knees. No one passing would have given them a second glance, except to note that they were women, and if they looked closer, that they were beautiful underneath all the dust and muck. But these were no ordinary riders. Nor were their horses, who they stopped to water at the stream, ordinary horses. They were Areion, sacred mounts of the order of the Aristene. They could have run for days without drinking, reaching speeds that would outpace the fastest of hunting cats. It was also said that the horses could speak, but only if one was worthy of their words.

Whether that was true not even the riders could say. They had raised the Areion from foals and never heard so much as a whisper. They had, however, caught many a hoof to the backside when the oats were late.

"Do you think we'll reach an inn tonight, or will we camp again?" the taller of the two riders asked, leaning back in the saddle to stretch her neck.

"Pft. Court life has made you soft." Her companion swung a leg over her horse's withers and jumped to the ground. She shook dirt from her dark gold hair. "I haven't been at any court for more than a decade"—she let the sand from her hair cascade from her fist: enough to make a small anthill—"and look at me now."

The tall rider, called Aster, laughed. "Indeed, look at you. But I didn't say that I preferred an inn to a field. It was only a question."

Her companion, Veridian, smirked and knelt to drink beside her horse before dunking her entire head in the stream. She looked well, Aster had to admit. Not lonely. Nor bitter, or at least not any more bitter than usual. Aster had not seen her in fifteen years, when Veridian had turned her back on the Aristene order and been labeled an apostate. But time didn't matter to them like it did to others. Its passing was of no more consequence than the passing of the water in the current, and Veridian looked the same as she always had: green-eyed and defiant.

"Perhaps I'll go into those woods and try for a grouse," Veridian said. "Roasted meat and crackling skin will ease the burden of another night sleeping on the grass."

"I wasn't complaining!" Aster laughed. But Veridian was already reaching into Everfall's saddlebag for her crossbow and bolts. It would be nice to have a grouse for supper. The country they rode through was unfamiliar and sparsely inhabited. Some roads had been left unfinished, suddenly ending in a patch of grass or a line of trees, or growing gradually thinner until they became little more than a game trail. But the birds in the region were fat, with a mild flavor from feeding on rice, both wild-grown and cultivated. The grouse had funny little tufted crowns and were depressingly easy to shoot, as if they were unused to being hunted. Aster had half a mind to snare a breeding pair and bring them back to the Citadel.

She was considering how nice they would be, a little flock of tufted birds, all her own to be baked or fried, when she looked down and saw the stain of red in the water.

The horses' heads came up.

"Do you smell that?" Aster asked.

Veridian tested the wind. "Ashes. Death."

Aster's hands gripped her reins until her knuckles shone white. "And *glory*."

Reed shivered, fists clenching and releasing as she huddled beneath the wreckage of her family's lodge. Panicked sweat had coated her and brought on a chill. She didn't know how much longer she could go unnoticed. She hadn't heard their language spoken in hours— only that of their attackers, a tongue that she didn't recognize, even from all her years spent living in the port.

The attackers were not from here. They didn't have the look of the Orillian people they had encountered. These men were tall and broad-shouldered. They painted their pale cheeks with blue mud. One, who she glimpsed by turning her body sideways and pushing slightly against the weight of the wall, had a long gold beard that ended in a braid. Now that the sun had come up, the beard seemed to bother him in the heat. He rubbed at it and scratched, and it dripped with water like he had wet it down.

Reed watched and listened, slowly moving beneath the wall. She had tested its weight in the night and found it not too heavy now that she was nearer to the edge. If no one found her under the debris, she might be able to escape when night came.

Except, she couldn't leave Mama.

Her mother still lay where she fell, her face turned toward Reed in the wreckage.

Throughout the settlement, the raiders were collecting what spoils they could. They slaughtered goats to roast and led donkeys away on ropes. They picked up shards of broken pottery and plate; one man with ragged, shoulder-length hair picked up a woven mat and bent it back and forth. Then he snorted and dropped it, and Reed wanted to break his teeth with a stone.

She knew they would never find what they sought: Mama's jeweled necklaces and gold hairpins were buried with Reed, somewhere under the fallen lodge. When the raiders were asleep, or after they had gone, Reed would dig until she found them, and then she would find her way back to the port. In the port, Reed had been entrusted with many errands, and many times she had traversed the city alone. But now there was no Papa to return to, no Mama to frighten a merchant who stated an unfair price. Maybe she should just stay in the wreckage. Lay her head in the cool dirt and wait until she stopped breathing and joined her family in the beyond.

It might have come to that. Reed was only a child, eight autumns old. None of the gods in the world would have condemned her had she simply decided to give up. A kind god might have even helped her along. But it was not a kind god who found her.

At the raiders' shouts of alarm, Reed jerked herself alert and shifted her position under the collapsed lodge to see, so the remains of the wall wobbled like a loose shell upon her back.

Two riders had come into the settlement. Two women, one on a bright red horse and another on a silvery gray. The raiders took up arms, and the one with the wet beard made his way to the front.

"The whole village annihilated," said one of the women. She

spoke in a common tongue, a language Reed knew well. "Is this really what you sensed?"

"And what you sensed," said her companion. "Don't deny it." Despite being in a circle of armed men, the riders kept moving forward, their horses pushing the raiders and the bearded man closer and closer to Reed and her collapsed lodge. The riders' clothes were filthy, but they didn't carry themselves like beggars. The one with wild blond hair, who rode the red horse, cast her eyes over the body of Reed's mother, prone and dead, her unarmed hands open. Reed's small arms shook with anger. *She is my mother*, she wanted to shout. *And she fought!*

"There is no glory here," the woman said quietly. "Only panic. No one put up a fight." She nodded to Reed's mother. "Except for that one."

The bearded man leveled a spear at them. He asked what sounded like a question, and the blond woman answered him in his own language.

Reed watched. At any moment, she expected the men to strike, and the women to be murdered before her very eyes. But the blond woman talked, and the men listened. Reed noted the weapons the women carried: short swords on their backs and a longer one in a scabbard affixed to their saddles—she thought she glimpsed the edge of a shield beneath the saddle's covering of leather. And then she realized that the gray horse was staring at her.

Reed didn't know how the horse had seen her. And she certainly didn't know why it should be so interested. But sure enough, the horse was staring.

"I know them," the blond woman said to her brown-headed companion. "They're Ithernan. Their lands are across the sea, to the northeast. They raid in the late summer and the fall for treasure and goods."

"These people had little of either."

The blond turned again to the bearded man and spoke a few words, then listened to his answer.

"It's been an unsuccessful campaign," she explained. "They make for home now to try again to the west. This"—she gestured to the ruined settlement—"was something they just happened across. And it's no business of ours."

Reed started to breathe hard. The women were going to leave. They didn't care that her family was dead. She looked at her mother, so fierce, murdered and cold on the ground, and screamed.

Reed sprang forth, legs aching after so long lying bent and still. She snatched a knife from the hip of the nearest raider, ready to drive it into their hearts. One of the men grabbed her by the neck and twisted the knife from her hand.

She struggled and snarled and tried to bite as she was hoisted up and her hands and feet bound. Over her grunts and shrieks of fury the bearded man spoke with the blond woman, and Reed twisted hard to look: the gray horse, and now her brown-haired rider, watched as she was carried off. Perhaps it was only a trick of her frightened eyes, but for a moment the woman didn't look like a dirt-streaked wanderer. For just a moment, Reed caught a glimpse of something else: a warrior, glowing brightly and gilded in silver and soft white fabric.

"Don't leave!" Reed shouted in the common tongue as the women turned their horses and rode away. But the man who carried her casually covered her mouth.

3.

TWO SPINDLE-LEGGED COLTS

They found her mother's jewels. It must have been small consolation to the raiders: a poor prize after all the trouble they had gone to sacking the settlement. But Mama's small bag of finery had been more to her than money—it had been memories. The pieces she kept back when all the others were sold off to buy supplies.

"Those are my mother's!" Reed shouted, and when a raider approached she kicked hard with her bound feet, kicking and kicking until he hauled her up painfully by her bound hands. He spoke words at her and squeezed her face hard. She jerked away and bit, digging her teeth into the meaty part between his thumb and forefinger.

"Ah!" he cried, and she grinned around his skin. Eventually he hit her in the side of the head hard enough to make her vision black in and out, and she slumped back into the dirt.

She came to later, when someone put a waterskin to her lips.

"I hate you," she said after she drank, and the raider grunted like he understood. "I wish you were dead." He grunted again. Then he cut the bindings on her feet and dragged her up by the arm.

He walked her past the charred wreck of the lodges, and as they passed a pile of bodies set to burn he made to cover her eyes. Reed shoved his hand away. They were her people. She had called many of them "auntie" and "uncle" even though they shared no blood. Now they lay stacked and covered in dark swarms of flies. On the top of the pile was old Orna. And even the sight of Orna, who she hated, made her sad.

The raider marched Reed out of the settlement to the riverbank. The donkeys were there, tied together and loaded with packs of goods all wrapped in leather and furs. In the water, slender wooden crafts bobbed, anchored to the bottom, and many more sat beached on the bank. They must have been able to travel quickly and quietly in crafts like those. No one must ever hear them coming.

The raider nudged Reed forward, through a patch of tall grass. Staked in the center, grazing, was a long-legged black colt.

"What is this horse doing here?" Reed asked. One horse. One horse, among the boats. And he was a beautiful horse, with a coat that shone and bright brown eyes and not a single white hair. She hadn't seen his like since leaving the port.

The raiders began to load back into their boats. One came to lead Reed and the black colt on the bank as the boats launched down the river.

Good, Reed thought. The river ran nearly to the port. Perhaps someone at the mouth of the river would recognize her. Perhaps they would rescue her and take her in.

But why would anyone do that? She was nothing now. Only another mouth to feed.

They hadn't gone far before they had to stop for the night—that they had tried to depart at all with so little sun remaining spoke of their eagerness to be out of the jungle. Once again they drew their crafts up onto the bank, and those that did not fit were anchored to the bottom. The raider who led her tossed her half a skin of water and a few strips of dried fish before tying her to a tree. She intended to kick them away, but the moment she sniffed at the fish she began to devour it, savoring the salty chewiness and draining the waterskin in a few large gulps.

Reed wiped her mouth and looked around. The raiders were distracted, but they were everywhere, and there were not many moments when one or another pair of eyes were not on her. She stared right back. Their faces were dispassionate, not even curious. She didn't understand why they had kept her.

Sand sprayed against her calf. There was no grass where they were tied, and the black colt was pawing crankily.

"I'd have saved you some fish, but you wouldn't have eaten it," Reed said. "Besides, you don't look like you're going to starve."

The colt was well-fed to the point of being chubby. It was odd that they would bring him on such a journey when he was too young to ride. He must have been taken in another attack. Taken from his home like she was taken from hers.

"Here," she whispered.

At the sound of her voice, the colt came closer to sniff at her. She put her hands to his cheeks and rested her forehead against his until he nudged her hard in the chest.

"Hey!" she said, but the colt continued to nudge, lips reaching for the pouch she had around her neck. The rice ball. She'd forgotten all about it.

She took it out of the pouch. It had dried up and been slightly crushed, but when she held it out the colt took it in one bite. For a few moments she felt almost well, almost happy, and as she watched him chew, a fierce wave of affection and protectiveness rushed over her.

"I will look after you," she whispered. "I don't know how. But I promise I will."

Aster and Veridian hadn't ridden far from the destroyed settlement. They hadn't really been able to—Aster's mount, the gray mare called Rabbit, had walked so slowly that her hooves left drag marks in the dirt.

"Eat your grouse," Veridian said, watching Aster poke at her meal, golden and roasted on a spit. She took a large bite of her own, as if Aster was a child and needed to be shown how. "What's the matter with you?"

"I can't stop thinking about the girl," she said. "Did you see the way she burst out from under that collapsed hut? The way she charged?"

Veridian grunted. "Of course I did. I was right there."

"She couldn't have been more than ten."

"Younger, I'd say," Veridian mused around a mouthful of bird. "Maybe seven or eight."

"So brave."

"So angry. And who can blame her? She probably saw her whole family slaughtered. And she will join them soon enough." Veridian threw a wing bone into the fire and watched it sizzle before tearing into thigh meat.

"What do you mean?" Aster asked.

"What did you think would happen to her?"

"I thought she would be traded off with the other goods. Or

kept as labor or a future wife."

"The Ithernan don't marry outside their kind. And they don't take slaves. If they did they wouldn't have killed absolutely everyone."

"The Ithernan," Aster said. She'd never had occasion to deal with them. "You know them well."

Veridian nodded. "One of their heroes, a long time ago, was mine. That blue they wear on their faces—it's to draw the eye of their war god."

"You know why they kept the girl, then?"

"To use as a sacrifice. They'll cut her throat over the prow of their leader's ship for a safe journey home."

Aster frowned.

"They must've been glad to find her," Veridian went on. "Normally they keep some of the prettier ones alive to choose from, but the attack must've gotten out of hand. Or they already had something to sacrifice. Another girl or a fast horse. They're an interesting people—they believe the soul resides in the eyes. So eyes are sacred. With my green ones I was nearly worshipped as a god." She went on talking, and eating, as Aster's roasted bird slipped lower and lower, until the spit was almost resting on the ground.

"What?" Veridian groaned finally. "What is it?"

"I felt Her there today," said Aster, and Veridian didn't need to ask who she meant. Kleia Gloria, the goddess of glory. The only god an Aristene answered to.

"No, you didn't."

"Just because you have turned your back on Her, and on the Order—"

"That girl was eight years old," Veridian said. "She's a child."

"You felt it, too."

"I did not."

But no matter what Veridian said or how she protested, she, too, was still an Aristene, down deep. And even if she truly hadn't sensed anything back at the settlement, she would know that Aster would not be moved.

"Fine," Veridian said, and threw away another picked-clean bone. "What do you want to do?"

4.
SACRIFICES

The man leading Reed tugged her forward, but it was mostly out of habit. Reed had stopped resisting, and even if she hadn't, he was too busy swatting flies to notice. She had woken before sunrise, her head resting on the black colt's soft, warm flank, and searched the bank for the citrus grass that kept the insects away. She rubbed it all over herself and the horse and laid back down before any of the raiders were the wiser. *Let them suffer and slap*, she thought. *Let them wonder why we don't and why we smell like fruit while they stink.*

Except instead of wondering, the raiders seemed pleased. And before they had set out they had fed her well, and given the colt a good grooming. They had been almost kind—until Reed had tried to bite them.

In the river, the raiders' agile boats moved with an effortless swiftness. They held more cargo than she thought would be possible, transporting the goats and lightening the load on the donkeys. They would reach the river port in half the time it took for her family to reach the settlement, bogged down with so many old people and children. Her father would have eagerly traded with them for one of those boats, had they come in the daylight with weapons sheathed.

At her side, the black colt lifted his head to scent the air.

"What is it?" Reed asked. The horse snorted and his short tail rose. He smelled something. Other horses.

Shouts broke out among the raiders, and paddles went upright in the river to slow the boats. It was a clumsily fast stop, full of bumping and curses, the raiders dammed up together like wayward logs. The man leading her gave her a sharp tug—a reminder to behave—and moved to hold tight to the black colt's rope halter. Reed craned her neck and pushed up onto her toes.

It was the riders. The same ones who came to the settlement after the attack. Two women, one on a red horse and one on a gray, waiting on the bank.

Like before, the shorter one with the wild blond hair did most of the talking. But she dismounted this time and greeted the bearded leader with a grasp of wrists when he waded onto shore.

Reed noticed that the gray horse was staring at her again. So was the woman on her back. The blond one gestured in Reed's direction and reached into a leather purse for a handful of silver coins. It was a lot of money. The leader touched his beard. He shook his head.

"They won't give her up," the blond woman called.

In the saddle, the tall brown-haired one sighed and lazily drew the sword off her back. *Was the woman stupid?* Reed wondered. The raiders were warriors, and in far greater number. But when the woman dismounted to join the other rider on the ground, the men didn't attack. They didn't even move. Finally, the man with the beard barked words and held his hand out for the coin. The tall woman put her sword away and came toward her and the colt, pushing past the man who held their ropes.

The woman bent to cut her hands free and Reed's knees clacked together. Since the settlement she had felt nothing but red flashes of anger and the cold emptiness of heartbreak, and now her heart pounded, ashamed to hope.

"My name is Aster," the woman said in the common tongue. "What is yours?"

"Reed," she said softly.

"Reed?"

"It's not my real, real name. But that's what I'm called."

"Well, then, Reed," Aster said, her voice steady and low, not unlike Reed's mother's. "My friend over there is Veridian. Would you like to come with us?"

"Come with you where?" Reed asked. A stupid question, she supposed, because what could be worse than to remain here, with her family's murderers?

"That will be up to you."

Reed hesitated. She reached out and stroked the black colt's neck—he was still focused on the riders' horses, his tail twitching with excitement.

Up the bank, the blond woman shouted, "What's happening? What's taking so long?"

"Is he coming, too?" Reed asked, and nodded to the colt.

"No. We've only enough silver for one of you, and I don't think they would let us buy him anyway."

"Why not?"

"Aster," Veridian shouted. "Get her up!"

Reed braced for a harsh hand on her arm or to be thrown over the big woman's shoulder. But Aster didn't move.

"You will be safer with us," she said. "I promise."

"Of course she'll be safer with us," Veridian grumbled, making her way down the bank. "With them she'll have her throat cut as soon as they make the port."

Reed blinked.

"They kept you alive to use as a sacrifice." Veridian bent down and looked into Reed's face. "A sacrifice to their gods for safe passage to their lands. Do you want to be a sacrifice?"

Reed blinked again.

"No, of course you don't. Let's go." She grabbed Reed by the wrist and started pulling.

"Wait, what about him?" Reed looked at the colt.

"They're happy enough with him. They were going to use him anyway, before they lucked into you."

They were going to use him anyway. They were going to sacrifice the colt.

"No!" Reed shouted, and dug in her heels, even though it felt like trying to hold back a two-ox cart. She didn't know how the woman could be so strong. "Let go of me!" Veridian dragged Reed across the sandy bank, through the raiders, who began to grin and laugh. No matter how she struggled and pulled against her it made no difference. So Reed jumped ahead instead and bit her.

"Ow!" Veridian cried, and the men laughed harder. The raider she'd bit before laughed hardest and held up his bandaged hand. "Aster," she growled, and released Reed to cradle her bitten arm. "She bites."

"I'm not going anywhere without him," Reed said.

"He's not even hers."

"He's mine now." Reed couldn't explain it. But he was.

Aster turned and looked at the colt. Then she looked at Reed. "He's a very fine horse." She smiled a small secret smile. "Maybe he isn't even really a horse."

"Aster." Veridian rolled her eyes. "You are not serious."

"Offer them more," she said to Veridian. "Offer it all."

"They won't take it," Veridian grumbled. But she turned and called out. The leader shook his head. She called out again. And again, he shook his head. Veridian's shoulders slumped. "They still refuse," she said to Aster.

Aster took the colt's rope from the man who held it, plucking it from his grip as easily as if he were a toddler holding a doll. She handed the rope to Reed.

"Take him," she said, "and wait for us over in the trees."

A ball of fear rolled in Reed's stomach. *Don't,* she wanted to say. *Just leave us, don't get hurt, don't make it worse!* But Aster gestured toward the trees, and Reed did as she was told. When the fighting broke out she started to cry and ran with the colt. They would get away together. They wouldn't stay and watch the women be cut down where they stood.

But the grunts and screams were not from the women. They were from the raiders, and Reed peeked out from behind a tree.

Aster and Veridian fought alone. Each had been quickly challenged by several men, and several men were knocked away just as quickly—their bodies lay prone in the sand. One appeared to have been tossed far enough to float in the water. In the port where she grew up, Reed had seen many scuffles. She'd even seen a duel with short, sharp daggers. But she'd never seen anyone fight so well or move so fast. She'd never seen a woman knock a man back on his heels, not even Mama when she was really angry.

The battle didn't last long. It was not, honestly, much of a battle. More than half of the raiders had stayed in their boats—some stood frozen with one leg in the water, as if they'd changed their minds about getting involved midway through.

"Enough," said the man with the beard, using the common tongue; the word sounded strange and almost pretty wrapped in his raider accent. "Enough, Aristene."

The two women sheathed their swords and let the men pick up themselves and their companions. As far as Reed could tell, they hadn't killed anyone.

"Reed," Aster called gently. "Come out now."

Reed stepped slowly from behind the tree. The black colt stomped and swished his tail; he whickered to the red and the gray horses for reassurance, but they ignored him.

"Give his rope to me," Aster said, and Reed let the rope go. She felt herself lifted easily onto the gray horse's back. "You'll ride with me and Rabbit. Your colt will be right behind us."

Veridian mounted her red horse and sighed as she tossed the whole purse of coins onto the ground. "They had better be worth it," she said. "For so much silver and combat."

TWO

THE INITIATE

5.

THE SUMMER CAMP—EIGHT YEARS LATER

Silver and combat. Eight years ago that was what Aster and Veridian had paid to save them. So that's what the horse was named. Silver-and-Combat. Silco, for short.

Reed leaned against the north pasture fence and watched him bite the other horses' legs and whirl away before they could bite him back. Silco was still a naughty orphan. He had grown up with sharp edges and a hoof-stomping temper. But he had also grown up strong, and fast, with the good looks that made most ignore the flaws in his personality.

If only Reed could say the same. But she had nothing to soften her edges.

Reed whistled, and Silco trotted to her, anticipating a piece of dried fruit or a handful of grain or even a honeyed biscuit. When he discovered that all she had was a scratch for his forehead, he snorted and stuck his face through the fence to check the folds of her clothing.

"I'm spoiling you," she said. "Look how rude you are." Rude, yes, as he grabbed the edge of her tunic with his teeth and tore a strip of it loose. Yet still the finest horse in the herd. Someday, Reed would be an Aristene, and the black colt would be her Areion mount, and it was a good thing he hadn't grown up to have knobby knees and a crooked back, lest they be the laughingstock of the order.

The black colt. Reed still thought of him that way, like she still thought of herself sometimes as the spindle-legged girl who had arrived at the Summer Camp so many years ago. But Silco was no colt anymore—he was a horse, and she a young woman, an initiate of the Order of the Aristene, about to embark on her Hero's Trial.

When she'd first come to the camp for her training, she hadn't really even known what an Aristene was, only that Aster was one and Veridian used to be, and they were strong enough to make an entire band of raiders lay down their swords. Back then all she'd known was that she'd lost her family and her place in the world. And that the order had promised her a new one.

If she could reach out and take it.

"That must be why Aster has been gone so long in Atropa," Reed said to Silco as he chewed on her tunic. "Because finally the time for the trial has come."

Reed had not been to the city of the Aristene since Aster had brought her to the Summer Camp, a seat of power in the Verdant Mountains, capped by a peak they called the Storm King. But Reed remembered Atropa better than she remembered anything from that time. Better than the blood-soaked blur of the settlement where Aster had found her, and sometimes better than even her own mother's face, a truth that made her stomach tighten.

Atropa, city of white and gold and unearthly quiet. City of warriors. A safe haven outside of the world. Aster had taken her there after the slaughter of her settlement. Together they had traveled through the black sickness of the Veil, so Reed could be taken to the Citadel to meet the elders. It had been full dark, but Reed still remembered how the gold dome of the fortress had glittered under the stars. One day soon, Atropa would be her home, and Aster and the Aristene would truly be her family. She would be like them and have what they had. Strength. Wisdom. Great purpose in service to Kleia Gloria. And all of that immortal time.

She looked at Silco and parted his long black forelock. The immortal horse part wasn't so bad either.

"Reed!"

It was Gretchen. Reed would've known even if she hadn't spoken. The other initiate's light, hurried footsteps on the path were unmistakable.

"Combat training," Gretchen said when she reached her. She leaned over the fence and gave Silco a smacking kiss on the muzzle; he shook his head and turned to swat her in the face with his tail on his way back to the herd. Not nice. He was a very not-nice horse. "You're going to be late."

"Now we're both going to be late," said Reed.

"Good." Gretchen rubbed her right shoulder. Her Aristene mentor, Jana, had Gretchen doing spear throws late into the night. "I'll never be as good at the spears as she is."

"Not without the Aristene magic. Not until you are a full member of the order."

"Not even then," said Gretchen. "I don't know why she bothers."

"Because Jana is one of the finest spear throwers. What kind of mentor would she be if she didn't try to pass on that skill?"

Gretchen tossed her brown braids back—two, one on each side of her head, perfect handles for her mentor to pull on when the girl did something wrong, so Reed didn't know why she wore them like that. "I don't see Aster driving you into the ground over her finest skill."

"That's because Aster has no finest skill," said Reed proudly. "She's good at them all."

"Good at them all but great at none," said the third initiate, the green-eyed and beautiful Lyonene. Lyonene stood in the path, her hands on her hips. "Aster is the perfect Aristene. Well-rounded in talent but with no talent too remarkable. Nothing that could steal glory from her hero and claim it for herself." She shook out her lion's mane of gold—she was aptly named—and jerked her head for them to hurry along.

Reed leaped up onto the path, large strides on long legs. It was all true, what Lyonene said, and no Aristene would have taken offense. But something in the way she said it made the palms of Reed's hands itch. Lots of things that Lyonene said made the palms of Reed's hands itch.

"Aster is also a pathfinder," said Reed, referring to Aster's special skill, an aspect of the magic that not all Aristene possessed. Aster saw the pathways of battle, hidden routes beneath fortresses, places to put their feet in a difficult climb.

"So she is as glorious as a map," said Lyonene, and Reed frowned.

"An Aristene is not meant to be glorious," said Gretchen. "We are only its vessels."

"Its vessel and its architect," Lyonene said. Few heroes would rise so high or reach so far, were it not for the Aristene's guiding hands. "Glory is ours to make, Gretchen, and ours to bestow."

"As its humble servants," said Reed. "Don't forget."

"As if any of us could, after all these years," said Lyonene. "And

I forget nothing; I am a sharper study than you, Reed."

"So you are always saying." But Reed smiled. It was true, after all. Of the three initiates in the Summer Camp, Lyonene was the fastest and the cleverest. The most deadly fighter. And she was the most beautiful, a weapon she knew well how to wield. Lyonene burned the brightest. Gretchen tried the hardest. And Reed . . . Reed was by far the most devoted.

"Now hurry up, both of you! I don't know why I let you drag me down." Lyonene laughed and tugged Gretchen along; the sleeve of Gretchen's tunic slid back to show the purple cloud of bruises.

"Gretchen." Lyonene stopped and pushed the fabric away. The bruises were old, already fading to yellow at the edges. Lyonene frowned. She looked at Reed.

"What did this?" Reed demanded, taking her friend by the elbow.

"Jana's war hammer. My shield broke against my shoulder." Gretchen tugged her arm away. "Do not do anything, Reed. I'm fine."

"Of course you are." Lyonene threw an arm around her and lightly flipped Gretchen's braid. But as they walked, she and Reed traded an angry glance. When they reached the area in the village used for combat training, no more than a horse corral and a length of green pasture—they split apart to select weapons. Reed grabbed a long bladed spear and spun it back and forth. It was nothing that an Aristene warrior couldn't handle, nothing that would do real damage. But if she swung it hard enough . . .

She stared into the center of the corral, where the mentors stood, waiting. Jana, Gretchen's mentor, leaned on a sword. She was tall and pale blond, a sharp contrast to Lyonene's mentor, Sabil, who was all short, fierce darkness. Reed's mentor, Aster, wasn't there, still lingering in Atropa. But that was good. If she'd seen what Reed was about to do, she'd have been displeased.

"Not a spear, you fool," Lyonene hissed quietly, and deftly twisted it out of Reed's hands. "You might actually cut her. Here." She gave her a wooden staff instead. But before Reed could curl her fingers around it, Gretchen yanked it away.

"I said do nothing," she whispered.

"I wasn't going to do much," said Reed. "Only feign a poorly aimed throw; she would have dodged it."

"What is the point of that?"

Reed shrugged. "It would make me feel better."

"It would make me look weak," Gretchen said, and tossed the staff aside. "I can handle my mentor myself."

"Someone ought to do something," Lyonene muttered.

"Then why not you?" Gretchen asked. "Why do you put the staff in Reed's hand and not your own?"

Lyonene looked down. "You know why. We are too near the Hero's Trial now—we could be taken to Atropa for the Granting Ceremony any day—stop sabotaging each other!"

Reed looked at Lyonene, whose face was pure innocence until she rolled her eyes. "Nothing would have happened to you, Foundling," Lyonene said. "You are Aster's, and you are the favorite."

Aster was the senior member of the order, and though Lyonene's mentor, Sabil, was fine and brave, she was not high up enough for Lyonene's tastes. Lyonene would not have truly been happy unless she'd been mentored by one of the elders: Ferreh, who they called the mind. Or Tiern, known as the teeth. But the elders rarely took on initiates. Nor did Aster; she wouldn't have taken Reed had she and Veridian not been the ones to find her, and had Ferreh herself not said that she must.

In the combat corral, Sabil sheathed the knife in her hand and slammed the end of her staff twice into the dirt.

"Lyonene."

The girl slipped quickly through the rails of the fence, taking up a small wooden shield and a blunt wooden sword on her way to face Jana, and nodding to her mentor as Sabil left the field. Initiates didn't fight their mentors in the corral. That was for individual training. In the corral, the mentor was only an observer. And of course, they were there to call the fight.

With Aster away, both Lyonene and Reed would fight Jana, and as Lyonene began to circle, her face was less a lion's than a wolf's. Even though she was smaller-framed than Reed, Lyonene's strength was elastic and tough as the green wood of a new tree. She was made for combat.

Along the fence-line, folk who resided in the Summer Camp village began to show up to watch: merchants from the market, house matrons, and shop workers. Any apprentices who had a view of the corral stopped what they were doing and leaned on their brooms. The training of the Aristene initiates was something to see in the quiet valley where—despite its small population of warriors—nothing much happened. As Jana and Lyonene took their positions, and Sabil took hers at the rail, coins from purses changed hands. Wagers, though not about whether Lyonene would be the victor—an initiate could not best a full member of the order. Instead odds were laid on whether she would end the contest on her back or on a knee. Whether the match would be called on account of a knife at a throat or due to Lyonene's unconsciousness.

"Water?"

A boy offered them a dipper, and Reed bent her head to drink. "Thank you," she said, and wiped her mouth absently before turning her attention back to the corral.

"Poor Emery," said Gretchen. She watched the boy walk away with a sympathetic expression. "He looks at you like you're the ripest fruit on the tree."

"I didn't even realize it was him," said Reed. She glanced at his retreating shape, the tavern keeper's son. He was nice enough, and kind to her since the day she arrived all those years ago when they were both still children. She took Gretchen's arm and directed her back to the fight. "Pay attention."

The sparring match began with Lyonene on the offensive, as was almost always the case. Her blows against the Aristene were hard with nothing held back—sparring with Jana was not like practice with Reed or Gretchen—they aimed to draw blood or leave bruises and were well enough placed to keep Jana on her guard. Over the course of her years of training, Lyonene had bloodied nearly every Aristene in the Summer Camp. Once, she had cut Sabil deep enough to require the wound sewn closed, another fact that lowered Lyonene's view of her mentor.

Reed's eyes narrowed with every strike of the wooden sword, *crack crack* against Jana's staff. She yearned for Lyonene to put the Aristene on her back in the dirt, to bruise her arm like Jana had bruised Gretchen's. An initiate's training must be hard, but Jana took it too far. Aster had briefly knocked Reed unconscious once, but when Reed woke, it was Aster she saw kneeling beside her, holding a wet cloth to her forehead.

In the ring, Lyonene used her shield to bash, and Reed's eyes flickered to Sabil on the rail. Sabil, not Jana, dictated how the fight would proceed, issuing subtle commands to test her initiate's weaknesses. A twist of a wrist was an order for the initiate to be turned toward their off hand. A twisted foot meant to sweep a leg. Every signal too quick and too subtle for the initiate fighting to track. It had taken Reed, Lyonene, and Gretchen years to decipher the code. But now they knew how to watch from the fence and see what was coming.

Reed gripped the wood. In the ring, Lyonene was still on the attack and doing well. She struck hard and fast and backed off, never exposing her weak side—which she did have, even though she denied it. To the average spectator, it would seem that the younger fighter would even win.

In the corner of her eye, Reed saw Sabil flick all four fingers. *Strip the shield.*

Effortlessly, Jana stepped in and knocked Lyonene's sword hand wide, then struck the low end of her staff behind Lyonene's shield. That fast, that easy, and Lyonene's shield lay wobbling in the dirt as she shook the pain out of her wrist.

Back off, Reed thought. One small blunt sword against the long staff was a disadvantage. A larger disadvantage given their already notable difference in size. And she was disappointed in Lyonene—it had been too easy to get her shield away. She should have been able to hang on to it.

Back off, Lyonene. But Lyonene rarely backed off. She fought on instinct, on her gut, and like she always said, training was a time to try things out. *Reed, Reed,* Lyonene would chastise her, *you are so afraid to fail. But if you don't fail here then your first failure will be real—and you will be dead.*

Lyonene attacked head on, striking low to sweep the staff and roll under Jana's legs. On her way past she rolled near her fallen shield and picked it back up, and Reed and Gretchen were not the only ones who cheered.

"Enough." Sabil clapped her hands. "That was a good recovery."

Lyonene nodded to her mentor and returned to her friends, slipping through the fence.

"Gretchen."

Gretchen's pretty face pinched as she ducked into the corral and Jana and Sabil traded places. The initiates all knew how Jana would call this particular match: with orders to exploit the shoulder. To teach her how to fight impaired. To fight through pain. But it wasn't right. Poor Gretchen could barely raise her arm.

"What is the point of this?" Lyonene muttered after Gretchen had limped onto the combat ground. "To punish her for mortal weakness? When she is an Aristene she'll have as much fortitude as any of them. Why test these temporary forms? It's like throwing a caterpillar in the air and being disappointed that it hasn't already mastered flight."

"It's not her body they're testing," said Reed. "It's her heart. If they threw *you* into the air, you would find a way to fly."

Lyonene grinned. "Yes, but not all of us are walking miracles."

In the oval, Gretchen subtly rolled her shoulder. The muscle looked so tight that even from behind the fence Reed could swear she heard it creaking.

"Sabil!" Reed called. "Let me fight next!"

Beside the fence, Jana tilted her blond head. She was no fool. She knew what Reed thought of her tactics. And Reed knew what Jana thought of Aster's. Many nights in the tavern the other mentor had admonished Aster for being too soft.

But before Reed could enter the ring, a messenger arrived and ran to Sabil.

The three initiates straightened tensely.

"Well?" Lyonene demanded when Sabil's pause went on overlong. "What was the message?"

"The message was that Aster will return tomorrow. And she is bringing the elders with her."

6.

THE VIRTUES OF INITIATES

"The elders," Gretchen said, staring down into her mug of ale. "There is only one reason for them to come here."

"The Hero's Trial. They come to invite us to the Granting of Heroes." Lyonene poured herself more ale from their pitcher. They had come to the tavern to gossip and guess, to worry about the elders' visit from the safety of their usual table, so well-worn that their backsides had rubbed the seats of the benches smooth and shiny.

"I need some bread." Lyonene reached for it and sniffed it before she ate, breathing in the comfort of the tavern's familiar grains and butter. Not much in the village was familiar that night; it was a rare day that the elders came to the Summer Camp and the regular folk who lived there had no idea how to prepare. They hastily cleaned floors and straightened stockrooms. They took out fine clothes from deep inside trunks. Most had never thought to lay eyes upon them in their lifetimes.

"Are you afraid?" Reed asked. "Lyonene, you're never afraid."

"And I'm not now," Lyonene said. "I just didn't expect they would come."

"No one did," said Gretchen, her fingers wrapped around the clay of her mug. They'd thought they would simply be taken through the Veil and to the city. She looked at Reed. "Do you think it's because of you?"

"Because of me?" Reed asked.

"Not all of us were marked foundlings discovered by two of the strongest members of the order," Gretchen said. "Some of us were dropped on the doorstep of the Summer Camp by our families with nothing but one good dress and a chest of riches like a dowry."

"What about Lyonene?" asked Reed. "She was found in a convent."

"A common enough story." Lyonene leaned back. "Many girls who are too brave are sent away to convents." She raised her eyes to Reed again. "But you were taken through the Veil as a child. You've been to Atropa. You are the vaunted foundling."

"The vaunted foundling," Reed said. "You keep saying that, as though I was lucky. As though I didn't lose my entire family in one night."

"Lost one and gained another."

"And all it means is that I have nothing to go back to if I fail."

Lyonene threw up her hands. "All I have is a convent!"

"You are never going back to that convent," Reed snapped, and Gretchen pounded her fist against the table.

"Enough! None of us are going to convents. I'm sure the elders are coming because there are three of us, because that is uncommon, and nothing more." She refilled their cups. "And none of us will fail. We will go to Atropa to stand before the sacred well. We will be granted our first heroes and lead them to *unimaginable* glory. And then we will take our places in the order. Together. You and me"—she looked at Lyonene—"and Reed and her mean black horse. Just like we've always planned."

"Just like we always planned," Reed and Lyonene chimed. They raised their cups. It would be like they'd planned and like Reed had always dreamed: the three of them rising through the ranks of the Aristene to become legends themselves within it. She saw Lyonene in shining silver, blood on her blade before a king who knelt on one knee. She saw Gretchen heaving a spear through the heart of a charging foe to save her hero from a falling sword. Her friends would be magnificent. Of course, their Areion wouldn't be as grand as hers, but they couldn't be faulted for that.

"I will miss this place," said Gretchen. She took both their hands atop the table. "I like being here. I don't like being chased around by an Aristene with a war hammer, but that's not *every* day."

Reed squeezed Gretchen's fingers fondly, but Lyonene yanked hers free.

"This place will always be here," she said. "Like we will always be here if we do not undertake our trials soon." She gazed down into her ale. "The longer they delay, the more stagnant we become. Stagnant and rotting. Wrinkly."

"Rotting and wrinkly? Not you; I do not think so." Gretchen smiled her bright, pretty smile. She was the calming one, the peacekeeper who could soothe and cheer even the blackest mood. It would serve her well when her heroes came upon difficult times. Lyonene also had some of that soothing quality, or at least she could fake it. Reed could not fake it at all. She could barely manage a "there, there," and a stiff slap to the back in the face of tears. But how often, really, did heroes cry?

"Gretchen's right," said Reed. "You've still got at least a few years before the wrinkles set in. Except for that one beside your eye."

Lyonene slammed her cup down on the table. "You've got gray hairs," she hissed, and Reed and Gretchen laughed. "I can't wait anymore," Lyonene said. "We've trained long enough. We can ride, we can hunt, we can survive. We have studied. All that's left for us to learn is out there." She pointed past their heads, past the walls of the tavern, past the peak of Storm King to the world beyond. Reed and Gretchen looked at each other. They'd heard this many times before. Were it not for the separation of the Veil, Lyonene would have set out herself for Atropa years ago.

But for all of Lyonene's bluster, the Hero's Trial also carried a shadow of fear.

Reed looked down into her cup. She was not Aster's first initiate. Long ago, Aster and Veridian had mentored another girl, named Selene. By all accounts she grew into one of the finest initiates the order had ever seen. But Selene didn't survive. She was killed, during her trial. It was that loss that had turned Veridian away from the Aristene.

We should drink to her, Reed thought. *To honor her, and for luck.* But what kind of luck was that, to bring up the name of a dead initiate in the days before their trials were set to begin?

"What do you think the elders want?" Gretchen asked. "I can't believe they're coming just to personally whisk us away on the backs of their saddles. Can't you tell us any more?" She and Lyonene looked at Reed. They wanted to know what she knew, what Atropa was really like and how it felt to cross through the Veil, the mystical barrier that separated Atropa from the rest of the world. But they would find out for themselves soon enough.

Reed still remembered the sickness of crossing over, the nausea that sat in her belly and the chills that crawled across her skin. Aster hadn't told her what the Veil was or what would happen. Reed had gone in unprepared, seated in the front of Aster's saddle, staring in wonder as the night fell and Aster's chanted spell grew loud in her ears, and all at once the trees and heat of Orillia were gone and the ground beneath the horses' feet was gone, and they tumbled through the endless blackness.

Reed reached for a chunk of bread and dragged it through the butter dish. Even now, the memory made her stomach feel like a cavern.

But Atropa had been worth the journey.

Since they were young girls, Reed had told Gretchen and Lyonene everything she could about the city—everything she could remember from her one dizzying visit. She'd told them of the Citadel, white and hulking atop the central hill, the massive dome capped in gold that glittered even under moonlight. She told them of how quiet it was, lit by candles and torchlight, how she had cantered through the streets on the front of Aster's saddle with little Silco dragging behind. She had told them of it all, so often and in such detail that she could no longer tell which memories were real and which she had embellished.

She just hadn't told them what happened when she reached the Citadel and Aster took her up inside the dome.

I met the elders and was given leave to train with Aster here in the Summer Camp was all she said. Then she would describe each of the elders in detail: Wise, regal Ferreh, who had dark brown skin and eyes that seemed to take in everything at once. Fierce, terrifying Tiern, clad in silver armor, and who had hair of every color: brown and blond, red and silver, and even black, gathered and braided together in a thick mass that made Reed think of a nest of snakes.

And the details were enough to satisfy them.

She didn't know why she held back the rest of the story. Maybe because the interior of the dome was a place of wonder and each initiate deserved to see it first for herself. Or maybe because to tell them what had happened felt like the breaking of a spell.

The sound of the sacred well opening was slow and granular, heavy stone against heavy stone. Aster was so strong, to be able to remove the golden cover on her own. Reed remembered the smell, mineral and somehow cold, and the sound of the water. The ripples of light it reflected onto Aster's face.

Aster turned away and Reed drifted closer, drawn to the sounds and the light. She looked down, and her arm dropped toward the water, her fingertips breaking the sacred surface—

—No! Reed, you are not to touch it—

"Reed," Gretchen said. "Are you with us?"

Reed glanced at Lyonene, who regarded her with a sideways look from over the rim of her ale cup. "I was only thinking the same thing that we're all thinking." She took a breath and a long drink. The ale's bitterness was tempered with honey, and the familiar taste settled her nerves.

"Who do you think our heroes will be?" Gretchen asked, to ease the tension. It was a common game and they'd played it many times around the table. Sometimes their heroes were pirates and took them to sea. Or they were beggars whose fortunes had to be made from nothing. Gretchen's heroes were often funny—when they were younger they'd imagined one was a rat-catcher on a glorious quest for the largest rat—and Lyonene's were always grand—nobles and warriors, all dazzlingly good-looking. But as for Reed, she didn't care. It was only a game. She already knew who her hero would be.

"I think they will be princes," said Lyonene, and cocked an eyebrow. "So they still have something to strive for."

"Princes," Reed teased with a quiet smile. "How many princes can there be in the world?"

"At least three." Lyonene laughed. "And I hope mine is"—she sighed with exaggerated wistfulness—"very handsome." Reed and Gretchen snorted. Lyonene was always going on about seducing her hero. Bedding her hero. Tossing a collar around her hero's neck and leading him about like a well-trained hound. It would be a good strategy. But it wouldn't be Reed's. Such things, such feelings, were messy and unpredictable. There would be plenty of time for it after, when her trial was over and her Joining complete. When her future was secure.

"But," Lyonene said with a dramatic sigh, "I suppose Reed will be granted the best of the lot. The most handsome boy, the most beautiful girl, and it'll be nothing but scraps for the rest of us. Gretchen will probably be granted a goatherd."

"And imagine how impressive that will be," Gretchen said, knocking into Lyonene and making her spill her ale, "when I turn that goatherd into the greatest hero the Aristene have ever seen!"

"True, true." Lyonene smiled. "And why would the well do that to Reed? A waste of beauty when she's never even looked at a boy. Or a girl. With her it is all swords and horses, swords and horses."

"I look," Reed said. "I have looked. I just . . . haven't looked as often as you."

Gretchen and Lyonene laughed.

"That is also true," said Gretchen. "By now Lyonene has kept company with most of the boys in the village."

Lyonene nodded and took a drink. "It is a good thing we're to leave soon. The pickings here grow slim."

They laughed and drank into the night, until finally Lyonene lay her head down on the table and fell asleep.

"Well," said Gretchen. "Now that she is out of trouble, I'm going to go find some for myself. Can you get her home?"

"Of course," Reed said as Gretchen twisted in her seat and nodded to the tavern keeper's son.

"Emery?" Reed asked.

"What? You don't think Emery is handsome?"

"He is, but shouldn't we all be getting some sleep?"

"He will help me sleep, believe me," she said. "Now go on."

Reed did as she was bid and helped Lyonene back to her hut, sneaking her in past an already snoring Sabil. When she finally made it to her own bed, she thought she would be asleep immediately. But instead her mind raced ahead, to the elders and the trial. To Aster's return. To the Granting Ceremony. And it also raced back to that night, eight years ago in Atropa.

"No time to rest," Aster said as they emerged from the Veil. She urged Rabbit down the sloping hill and Reed took deep breaths. Her stomach clenched from traveling through all that darkness, but the breeze was sweet here, as if from night-blooming flowers, and below she could make out a city of pale buildings set into the valley. She saw herds of sheep and goats dotting the hillsides.

"Where are we?" she asked as her vision swam.

"We are in Atropa," Aster replied. *"My home and the city of the Aristene."*

Reed twisted in the saddle as the nighttime streets went by. Atropa wasn't like the port city where she grew up, that place of ramshackle slums and houses painted many colors—every inch of seaward-facing wood stained white by the salt. And of course it was nothing like the settlement. Sometimes, Mama told stories about the great cities of their home country: buildings of marble and grand gilded columns, great statues erected in the public squares. She told of walls painted with ornate depictions of battles and vines of flowers. It had seemed to Reed like a fantasy, but now she imagined that this was what Mama had spoken of.

"How did we get here?" Reed asked. *"Where is the river?"*

"We've left that far behind," Aster replied. *"The port at Preta, the country known as Orillia—all are unknowably distant now."*

Reed blinked. It had been a long, strange ride, and it had seemed like a dream, but how far could they have gotten?

"I wish Papa had known about this place," she said. *"And brought us here to settle instead of in the jungle."*

"He couldn't have found it, I'm afraid. Only a member of the Aristene can find the way. And even she must do so deliberately." Reed turned to look up at Aster and gasped.

Aster was not the same. Her clothes of leather and worn-thin hemp were gone, replaced by a white tunic and cape, silver armor at her chest and shoulders. Reed looked down and glimpsed the glint of silver greaves upon her legs. Even Rabbit was different: the horse had gained a silver plate of armor over her face.

"What—?"

"Quiet, little one," Aster whispered. "The city is sleeping. And we are not really supposed to be here."

They rode farther into the city, on streets paved in gravel and then in rough, flat stone. They seemed to be heading for a pale fortress set into the central hill, enormous and crowned with a vast dome of gold.

When they reached it, Rabbit came to a halt, and Reed felt herself whisked from the saddle and quickly carried up the broad marble steps.

"Silco," she said, and looked back over Aster's armored shoulder at the colt milling around behind the gray mare.

"He will be fine. Rabbit will look after him."

Reed looked up. "What is this place?"

"This is the Citadel." The Citadel's dome loomed over their heads like a great golden eye bathed in moonlight, and as the exhaustion of the Veil began to fade, Reed felt silly being carried. She was too old for it, even if it was no trouble for Aster. Still, watching the many, many steps go by, she didn't ask to be set down.

Aster didn't let her walk on her own until they reached the top and were inside a great hall lit by torches. The hall was filled with statues on both sides. Marble warriors in poses of battle. Some were mounted on fierce horses. Others depicted on foot. Reed saw bows and arrows, spears, and short broad-bladed swords. Many variations of armor. And all of the warriors appeared to be women.

"Are those Aristenes like you?" Reed asked.

"Yes," said Aster. "In the world of men we take no glory for ourselves. Our names are not known; our deeds are not preserved in song. But Atropa is our city. And in the Citadel we revere those who have come before."

"Who arrives in the Citadel so late?"

Aster stopped short and tugged Reed close. Out of the shadows came *a tall woman, striding toward them with sword drawn.*

"Aster!" The warrior sheathed her sword. She was big, bigger even than Aster, and had a thick braid of the darkest black hair Reed had ever seen. As she stepped into the torchlight and bent to peer into Reed's face, Reed realized that her eyes were even darker still. The woman's eyes were as black as Silco's coat.

"Gloria Thea Matris," the woman muttered.

"Gloria Thea Matris, sister," Aster replied. The woman stepped back and they grinned and embraced each other; the big woman hugged Aster so tight she was lifted briefly off the floor.

"You weren't expected. Is she with you?" the woman asked, and Reed didn't think she was asking about her.

"No," said Aster. "Veridian would not come."

The black-eyed Aristene sighed. "But you saw her? She is well?"

"She is well." Aster shrugged. "She is Veridian."

"And who is this?" The black-eyed woman bent down again. There was a thin black band across the woman's forehead, and it wasn't a tied bit of leather or fabric—it was dyed right into her skin.

"This is Reed," said Aster.

Reed stood still as the big Aristene stared. Her armor was similar to Aster's, but slightly heavier, and she bore a sword and shield upon her back. She carried several ornate daggers strapped to her calves and hung at her waist. There was something innately dangerous about her, and despite her warm greeting, Reed began to feel threatened. She tucked her chin and made a noise deep in her throat.

"She is growling at me," the woman said, surprised. She stood and threw her head back to laugh, then placed her hands on her hips. "I like her."

"I am taking her up into the dome."

"To the dome?" the woman asked. "Shall I fetch the elders?"

"Please, sister. And quietly."

The woman nodded and disappeared down a corridor.

"Who was that?" Reed asked.

"That was Aethiel," Aster said. "She is relatively new to the order, but she has always been a friend to Veridian and me."

"She's . . . ," Reed said, and searched for a word that was not too insulting. "Rough."

"She is indeed. But before she was an Aristene, she was once a queen. Hurry now."

A queen, Reed thought as Aster led her quickly through the halls of statues. A queen of what? She didn't look like any queen that Reed had ever imagined or like Mama had described in stories. A queen should have gowns and flowing robes. A crown. But then, Reed supposed she'd never actually seen a queen in person.

The way to the dome was long, and when Reed's tired legs began to falter, Aster scooped her up again and carried her the rest of the way. Much of the journey was a blur, through darkened passageways, past rooms and up stairs, stairs that twisted around and back until Reed lost all sense of place. By the time they stepped up into the open, for all Reed knew they'd gone back to the beginning.

The inside of the dome was dark. Aster held her by the shoulder to keep her from falling back down the steep steps.

"I will light a torch," Aster said, and Reed heard her move away. After a moment, she could see that there was moonlight here, too, and stars—the dome was ringed by cut windows. She could make out the shapes of roosting birds, rustling on the ledges.

The dome was enormous. So large that half of the port marketplace *could have set up inside. It seemed an open, empty space, except for a long oval table set to one side and an odd stone formation rising from the other. Aster lit a torch, and Reed saw that the formation was made of many different kinds of stones and covered with a heavy stone circle that was capped in gold much like the Citadel itself.*

"That is the well," Aster said. "Come. And take care not to step upon the silver circle." She cast the light of the torch onto a large silver circle, set into the floor.

"What is that?" Reed asked.

"The World's Gate. And it is not to be tread upon."

As they walked to the well, the torchlight illuminated the walls and Reed's eyes widened. The entire interior was painted in beautiful murals of land and sea, green rolling hills, and white sand beaches. And set against the landscapes were warriors and kings, queens and nobles, some in ships and others at the heads of armies. Her eyes caught upon a depiction of fine horses painted so large they were almost life-size, necks arched and glossy, grays and bays and chestnuts and even a Silco black.

"Those are the Areion," Aster said. "The sacred mounts of the Aristene."

"Like Rabbit," Reed said.

"Yes, like Rabbit. And that one in the center"—she gestured to a great bay stallion, his coat painted a deep reddish brown and his mane and tail long and black—"he is Amondal. Desert Fire. The lord of all Areion and the mount of one of our elders." Aster went ahead to the well and uncapped it with one muscular motion, even though the stone covering must have weighed as much as Reed three times over.

Reed went to her, and Aster lifted her by the waist so she could lean over the many-colored stones and look down. The water inside was high and black.

"In this well," Aster said, "an Aristene may see the heroes they are destined to guide. And in this well, the goddess sees us. Kleia Gloria, the goddess of glory. I would let her see you, tonight, Reed. And speak to the elders to know if your mark is true."

She turned away, and Reed felt herself pulled toward the well as if by invisible strings. Before she knew it, she was leaned over the side, staring down at the water.

Even cast in torchlight it showed no reflection. It smelled of minerals and the cold deep mud of the river. It smelled of the salt of the sea, and the wet paving stones of the port. She reached out her hand.

It seemed to take a long time before her fingertip broke the surface, and the water of the well stirred and rippled, slow and thick like oil, smooth as silk.

"No! Reed, you are not to touch it." Aster pulled her back, but not before the surface changed. The water turned blue as the daytime sea, and Reed saw the face of a boy with rough, sandy-gold hair and serious eyes.

7.

THE ELDERS OF THE ORDER

In the morning, Reed woke from a dream of the boy. He had been handsome even then, with wild hair and stormy eyes, and over the years his image had grown with her. He became a child no more but a young man, good-looking enough to please even Lyonene.

Reed turned over on her sleeping mat to stare at the thick beams of dark wood that crossed the ceiling and ran down at the corners. That boy could be another Aristene's hero by now. Perhaps what she'd seen in the well was only a vision of chances missed and paths not taken. A mistake shown to a naughty child who had sought to see before her time. For eight years she had wondered and fretted and hoped that he would be hers. Her first hero, the boy she had always imagined by her side. The boy she had come to know. But no amount of hoping would change what she would see when she looked into the well at her Granting Ceremony.

Reed rubbed her eyes and got up. The home she shared with Aster was little more than a hut: two rooms, one for sleeping and another for cooking and eating around a central hearth. The walls were slabs of mudbrick, a mixture of clay, silt, and straw. It was less sturdy than the buildings in the village, and nothing compared to the stone city of Atropa. But the huts of the Summer Camp didn't need to withstand much. The Summer Camp was not so named because it was used only in the summer. It was called such because the weather in the valley remained temperate year-round.

All year long rains were short and the air was warm. Waters were full of fish and forests full of game. There were hayfields to lie in. It seemed a strange place for the training of an Aristene warrior, but perhaps that was the point. The Summer Camp made it harder for Reed to become what she needed to be: quick-eyed and disciplined, tough and springy with muscle. If you could become such a person in a place that lulled you to sleep, you could become one anywhere.

Reed stoked the fire and put on some nice strong tea to soothe the headache from last night's drink. Then she quickly but dutifully did her chores: sweeping the hearth, placing the ash into a small pot to spread in the garden to ward off snails, and cooking the day's flatbread before hurrying to find Lyonene and Gretchen.

Like the rest of the village, the initiates positioned themselves along the road to wait for the elders. It was easy to know when they were coming by the growing ripple of noise flowing up the street. Reed craned her neck, never so glad to be the tall one.

The elders rode two abreast, garbed in the silver armor and white capes of the order. Ferreh, the mind. And Tiern, the teeth. Tiern sat straight-backed in the saddle. She did not speak or acknowledge the greetings of the village folk. To the Aristene present, she only nodded, and the initiates, when they came into her view, she fixed with hawklike gray eyes. Anyone could see that Tiern was fierce, and ancient, with pale skin like marble. Her hair of many colors, worn loose and long, was, in Reed's opinion, strange and ugly, just as strange and ugly as she remembered it being eight years ago.

Ferreh, on the other hand, was beautiful. She had dark brown skin and short brown hair that framed her head like a crown. She reminded Reed of many of the merchants in the port city where she'd grown up. The first time they'd met she had tried many greetings, in many languages, only to have the elder shake her head. Ferreh hadn't been unkind, but thinking of it now, Reed's cheeks still burned.

To one side of the elders, and riding just behind, was Aster on her gray mare, Rabbit. Reed stood up as tall as she could, hoping Aster would see her and give something away about what to expect. But whatever they expected, it had been too much. The elders rode past the initiates without a pause or a word of acknowledgment.

"That's it?" Gretchen asked as the procession moved down the street.

"Perhaps they're not here for us after all," said Reed.

"Nonsense." Lyonene placed her hands on her hips. "It's only ceremony. They are the elders. Did you expect to speak with them? To share a pitcher of ale?"

"It would have been nice," Gretchen said as Reed watched the Areion's tails disappear around a corner.

"Well, I'm not going to just wait here." Reed slipped into the street. "Let's go and spy, at least."

Lyonene and Gretchen followed closely as they tailed the elders. They hadn't truly needed to trail them: the village in the Summer Camp was small; the tavern the elders went to was the only one, with the sole stable for visiting horses nearby. They waited in the shadows as the elders and their mentors went inside and then skirted around upwind of the stables. All three girls knew how to walk like hunters and to keep from alerting game, but the horses in the stable were no grouses. They were all Areion.

Reed peered around the side of the stable door. She saw swishing tails and heads lowered to piles of hay. She saw Amondal, the mount of Ferreh, standing untied and still as a statue. Amondal, the Desert Fire, as ageless as his rider. The horse was more of a legend than the three initiates could ever hope to be.

Just as she was about to duck back down, Rabbit's long face slid into view. The mare chewed through a mouthful of hay and stared at her, and Reed made a pleading expression and shook her head. After a long moment, the mare seemed to say, *Oh, very well*, and walked a few steps ahead, using her big gray body to give them cover. The initiates hurried past and pressed themselves silently to the side of the tavern to listen.

"She has grown tall."

Reed looked at Gretchen and Lyonene and mouthed, "*Ferreh*."

"Tall and broad," said another strange voice they would know as Tiern. "And she still looks like a scowler. She is not still biting?"

The mentors laughed, and Lyonene nearly did as well; she had to cover her mouth and Reed cast her a sharp look.

"But the tawny girl," Tiern went on. "The beauty. She is the best?" There seemed to be general agreement about that, and Reed ached to peek over the edge of the window to see whether Aster had joined in.

"She will come," said Ferreh. "It is time."

"They will all come," said Tiern, and below the window, the girls joined hands.

"We cannot rush the foundling," Ferreh said.

"The foundling is strong," said Aster. "She is ready."

"She is," Sabil added, and even Jana agreed, to Reed's slight surprise. But it seemed that the elders would not be convinced.

"As mentors your words are valued," said Ferreh. "But Aster has not taken on an initiate in many years. And your mind is often elsewhere, is that not so?"

"You bid me stay here to train her and so I have."

"I did not bid you stay here as punishment! I gave you the foundling because you wanted her. It was plain the night you brought her to us. And besides, you have not always remained here. Tell me: when have you last seen our Veridian?"

Their Veridian. The fearsome blond warrior who had fought to free Reed beside the river, who had paid for her and Silco in silver and combat. But Veridian was not theirs anymore. She had turned her back on them. The only thread that remained tethering Veridian to the order was the thread that ran between her heart and Aster's.

"I haven't," Aster replied. "I have not been able to find her. Not since Reed." There was a heavy pause. "When Reed's Joining is complete I will search again. I won't stop until I bring her home."

"She must return," said Tiern. "Our patience for her absence is near its end." She paused, and it sounded as though she took a drink, and when she spoke again her words were muffled as if through bread. "Let us eat now. Afterward go and bring your initiates. We've come all this way; we will see what they can do. Then we will decide about the foundling."

"'Come all this way,'" Lyonene scoffed when they had put some distance between themselves and the tavern. "They've only had to ride through the Veil; it's not as if they had to board a ship or ride overland on a nine-day journey."

"You may prefer a nine-day journey," said Reed, "after you've gone through the Veil yourself." Beside her, Gretchen paled. She feared the Veil, even though Reed had survived it and even though Aristene rode through it anytime they traveled to Atropa. But Reed barely noticed the way Gretchen swallowed or how the sweat broke out on her upper lip. She was too distracted by what they'd heard. Would they really not allow her to undertake the trial? Would they take Lyonene and Gretchen and leave her behind?

Impossible. She wouldn't allow it. She would ride after them through the Veil on her own.

"What did they mean when they said their patience for Veridian's absence was at an end?" Gretchen asked.

"What do you think?" Lyonene said, walking quickly along the road to their huts, where they would innocently wait for their mentors. "Veridian is an apostate. And apostates are killed. In every church in every faith, by every god I have ever heard of."

"Not by ours," Reed said. "Kleia Gloria is mother to us all. Why would she demand the head of her own daughter?"

"It doesn't matter anyway, does it?" asked Gretchen. "Aster will find her and bring her back."

But what Reed remembered of Veridian was a fierce, headstrong woman. She rode a red horse named Everfall, named so because he had been clumsy as a child and she hadn't thought he would survive to become an Areion but would break his leg first. She had shot two grouse for their supper, clean through the heads. And she had fought Aster against bringing Reed to the order, offering to take Reed to a port and put her on a ship instead.

"I should not have given in to you; she would have been better left where we found her, even if it meant a cut throat."

Had Veridian really said that? Or were the words that flooded back across time a trick of her imagination? Reed couldn't remember Veridian's voice. She couldn't be sure.

It doesn't matter if she said it, Reed thought. She was wrong. The order was Reed's family. The order was where she belonged.

"That's not what bothers me anyway," Lyonene muttered as they walked. "What bothers me is what they said about Reed. They cannot mean for us to leave her behind!"

"Of course they can't!" Gretchen exclaimed. "We wouldn't go. We would remain in the Summer Camp until it was time for all of us."

"And go against the elders? Go against the goddess?" Lyonene picked up a rock and threw it, pinging it expertly off the rail of the pasture fence. "It won't come to that. Reed is ready; and we will make sure they know it. Whatever show they ask of us, whatever task or demonstration—" She looked at Reed. "You must perform well."

"What if they mean to never take me at all?"

Gretchen's eyes widened. Lyonene picked up another stone.

"If they mean not to take you," Lyonene said, "then we will stay until they change their minds." She threw the rock, harder this time, and it sailed past the fence, flying so far that they couldn't see where it landed. Lyonene hated this place. She was trapped in it. And so was Reed.

"No," said Reed. "None of us will stay. Whatever they ask of us, I will make sure they cannot deny me my place."

8.

THE INITIATE EXHIBITION

When Reed heard Rabbit's hoofbeats outside the hut, she wanted to burst through the door and drag her mentor out of the saddle. Instead she brushed a bit of ash away from the hearth and swung the teapot back over the fire to heat.

"Hello, Reed."

"Aster." Because the elders were there, her mentor still wore her armor and cape; normally she would have let them fade into the aether, where the regalia of the Aristene always remained to be called upon at will. "Is there tea? My journey has been long and taxing."

Reed pulled the pot away from the fire so hard that it clanged against the stone and bounced back.

"What did the elders say?"

Aster looked at the teapot, amused.

"They've come to tell us the time of the Hero's Trial is here? To take us to the well, for the Granting?"

"They have."

"And they . . ." Reed swallowed. "They don't think I am ready."

"You and Gretchen and Lyonene were listening," Aster said. She walked to the hearth and warmed her hands. "I thought so. Rabbit must have spotted you."

"Did she tell you that?" Reed asked, knowing that the horse had done no such thing.

"No. But she seemed very . . . smug as we were riding out here. How much did you hear?"

"All of it," Reed said. "They do not mean to take me."

"They mean to discern your readiness. That is not the same thing."

"I don't understand. Have I not done well?"

Aster turned and reached out to touch the ends of Reed's long dark hair. "You have done more than well. You are an Aristene born. I knew that the moment we found you in that wreck of a settlement. But if the elders say you must wait, then you must wait."

Reed frowned. How long? Another year? Two? She tried to tell herself it didn't matter, that as long as she passed her trial, she and Gretchen and Lyonene would be reunited in the order. But it did matter. It was meant to be the three of them, just like it was meant to be her and Silco, when they'd been found together all those years ago. The marked Aristene and her Areion mount. Two sacrifices. Two foundlings. She swallowed the rising lump in her throat.

"How long would I have to wait?" Reed asked.

"I don't know."

"What about Silco?" Most horses were selected to be Areion in the prime of their lives; how many years until he was deemed unfit for the honor? Rabbit was chosen when she was five, so young that her gray coat was still darkly dappled, and Everfall had only needed to survive without injury for four. Silco was already nine. "I promised him, like you promised me. I won't join the order without him!"

"Reed," Aster said. But Reed knew her mentor too well. She could see that it had already crossed her mind.

"Is it because of you? Do you not want me to go because of what happened to Selene?"

Aster looked down, and Reed regretted asking.

"You and Selene are not the same," Aster said. "And even if I am afraid, it isn't up to me. It's up to the elders. So tomorrow you had best show them what it is that they want to see."

They wanted her to fight. Lyonene would demonstrate her skill as an archer, and Gretchen was to throw her spears. But Reed they wanted to fight. She stood inside the arena, watching the elders at the rail, laughing and conversing with the mentors and a few of the other Aristene who resided in the camp. Out on the training field, Gretchen had completed her spear throws, heaving with her good, unbruised arm and giving a very good show—Reed had been worried Gretchen would buckle under the weight of the elders' eyes, but she had never thrown better. It made Jana lean back and nod, and she managed to look only a little surprised.

"You taught her well," said Ferreh, and the tall, pale blond shrugged.

"As I teach them all."

Reed glanced at Aster. Her mentor had barely looked at her since they'd arrived, perhaps feigning indifference to hide her worry. Or perhaps to avoid being seen as coddling. Had she been coddled? Reed wondered. She hadn't felt like she had. There'd been no shortage of chores, no lesser hours of practice. She had studied the same subjects, pored over the same maps, sparred and trained just like Gretchen and Lyonene. But Aster loved Reed. That was the difference. The other mentors were fond of their initiates. But

Aster treated Reed like a daughter.

Just once, Aster's eyes met Reed's, and the worry she saw in them only made her more nervous. Her mentor had already lost her first initiate, and her love. If she lost another person, she would do something foolish. She would get herself into trouble.

"Reed, look!"

Gretchen had returned from the spear-throwing course and waved to her from the rail, where she had tied a snorting, pawing Silco to the fence.

"I brought him down from the pasture," she said as she ducked through and jogged over. "For motivation. For luck." Reed watched as the black colt leaned back, testing his rope to see if he could break it. He was a terrible, cranky creature. She couldn't leave him behind; who else would take him?

"Thank you," she said, even though having him there only added to the seething flies in her stomach. She wanted to vomit but feared she'd look down and see a pile of wings.

Out on the training field, attendants assembled a line of targets, two low and round, and three higher: straw formed into the shapes of men. To one side, Lyonene waited astride a slim brown horse, and when Sabil gave the sign she put her heels to it. She drew her arrow as she thundered past and fired, the arrow sinking easily into the first low target. She reached the end and whirled the horse back around, taking aim and firing again with the same result.

Reed glanced at the gathering of Aristene observers. As was the case with Gretchen's demonstration, they appeared to only passively be paying attention, clapping and nodding at each good shot before going back to their chatter. No doubt they had seen many such displays. Why, then, have the exhibition at all? Unless it was only an excuse to deny Reed's acceptance.

On the field, Lyonene kicked her horse hard. Before she reached the remaining targets she pushed herself up in the saddle to stand and then dove from the horse's back to roll across the grass. She came up and shot arrows into the straw men: one, two, three, as fast as any shots Reed had ever seen fired.

That made the elders take notice, and as they clapped, Lyonene turned to her friends and gave them a wink.

"After she has the Aristene magic, she will be as good a shot as Veridian," said Aster, but Tiern, who looked happy for once, only laughed.

"No one is as good a shot as Veridian."

Lyonene put up her bow and joined Reed and Gretchen in the arena.

"Well, that woke them up," she said with a smirk, and Reed grinned.

"You're lucky you didn't put an arrowhead through your own knee."

"If I had, I would have ignored it and gone on. Now get out there. Everyone's waiting."

Reed lifted her sword and shield. There were no practice weapons today. No wood or blunted edges. She would cut and be cut. She walked to the center of the corral and faced the elders to bow. Then she waited for her opponent to appear.

"Who am I to fight?" she asked after a long moment.

"Whomever you like," Tiern said, and nodded toward Gretchen and Lyonene.

The initiates glanced at each other. Reed had assumed she would face one of the mentors, but she knew Gretchen's and Lyonene's skills well, and she knew which one she could beat. Not Lyonene. Lyonene might make her look better than Gretchen could, pushing her to higher heights, but the match would end with Reed disarmed, and she couldn't afford that today.

"Gretchen."

Gretchen nodded soberly and took up a spear and shield. Smart. She was smaller than Reed was by far and would need the extra reach. She walked to Reed's side and bowed to the elders.

"I will make you look good," she whispered from the side of her mouth. "But do not make me look *too bad*."

Aster called for them to begin. At every sideways step Reed felt the weight of a different pair of eyes. Aster's. The elders'. Lyonene's. Even the eyes of her horse. Gretchen thrust out with the spear and Reed knocked it aside. It was only a testing blow. Gretchen paused for a moment and smiled. Then she attacked for real. They traded in the center of the arena, blow, shield, blow, the heavy sounds of weapons meeting ringing in Reed's ears. Reed got the better of the exchange and ended it with a shield bash that rocked Gretchen back on her heels. Her friend blinked, but the corner of her mouth curled up.

"This is for you," Gretchen said quietly. "Don't hold back!"

But she didn't know what she was asking. Reed outmatched Gretchen in all things: size, strength, and skill. With the Aristene magic, Gretchen would be an excellent fighter. But without it . . .

"Come on!" Gretchen thrust her spear. Reed blocked it and swung, landing a blow hard enough to rattle Gretchen's teeth. She shook her head, dazed, and nodded for more. So Reed gave more. Gretchen feinted to one side, but Reed didn't take the bait, bashing again with her shield. When Gretchen reeled, Reed rained down blows, swinging her heavy sword again and again. She struck and struck, until finally the shield shattered against Gretchen's already badly bruised shoulder.

Gretchen wanted to drop her spear and hug her arm. Reed saw it in her eyes yet still she attacked, piercing Gretchen's defense, knocking the spear wide, pushing her around the arena mercilessly until the girl fell to one knee. Everyone watching must have seen that Reed could have killed her opponent five times over. But just in case they hadn't been paying attention, Reed shoved Gretchen down, crushing her spear into the dirt with her heel so hard that it snapped in two.

Outside the arena, the elders stared. Reed looked down at Gretchen, who sat panting on the ground, her lip bloody and strands of her pretty brown hair stuck to her cheeks.

Reed sheathed her sword and reached down to pull Gretchen up.

"I'm sorry," she said, and hugged her tightly. "I had to, but I'm sorry! Are you all right?"

"I'm all right," Gretchen replied. She smiled, but her smile wasn't the same as it was before. "You fought well!"

Reed scoffed. "You let me."

At the fence, the elders and the mentors whispered, Aster the most fervently. They seemed to be arguing—all but Ferreh, who stood still and thoughtful, her brown eyes fixed on Reed. Reed stood straight, breathing hard. Finally, Ferreh nodded.

* * *

"Hush, Reed. The elders are coming."

"Who are the elders?"

"Ferreh, who we call the mind. And Tiern, who is known as the teeth."

"Why do they call Tiern 'the teeth'?" Reed asked.

"I do not know. Maybe because she has a bite. Like you."

Aster smiled. When footsteps sounded on the stairs she pulled Reed to her side, and tugged her up as straight as she could.

The women who entered the room were dressed like Aster, in white capes and silver armor. There were two of them: one with pale skin like the traders who came to the port from the seas to the north—the ones that burned pink in the sun and then went straight back to white without tanning—and another with dark skin like many of the merchants in Preta.

"Gloria Thea Matris, elders," Aster said, and bowed.

"Gloria Thea Matris, sister," said the dark-skinned woman. Her hands were joined before her stomach and she was smiling. The other woman, however, looked down on Aster and then on Reed with a frown.

"This isn't Veridian," she said. "We hoped you would return with her."

"Perhaps if I'd had more time," said Aster.

"But it was not to be," said the dark-skinned woman.

"Not yet."

The woman looked past them, over their shoulders, so intently that Reed turned to see what she was looking at, but there was only the shadowy wall. "I'm imagining her here. I so wished to see her."

"Well," said the pale woman. "What have you brought us in her stead?"

"This is Reed," Aster said. She placed her hands on Reed's small shoulders. "Reed, these are the elders of the Aristene. This is Ferreh." She gestured to the dark-skinned woman. "And this is Tiern." The pale woman, Tiern, bent down to look at her, much like Aethiel had, *though with a less birdlike expression.*

Ferreh, on the other hand, looked familiar to Reed, and amid all this strangeness, anything familiar was good.

"Noté ashé," Reed said to her, using a greeting she had spoken with the port merchants. But though Ferreh smiled, she shook her head.

"I'm not of that country, child."

Reed tried again, other greetings in other tongues. But Ferreh shook her head at each, and eventually Reed stopped, feeling foolish.

"It's all right," said Ferreh. "I come from far away. And I'm very old."

Ferreh didn't look any older than Reed's mother. She reached into a pouch behind her back and held out a seed cake. Reed's stomach grumbled. She took it and shoved it into her mouth to keep from saying anything more.

"Where is she from?" Tiern asked. During Reed's attempt to discern Ferreh's language, Tiern had begun to walk around them. She looked Reed over, taking in her bony frame and tan skin, her dark, softly curling hair. Mama always said she would grow up tall. She wished she already was so Tiern might stop squinting at her like she was a stray cat.

"We found her in the middle of a massacre," said Aster. "She was the only survivor."

Ferreh's brow knit, but Tiern only clucked her tongue.

"That explains why she's got that sour face. She's angry. Maybe too angry to train."

"Train to what?" Reed spat. Literally spat, her full mouth sending crumbs flying. "What are you?"

"What I am is bigger than you," said Tiern. "And the mistress of this place. She's headstrong," she said to Aster.

"But she is marked."

"She is marked." Ferreh sighed. "Shining brightly." Aster and Tiern

turned to Ferreh, waiting for her words. "Her light is like midday. It hurts my eyes." At that, Tiern seemed to consider Reed afresh. After a moment, she shook her head.

"I do not think so."

"But the mark," said Aster, and Tiern's head twisted like a snake's.

"So you would take her, then? You who have not taken an initiate since—" She stopped when Aster lowered her eyes, and she amended her words. "You, who do not take initiates."

Listening to them argue about whether or not to take her, Reed began to grow upset. She didn't ask to be anybody's burden, any more than she'd asked to be taken to the settlement in the first place or asked for her family to be killed. Quietly, she took the remains of her seed cake and ground them to dust in her fist. Ferreh watched as they cascaded to the floor.

"What do you want, child?" Ferreh asked. Reed gritted her teeth. There were many things that she wanted. But only one she could still have.

"I want my colt."

"Colt?"

"A black colt who was taken with her," Aster explained.

"She comes with her own mount," Ferreh said. "That is a good sign."

Tiern strode toward the torches and took one from the wall. The light caught the steel sword strapped across her back and another, shorter bronze one hung at her waist. Her long multicolored braid swayed like an agitated tail as she handed the torch to Ferreh. Ferreh held out her arm, and after a nudge from Aster, Reed followed the elder around the outskirts of the dome.

As she held the torch out, Reed took the opportunity to look more closely at the murals, until Ferreh stopped before the painting of the horses.

"The one in the middle there," Ferreh said, and pointed. "He is mine.

Amondal is his name. Desert Fire. And that one"—she pointed to a dappled gray—*"looks a little bit like Aster's mare, does it not?"*

Reed nodded.

"To be so fond of your colt you must know horses well," said the elder. "How old would you say Aster's horse is?"

Reed thought a moment. "Three?" she guessed.

"Older."

"Four?"

Ferreh shook her head and looked at Aster, who replied. "Rabbit is more than one hundred years old."

Reed blinked. Then she smiled. It felt strange to smile, her first in days. "No."

"Yes," said Aster. "And so am I."

Reed looked at Ferreh. Soon the elder would start to laugh and reveal the joke. But Ferreh only watched her quietly.

"You're ageless," Reed said. "You don't die."

"We do die," said Ferreh. "We may be killed. But we live far longer than any mortal." She cast her torch back to the murals.

"Look upon these walls, Reed. Upon these deeds and heroes. It is the duty of our order to guide these mortals, to elevate their stories, to make their names live on forever even if they do not. It is our task to push heroes to greatness, to put kings and queens upon their thrones and ride with generals into war."

"Can you do that, child?" Tiern asked. "And think before you answer. It is not easy. And it is not always kind."

Reed looked upon the murals. It didn't seem possible that she could be among these swords and crowns. That she could ride into such battles.

"The mark you carry tells us you can," said Ferreh. "And if you prove it

to be true, you could take your place here with us. You and your black colt."

"Me and Silco," Reed whispered. Here, with Aster and these untouchable warriors. No death, no separation. Safety. Peace. It sounded like a dream, what they were offering. But her mother had not raised her to be foolish. It wouldn't be given for free.

"How?" Reed asked.

"When you come of age, when you have trained and are ready to take the test of proving"—Ferreh gestured to the well that Reed had mistakenly touched—"you will come to this well and be granted the first hero of your own. And you will be in service to Her."

Ferreh cast her torch upward, to the ceiling of the dome, and Reed looked up. The face of a goddess was painted there, brightly as if lit by the sun, her eyes at once fierce and tender, firm and nurturing. She was beautiful like Reed's mother had been and beautiful like Aster was, though she didn't look like either.

"That is Kleia Gloria," Ferreh said. "The goddess of glory. Train hard, become strong, pass our tests, and you will be one of us, and you will belong to Her, and you will have a place, forever."

9.

THE BLESSING OF KLEIA GLORIA

They were going to let her come.

Tonight, at nightfall, the mentors would open the Veil and lead their three initiates to Atropa, where they would go before the sacred well for the Granting of Heroes and be prepared for the missions they would undertake to successfully complete their Hero's Trials. There would be feasting and stories. They would meet other members of the order. Reed had waited for this day so long she'd feared it would never arrive, yet now that it had, she felt uneasy. The doubt of the elders had shaken her confidence. Something that had once seemed fated now felt like it could slide right through her fingers.

And she couldn't stop thinking of the look on Gretchen's face when she was knocked down in the arena. *Do not make me look too bad.* Reed closed her eyes.

When she had finished her chores—Aster had not returned last night, off somewhere with the elders, or perhaps she didn't want to be near her either, after what she'd done to Gretchen—she took some dried fruit and left the hut to find Silco in the pasture. After he had emptied her tunic of fruit, she threw a rope halter around his head and rode him up the windward side of Storm King, deep into the trails of the lower mountain. These trails were lush and shaded, thin and winding in places, full of rocky outcroppings that had made Silco as sure-footed as one of the white goats that dotted the hillsides farther up. She rode until the air turned crisp, past vast flats where the river ran by, fat and sparkling and cold. She didn't stop until they reached the shores of the ice lake embedded in one side of the rock. The villagers said that the water was the mountain's heart's blood—Storm King's heart of ice, melting and leaking out to pool between the peak's foothills.

Reed slipped from Silco's back and he walked into the shallows to splash his lips around in the water. She bent near the bank to cup her hands to drink and dashed some against her face and neck. But Reed hadn't come for the water or the breeze or even the solitude. She came for the goddess's blessing.

When she was an Aristene, she would never need to search for Kleia Gloria; she would feel the beat of her heart through her own veins. She would see with her eyes the threads of glory that raced through the veins of mortals. But Reed was not an Aristene yet, and when she sought the goddess, she had to do the same as any other follower would do for their god. She went to sacred spaces, and she prayed.

It was silly, really. There was no legend that said Kleia Gloria dwelled upon the peak of Storm King or that she raced through the mountain's forests. But unlike other deities, Kleia Gloria had no temples. The order was her temple, and so Reed had to make do. Sometimes beside the lake, when the wind would still and the birds would pause, it seemed the goddess might hear her, and those moments filled her up, like the first time she'd seen through Aster's mortal disguise to the shining armor underneath or like looking into the gold-capped well and touching a finger to all that darkness. Like seeing that boy, reflected in the ripples.

"This is a long way to come, just to shoot something for supper," Aster said, and Reed turned as she and Rabbit stepped into the clearing.

"Did you follow me?" Reed stood. Aster had brought her bow and a quiver of arrows; she took them from the back of her saddle and tossed them down.

"Of course I did. I thought we might hunt together. One last time in the Summer Camp." She smiled. "What are you doing here?"

Reed shrugged. "Seeking guidance."

"I am your mentor; I'm your guidance."

"I was seeking the goddess's blessing. Or perhaps her forgiveness."

Aster looked up to the peak, as if she too thought the goddess might reside there, reclining atop the mountain on a silver throne. "Kleia Gloria does not demand repentance. She's not that kind of god." She looked at Reed. "What is it you need forgiveness for?" She already knew, of course. Aster knew Reed as well as anyone. But she liked Reed to give voice to her own lessons.

"For Gretchen. It was unkind, what I did to her yesterday. And it was unfair. I broke that shield against an arm that was already badly injured. She could have fought me off, had it not been for that."

"She could not have," Aster said. "You talk like I haven't also been here for all of Gretchen's training."

"But it was a poor victory." The familiar lump of anger rose in Reed's throat, the same anger she'd felt since the murder of her family or perhaps even before. Perhaps she'd always been angry and that was why she always bit, and why that old wise woman had hated her from the start. Orna. Reed hadn't thought of Orna in many years. The only memories the thought stirred were of a mean-spirited curse and an aged, broken body tossed onto a pile.

"Don't you understand?" Reed snapped. "I cheated my way into the trial."

Aster laughed. "No, you didn't. You are a very good initiate, Reed, but you are not so good that you can fool the elders.

"And in any case, it wasn't your victory over Gretchen that made Ferreh change her mind. It was the way you embraced her afterward."

"What?"

"Your love for your sister. Fierceness is not the only quality the Aristene reward, and it is not the only quality we require. Ferreh sees into your heart, and that is what she judged. Not the way you bashed her down mercilessly when she was already beaten."

Reed frowned, and Aster leaned down and pulled her against her leg. She smoothed Reed's hair away from her eyes.

"Gretchen is angry with me," Reed said.

"She is hurt, but you can fix it. And fix it you should. When the trials begin, you will be on separate paths, each guiding your own heroes. And only the goddess knows when or how or even if you will all meet again."

"Why do you say such things? *If* we will all meet again." Reed gave her mentor a teasing shove. "You will give us bad luck."

"I assure you, an Aristene gives only one kind of luck." Aster grinned, but then she touched Reed on the chin and grew serious. "Make your peace before you part. Don't leave things unsaid. But before you do that, let us shoot some grouse for supper."

They took the horses into the trees. It wasn't long before they found what Aster was looking for: a small fat grouse with a tufted crown. The same kind that Veridian had shot for them after she and Aster had rescued Reed from the raiders. Some years ago, Aster had returned to Orillia and trapped several breeding pairs to introduce into the valley. They tasted different there, as their diet in the Summer Camp was not the same, but they were still delicious, and still depressingly easy to shoot.

Rabbit flushed this one from a shrub, and Reed took careful aim as the grouse trundled out from the brush. She fired, and it fell to the grass without so much as a chirp.

"I am realizing now that I should have been less impressed by Veridian's shots that day," said Reed as Aster went to collect the bird. "A bolt through a grouse's head is not such a feat if you're standing directly behind them."

"It does seem a waste of an arrow." Aster hung the bird across Rabbit's saddle. "Perhaps we could just sneak up behind them and scare them to death."

"Aster," Reed said. "I heard what the elders said about Veridian. I'm sorry if I've kept you from her. I can't help but feel that, if it wasn't for me, she would have returned with you that day."

Aster didn't look at Reed as she finished tying the bird and took another arrow from her quiver.

"No," Aster said, her expression hard. "You or no you, Veridian wouldn't have come. Veridian is Veridian. She will return in her own time and not a moment sooner."

"So what the elders said—"

"Don't worry about that. Veridian is safe. If she was not, I would know it." She turned to Reed and smiled softly. "As much as any hero has been mine, Veridian is mine. We will see her again, I promise. And when we do"—she searched the bushes—"we ought to have named these birds." As she spoke, another grouse poked its tufted head from a shrub and looked at Reed, then came out of hiding completely to toddle over to Silco and peck at the grass beside his feet.

"The Orillian crowned grouse," Aster suggested. "Or perhaps the Orillian noblebird."

"They would make for very stupid monarchs," said Reed.

"Like many people do. And some you will have to put on thrones. Glory does not always come from the best. Not always the brightest. Our heroes are determined only by the goddess, and it will be up to you to guide them to their right time and place, to make the most of their feeble hides."

"Heroes? Feeble?"

"All have moments of weakness. If they didn't, they wouldn't need us." Aster shooed Silco out of the way to take aim at the grouse by his feet.

"When you went back for these birds, were you looking for Veridian?"

Aster lowered her bow. "Yes. But I found no sign of her."

"Did you see . . . anything else?" Reed swallowed. She knew the raiders had burned the bodies in her settlement, but in her mind they were all still there, forever rotting. Her mother's body was still beside the collapsed wall of their lodge, her bones wound through with growing vines.

"I did go back to your settlement, Reed," Aster said quietly.

"But there was nothing there. In that heat and those wilds, the land reclaims itself quickly."

"Good." Reed straightened and took aim at another noblebird flushed by Rabbit and actually deigning to fly. She missed, and Aster fired a shot in her wake, fast as lightning. The bird dropped into the grass. "I don't remember much of that time," Reed said. "My mother's face. The sound of Papa's voice when he sang. Reed isn't even my name, you know. I had another one. A real one. And now I have no idea what it was."

"Ferreh can recover that, at your Joining Ceremony," Aster said. "When you become an Aristene, she can delve into your memories. Your old name can be reclaimed, if that is something that you wish."

"No," Reed said. "But perhaps she can give me a new one. Reed seems a poor name for an Aristene. That is, if I make it to the Joining and do not die."

"That is not funny."

"You were the one who brought it up!"

"Because I fear it, Reed."

"It wasn't your fault, you know," she said quietly. "What happened to Selene. Not yours or Veridian's."

"You were not there," Aster replied. "But I know that it wasn't."

"And it won't be again if anything happens—"

"Nothing will happen. I won't allow it."

"You won't allow me to die?" Reed clucked her tongue. "They'll say that you are coddling me. . . ."

"I said it is not a joke!"

"It is a little bit of a joke," Reed said, and tossed her the second grouse. Aster's face grew red, and her lips had drawn into a dire thin line. But when she caught the bird, she let all her air out and waved Reed away like a bothersome fly.

"Get out of here, my brat of an initiate," she ordered. "Go and make your peace with Gretchen. And then come back home, for one last supper."

10.

THROUGH THE VEIL

When Reed went looking for her friends, she found herself swarmed by well-wishers. Word of the initiates' departure had spread quickly, and it took her twice as long as usual to reach the tavern, because so many villagers came out of their shops to touch her arm or tell the story of their first meeting. Melita, the butcher, even gave her a gift: a gruesome little necklace she had strung through with goats' teeth. "For hardiness," she said.

When Reed finally reached the tavern, Lyonene and Gretchen were already at their table. Reed paused. Should she go over? Or ask Gretchen outside to apologize first? But Gretchen half stood and gave her a wave.

"Gretchen, I—" Reed started when she reached them.

"Never mind," Gretchen said. "You were the one in danger of being left. I understand. Though if you had gone too far and broken my arm, we'd have all been waiting longer."

"And I'd have broken your arm in kind," said Lyonene, regarding Reed over her cup with serious eyes. Then she sighed and gestured for Reed to sit. "Well? What did you get from Melita? Gretchen received that fine leather pouch." She nodded to it, lying on the table. It had been colored by the red-orange dye derived from the bark of the trees in the valley. Reed held up her necklace of teeth.

"What about you?" she asked Lyonene.

"A packet of dried berries. She said they're good for the eyes and will help my arrows fly straight. As if I need the help. Trade for your teeth?" Reed nodded, and they swapped.

"It will be hard to go," Gretchen said, touching the leather pouch fondly. "Hard to leave them all, and our home."

"But go we must." Lyonene poured Reed a cup of their beloved, honey-sweetened ale. "It is why we are here in the first place."

"I'm afraid of the Veil," Gretchen blurted out. "I'm worried I won't make it. That I'll be lost there. Or that I'll throw up all over my saddle and Jana will beat me with her staff."

"Jana has never beaten you with her staff," said Lyonene. Then she narrowed her eyes. "Has she?"

"No. But sometimes I can tell that she'd like to."

"It will be fine," said Reed. "We are all going together. We won't let you be lost."

"And we'll cover your mouth if you start to look poorly," Lyonene teased. But none of them were looking forward to that part of the journey. The way the world tilted in the dark. How it had seemed to go on forever, longer than the night.

"I was eight autumns old when I went through the Veil," Reed said. "That's how we tracked ages. By seasons. I was born in the autumn, and my mother used to say that autumn children were changeable in mood, that they were wild, that they would fly away with the wind if you didn't hold them close." She closed her mouth. It had been a long time since she'd thought of that.

"That doesn't sound like you at all," said Lyonene. "What season's child is chained to the ground, hugging the same stone that they're rolling along in front of them?"

Reed laughed. She dipped her fingers into her cup and flicked ale into Lyonene's eyes.

They drank in quiet for a few moments, and waved to a few villagers who came in. The villagers tried to buy them another pitcher, but Reed declined, to Lyonene's dismay.

"What do you think it'll be like?" Gretchen asked.

"What what will be like?" Reed asked, even though she knew.

"The trials. What do you think it will be like when we pass? Will we know for sure we've done it? Or will we keep on pushing them for more and more greatness until the mentors come and claim us, or the heroes kick us out of their castles?"

"Castles." Lyonene raised her brows. "Gretchen thinks she's going to a castle."

"I said 'we,'" Gretchen said, and shoved her.

"Well. Sabil says there's nothing like the feeling of bringing glory to the goddess. She says it bursts forth from your hero and flows through you up into the sky in sparks of bright gold. Or beams. Or dust. She's said different things at different times. But always that there is nothing like it."

"But will we feel that?" Gretchen asked.

"Of course," said Reed. After the Granting of Heroes, they would each be gifted with a borrowed share of Aristene magic. Not enough to make them full members or make them immortals. But it would make them stronger, and faster. Better with their weapons. It would be just enough for Kleia Gloria to see them, a golden string tying goddess to initiate. They just didn't know how it would be given, or for how long it would last.

"Have you chosen the horses you'll take with you?" Reed asked. "Or will you ride on the backs of your mentors' saddles?"

"If I rode with Jana then at least I could vomit on her and not only myself," Gretchen said, and Reed laughed. "But I will let Jana choose my mount."

"Is that wise?"

"Not all of us have been with our horses since childhood," said Lyonene. "We didn't come to the order with our fated mounts. And speaking of fated mounts, have you said your goodbyes to Silco?"

"Goodbyes?" Reed asked.

"Surely you don't intend to bring him on your trial. It will be too dangerous, Reed. What if he's killed? What if he takes an arrow? You know that to be accepted as your Areion he must be perfect—"

"I don't intend to ride him in the first charge," Reed sputtered. Except she had. Foolishly, ridiculously, she had imagined Silco with her for every part of the journey. Because it was his journey as well. "And I need him. He is my luck."

Lyonene seemed dubious, but she nodded and sighed. "The vaunted foundling and her vaunted mount," she said, and drank.

"You mustn't say that anymore," said Reed quietly, and Lyonene and Gretchen quieted, too. She mustn't say it since it wasn't true. It couldn't be, since the elders had almost left her behind.

That afternoon, Reed and Aster ate a final meal before their hearth. After today, neither would return to it. Not for years, and perhaps never again together.

"My aim was memories," Aster said, licking her fingers of the last of the Orillian noblebird. "A nod to your origins. But perhaps we shouldn't have eaten such greasy birds just before a crossing of the Veil."

Reed smiled nervously. "I could have eaten a meal of dry bread and it wouldn't have made much difference. My stomach is already up and down and sideways."

Aster reached out and pushed Reed's hair back to keep it from dropping into her mostly untouched meat. "You've nothing to fear. You were not sick the first time, nor the second when we came to the Summer Camp, and you were only a child."

"But a child who had just seen her family killed," said Reed. "What is the Veil in the wake of that?"

She said it lightly, but Aster nodded. "I don't know why I have felt such a need to protect you all this time, when you had already survived so much. But perhaps that is why." She looked away from Reed and into the low-burning fire. "I would never have you suffer more."

Aster leaned forward for bread, her tunic falling low to reveal the bright, thick scar on her chest. She did not have many scars— three on her shield arm from deep cuts, each made by a great sword with a name, and one puckered circle on her right calf from a lucky arrow. Other, smaller scars from her time as a mortal had faded to almost nothing, though she had told Reed what stories of them she could recall. But of all her scars, the scar on her chest was by far the worst.

Reed had never asked about it. It took much to kill an Aristene, but it could be done, and the thought that another mother could be wrenched away, even an immortal one, filled her with fear.

"Aster," she said as her mentor wrapped the pot handle in a cloth and tipped more vegetables onto Reed's bread even though some still remained from her first helping. "Tell me about your first hero."

"Again?" Aster chuckled and hung the vegetable pot back up to trade it for the teapot. She poured tea for herself and for Reed and motioned for the girl to eat up. "Surely there are other heroes I could tell you of. What about Ankare, the queen who was torn between two suitors and ended up facing both in war? What about Nevien, the hunter who sought vengeance for his murdered father and gained the allegiance of a great panther who was similarly wronged? Now that was a story. I don't know whose glory shone the greater, the man's or the cat's."

"Please." Reed dutifully took a bite of stewed vegetables and wrapped both palms around her cup of tea. She had heard the tale of Aster's first hero many times. But tonight felt right for another telling.

"Very well," said Aster with a deep breath. "My first hero was a young woman. Meryn. She was a leader in her lands, a chieftain in a land that didn't allow women to become chieftains."

"So how did she become one?" Reed asked, same as she always did, and Aster's lips curled up at the corners.

"You know how—the same way any woman becomes anything in those places: her husband died. Her husband died, and I was sent to the side of this frightened girl, not much older than I was. My mentor arranged to have me delivered there as a gift: a gift of servitude to ease her time of mourning." Reed smiled. She loved that part. She liked to picture young Aster—though she wouldn't have looked much younger, as Aristene warriors ceased to age— standing before the young chieftain dressed as a fancy handmaid, skilled in the arts of dancing and singing, of healing touch.

"Sing me the songs you sang to her," Reed teased, and Aster smiled.

"I feigned a cough," she said. "So she wouldn't know that I had the voice of a scrub jay. But I could dance. I can still. Perhaps when we feast in Atropa, you will see it." Reed couldn't imagine. All she had known of Aster was the teacher, the warrior, the wielder of weapons. And of course, the cook and the hunter, the sweeper of hearths. But Aster had been in the order a long time. She had gained many talents.

"When I arrived, I found my girl sequestered in a hut of mourning. All day she cried laments and all night she wove her husband's death shroud, even though he'd been unkind and many years her senior. She'd had the courage to assume her husband's title, you see, but not much else—she had not the loyalty of his people, nor the armory to defend the claim. So she remained in that hut, wailing and stalling.

"Part of me, of course, wanted to join her. I was unsure and untried, with only a small amount of borrowed magic. Looking back, it's a wonder we were not both killed, strung up by our heels from the highest tree. But my mentor had prepared me well, and I knew which chieftains were likely to be rivals, and which could become allies."

"Tell me about your mentor, Emaleth."

"You know—" Aster began.

"Tell me something about her that I don't." That might be difficult. Reed already knew much. She knew that Emaleth was second in the order only to Ferreh and Tiern, and that she was ancient, from the days when men fought with stones and wood.

Aster looked into the fire. "I will tell you this: you will never meet her. Emaleth is gone."

Reed straightened. "She was killed? You never told me that!"

"She disappeared years ago. Long before you. Not all Aristene die by fate's hand, Reed. Some of them choose to go. Immortality is a long bargain. You do not yet understand the passage of that kind of time."

"Do you think my first hero will know of the order?" Reed asked.

"Perhaps. It depends on the lands. Our numbers are few, and we are not sung of in the songs. Our names die out, as is our way. Some parts of the world know we exist. Others have never heard of us. And to some, we are little more than rumor."

"Should I hope that they do?"

"You shouldn't hope for anything. You will have to find a way, whether they do or not."

Reed sipped her tea. Her mind wandered back to Aster's first hero, that young chieftain of so long ago. She wished she could have been there, that she could have seen it: the way Meryn and Aster charged onto the battlefield, the weapons they won during an expertly intoxicated round of gambling. Aster had guided many heroes since then, but the first was always special. She and Meryn had remained friends for a long time afterward, and after Meryn was gone, Aster had even watched over her children, and her children's children, when they had a need.

"When was the last time you saw her?" Reed asked. "Meryn."

"Oh, Reed," Aster said, and sighed. "I can hardly remember." She reached out and touched the pad of her thumb to Reed's chin. "Now, enough storytelling. Finish that bread and go and ready Silco."

At sundown, the mentors and initiates gathered at the mouth of the river, below the peak of Storm King and windward of the Sisters, a set of three smaller peaks that huddled together like sorceresses around a fire. Lyonene rode the brown mare she had ridden during the archery demonstration, and for Gretchen, Jana had taken pity and selected a stout, steady gelding who wouldn't mind having his neck clung to or being thrown up on. Reed sat astride Silco.

She hadn't been certain about bringing him when she went to catch him in the pasture. She knew it was dangerous. But the horse had been with her so long, and he was wrapped up in her dreams.

"We are each other's luck," she said to him in the pasture, and he seemed to agree, not fussing a bit when being saddled and cantering gamely to the river with his tail high.

Kleia Gloria has put us together, Reed thought. *And Kleia Gloria will keep us that way.*

"Are you ready?" Sabil asked from atop her tall bay Areion.

Lyonene nodded. Aster looked at Reed, and Reed nodded as well. When Aster had taken her through the Veil the first time, she hadn't known what to expect. This time it would be easier. But even so, her stomach felt tight as a clenched fist.

"I feel bad for these horses," Gretchen said nervously. "They are even less prepared than we are to be dragged into . . . whatever it is we're about to be dragged into."

"You are not 'dragged,'" Jana said, irritated. "But do not worry for the horses. All have traveled through it before."

Reed looked to Gretchen and gave her a closed-lip smile. It would be all right. They were together.

"Darkness falls," said Jana, with an eye to the west. "It is time. You must keep quiet now, do you understand? Once we start there is no stopping."

"Yes, mentor," the three initiates responded.

Jana, Sabil, and Aster clicked to their Areion. They rode along the riverbank, mentors ahead and initiates behind, into the forest, the darkness growing until the trees were mere silhouettes. Soon their surroundings were nothing but a void—sounds and hoofbeats and a soft wind that turned cold and stuck Reed's damp clothing to her skin. Silco snorted, perhaps remembering what had happened the last time. And the mentors began to chant.

They chanted together and on top of one another, muttering and singing, sometimes seeming to hum as they opened the way to Atropa. It was so dark that Reed couldn't see the hand before her face, but she knew the moment that they stepped through: the earth shifted beneath Silco's hooves, and her stomach tilted like she'd been dropped. They were inside the Veil, and when they emerged, they would be in another world, outside of time.

11.

CITY OF WHITE AND GOLD

Atropa was just like Reed remembered. Time was slippery here, and they had emerged from the Veil to the light of early morning. Below them, the buildings of white stone nestled in the green and the city seemed to glitter. And there, upon the central hill, stood the massive gold dome of the Citadel.

"Look at that," she said breathlessly.

"Like coming home," Lyonene agreed, but her voice was gruff and she looked slightly sick.

The journey through the Veil had been as unpleasant as it had been for Reed the first time. Their horses' bridles had been tethered to the saddles of their mentors, but in the unending dark the ropes seemed to stretch, and many times Reed was certain they would snap and she and Silco would wander until they died. Each step the colt took felt like falling, and she regretted that his coat was so black, with not even one helpful white hair to focus on.

But they had plunged ahead. Blindly, listening to the Aristenes' chant, the constant, sacred words spinning through their heads until they could no longer remember what silence was.

And then there was light.

And then they arrived.

Gretchen immediately threw up all over her own leg. But for

once, Jana was gentle and patted her shoulders.

"You will get used to it," she said, and wetted a cloth with her waterskin so the girl could clean herself.

"We'll have to do that again, won't we?" Gretchen rode up beside Reed and Lyonene, still pale. "To get out?"

"The way out is easier," Reed promised, lying.

"It's not fair that we must arrive looking like this," Gretchen said, "and they arrive looking like that." The mentors sat astride their Areion, basking in the warm light. Their Aristene regalia had emerged as they came into the city, and their white cloaks and silver armor were spotless. Even their horses seemed reinvigorated. Rabbit tossed her head and flashed Reed in the eyes with the plate of silver over her face.

"We'll look like that soon enough," said Lyonene.

"Reed already looks well," Gretchen said, frowning.

"Only because I've done it before. And I'm older than I was the first time."

"Not if you count your age by the seasons." Lyonene's color had begun to return, and the sweat in her tawny gold hair was nearly dry. "You're an autumn child and autumn never really comes to the Summer Camp. As far as I'm concerned you're still eight."

"Shut up, Lyonene."

"Shut up, all of you," said Jana. "Let's go."

The girls nudged their mounts forward and Reed patted Silco's neck. During the journey he had flecked white foam and nervous spit all over Reed's trousers.

"He'll need a good rubdown when we reach a stable," said Gretchen. She looked over the white city and whistled. "Look at this place. I bet the horse stalls are more comfortable than our huts in the valley."

Reed stared out at Atropa, trying to take it all in without blinking. Some things felt familiar: the way the streets curved and the shapes of the buildings and homes, but most things were completely new. In the daylight she could see how far the hills stretched and the high white cliffs around the side of the bay. She could see the colors of the stalls in the marketplace, their shades dyed brightly in yellow and blue and orange and purple. They rode through a herd of sheep, and Silco gently booted a few of their woolly rumps, seemingly amused by their bounce.

"This place is strange," Gretchen noted. "So many empty buildings. And so quiet."

It wasn't quiet, not really. It seemed so only because the people stopped speaking at their approach. Atropa was like the Summer Camp, where the order was known and the members revered. The people would know what day it was and who they were: the initiates who had come for the Granting of Heroes.

Reed nodded to them as they passed. They seemed a varied citizenry, with many tones of skin and many colors of eyes, but wore garments cut from similar cloth: shifts of pale linens or woven hemp, tunics or loose trousers, and all overlaid by some amount of light blue cloth. Some women wore the light blue as a veil. Others as a scarf around their shoulders. Men and boys cut it into their shirts or wrapped it about their waists as a sash. The light blue marked them as acolytes of the goddess. It bound them together and gained them her protection. Though what protection they could need in the sanctuary of Atropa, Reed didn't know.

"So quiet, and curiously clean," Lyonene said, and sniffed the air. "They must have very good drains."

Reed laughed. "Go ahead and pretend. But we know that even you are impressed."

"Pft. I am impressed by nothing that isn't handsome and shirtless."

They stopped in the wide square before the Citadel, and the mentors dismounted to hand their reins over to the waiting acolytes. Gretchen and Lyonene followed suit, but Reed hesitated until Aster said, "Give Silco over to them, Reed. They will see him settled. And I've already told them that he bites."

Reluctantly, Reed swung down and took his reins from over his head. "He really does bite," she said to the boy she handed them to.

"And so does his rider," Lyonene teased as she shouldered past. Reed watched as the horses were led away to the stable, a long wide building set to one side of the Citadel steps. It, too, was strangely quiet: there were no neighs and no stomping feet. Reed wanted to follow them and warn the grooms about Silco's temper and where to stand to avoid being bitten, but she pulled herself away to join her friends at the feet of the Citadel steps.

"The acolytes will take you to the baths and dress you for the ceremony," said Jana. "Then we'll await you at the top of the Citadel steps."

"The baths," said Gretchen. "That sounds nice. I would like to be properly clean after . . ." She made a sheepish face and hid the stain of her sickness by crossing her leg behind the other. The mentors traded glances, and Sabil chuckled.

"You will indeed be properly clean. We'll see you soon."

"The mentors are even stranger here," Lyonene muttered as they followed a slim, young acolyte in a light blue gown. Reed turned around. Aster, Jana, and Sabil didn't immediately go up into the Citadel. They went down the street and disappeared around a corner. The last time Reed had been in Atropa she had never strayed from Aster's side. She remembered the sound of Rabbit's hoofbeats clattering across the stones of the square. She remembered the breathless feeling of being carried up those endless stairs.

"Reed," Gretchen whispered. "Keep up!"

Reed turned and hurried along. This is how it would be now. They would be on their own.

12.

CEREMONIAL PREPARATION

The baths were located not far from the Citadel and were comprised of several small private soaking pools and a larger communal bath. The initiates were directed to the communal pool, and the acolyte pointed to a doorway beside it, past a colonnade of white pillars.

"Initiates may leave their clothing inside. You will find a white bathing garment to wear in the soaking pool."

Reed and the others went quickly through the door to get out of their sweat-stained buckskin trousers and tunics. The bathing garments were pale linen and felt like wearing nothing at all.

"Oh my," Gretchen said as she stepped into the heated water and sank down to her shoulders. "I hope they do not expect us to hurry. I could linger here all day." Reed stepped in behind her and watched Lyonene swim toward the center and dive below to come up on the other side. The water was so warm it was almost hot and instantly leached the nervous tension from her body. It smelled faintly of sulfur, but not enough to stink, and took on a greenish-blue hue from the mosaic of colored tiles that lined the bottom.

But the respite was not to last. Three attendants emerged from the interior and joined them to kneel before each girl and vigorously begin to scrub. They used rough cloths to scrape away any filth that lingered on their skin and sharp, metal tools to pick dirt from under their nails. By the time they were finished, Reed had never been so clean, and Gretchen and Lyonene looked almost injured, their pale skin gone red as a boiled crayfish. Now they knew why the mentors had snickered.

"That's enough," Lyonene said finally as she pulled her hand away from her bathing attendant. "I am clean. I am so clean I am a whole new person." The attendants looked at each other and nodded. Reed flinched when one of them came at her with a cloth, but thankfully, the drying was gentle. Afterward, they were folded into lovely white tunics edged in silver thread.

"This way."

They followed the acolyte out of the bathhouse and past another colonnade of pillars to a small building of white brick. Inside, another acolyte waited, an older woman this time, dressed in a belted tunic with short sleeves.

"Greetings, initiates," she said. "I am Sarah, and I will be preparing you for the Granting."

"We can't get any cleaner," said Lyonene. "What more is there to prepare?"

Sarah smiled. "Do not fear. The painful scrubbing is over. The rest of the preparation you will find more pleasant." She stepped around the back of Reed and lifted her long dark hair. "This will need much wax, to straighten the waves," she said. "And you—" She ran her fingers through Lyonene's mane, wilder than Reed's, that had begun to curl at the ends as it dried. "But you—" She ran a palm over Gretchen's head; her brown hair out of its braids was smooth. "Leska and Raven will see to you. I will prepare the tall one. Choose a place and kneel."

Reed looked around. The room was small and open, and low tables had cushioned pillows placed before them. It smelled of incense, and the walls danced with flickering light, thanks to garlands of thin-pounded silver and gold hung from the ceiling. Reed selected a table and knelt upon the pillow. Sarah knelt behind her and began to comb her hair. Combing and pulling.

"What are you doing?" she asked as her scalp burned.

"Applying the wax."

Each initiate grimaced as the combs moved through their hair, coating it in wax all the way to the ends. It hurt terribly, and it only hurt worse when the acolytes began to yank the hair together to form a tight, waxed bun. Then they secured it with what felt like a hundred pins, each sharp and scraping against Reed's head.

"I thought you said the rest would be pleasant."

"I said, 'more pleasant,'" Sarah replied. "The baths are quite horrible." She placed the final pin and pressed her warm palms to the sides of Reed's head. It felt so soothing after the pain that Reed nearly fell asleep. "Do not rest on this bun," Sarah cautioned. "It must last until the ceremonies are finished. If you ruin it, we will have to do it again."

"Again," Gretchen murmured. "Never again!"

Reed looked at her friends. The buns were so tight that they stretched the skin at their temples. It had been many years since they had been groomed in such a way. Reed had never done it: she had never worn gowns or had her hair twisted into plaits. She'd thought it would be luxurious, that it would make her close her eyes like the cats in the Summer Camp when someone stopped to stroke their backs. Instead, her teeth were bared and Gretchen's face was streaked with tears. Only Lyonene, who had grown up in gowns before being sent to her convent, was able to endure it with any grace.

"There now," said Sarah, looking at them. "The three of you go before the goddess as great beauties." She snapped her fingers, and the other acolytes, Leska and Raven, brought forth small glass bottles and set themselves at the initiates' feet. It was only hot oil, to be rubbed into their skin, but every one of them flinched at the first touch.

"This is nicer," Gretchen said as Leska gently cleaned the tearstains from her cheeks. But it was more than that. After the journey through the Veil and the horrors of the bath, to be touched with kindness felt like floating. The oils smelled of sweet flowers, and the acolytes' hands were soft and practiced. Reed felt her eyes slip shut and awoke to the feel of Lyonene's slap.

"Don't be fooled," Lyonene said, settling back into Raven's soothing touch. "This is really just another form of torture, to lure our exhausted bodies to sleep so we ruin our buns."

After the oil treatments were completed, they made their way wearily out of the building and past the colonnade, toward the many, many steps of the Citadel.

"I'd take combat training over that any day," Reed said, stretching her back. Gretchen agreed, but Lyonene just smiled and examined her feet in their new leather sandals.

"We look like initiates, finally," she said. "We look . . ." In their waxed buns and identical tunics, scrubbed clean and purified, they had never looked more like sisters.

"Wait," Gretchen said.

"What's wrong?" Reed asked.

"Nothing is wrong." Gretchen smiled her usual bright smile. "I just wanted a moment. One last moment before." She slid her hands down their arms and squeezed their fingers. Only Kleia Gloria knew how long their Hero's Trials would last. Lyonene boasted that hers would be over in one battle—and some were. But others took seasons. Or years. There was no rush to greatness in an immortal order, Aster liked to say.

Together they walked up the steps and reached the summit slightly breathless. They stood in the hall of warriors, lined by statues of famous Aristene, marble figures in poses of battle. Lyonene, the scholar, was trying to discern who was who from the legends that she knew, leading Gretchen to this one and that, their mouths slightly agape.

Reed didn't follow. She was remembering the last time she had been there, when it was lit only by torchlight and she had been pulled through it so quickly, still sick and reeling from the Veil, her small legs burning as they tried to keep pace with Aster's longer ones. Back then it had been mostly a blur; she hadn't realized just how many statues there were, how many legendary warriors, tucked into every alcove and stretching into pathways right and left. Curious, she explored, walking past marble figures caught in midbattle until she stopped at one: a statue of a warrior standing still with feet apart. She held a stone hammer in one fist and a bone knife in the other. Half of her head was shaved, the hair on the other side long and blowing in a wind. Reed read the name engraved in the block.

"Emaleth."

"The mentor of your mentor," Ferreh said. Reed jumped back and quickly dropped into a bow. The Aristene elder was deadly silent and still; Reed could have passed her in the shadows and mistaken her for another statue.

"Ferreh," Reed said. She looked around; she hadn't realized she'd wandered so far from Gretchen and Lyonene.

"The mentor of your mentor must always be a wondrous thing to see. For our mentors are so wise and learned; it is impossible to think that they, too, were once initiates." Ferreh moved to stand beside her and studied the figure of Emaleth. "Stranger still to stand before a woman of stone when you knew the woman of flesh." She crossed her arms and her silver armor winked in the light streaming in through the columns. "I miss her."

"I didn't know she was gone," Reed admitted. "Aster just told me." Ferreh didn't seem surprised by that. She only nodded.

"Ancient Emaleth."

"But you are even more ancient," Reed said rudely, and the elder laughed.

"There you are," she said quietly. "That spindle-legged girl who tried to bite Tiern and spat crumbs at my sandals. I hardly recognized her under the initiate you've become." Reed flushed. She didn't remember doing any of that. But she could see herself doing it. "Long have I wondered how you fared. Many times I wanted to cross the Veil into the Summer Camp, to look in upon you and your little black colt. But I did not. It was only now, at the time of your Hero's Trial, that curiosity got the better of me.

"You must know, Reed, that it is not common for the elders to visit an initiate."

"We thought it was because there were three of us."

"That, too, is uncommon. But it is not why."

"Why, then?" Reed asked.

Ferreh reached out a long-fingered hand and touched the side of Reed's face, like Aster sometimes did.

"When you were brought to us those years ago, we did not know what to do with you. You were young, one small lone survivor of an awful massacre, too young to begin your training and we'd not yet been called to your mark—Aster had not been sent to claim you, and many marked girls perish in the world before we can find them and summon them to us. Coming upon you was a stroke of fate. And though you were angry and frightened and all teeth and claws, I saw something more." She turned away and faced the sun, letting the gold fall upon her brown cheeks. "That night in the dome, Kleia Gloria shone upon you as bright as this. As clear as the light that pierces the water of the stream to bounce across the rocks below."

"What did it mean?" Reed asked.

"I didn't know," Ferreh replied. "So I was curious. Curiosity was why we took you in, Reed. I wanted to know what you would do. What you would become."

Reed looked again at the statue of Emaleth. Even in stone the warrior's scowl was deep and her fists so tightly clenched that it seemed a wonder her depicted weaponry didn't crumble. Aster spoke of her as kind and wise. But seeing her, she looked hard and frightening. "Are you disappointed?" Reed asked.

She turned to Ferreh, but the elder was gone. Vanished like she had never been there. Reed spun as Aster rounded the corner.

Aster held her arms out and kissed Reed on the cheek. Reed jerked away sharply.

"Take care for the bun! It was . . . difficult to achieve."

"Consider yourselves lucky. When I was an initiate, they used to shave our heads."

Reed's eyes widened, and Aster chuckled.

"Not really." She glanced at the stone figure of her mentor. "I imagine this hall must look different in the light of day."

"Everything looks different. Yet it feels the same. Where are the others?"

"With their mentors. It is time to go below and take the oaths. Time to be granted a share of our magic." Aster rubbed her thumb along Reed's cheek as if she'd seen a smudge. "What are you doing here, off so far on your own?"

Reed looked into the shadows, making sure no elder was there crouching in the darkness.

"Nothing," she said. "I was led away by the statues. I hadn't realized I'd left them behind."

"Well, then." Aster stepped back and Reed squared her shoulders. They were the same height now, but she would always think of Aster as tall and towering. "My Reed. Are you ready?"

13.

MAGIC IN THE BLOOD

Reed followed Aster through the curving halls, up one staircase and down another. It didn't take her long to become completely lost. Some things in Atropa had seemed smaller than they had in her memories but not the Citadel. The Citadel would never be anything but enormous and unknowable.

When they reached the darker corridors, Aster took a torch from the wall to light their way. Reed glanced back and saw that it was replaced almost instantly, the acolyte there and gone like a ghost. She couldn't imagine being so aware, knowing the inner goings-on of the Citadel well enough to be precisely where she was needed at precisely the right moment. Yet the acolytes managed it without a drop of the goddess's magic. They were not immortal—some even returned to the regular world after their time of service. But most lived and died as citizens of Atropa. Reed didn't know where they came from or how they came to be devotees. Perhaps they came from the Summer Camp or another of the Aristene strongholds—

"Are any of the acolytes failed initiates?" she asked suddenly.

"A few initiates who did not join the order have chosen to spend their years in service," Aster replied. "But not many."

At the end of a long hall, Aster stopped before a door of dark wood strengthened by fat bands of iron. Yellow light emanated from beneath it and illuminated the tips of Reed's toes.

"Inside this door you will take your first oaths, Reed. And I will give you a drop of my magic."

"Your magic?" Reed asked.

"The sharing of magic between mentor and initiate maintains the bond between them during the separation of the trial. I will not always be with you, Reed. But through the bond of magic I will never be far." She looked at Reed in the torchlight, and Reed swallowed. She should say that she was honored by that gift, that to be mentored by an Aristene as great as Aster was something she didn't deserve. She should thank her for all she had done, the thousand small kindnesses over the years. Instead she nodded, and Aster opened the door.

Inside the room was close and quiet. Light from candles flickered upon the stone walls and made shadows of every curve and crevice, and as they walked past, the tiny flames moved with their breaths and the movements of their bodies. Aside from the candles the room was mostly bare: there was only a small circular table set in the center and draped in white cloth. It was set with many candles and held a cup of glazed clay pottery. Beside the cup rested a knife, the handle inset with red and green stones.

Reed knew the words to the vows she would take. Aster and the other mentors had tutored them, made them commit them to memory. She knew what Aster would say so well she could have said it all herself. Yet standing there in the low light, with the jewels in the knife handle glinting like eyes, Reed feared she would forget and get it all wrong.

"Shouldn't we begin?" Reed asked.

"Soon. We must wait for the elder."

"The elder?"

"Either Ferreh or Tiern will come. We may have to wait a while if they decided to administer Lyonene's and Gretchen's oaths before yours."

But Reed was unsurprised when the door opened a few moments later, just as she was unsurprised to see that it was Ferreh who walked through it. The elder didn't look quite the same as she had above, when they stood together before the stone statue of Emaleth. Now she wore full battle regalia, with a long sword strapped to her back across a studded shield and knives strapped to her waist in leather sheaths. Her deep brown skin had been painted with white, swirling symbols at her wrists and throat, and her eyes above the candles looked through Reed as through a stranger, as if her fond words had been a figment of Reed's imagination.

Ferreh positioned herself across the table from them.

"What do you wish?" the elder asked.

"To be an Aristene," Reed replied smoothly. "To join the order and dine at the Citadel and send tribute to Kleia Gloria." Beside her, Reed felt Aster relax. She remembered the words and felt their weight, no longer mere phrases to be learned and regurgitated on command. The oaths were real now, her first before the goddess.

"To be an Aristene is to give up your mortal life," said Ferreh. "And to be granted a new one. To be an Aristene is to forfeit everything else. You will have no husband. No children. Your bloodline will end. Do you understand?"

Reed's jaw tightened as each supposed cost dropped from Ferreh's lips. She had no use for a husband. And she was all that was left of her bloodline. There was no blood to go back to.

"My bloodline will end," Reed said. "But I won't." She met Ferreh's eyes. Did she really think that any of this could change her mind? Prices and consequences hung suspended in the future as blurry and distant as clouds in the sky. The order was her path. The order was everything.

"You will be strong and you will be fast. You will be a maker of destinies, shaping the rise and fall of kingdoms. What will you be?"

"An Aristene," Reed said. "A servant of Kleia Gloria."

"A servant?" Ferreh asked.

"A servant. Her will before my own."

Ferreh took up the knife. She turned to Aster and pointed the tip at her chest.

"Aristene, will you accept the burden of this initiate and watch over her during the Hero's Trial?"

"I will."

Aster held her arm out over the mouth of the clay cup and Ferreh slashed a fast cut between her wrist and elbow. It was deep, but not deep enough to scar a member of the order—Aster would heal in a matter of days. Her blood ran dark in the candlelight, falling into the cup.

Ferreh turned to Reed.

"Do you accept this offering of your mentor?"

"I do."

Ferreh waited, and after a few breaths, reached out to gently tug Reed's arm over the rim of the cup. Reed flushed. They hadn't taught them what the magic-sharing ritual entailed, nothing past the oaths, but she should have known what to do. Lyonene had probably put her arm out so fast she had pushed Sabil's away still bleeding.

Ferreh cut. The sting of the knife was sharp. She held Reed's arm steady as the blood dripped down, then wrapped it in a bandage of white, careful to keep any blood from falling onto the tablecloth. The knife she had already set beside the cup—her cuts had been so fast that the blade hadn't even been soiled.

Aster took up the cup and drank, and Reed's stomach turned when she lowered it and saw her lips tinged red at the corners and shiny in the center.

"And now the initiate will drink," Ferreh said.

Reed had tasted blood before, many times when she had taken a hit from Jana or Lyonene, or even Aster. But this was different. It wasn't only her blood, and it wasn't only blood—it had been mixed with some kind of oil and a fine dusting of chopped herbs. When it hit her tongue, her throat locked and refused to swallow, so she took all of the blood into her mouth and held it puffed out in her cheeks, like the cheeks of the pale white fish they kept in the pond beside the north pasture. The taste was fatty and salty. Metallic. She wanted to retch and sucked air through her nose. Finally, she swallowed hard. The mixture of blood reached her stomach and bobbed there a moment as if it were solid.

Ferreh smiled warmly, signaling that the ritual was at an end.

"You did well," Aster said. "For a moment I thought you'd be sick, and we'd have to start all over again."

"Is that what would have happened?" Reed asked. "We'd have just started over?"

"Of course." Aster clapped her on the shoulder and went to open the door, but Ferreh put a hand on Reed's arm.

"A moment with your initiate," she said, and Aster bowed and left them alone. At the table, Ferreh took up a stone pitcher and poured water into the bloodstained clay cup. She swirled it out and tossed the liquid into the corner. Then she held her own wrist.

"Wait," Reed said before the knife could bite into the elder's skin. "I don't want this. I can do it on my own."

Ferreh looked at Reed with calm brown eyes. "This is not for you, child. It is for the order." She sliced fast and deep; her blood ran down in a ribbon of red. "Now," she said, and held out the cup. "Drink."

Reed hesitated. An elder's blood. She didn't need to be told that it was not commonly given.

"It will not tie me to you," Ferreh said. "It is not like the tie between mentor and initiate, where both drink."

"Then what will it do? Why am I being given this?"

"Why do you question the elder of your order?" Ferreh asked.

Reed took the cup. But she couldn't bring it to her lips, and the elder sighed.

"Something is coming, Reed. That may threaten us all." Ferreh stepped closer, her voice low. "Three initiates is uncommon. A foundling girl is uncommon. And the movements of men have become *uncommon*. Tonight we send three initiates into the world for more than their Hero's Trials. I do not wish to ask an initiate for this kind of faith. But for the order I will ask it."

"Will you ask the same of the others? Lyonene is the fastest, the cleverest, if the order has need—"

"Lyonene was not the one I saw in the waters of the well. She was not the one delivered to us in the night, shrouded by death and blood."

"I don't understand, elder," Reed said. But Ferreh said no more. She was the mind, as they called her. She was the leader.

Reed tipped the cup back and drank until it was empty.

14.

THE GRANTING OF HEROES

When Reed and Aster climbed up the winding stairs and stepped into the interior of the dome, Lyonene and Sabil were already there. Lyonene had the same white bandage on her arm that Reed had and kept that hand clenched in a tight fist, as if she was trying to squeeze more blood into the cloth. She raised her chin when Reed entered, and she winked. *I'm glad to see you*, that wink said. *And I'm glad that I beat you here.*

Reed wrinkled her nose at her, and Lyonene stifled a smile. The initiates separated from their mentors and wandered around the space of the dome.

"What do you think?" Reed asked as Lyonene's eyes drifted to the curving walls.

"What do *you* think," Lyonene countered, "now that you're seeing it in the light?"

Reed followed the progress of the murals until she found the one she remembered best: the mural of the Areion. She was relieved to find it looked just how she thought it looked, but there was a dimension of strangeness to it now that she had met the bay stallion at its center, face-to-face. Ferreh's mount, Amondal. Desert Fire. And prettier, even, than his painting.

"There isn't much to it, really," Lyonene said, though her gaze caught upon the different-colored stones of the sacred well and stayed there as if she thought it might move. "And yet—" Her footsteps slowed to one side of the World's Gate, the great engraved silver disk set into one part of the floor. "Even the air here feels heavy. Heavy and charged."

"Gretchen isn't here," Reed whispered.

"I hope she didn't throw up again," said Lyonene. "That blood was the worst thing I've ever had to drink."

The worst thing, Reed thought. *And you only had to do it once.* How jealous Lyonene would be if she knew that Reed had drunk from an elder. But it didn't feel like something to be boasted about. She touched her belly, where Ferreh's blood mixed with Aster's. She should have spat it out. She didn't need the elder's help in the trial. But she'd taken it anyway. And now her excitement was mixed with a cold, dark dread.

"Reed? You're not going to be sick, are you?"

"Of course not." Reed steered Lyonene away from the World's Gate and looped her bandaged arm through her friend's. This was the day of their Granting, the Granting of Heroes. It was always going to be a day of mysteries, and she wouldn't let questions spoil it. "Did you remember all the words to the oaths?" Reed asked. "Or did Tiern frighten them back down your throat?"

"Ha." Lyonene snorted. "She is not that frightening. Or maybe she is, and I am just that steady." Tiern indeed was that frightening. No matter what had happened, Reed was relieved that it had been Ferreh who'd administered her oaths. Ferreh whose blood she'd had to drink. Tiern's would have probably burned her throat or seethed like snakes all the way to her stomach.

As they walked, easing their nerves and studying the murals, their eyes kept flickering toward the well. It stood just as Reed remembered it, alone and off-center, though it had seemed taller then. Stones of differing colors and thicknesses stacked atop one another in no discernible pattern. Most were plain, but some sparkled with quartz or were veined with shining metals. Aster had told her that the stones of the well came from many places. Some that no longer existed. "Fallen cities?" she had asked, but Aster had said no more.

They turned suddenly as the elders stepped up into the dome. Tiern swept past them, her hair of many colors twisted back into a mottled braid. Ferreh swept past them as well.

"We should begin," she said.

"Shouldn't we wait for Gretchen?" Reed looked to the door, at the stairs coming up through the marble.

"No," said Tiern. She reached over the well and slid the heavy cover of gray stone to the floor to rest gently against the well's base. Reed had seen Aster do the same, but it was still strange to watch Tiern's slender arm move the stone with such ease. What it must be like, to wield that much strength. The thought made her dizzy.

Beside the well, Ferreh held out her hand. "Come, Reed."

Lyonene frowned, and despite her nerves, Reed felt a whisper of triumph. She could understand why Lyonene would expect to go before her, but Reed was pleased that she hadn't. Reed had been there first, after all, eight years ago.

She stepped forward, her heart loud in her ears. *I will see the boy*, she thought. *The boy with sandy-gold hair. I will see him again, finally.* But what if she didn't? If she saw another face inside the well, would it spoil this moment?

"Bend to the water, and drink," Ferreh said. "Let the droplets fall from your hand back into the well and spill not a drop past its edge."

Reed bent. The last time she had been there she had been so small she'd needed to lean over the edge to see. She still remembered the feel of the stones against her chest. Her hands ran over them now, some rough and others pale and smooth as milk, some cut to straight edges and others seemingly torn whole from their bedrock. Looking down, the water was high, higher than it had seemed when she was a child, but no less thick and strange-looking. She remembered the way it had shimmered, how it had moved beneath her finger like smoke. She hadn't known the rituals would require she drink so much. But not even the strange water could be worse than the blood.

Reed dipped her hand beneath the surface and brought a cupped palm to her lips.

It was cold, colder even than the water of the ice lake that flowed from the heart of Storm King. The ripples left by her hand were thick and slow, but the water didn't feel thick or unpleasant. It felt like water and tasted slightly of minerals, perhaps leached from the multicolored stones. Droplets fell and broke the surface in a small shower. As she and Ferreh and Aster watched, their reflections wavered away, and her hero was revealed.

Sandy hair. Fierce eyes. The same serious expression he'd worn as a boy, but in the face of a young man. The image in the well shifted to show him in the tunic and scant armor of a soldier, mud and blood streaked across his cheek. With the water in her belly Reed knew that he was brave—nearly fearless—and she sensed a fierce love in him for someone he admired: an elder brother.

Reed held her breath. What strange tether had bound them together so long ago? What strings of fate had linked them even as they were children? Whatever string or tether it was, Reed felt it wind through time and tighten. *He is mine*, she thought. *He has been mine since the beginning.*

"What is his name?" Ferreh asked.

"Hestion," Reed said. "He is Hestion, of Glaucia."

Glaucia. It was the name currently given to the vast wildlands that lay between the western side of the Sendel Mountains and the Priaspian Sea. It had also been Glaukia and Glaukos, the name changing as wars over it were fought and rulers changed. Or so Reed had learned in her teachings.

She looked from Ferreh to Aster and finally to Lyonene, who gave her a smile despite being so eager to be called forward that she was going to gnaw through her own lip. Beside the well, the elders traded places, and Reed and Aster walked back to the others.

Tiern held out her hand.

"Lyonene."

The girl walked forward and reached into the well with both hands. Reed rose up a bit onto her toes as Lyonene stared into the depths. Tiern and Sabil leaned over the side with her, and Tiern's stern face stretched into a frown.

"What is his name?" she asked.

"His name is Alsander of Cerille," Lyonene replied. She straightened. "The king's son. The crown prince."

The king's son. Of course. And from the wealthy country of Cerille. Cerille was actually not far from Hestion's country of Glaucia—it lay to the east across the sea, where the crossing was the narrowest—but it was far more civilized, a true nation of allied cities, rich with exports. Cerille was a country of clever scholars and innovators, and worshipped a god of poverty at the same time as they aimed to enrich themselves. Lyonene would fit right in.

"A crown prince," Reed whispered when Lyonene returned to her side. Lyonene grinned, probably thinking that with the leg up she would be back in Atropa before the seasons changed.

"Glaucia and Cerille," Sabil said. "Can this be a mistake?"

The initiates looked up.

"The well doesn't make mistakes," said Ferreh.

"But . . . Glaucia and Cerille are headed to as large a war as the world has ever seen. Is this truly a trial for initiates?" Sabil glanced at Aster, perhaps for agreement, but Aster said nothing. Of course she didn't often train initiates, so perhaps she did not know. "Elders—"

"The well knows to whom the heroes are granted, Sabil," said Tiern, her eyes glittering. Reed looked at Lyonene. *Tonight we send three initiates into the world for more than their Hero's Trials.* That's what Ferreh had said.

"Very well." Sabil relented.

"Go now and brief your initiates before the feast. And do not tarry," Ferreh said, and smiled. "I am hungry." The elders brushed past Reed and Lyonene as they left, disappearing smoothly down the steps.

"Did you hear that?" Lyonene whispered as the mentors talked beside the well, and Reed nodded. "Does it not make you wonder what it is she has planned?" Lyonene cast her eyes overhead, where the mural of Kleia Gloria had been painted upon the ceiling. Reed looked up into the face of the goddess, painted brightly and lit by the sun. Kleia Gloria's eyes were at once fierce and tender, firm and nurturing. Reed took a breath.

"I only hope that whatever it is, I am equal to it."

15.

THE OUTFITTER

"Wait," Reed said as Aster and Sabil led them down from the dome. "What about Gretchen?"

"Gretchen has been delayed," Sabil replied. The mentor sounded terse, perhaps still uneasy about the assignment of their heroes. Reed could barely believe it herself. But it was real. The day had come, and they were going to war.

As large a war as the world has ever seen.

At the bottom of the stairs the mentors turned them through a maze of corridors, past storerooms and broad, open balconies, through a tall doorway with doors made of thick dark wood. They followed the mentors into the outward-facing chamber. Behind them, the wall on either side of the doorway was lined with books and scrolls. An upright musical instrument sat in a corner, strung with silver wire. There were many tables, chairs, and benches, and pretty vases of white flowers. Cups of quills for writing and gold pots of ink. On another table across the room sat a game board laid out with pieces of black and white stone.

Reed walked toward the open wall of columns to look down upon the city, where the light was softly fading. The white of the buildings turned to gold and eventually to soft pinks, and on the hills the sheep moved down toward the city in fat, grayish lines.

"Reed."

She turned at the sound of Aster's voice and joined Lyonene at the table where the mentors had laid out a vast map. Sabil used pieces from the game board to weigh down the edges and ran her hand across the images of land and sea as if she was wiping the borders clean, leaving the map fresh for the Aristene to shape anew. She placed a white stone game piece into Lyonene's hand, and a black one into Reed's.

"You will meet Alsander of Cerille in his capital city. Show me," Sabil said, and Lyonene deftly placed her piece in Cerille near the southern port.

"Reed," said Aster. "We will find Hestion in Glaucia, in the seat of the king's region. The king's men are the fighting elite known as—"

"The Docritae," Reed said. "I remember." She studied the map. It was an area she knew rather well, a region of the world that excelled in trade and which frequently broke out in skirmishes, and of the men there, the Docritae were the most wild. They had the bravest soldiers and were the ones most likely to lead a charge. Lyonene would know that too and be counting on her prince's crown to earn him a place at the front. But Hestion was a prince as well. He was just a younger son, not the one who was to inherit.

She slid her fingers across the blue ink of the sea to the northwest, where Glaucia lay, and placed her piece.

"Very good," said Aster.

"The city to be sacked lies here." Sabil tapped her finger in the middle of the map, on the country of Rhonassus, and its capital, Roshanak. It lay to the east of Cerille and to the southeast of

Glaucia, across the sea. Rhonassus was as rich in coin as it was in soldiers, and Roshanak was a fortress. It had never been conquered.

"The land between is too mountainous to easily move an army." Sabil moved her finger in a line between Cerille and Rhonassus. "And of course Glaucia must come by ship. So the forces have decreed that they will meet here." She tapped her finger near a large bay to the southeast of all. "The Port of Lacos. They will supply there and arrange for transports of goods to support the siege. And there the armies of Cerille and Glaucia will join forces to sail directly into the port at Roshanak to take the city.

"But there is more." She tapped again upon the Port of Lacos. "Cerille and Glaucia have their own complicated past, and already they squabble over who will lead. They have devised a way to settle this when they reach the port." Reed looked up and Lyonene grinned at her, green eyes sparkling. The Hero's Trial was not a competition, but she was determined to make it one.

"The Port of Lacos is known for many things," said Aster, taking control of the map. "Imported spices. Dyes. And horses. Lacos is home to a herd of legend, and when the armies arrive, they will hold a great race. The kings, both of Cerille and of Glaucia, have determined that the winner will lead the armies"— Aster glanced at Reed—"and his country will have his pick of the finest of the horse."

Now it was Reed's turn to grin. The things she could best Lyonene at were few, but one was horses. She knew them better and she was the better rider. She and Silco could win that race themselves and give the honor of leadership to Hestion as a gift. "A fine prize," she said, her voice casual. "In open battle the army with the strongest cavalry always has the advantage. I am sorry, Lyonene."

"Sorry for what?" Lyonene said, and smirked. "You've not won anything, yet. And you must not forget Gretchen; if the initiates are being sent to this war then she will also have a hero in the fray—"

"You think I can't outride Gretchen?" Reed asked.

Lyonene narrowed her eyes.

"So *you* will ride?"

"Enough." Sabil brushed the pieces from the map and rolled it back up. "This is not a game. This is glory to be won. More glory than any initiate has the right to covet," she muttered, "and yet perhaps not enough for the both of you."

The initiates quieted.

"Sabil," Reed asked softly. "Why do they go to war with Rhonassus? Roshanak is a rich jewel, but it has been left alone for a hundred years."

The mentors looked at each other, and Sabil went to the shelves and selected a book.

"The nations of this region worship different gods," she said, and set the book down to flip through it. "But for generations they have been united under one prophet: a familial line of prophets who can speak with all of the gods' voices. This prophet is known as the Prophet of Scylloi—the Prophet of All. During the winter months, the Scylloi Prophet made his pilgrimage to Roshanak, to prophesize for King Oreas. This is King Oreas."

She turned a page and planted a finger upon an ink drawing of a man with golden skin and long curling dark hair. He was draped in a cape of green and weighed down with so many pieces of jewelry it was a wonder he could lift his hands.

"And when the prophet tried to leave, King Oreas cut off his head."

Reed looked again upon the man in the book. The knowledge of what he had done infused his visage with an evil glint. The mouth that at first seemed to smile now appeared to snarl. His eyes were narrowed with calculation rather than with mirth.

"A holy war," Lyonene remarked. "Passions will run high."

"Passions and tensions." Sabil slapped her palm down across the image of King Oreas's face. "Use your heroes to slay this monster," she said, "and you will complete your Hero's Trial."

The mentors kept them in the library a while longer, separating them to pore over more detailed maps of their respective nations. Aster pulled books from the shelves, including one that showed the line of succession to the Glaucan throne. It was broken many times and had branches reaching in all directions; Aster had to unfold several flaps of paper in order to view the whole of it. In a few generations more it would need to be redrawn onto an even larger piece of parchment.

Hestion's family, the men who led the group of soldiers known as the Docritae, had held power only since his father's youth. But unlike many Glaucan ascensions, King Arik had come to the throne peacefully, through marriage to the only daughter of the previous king. The queen, a woman named Iska, had borne two living sons: Belden, the eldest, and Hestion, who was Reed's hero. She had also borne a living daughter, but the child had only survived to infancy. When the queen herself passed some years ago following a long illness, King Arik had fully inherited the crown.

"He has lost a mother," Reed said quietly.

"Yes," said Aster. "You both have; you can use that."

Reed flinched, and Aster softened at the stricken look upon her face.

"It is not cruel," her mentor said. "It is commonality. You will understand one another. And you must find ways to endear him to you, Reed. You must earn his trust and his affection." She glanced at the girl slantways. "Just . . . not too much."

Reed smiled at her mentor's teasing. How many times had she heard the caution? *Over your immortal years you will love many heroes. But be on your guard against the first one.* A Hero's Trial was too fraught with nerves and desperation. Better to save those feelings for after the Joining, when Reed was an Aristene, and her heart was not so tender and mortal.

Still, Reed allowed herself a moment to think about him: Hestion of Glaucia. It was nice to have a name to put to the face she'd carried in her mind for so long. She wondered if he felt it on the other side of the Veil when she saw his reflection within the well. She wondered what his stormy eyes would look like filled with surprise. And then she shut him away as Aster shut the book.

"These histories are here," she said. "They are here for you to peruse and are frequently updated by the acolytes and by our Aristene scholars. But they are not all you will need." Across the room, Sabil and Lyonene finished their lesson and straightened to listen. "There are skills an Aristene must have when she travels to the far reaches of the world. Tools and weapons specific to the task she must undertake. And for all of those, you must go to the Outfitter."

"The Outfitter?" Reed asked as she and Lyonene followed their mentors through the Citadel. She reached up to rub a sore spot out of her tired neck, and her fingers itched to tear into the tight, waxed bun.

"Don't," Lyonene cautioned. "It's still supposed to last."

"The Outfitter," Sabil called back over her shoulder, "is imbued with magic to give an Aristene the gifts she needs to navigate any circumstance. She has magic to charm rhythm into a dancer's feet, magic to coax languages from an Aristene tongue. She has knives meant to be concealed and daggers for display. Often an Aristene will learn as much about the nature of her mission from the Outfitter as she does from the sacred well."

"I—" Reed began, and Aster looked back.

"You will understand soon enough."

They had reached the hall of warriors, where the great steps of the Citadel stretched down toward the square. But instead of exiting, the mentors led them aside to a slim, stone doorway. The steps below it led into the utter dark, yet the mentors took no torches.

"Tread carefully," said Sabil as Reed reached out to feel her way along the wall.

"What is this leading to?" Lyonene asked. "A pile of initiate skeletons with all of the bones cracked off at the ankles?"

The mentors didn't reply. They led them down and down, far below the Citadel where the air smelled damp. When they reached the bottom, Reed felt the crunch of straw beneath her sandals. But ahead was a glow of light. They followed the mentors to a door, and Aster lifted the heavy latch and shouldered through.

Inside was . . . a home. A home as if hollowed out from a rock, with high arching ceilings that angled back into the darkness.

There were a table and chairs and vases of wildflowers, and the light from the hearth was yellow and warm.

"The air smells fresh," Lyonene commented. "How is that possible?"

"The Outfitter is blessed by the goddess," said Sabil. "She is an acolyte but not like the others. She serves Kleia Gloria—not the order. When you come to her, you must do as you are told and show her respect. She is ageless. And she is strong."

Reed stiffened as the sounds of footsteps echoed from the rear of the dwelling, where the ceiling slanted down to shadows. What sort of being was the Outfitter? The mentors made her seem more frightening than Tiern.

"She approaches," said Sabil. "You may go."

"What?" Lyonene asked.

"You may wait outside. You are only initiates—you are not privy yet to these secrets."

"Then why did you make us walk down those treacherous stairs?" Lyonene thrust her arm past Reed, gesturing to the corridor.

"So you would know the way when it was time." Sabil and Aster drew their knives. They held up the arms they had cut during the oaths, and Reed knew that whatever the Outfitter was, she would require more blood. So much of the order, so much of glory, was blood.

She and Lyonene went into the hall to wait. Lyonene left the door cracked to give them a hint of yellow light, and perhaps to see what she could of the Outfitter through the gap.

"What do you see?" Reed asked.

"A shambling shape in a cloak." Lyonene straightened and sighed.

They heard laughter from the chamber and hushed voices. Then nothing but silence.

"Well," Reed said, "I wonder what the Outfitter will give us."

"Probably nothing of any more use than Melita's bag of berries and goat-tooth necklace," said Lyonene. "We are only initiates, after all. Kleia Gloria would have us tested without the full aid of magic." She touched the sides of her tawny bun. "If she is kind, she'll give us oil to loosen the wax from our hair. I swear they will send us to our heroes looking like crazed, wet cats."

Reed chuckled and leaned against the cool stone wall. The back of her bun crushed slightly, but she had grown so weary that she didn't care.

"Lyonene, you don't think Sabil meant there wouldn't be enough glory to go around?"

"Of course not. She was just shutting us up, calling us greedy. Which we are."

"But you don't think that it has to be either me or you. It's a war! There will be glory to spare!"

"There will be more than enough for us both," Lyonene said brightly. "There is just more for me. And the smallest share for Gretchen. Where is she? What could be taking her so long?" She sighed. "I suppose you're quite happy about the horse race in Lacos."

"Of course I am. You know you can't outride me. Did you somehow know already? Is that why you encouraged me to leave Silco behind?" She heard Lyonene's scoff in the dark. "Would you like to make wagers about who will place first?"

"I will make you a wager that, despite some stupid horse race, Alsander of Cerille will be the hero of the war. And I will be an

Aristene before you are." She stuck out her hand. "If I win, you must declare yourself second to me before the goddess and muck out my Areion's stall for a year."

"A year?"

"We will be immortal." Lyonene shrugged. "What is a year?"

Reed took her by the wrist.

"Done. And if I win?"

"You won't. But if you do . . . I will give you my silver bracelet that you like."

"That bracelet was your mother's," said Reed.

"I know; I'm not going to lose."

Reed laughed. They released each other as Aster and Sabil emerged.

"Well?" Lyonene demanded. "What do you have?"

"Gold and silver coin," Aster said, weighing a sack in her hand. "And clothes." She and Sabil tossed them each a bundle, and they looked them over in the light cast from the Outfitter's door. To Reed she had given a finely woven but simple tunic and leather leggings and a belt of bright blue cord. The pins at the shoulder of the tunic were gold but bore no jewels. The clothes of a noblewoman but not of a royal. For Lyonene she had provided a deep red gown, pins of red jewels, and a long ornamental dagger. Reed didn't need to see her in it to know what she would look like and that Alsander of Cerille would not be able to take his eyes off of her.

"There is also this." Sabil tossed Lyonene a circlet of silver to wear upon her head. "You go as royalty to gain access to the prince."

"We go as mercenaries," Aster said to Reed.

"Mercenaries," Lyonene whispered as the mentors led them

back up the dark steps. "*I* am a princess."

"I prefer being a mercenary," Reed hissed as Lyonene snickered. A mercenary was horses and weapons and coin. Though Lyonene was a princess with a very nice dagger, she had to admit.

"And there is this." Aster passed them each a small silver canister. "It is a salve, to heal the cuts from the Granting."

Reed removed the cover and sniffed. The ointment glowed faintly in the dark and smelled of mint.

"Now come along," Sabil said. "And step lively, initiates."

"Why?" Lyonene asked as she and Reed tried to keep up without stumbling and falling to break their necks.

"Because the rituals are over," Sabil replied. "And now we feast!"

16.

FEAST AND FAREWELLS

The Feast of the Initiates had begun without them. The acolytes had set it into the square below, dragging tables and benches, lighting braziers to illuminate the square and the steps of the Citadel. There were loaves of bread and great hunks of cheese, bowls of honey and berries, and slabs of salted fish. Upon the main table lay a roasted boar. Aristenes and acolytes alike took part, and the firelight glinted off silver armor and turned white capes and linens orange.

"Is that everyone down there?" Reed asked. She tried to count the number of white capes and gave up, but there had to be at least fifty.

"Not everyone. The square isn't large enough for that. People will spill out down the side streets and into the taverns. But all of the Aristene are there. Or at least all who are here and not away with some hero or another." Sabil waved down, and Reed saw Ferreh and Tiern nod. The elders were seated at the central table, where the celebration seemed the most restrained. There must have already been much wine—there was an Aristene stretched out across a table like she was another roasted boar. She rolled onto her back and the boom of her laughter carried all the way up.

"There's still no sign of Gretchen," Reed said, scanning the crowd. Aster looked down to check for herself.

"I will speak to the elders and see what's keeping them," she said.

"But Jana is there." Sabil pointed. The pale blond mentor was easy to pick out, laughing beside one of the braziers.

"What's happened?" Lyonene asked. "Where's Gretchen?"

"Come," said Aster.

The mentors led them down the steps. As soon as they were spotted, the gathering gave a great cheer, and Reed and Lyonene found themselves crushed within the crowd.

"This one is fine and tall," someone said, grabbing Reed by the shoulders. "She will have no trouble."

"But this one is so lovely," another said of Lyonene. "So she is sure to make some!" Reed and Lyonene looked at each other. Cups of wine were thrust into their hands and Reed drank quickly; her throat was so dry, and she'd not had a drop of anything since the blood of the oaths and the water of the well.

"Take some bread." An acolyte pressed a piece to her chest. "Eat!"

She and Lyonene both tried. The food was good: the bread soft and the cheese rich, the meat tender and glazed with spiced honey. But the sea of faces was overwhelming, and Reed barely tasted any of it.

"Look there." Lyonene pointed to the Aristene Reed had spotted lounging across an entire table. Up close she seemed no less massive, with a broad smile of white teeth beneath a shock of black hair. There was a stripe of black running across her forehead.

"Who is that?" Lyonene asked. "Why does she have that"—she gestured to her forehead—"paint across her face?"

"That is no paint," Reed replied. "It is inked permanently into the skin. I know her—that's Aethiel. The one who Aster says used to be a queen."

"A queen of what?" Lyonene asked, and Reed recalled wondering the same thing. "And how is it allowed?" Within the order, crowns were forbidden. An Aristene must wear no crowns and make no marriages. They were the only rules: no oaths and no vows, save those made to the goddess.

"She must have given up her country in favor of Kleia Gloria," Reed said. As they stared at her, Aethiel spotted them and leaped down from the table.

"There they are!" She shoved her way through people and greeted them with a large hand clapped to each of their shoulders, knocking them together hard as if she was too intoxicated to be wary of her strength.

"Aethiel," Lyonene said, and bowed her head. "It is an honor."

"You know me. They know me!" she shouted to the crowd. "And I know you. Particularly this one." She peered at Reed, and Reed remembered that there was something odd about her eyes: they were black all the way through. "You are Aster's. The girl she and Veridian found and brought back. You probably do not remember this, but I met you the night that Aster brought you here."

"I do remember," Reed said. "You tried to pat my head and I growled at you."

Lyonene rolled her eyes in embarrassment. "Reed."

But Aethiel only laughed.

"Join me at my table." Aethiel shoved them forward. "And hear some stories." But before they could sit, Aster appeared, and Aethiel wrapped her in a great hug, so tight that it lifted her off her feet. "Aster!" Aethiel exclaimed as the mentor laughed. She was odd and boisterous, this Aristene. She seemed so friendly, but her features were those of a hawk, and she carried more knives strapped to her person than any of the others. "Gloria Thea Matris, sister," she said in the order's traditional greeting. Glory to the mother goddess.

"Gloria Thea Matris, Aethiel! It is good to see you."

"And you. It seems no more than a blink has passed since you and Veridian took on this little one." Reed raised her brows. It had been a long time since anyone had been able to refer to her as "little." "Have you seen her since?"

She spoke of Veridian, and Aster shook her head.

"I have not either. And I have been looking."

"Forgive me, old friend," Aster said, "but I must speak to the initiates."

Aethiel nodded, and worry crept up Reed's spine as Aster led them away to a quieter corner near the stable, where Sabil waited with a somber expression.

"What is it?" she asked. "What happened to Gretchen?"

The mentors looked at each other.

"Nothing happened to Gretchen," Aster said gently. "But she will not be undertaking the Hero's Trial."

"What?" Lyonene gasped.

Reed squeezed her eyes shut. Perhaps she had drunk the wine too fast or perhaps her stomach had been empty for too long, but the square around her began to spin.

"What do you mean? Did she . . . Was she ill? Was she afraid? The elders shouldn't discount her for that; she's brave even if she isn't always hardy—"

"Reed."

"She's better than I showed them! Did you tell them, Aster, that her arm was already injured that day?"

"That was not why," Aster said. But Reed wheeled away. She had to find Gretchen. There had been some kind of mistake, but mistakes could be undone. Reed hurried through the crowd, asking all she passed if they had seen Gretchen. She was another initiate, one of only three in Atropa clad in a white-and-silver tunic and painfully tight bun, but no one had seen her.

"Jana!"

Reed burst into the mentor's circle, and Jana looked at her in surprise.

"Reed," she said. "I've heard that you and Lyonene have been granted—"

"Who was Gretchen granted?" Reed interrupted.

"Gretchen was granted no one. I'm sorry; I thought she would have told you. She elected not to undertake the trial."

Elected? That wasn't right. That was impossible. "Why would she do that?"

"She—" Jana started, but again Reed cut her off.

"Where is she?"

"I don't know. I thought she would stay to congratulate you and Lyonene. But she said she might find another escort back through the Veil to the Summer Camp."

Back through the Veil to the Summer Camp. And then to where? Reed plunged away through the feast, ignoring Jana's offers to help her look. They weren't telling her something. Something had to have gone wrong. Why else would Gretchen have suddenly disappeared? She wouldn't have just changed her mind. With a flash of guilt, Reed saw Gretchen down in the dirt of the training arena.

"No." She shook away the image. It couldn't have been that; Gretchen said she understood!

In a blur, Reed found herself in the stable, saddling Silco. She had to find her friend. And if she had already gone back through the Veil . . .

Reed had the borrowed Aristene magic now. She could open it herself and follow her.

She swung onto Silco's back and put her heels to his sides, galloping through the nighttime city, leaving the sounds of celebration behind. Opening the Veil was foolish, she knew that. She knew it as well as she knew the words and knew the chant. How to focus to find her way. She rode up into the hills and sang out the sacred words, afraid to hesitate and lose her nerve. She called louder, over and over, half expecting that the chant would fall from her lips straight down to the ground. But as soon as the first phrase was complete, the air rippled and a shadow formed before her like black fog. Silco snorted, but she would look after him, like she always did.

"Reed!"

Too late, Reed looked back. Lyonene had already found Gretchen, and they were each on a horse and galloping after her. She pulled sharply on Silco's reins and stopped the chant, but not before she and her horse fell into the Veil, and the dark.

17.

PARTING WAYS

Reed awoke in the familiar comfort of Aster's arms.

"Gloria Thea Matris," Aster whispered when she stirred. "She wakes. Thank you, goddess." She adjusted Reed's head where it lay on her lap. "It's all right, Reed."

Reed's eyes cracked open. It was day again. Light streamed into the room bright and clear. She remembered what she'd done, impulsively opening the Veil, but lying in the soft bed, she could have thought it all a dream—were it not for the ache in her limbs and the sickness in her belly.

"What were you thinking?" Aster asked. "You are lucky Lyonene and Gretchen found you. You would never have made it through the Veil on your own, exhausted after the rituals and half-drunk on wine. Lyonene rode up onto the elders' table in the square to get them to pull you back out."

"The elders pulled me out?"

Reed prodded her memories gently, tiptoeing around the edges of her time in the blackness. Aside from the cold and the hopeless dark, there was something else, just at the last—something warm and with a heartbeat, strong and bright as the dawn. A dark-skinned woman charging in on a blood bay stallion. Ferreh and Amondal.

"That's right," Lyonene said from the doorway, where she and

Gretchen stood, their faces drawn and worried. "Be ashamed. You could have been killed. And worse than killed. You could have been lost."

"Where is Silco?" Reed asked. She sat up and winced. Her whole body felt like a bruise.

"Good," Lyonene said. "I'm glad it hurts."

"Lyonene," Aster chided, and the initiate crossed her arms.

"Ferreh says there is no lasting injury," Aster murmured. "You should be back on your feet before the end of the day."

"But Silco," Reed said. "Where's Silco?"

"He's fine," Lyonene replied, looking away sulkily. "I told Ferreh not to bother bringing you back if she couldn't get the horse, too. I told her you'd be insufferable otherwise."

Reed smiled at her. "Thank you."

"You're welcome, idiot."

"I'm sorry." She looked back at her mentor, who couldn't seem to look at Reed anymore now that she was awake. "Aster?" she asked, but Aster slipped from the bed and walked to the door.

"Stay with her." She touched Lyonene's arm as she passed. "I will be back later."

"Where are you going?" Reed asked.

"Where do you think she's going?" Lyonene said after Aster had gone. She sat down heavily on the edge of the bed as Gretchen perched on the other side. "To the elders. To plead with them so that you might go on to your Hero's Trial. And to take every lash meant for your back across her own."

"They wouldn't do that."

"How do you know? Have you ever seen an Aristene punished?"

Reed looked down. The Hero's Trial. Fresh from the Veil it felt hazy and far away. But Gretchen—

"Gretchen! I knew you couldn't leave! I knew they—" But beside her on the bed, Gretchen shook her head.

"I have decided instead to go home," Gretchen said with a small smile. "Back to my country of Centra. My parents will be somewhat disappointed, but they will still make me a good marriage, and Jana said the elders have given leave to return their trunk of riches. Nearly as full as it was when it was given."

"But you can't just quit. After all this?" Reed turned to Lyonene, but Lyonene stared at the floor.

"All of this has given me friends such as you," said Gretchen. "And I would never trade it. But in the end the order was not what I wanted. I don't love it like you, Reed, and I wasn't born for it like Lyonene. Everything here has been a struggle for me. And I do not want to struggle. I want to bear children and grow old listening to their laughter."

"This," Reed whispered, "does not make any sense. Is there a boy? Someone in the Summer Camp?"

"Oh, for the goddess's sake, Reed," Lyonene snapped. "If it was a boy, do you think I wouldn't have already tied her hands and thrown her over the back of my saddle?" Lyonene's words were harsh and hurt, and made it plain that she and Gretchen had already spoken of this at length while Reed lay in the bed unconscious. "It is a life for a life. This life or that one. And she chooses that one."

"So you . . . will go," Reed said slowly.

Gretchen nodded. "Jana gave me one of her finest spears as a parting gift. I am actually going to miss her, can you imagine?"

"We will drag her with us, then," Lyonene said gruffly. "When we come to visit you."

Reed sat numbly between her friends. She couldn't believe that Gretchen was going. That Gretchen would not always be there.

"I know you think less of me," Gretchen whispered. "Because I want the life that other people have more than I want a great destiny. I know you think I lack the heart."

Reed looked at her. Gretchen, who at times seemed so timid but was truly so brave. The girl who stood before an Aristene and took the falling strikes of a war hammer, and who dulled the sharpness of any argument with a laugh and a smile.

"I do not think any such thing," Reed said. "It's only . . . that I'm going to miss you, Gretchen."

Beside Reed, Lyonene brushed at a tear, and Gretchen threw her arms around them.

"I'll miss you, too. I love you. But your lives will be long. You'll come and see me. Meet the children I will have so I can tell them stories about their aunts Reed and Lyonene, still young and beautiful when their mother is ancient and wrinkled." She smiled wide through her own tears. "But you must promise me," she said, "that as you depart on your trials you will be careful. Promise me that you'll survive."

"Of course we will," said Lyonene.

"No young warrior thinks they are going to fall—"

"Most young warriors are not blessed by the goddess of glory." Reed wiped at her eyes. "We will be fine. We will be Aristene. And you will always be one, too, Gretchen. At least to me."

Gretchen hugged her and kissed both of their cheeks. Then she slipped from the bed and walked to the door.

"Gretchen!" Reed cried out. "It's not . . . it's not because of what I did? During the exhibition?"

Gretchen paused with her hand on the wall. "Of course not. You did what you had to do, like we always knew you would. Besides, if anything were to drive me to quit, it would have been the baths."

Lyonene laughed. "I can't believe you endured the making of this bun just to leave."

Gretchen laughed, too. She looked back at them one last time. And then she turned and walked through the door.

"She's gone," Lyonene said, and Reed held her tightly.

"She will never really be gone," Reed whispered. "Not as long as you and I are still here."

That evening, Reed and Lyonene stood together in the low, gold light upon the hills above Atropa. The elders had been right, and Reed felt completely recovered from her mishap in the Veil. The only ailments that remained were a sore scalp and the cut from the bloodletting of the Granting Ceremony. She'd applied a thin layer of the Outfitter's salve to it under the bandage. And now it itched.

"It is lovely here," she said, looking out across the city. The time had come to separate: Lyonene to her prince in Cerille and Reed to hers in Glaucia. It felt far too soon, and after Gretchen it felt like one goodbye too many.

"Do not weep again," Lyonene warned. "Not when we're about to part. Don't make me worry about you."

"It's not that." Reed blinked. Hard. "I'm crying because I have to go through the Veil again."

Lyonene laughed. "I am going to worry about you, you know. You are big as an ox, Reed, and strong as one, too. I'm not afraid you can't fight. But I worry about the battles you may choose."

"I'm not a child, Lyonene. I have trained just like you."

"But for different reasons. I have trained, and excelled, because it is my nature. Because the Aristene are my destiny, and I accept that. You have trained because you want it. Because in the order you have found something that you lost." She glanced at Aster standing with Sabil farther down the hill. "It is about love for you, Reed, and I worry where that might take you."

"It will take me to the same place as you," Reed said. "And it will take me there sooner, so I may have your silver bracelet."

Lyonene grinned. "I hope so, Ox. Because that future we dreamed of, of you and me and Gretchen—you weren't the only one who dreamed it."

"Don't call me 'Ox.' You're not going to make that stick," said Reed, and Lyonene laughed again as she stuck her finger into her bandage and scratched.

"Did you use the salve as well?"

"Yes, and now it's driving me crazy!" Lyonene tore the bandage off and stared at her arm in wonder. "Reed! Look!" Lyonene's arm was healed. With no scar nor a scab nor even a red mark. Reed removed her own bandage and flexed her forearm. It was like the blade had never touched the skin. Except for the odd, uncomfortable itch that persisted down deep, as if it was the bone itself that needed scratching.

"Initiates," Sabil called.

Reed and Lyonene turned. With deep breaths they led their horses to their mentors. Sabil and Aster looked upon them with pride. Lyonene in the red gown given by the Outfitter, the jeweled dagger shining at her belt, her hair somehow lustrous and without a trace of wax. And Reed, noble in the embroidered tunic and soft leather leggings. She had strapped a hunting knife to her waist below the tied cord of blue.

"Today your Hero's Trial begins," said Sabil. "Today you will live as Aristene warriors. Atropa will be here—the Veil may be opened from anywhere after dark—but you are forbidden from returning except in the most dire of circumstances."

"Yes, mentor," the initiates murmured.

"Then there is only one more thing to do." Sabil held out her palms and stepped back. Reed and Lyonene looked at each other, confused, until the mentors began to laugh.

"You must learn to call your armor," said Aster. "I can't believe you didn't try to do it the moment the magic was shared."

Armor. The Aristene armor of silver and white. With the magic coursing through them it was waiting, invisible in the aether between worlds.

"How?" Reed asked.

"You have simply to ask," said Sabil. "You have simply to wish. To be a warrior, for Kleia Gloria."

Reed's heart began to thump. That was all she had ever wished. But it felt different now. There was an aura or an energy, just out of reach. Warm as a beam of sunlight she could slip her arm into. She took a breath and focused, trying to draw that glowing warmth upon her body.

She heard Lyonene's delighted squeal and knew that she had

done it first. But she refused to be distracted. It was almost there.

And then she felt it: the weight of the armor and the sweep of the cape hanging down her back.

For a few moments the initiates could do nothing but cling to each other's wrists and hop about. The feeling of the armor was indescribable. So light and so movable but more than that—it made them feel strong. Invigorated. Reed felt as though she could run for miles, as though she could lift Silco with her bare hands. All of her muscles felt tighter, her reflexes quicker. She couldn't wait to test them in battle.

"All right, all right," Sabil said, grinning. "Save some of it for the trials, will you?"

Reed smiled at Lyonene, and they let each other go.

"I will see you at Lacos," Lyonene said as she and her mentor walked away. "Where my prince and I will steal that race."

"You decided to let her go."

Tiern stood beside Ferreh high in the rooms of the Citadel as they looked down upon the initiates and their mentors on the hill.

"Of course I did," Ferreh replied. "She had to go."

"You are making a mistake. She is the wrong choice. She is weak and emotional. She nearly killed herself trying to run away through the Veil."

"That only means she is brave. That she will do what she feels she must." Ferreh turned and looked at the other elder, eyebrow cocked. "And if it is a mistake, it is only the same mistake that you have made."

Tiern scowled, a scowl so deep that on a great warrior like Tiern it would have sent the acolytes scurrying for cover. But to Ferreh it was only cause to chuckle. She was not wrong, after all. Years ago, Tiern had made the choice, and her choice had been Veridian. And all knew how that had turned out.

"If you ask this of her, Ferreh, she will break."

"She will not." The elder pulled her red wrap close about her shoulders. The initiates gone and ceremonies over, she had allowed her armor to recede and wore only a simple linen shift above flat, winding sandals. She felt tired, but the weariness was the satisfying kind, a heaviness in her limbs that spoke of work well done, a stillness of mind that reflected time passed in laughter and good conversation. So many years they had prepared for this. Some things, like the departure of the third initiate, they had counted on. Ferreh had seen the doubts in the girl's tender heart since the moment she saw her in the sacred well. Others, like Reed's flight through the Veil, they had not. But it didn't give her any pause.

"How do you know?" Tiern asked. The other elder peered into Ferreh's eyes. They had known each other for so long. For an age. For more than that. They had known each other through falling worlds and back again. But still, the mind could keep her secrets.

"I knew the moment I asked that spindle-legged child if she would join us and she said that she would," Ferreh replied. "Without hesitation."

"But why would she hesitate," said Tiern, "when you dangled salvation before her little eyes?" The younger of the two elders faced Ferreh with crossed arms, still protected by silver bracers. It was a rare day, when Tiern was caught out of her armor. "You promised a family to a child who had none. You promised strength to a girl fresh from slaughter. No death. No fear. And you promised to make her pony live forever." Tiern snorted. "You lied, old friend. And one day she'll come to know it."

"It does not have to be a lie," Ferreh said, but Tiern went on as if she hadn't heard.

"And then to give her to Aster. Aster, whom mentorship has already broken—"

"That is *why* I gave her to Aster." Ferreh's voice rose ever so slightly. A warning undetectable to anyone but Tiern. "Did you not see the way that Aster looked at that girl? The way she begged for her cause?"

"And how will Aster's affection help when it comes time for the girl to do what we ask?"

"It will help," Ferreh said, watching the Veil open upon the hill to swallow up the women and horses who stepped inside, "because when we ask she will do it not for ambition or for devotion to the goddess. She will do it because she loves us. And even if it does not help, it is too late. I have already given her the blood."

THREE

THE HERO

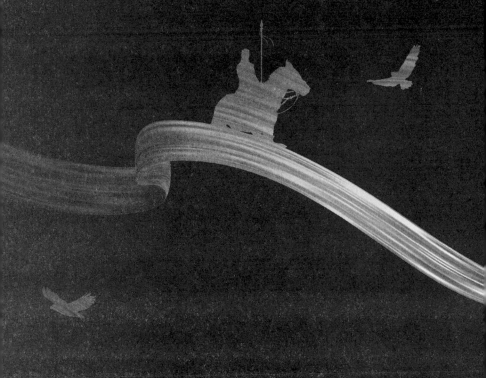

18.

SOLDIER IN A FARAWAY LAND

When she and Aster stepped into the sunlight, Reed looked back at the disappearing darkness of the Veil. Then she promptly bent over and was sick off the side of Silco's saddle.

"Reed," Aster said, surprised.

Reed righted herself and wiped her mouth. "I'm fine. It was only an ode to Gretchen." And indeed, she understood how the girl had felt now. It was different passing through the Veil when she knew what it was like to get lost.

"Don't worry," Aster said. "Soon enough, stepping into the Veil will be no different from stepping out your front door."

Reed nodded. "Just don't tell Lyonene." She took up her reins and nudged Silco forward.

The Veil had dropped them into a green field. Small flowers of blue and yellow bobbed here and there on the ends of long thin stems, and from the slope where they rode, Reed thought she could see for forever, a very different sight from the closed-in mountains and high foothills of the Summer Camp. Everywhere she looked, shadows from fast-moving clouds moved across the ground like great dark fish in the ocean, and the air was cool and wet. Glaucia was so lovely and distracting that she was nearly pulled out of her saddle when Silco yanked his head down for a mouthful of grass.

Aster let Rabbit have her head to graze, too, and as they sat, their silver armor and white capes receded, and tunics and stitched leather leggings settled upon them like dust. Aster sniffed the air. "Do you smell that, Reed?"

"Smell what?"

"The cusp of war. Blood on the air. Do you feel it?"

Reed slowed her breath and listened, tried to focus on every scent and sensation: the wildflowers and the wind through her still-waxy hair. "I mostly smell Silco." He needed a bath after all that Veil travel.

Aster chuckled. "When you are an Aristene, you'll be able to sense it. The growing excitement of people from different lands converging."

"We—" Reed began, and then had to grab her saddle when Silco twisted in a tight circle. He wanted to roll, and she had to jump off to avoid being crushed in the fun. Reed scowled at him, but Aster shrugged and walked with Rabbit to wait a short distance away. As her horse flopped on the ground, getting grass stains on her saddle, Reed watched Aster and Rabbit as the Aristene and the Areion conversed, Aster in words and Rabbit in gesture. Aster pointed to a valley and Rabbit looked where she pointed. She made some small joke and Rabbit shook her head as if laughing.

"Get up," Reed said, and prodded Silco with her toe. "And when you're an Areion you will ask if you may roll."

"He may be an Areion but he'll still be Silco," Aster called, overhearing. When Reed and Silco rejoined them, Aster made a show of dropping Rabbit's reins and letting her navigate them to the road. "Rabbit remembers these lands better than I do," she said.

"Someday Silco will hold maps in his head as well."

Reed righted herself as he tugged hard after another mouthful of grass. Silco holding maps. That would be the day.

"You and Rabbit have been here before?"

"We have. Veridian had a hero in Glaucia once, though he is long dead. And I had one myself, in Rhonassus."

"It must be a strange thing sometimes," Reed said. "To help cities rise and then help them to fall."

Aster smiled with half of her mouth.

"It's not that simple, Reed. And it is not for us to take sides. We serve one goddess and one thing. Heroes, not countries."

They reached a road, and their pace settled to an easy amble. They would reach the city of the Docritae before nightfall, and as they drew nearer, the road became crowded. It wasn't long before Aster tensed, and Reed looked back to see a fast-moving band of thirty riders coming up behind them.

"Easy, Silco," Reed whispered, and held his reins tight. They kept to one side of the widening road as the riders reached them and slowed. A few of those nearest greeted them in a language that Reed didn't know. Aster probably did, but she chose to respond with no more than a polite nod before returning her eyes to the road, like any noblewoman might do. Reed kept her head down and watched from behind the cover of her hair. The men were excitable—full of energy. Dirt and dust coated their chests and the flanks of their horses, and they wore helmets of dark metal with a band that came down to cover the nose. They were only thirty men, but all were equipped for war.

One of them rode his horse around Silco's hindquarters, close enough to bump into the back of Reed's leg. Silco bared his teeth to bite, but the man only laughed, calling to his friends as Reed pulled Silco's head away. She didn't need to speak the language to know what he was saying: *The girl's horse has a bite—I wonder if she does, too!*

Reed ground her teeth. *I have more than a bite*, she wanted to say. *I have sword and fist and shield, and a woman beside me who could cut you to ribbons.* These men were brutes. They were the kind of men who killed and pillaged, who stole into settlements in the dead of night.

Aster put her hand over Reed's on the reins. She shook her head and kept her eyes down. Eventually the band rode off, but before they did, one of the men dragged his fingers across Reed's bare cheek.

"Are you all right?" Aster asked. She wiped at Reed's cheek as though he had left a mark.

"I'm fine," Reed replied, shaking off her anger and the sharp twinge of fear. "What were they saying?"

"Never mind," Aster replied. "What matters is that they decided they had more important matters to focus on than women."

Reed glared up the road. "You looked like you were afraid. But you weren't really."

"If I was it is nothing to be ashamed of. Fear is useful and it is often smart. But you're right: I could've ground them into a red paste." She chuckled and shoved Reed lightly. "Stop curling your lip like a badger—we will see those men again in the city and you may end up fighting side by side."

Reed made an effort to lower her hackles, and beneath her Silco shook his head and pulled his reins loose.

"Did the Outfitter charm your tongue so you could speak so many languages?" Reed asked. "Or did you learn them?"

"I learned them. In the beginning, the Outfitter may use her magic to weave languages into you, but an Aristene has nothing but time. You will learn. And you'll be glad, for the weaving of the Outfitter is not pleasant. We are lucky you had no need of that." In Glaucia and the surrounding region, nations spoke a common tongue when they met. The same that the Aristene spoke.

"Why didn't we just show those men who we are?" Reed asked, eager to show off her silver and white. Glaucans were likely to know of the Aristene; the whole region was warlike and through places like that, rumors of the Aristene were often whispered.

"I might have, if it came to that. But I'd rather we keep our identity to ourselves until we see the king and discern whether he will look upon us kindly."

They reached the city of the Docritae just before sunset. But Reed wouldn't have minded if they'd arrived in the dark.

It wasn't much to look at. Inside the border of the wall of stones were the huts and hovels of farmers. Farther up lay the city proper: a hill fort of defensible banks and ditches where the buildings were made of stone. It was no grand city of marble and aqueducts and terra-cotta piping but wild and vast and well-forested, the kind of country for hunters, which was hard to survive in and produced hard, surviving people. The villagers they passed regarded them with stony eyes, leaning against their rakes as they stood inside stock pens of hogs with coats of dark, wiry hair. Up and up the hill they went, and what started out as a road of firm mud ended up a slippery mess after being churned up by the many horses and soldiers who had already arrived. Soon Silco and Rabbit were brown to their knees.

"This is the city of the finest warriors in Glaucia?" Reed asked doubtfully.

"Yes," Aster replied. "And there is the king's lodge."

Reed looked upon the long, low building lit by torches and constructed from thick timber. That is where they would find him. Hestion. The boy from the well.

They tied the horses to a post and made their way inside; when the door opened, the sounds of raucous celebration spilled out, and Reed slunk behind Aster as they threaded through the crowded space. The air was hot and smelled of leather and spilled ale. She didn't like being shoulder-to-shoulder with so many strangers; it brought all her old anger and fear to the fore.

"Look sharp," Aster said as she deftly blocked a thrown elbow that would have given Reed a black eye. Reed tried to be on guard as they found a place to stand along the wall. The tables and benches in the middle of the room were swarmed with men, and though the gathering seemed friendly, the air felt too excitable, as if one wrong word could turn a laugh into a scream of fury.

Reed scanned the room, searching for Hestion's face. She feared she wouldn't recognize him in the firelight or in a helmet. The king was there, King Arik, seated on a fur-covered throne at the far end of the lodge. And beside him a young man who must be Hestion's brother, Belden. They had the same look. But Belden's eyes were not the same, and his hair was shorter and darker, like the king's.

"I don't see him," Reed said into Aster's ear. "Is he not here?"

The door behind them opened, letting in a blast of fresh, cool air, and as if her voice had called him forth, Hestion entered the hall. He carried a young, field-dressed stag slung over his back and he came with a small band of warriors. The crowd parted for them happily for they had brought the feast: when Hestion dropped the stag at the feet of his father, a bit of blood trailed down his white cape of fur.

"Finally," King Arik said. He rose and took his younger son in a brief embrace, clapping his back. "The feast may begin."

Reed swallowed. There he was. The child she'd glimpsed in the ripples of sacred water. The young man she'd seen in the well. He had passed so near to her when he'd come with the stag that there had been not even ten bodies between them. She watched as he joined his brother at the nearest table. His sandy-gold hair was wild and hung to his shoulders, part of it tied back in a braid and secured with a strip of leather. When he smiled he looked like Belden but not quite—Hestion's smile was a guileless grin, a hallmark of a younger heir who had fewer responsibilities. To Reed he looked as fresh as the stag he'd killed.

See me, Reed thought.

But when Hestion scanned the hall, she ducked behind Aster and her cheeks burned.

"Well done," Aster said quietly. "Remain invisible, for now."

Reed frowned. She hadn't done it on purpose, but it did seem that they were invisible; at the back of the lodge no one paid them any mind even though they were the only women who weren't there to serve. As she watched, a tall woman with a golden braid wound through with gray approached King Arik. She wore a finely spun gown of blue, but Reed didn't think she was the new queen. She had a similar look to the king and to Hestion. She must be a relation.

"The king's sister?" she asked as the woman directed servants with a pointed finger. Then she took a basket of bread upon her hip and waded into the fray herself.

"Perhaps."

"She seems half a servant."

"The women of Glaucia work as hard as the men," Aster said. "Even royalty, when war approaches."

The hall quieted when the princes rose to their father's side, and Belden began to speak.

"Welcome, men of Glaucia to the hall of King Arik, lord of the Docritae," he said. "Welcome to archers and shield-makers. Ale drinkers and wild men. And those who have come from the Salt Flats, great and seafaring. That you go with the Docritae into war is to ensure a victory for all of Glaucia."

Reed wondered why Belden spoke instead of the king, though he spoke well and she liked his voice. He had kind eyes that wrinkled in the corners.

"It is right that we gather here in the days before we sail across the sea," Belden went on. "For it was here that our nation was formed, long ago, when King Docran slayed the First Stag, pursuing him for twelve days and twelve nights to the summit of this hill. Here they fought, dagger to antler from sunrise until sunset, until the stag's antlers were cracked and stained red with Docran's blood, until Docran's dagger was lost and his strength nearly broken. And when the stag charged once more, he dove between the beast's front legs so fast that when the stag turned his head to pursue him he gored himself instead, the sharp tips of his great cage of bone tearing through his own stomach. King Docran stayed with the stag as his life bled into the ground, and all the forest came to mourn the stag's passing. He buried the First Stag deep beneath this hill. He ate none of his meat. Kept none of his hide. Made no trophies of his antlers. And that honor is repaid by the creatures of these lands with good hunting and plenty of game." Belden grinned. "Like this little deer, speared through the heart by my baby brother."

The men laughed, and Hestion reared up in mock anger, a cup in his hand.

"Little?" he asked. "He is a monster!"

"Looks like a stretched rabbit!" someone shouted, and they laughed again, and Belden and Hestion laughed as well.

As the men returned to feasting and talk, Reed began to grow restless.

"Did we come here only to hear stories and eat?" Reed asked.

"This is your Hero's Trial, Reed. And there is your hero. It is up to you what we do."

Reed pressed her lips together. Despite her restlessness and her eagerness, part of her wished to remain hidden in her mentor's shadow. But Aster was right. "Then it's time we were seen."

"Very well."

Aster stepped away from the wall. She made her way through the crush of men, and then through the tables of feasting. Reed followed behind, watching heads raise and hearing the room quiet. When they passed Hestion's table, he looked up at them and she kept her eyes firmly fixed upon the king and his throne.

King Arik leaned forward. There was gray in his beard, but he was not yet an old man. The breadth of his shoulders spoke of past strength and his large hand, curled around the arm of his throne, was flexible and sinewy. Still, there was no light in his eyes when he looked at them.

"And who is this?" he asked.

"I am Aster. This is my apprentice, Reed. We are mercenaries from the west, and come to the hall of King Arik to offer our aid in the war with Rhonassus."

The announcement was met with silence. And then with laughter.

"Women mercenaries?" someone called out. "What use is a woman mercenary?" Reed clenched her fists, searching for the source of the insult as the laughter grew.

"We seek a claim of the spoils," Aster said, raising her voice above the noise. "In whatever portion you feel we are entitled, after the war is won."

"After the war is won you will be dead," called another voice, but as King Arik studied them quietly, the joking turned to dissent.

"We'll not lose our lives protecting women on the battlefield," said one. "And I've no desire to see their pretty heads run through with spears or their pretty breasts shot through with arrows," said another.

"We don't need your protection!" Reed shouted. But of course they only laughed. One, a tall soldier with a long red beard, raised his cup to her from his place on the wall.

"And they're unarmed," he said. "What kind of mercenaries are fool enough to come into a hall of fighting men unarmed?"

Reed reached down to the table beside her and picked up a knife. She threw it so quickly that the man against the wall had no chance to lower his arm, and the knife shattered the clay cup in his hand on its way to sink into the wood behind him.

"The kind who don't wish to insult a good king by bringing steel and blood into his hall," she growled. The men fell silent, and fast as her temper rose, it also deflated—she glanced at Aster, expecting to see disappointment, or perhaps an angry mentor in full Aristene regalia, but Aster only shrugged.

"My apprentice is of an unruly disposition," she said. "If she does any damage to your arms or your men, I will pay for it from my share in the spoils."

"Your apprentice throws a good knife," King Arik said thoughtfully. "But is that her only talent?"

"Reed possesses many talents. As do I."

He studied them again as the men in the hall grumbled.

"My son Belden will lead the army. It should be he who decides his companions."

Reed turned to Belden, who was clearly the young king in all but name. He looked strong and full of ease; as he studied her, he popped a bit of meat into his mouth and chewed, feeling no need to speak in haste. Reed felt her borrowed Aristene magic quicken at the sight of him.

"I would be honored if the mercenaries were to sail with us," he said finally.

"I am telling you, they will both be dead," grumbled a man near the back.

"If they are both dead," said Belden affably, "then their help will come cheap." He smiled at Reed. "We will not turn away a good sword. You can be sure that in Rhonassus, we will need every one."

Aster bowed and led her back through the lodge, and Reed

finally let her head turn toward Hestion. She'd felt his eyes on her since she threw the blade, and they burned over every part, so hotly that she'd wanted to throw another knife into his bread to give him something else to look at. But his attention had returned to his brother, and no matter how long she stared, Hestion didn't look at her again.

19.

SHADOWS OF THE PAST

Reed and Aster kept to themselves as they ate. After the thrown knife none of the men seemed particularly friendly, though one of the sailors from the coast known as the Salt Flats did get drunk and tell them of how he slayed the great sea serpent who crushed ten of their ships before he heaved a spear down the beast's throat hard enough to emerge through the tail.

"An amusing story," Aster said after the sailor had put his head down onto his bread and fallen asleep.

The lodge began to empty as the thin moon crested in the sky, and without the crush of bodies the great size of the lodge was more apparent. Reed marveled at the intricate carvings of fish and wolves in the wood columns supporting the ceiling.

"Travelers, you must be weary."

Reed looked up. The woman with the gold-and-white braid stood before them.

"I am Morna," she said. "Sister to the king. Aunt to the princes, Belden and Hestion."

"I am Aster," Aster said, though Morna must have heard them introduce themselves already. "This is Reed."

"King Arik invites you to stay with the ranked women, the ladies of his former queen. The inns and taverns will be full and the nearby meadows claimed by the tents of soldiers. We would be happy to offer you a warm place by our fire and soft furs to lie upon."

"That is most kind," said Aster. "We would be happy to accept."

Reed's eyes darted toward the open doors of the lodge. She wanted to know more about the men, to learn more of the people she would fight alongside. And she wanted to know just where Hestion had gone off to and how he was spending his night. But there was no escaping an offer from the sister of the king.

Morna led them through the rear of the hall, which connected to a large house: the quarters of the king and his family and servants. It looked to be the oldest structure in the city and was comprised of stone walls, though some were clay brick, probably installed as repairs after a stone section fell. Morna's torch shone on fine woven tapestries, many depicting a large stag with a great cage of antlers—the Father of the Forest, whose story Belden had told before the feast.

"Here you are," Morna said. She opened a thin wooden door and led them into a room with a hearth and four beds. There was a small loom for weaving in one corner and low shelves of bowls and clay pottery. Near the fire three bowls sat unattended, two of nuts and another of hulls, as if someone had been interrupted in the middle of shelling them.

"Whose beds are these?" Reed asked.

"This room is shared by the youngest of the queen's ladies," said Morna. "Any may return, but I think all four will find a soldier to share furs with instead." She put her hands on the hips of her light blue gown of woven wool. She was King Arik's older sister, judging by the look of her stern face and the wrinkles beside her eyes. "If you need me, I will be in the kitchens, preparing tomorrow's feast. In Glaucia we feast for three nights before departing for war."

"But don't you need to sleep?" Reed asked.

"I may stumble in at some point." Morna smiled. "I'll try not to disturb you. Perhaps tomorrow you may wish to visit the altar of the Scylloi Prophet. There is a stone path that leads to it in the western wood."

"The Scylloi Prophet was murdered by the Rhonassan king," Reed said. "Why pray to a dead prophet?"

"Forgive my apprentice," Aster said gruffly. "She has had a long ride and can no longer curb her rudeness."

"It's all right. You are not from here, are you, despite the clothes? Your accents are strange. Mixed. But yours," she said to Reed, "is almost familiar. We had a traveler here years ago, from a land called Sirta. You sound a bit like he did." She looked deep into Reed's eyes, and Reed looked away. She must have known, once, where her family had come from. But so much of her past was hidden in her own mind, lost in the darkness that bled across her memories after the night of the raid. Sneaky how that fog had spread. But that was how it was with all forgetting: one didn't know what was lost until it was far too late to recover.

"Well," Morna said, and sighed. "The Scylloi Prophet was a walking god. So I suppose it can't hurt to continue to pray. In any case the altar is a place of beauty—it was constructed by our queen."

"A woman of many talents," said Aster.

"A great woman indeed." Morna performed an odd, bent-kneed bow. "Sleep well."

But Reed couldn't think of sleeping. She stoked the embers in the hearth as Aster inspected each of the four beds, inhaling sharply over the third.

"What?" Reed asked.

"This one." Aster waved her hand through the empty air. The bed didn't look like anything special to Reed—only a cot stuffed with straw and covered in stitched-together rabbit pelts. "This one may be a queen."

"You can see that?" Reed asked. "How? What glory is there to be had in that?"

"A crown is a crown. Glory can be found in marriage." She loosened the belt of dyed cord at her waist. "I've been in enough courts to know that marriage can be a sport, a hunt with deadly consequences. You will be surprised, Reed, by all of the glories to be found in this world, large and small, and all of them sacred."

"Are you telling me that one day I must be a marriage broker?"

"I guarantee it," Aster said, and flopped down upon the bed. Reed watched her with frustration. She paced loudly until her mentor broke into a closed-eyed grin. "Get out, then, and go see to the horses."

"Thank you." Reed darted for the door.

"Silco is fine, you know," Aster called drowsily after her. "Rabbit is fine, and so Silco is fine. She won't let him come to harm. . . . He is like . . . her initiate." She chuckled. "And Reed. Stay out of trouble. We were not offered these quarters only out of hospitality. They're worried we wouldn't be safe with the men."

"Do I need a dagger?" Reed asked, and Aster shook her head, eyes still shut.

"If you're in danger, I'll know. The blood and borrowed magic bind us."

Reed stepped through the door, then ducked back inside. "Aster, what would we have done if Belden and the king had ordered us to leave tonight?"

"Then," Aster mumbled, curling into the bed of the future queen as if the hint of glory there were warm as a blanket, "we would have had to get very creative."

Outside, the blackness of the night was impermeable. The glow from fires reached only a few steps, and the sliver of moon and scattered stars were about as helpful as Aster, passed out back on the cot. Reed wandered the unfamiliar streets, which despite the mass of soldiers gathered, were mostly empty—people had found their way to their beds or to sit around fires in the surrounding meadows and woods. Occasionally a sound would ring out: a burst of gathered laughter or a delighted squeal, perhaps from some future queen finding her future king.

Some future queen, Reed thought. Was the girl to be Belden's wife, perhaps? Morna told them that the room was shared by former ladies of his mother but that didn't mean they were blood relations. It wouldn't be surprising if he were to choose his queen from among his beloved mother's favored companions.

"Good goddess," Reed muttered. "I've become a marriage broker already. Silco!" She hissed. "Rabbit!"

No answer. She continued on, calling to the horses softly and trying not to break a leg in the dark. She kept the king's lodge at her back, but it wasn't long before the hall was out of sight and the roads beneath her feet changed from stone to soft, damp dirt. To her left she sensed the shadowy shapes of distant lower hills. To her right were trees and shrubs and the shifting sounds of animals. She was never going to find the horses.

"Silco," she called out, her voice defeated.

And so of course, he whinnied back.

"Silco!" She squinted and stepped off the road into she knew not what. A deep ditch, maybe, or a bush full of poisonous leaves and berries. "Silco!" He whinnied again, and she saw the strange double shape of him and Rabbit joined together and trundling toward her through the trees. "You're safe," she said, and hugged him.

As if there was any doubt, Rabbit seemed to say. Reed stroked her forehead and realized that she could see their eyes, lit up by the reflection of a bonfire.

Stay out of trouble, Aster's voice said in her head. But she wasn't going to get into trouble. She had her fists and two fast horses—if trouble arose, she would punch fast and ride away, never to be heard from again.

"I know, I know," she whispered to the Aster in her conscience. "Don't joke, Reed."

She crept toward the fire, using the trees and the obvious drunkenness of the men gathered around it to her advantage. There were nearly a dozen on logs or large stones, and in the shadows cast by the fire they looked like older men. But then they smiled and were boys again, and she forgot why she should be wary. They were passing a jug of something back and forth; one drank too much and sprayed it from his nose when he laughed. He leaned forward to wipe his face and when he did, Reed saw the Ithernan.

He was seated in the middle of a log with his elbows upon his knees. He didn't look like the other soldiers, though he wore a similar tunic. His light hair was shorn close to his head, and his cheeks— Reed gasped. His cheeks were painted with streaks of blue, just like the raiders who had killed her family.

For a moment it was as if she was back in the settlement, shaking through that long, cold night beneath the wreckage of her hut. She couldn't move. Couldn't speak, at once deadly angry and immobile with fear.

"Greetings, mercenary."

Reed turned, and Silco did, too, bumping up against Rabbit in the dark. Hestion leaned toward her with his arm wrapped around a tree.

"I'm sorry. I didn't mean to frighten your horse." He reached out to stroke Silco's nose. "Or you."

"Do princes of Glaucia always sneak up on women in the woods?" Reed asked.

"Always." He grinned. "It is custom." He nodded to the soldiers around the fire. "I wished to speak with you without attracting attention. And besides, I didn't think it was possible to sneak up on such a deadly mercenary as the one who threw that knife.

"You know who I am?" he asked.

"Prince Hestion," she said. "And my name is Reed, not 'mercenary.'"

He smiled again, a flash of white teeth. Facing the fire she could see more of him than he of her, and she was struck by how handsome he was, and the ease with which he moved. If he was drunk like his friends, he hid it well. His voice was almost how she imagined it would be, though he spoke a little faster. And his smile was disconcerting; where was the serious boy with the troubled eyes?

"I didn't know the Glaucans feasted with the Ithernan," Reed said. She gestured over her shoulder to the soldier with blue-painted cheeks.

"Ah, yes, well." Hestion looked past her. "That is Sar, and he is nearly a Glaucan by now. He's been with us since we were boys, and my father defeated the Ithernan raiders."

"He is a hostage?"

"No. The Ithernan king gave him to us as a ward. For peace. He is a prince."

Reed turned to watch the raider, though she didn't like to look at him. His grin was sharp and the shadows thrown from the fire made it sharper. Above the blue paint his eyes were deep-set and cold.

"Almost a Glaucan," she said. "But he still paints his cheeks."

"As he always will. And it is not about the cheeks but the eyes." Hestion pointed. "To the Ithernan eyes are sacred. Even without the blue paint you won't find him without rings of kohl, the lids black. You sound like you know of them."

"Not much. Only that they are a brutal people. And not terribly smart." Reed turned back. Hestion stared at her, and too late she realized her folly, insulting one of his companions. Luckily, he only laughed.

"I will be glad to tell him so." He chuckled and closed his mouth, though his eyes were still smiling. What did he see when he looked at her? A stranger, a mercenary. But to Reed he had long been a friend. Suddenly she wished to tell him all of it, that she already knew him, that seeing his face in a well so long ago had made a frightened child feel less alone. But he wouldn't have understood.

"Reed," he said, and crossed his arms. "Are you really a mercenary?"

"You saw me throw the knife."

"I did. But you do not seem the type to sell your sword for coin, to take payment for blood."

"Because I am a girl."

"No." He smiled again. "You are big for a girl and I don't doubt that you can fight." Reed frowned. It had never bothered her to be called big, for that was what she was. But somehow when he said it she found herself wishing she was small and lovely like Lyonene. A treasure that men would protect, not an ox they would send to pull their carts.

"But when you threw that knife, there was something in your eyes. Anger. Mercenaries aren't angry. They are detached and cold."

"Have you known many mercenaries?" Reed asked with a dubious look.

"I only seek to know if coin is truly your motivation." His eyes rose to hers, no longer laughing. "And I don't like sellswords fighting close to my brother. They can't be trusted."

"Perhaps I don't wish to fight close to your brother," Reed said. "Perhaps I'd prefer to fight close to you."

He paused, like her boldness surprised him. It had surprised her, too.

"Is that so?" he asked. He looked at her. When she looked away first, he laughed. "Find me tomorrow. I will take you to the altar of the Scylloi Prophet, and you will see why it is that we fight: a cause beyond coin. Now you should go. Before the men see you."

"The men are no threat to me."

"Yes, I know. You are a fierce mercenary." He teased, but that was all right. He'd discover his mistake soon enough, and she would delight in bashing the shields of his men and bringing them to their knees. "Here. Take your horses to my stable." He removed the pin from the shoulder of his cape and handed it to her. "The others within the city are full. They'll know you come by invitation." He walked past her, barely brushing her shoulder with his own.

"The horse's name is Silco," she said, and he turned. "The mare is called Rabbit."

"She doesn't look much like a rabbit."

"I think . . . when she was young her ears were big."

Hestion smiled. "Take your fine horses." He walked away. "And then go and find a bed."

"Go and find yourself a bed," she half shouted, irritated by his orders.

"I will find someone's," she heard him mutter.

Reed smirked and led the horses back toward the square. It wasn't the first meeting she'd imagined. But in some ways, it was better. He was real, and unpredictable. He looked like a hero, carried himself like a hero. And before the war was over, she would make him into a legend.

20.

COMPANIONS OF THE WORTHY

Reed woke to the sound of Silco munching hay. She opened her eyes and found no hearth, no smells of warm bread or boiled barley, only the smell of horses and the poke of straw into her shoulder. She'd spent the night in the stable.

"Finally awake," Aster said as she brushed out Rabbit's tail.

"I only sat down for a moment."

"The stable boy said you came with the prince's badge," Aster said, and cocked an eyebrow.

"When I found the horses, they were near him."

"Mm."

Reed hadn't considered that Aster had sent Rabbit to Hestion in order to force a nighttime meeting—could an Areion follow such an order? She narrowed her eyes, and Rabbit gazed back at her and blinked. A very slow blink.

"I thought you wanted me to stay out of trouble."

"Your hero isn't trouble. And you got the pin for these fine stables—so you must have done something right. How did you find him? What do you think of him?"

"I don't know what I think," she said honestly. "But I know what I see, and that is what Kleia Gloria sees. Potential.

"He has a companion," she added. "He's an Ithernan."

Aster stopped brushing, then started again without looking at her. "I know. I saw him. But you are safe, Reed; I would never let him touch you. And he wasn't among those who attacked your family that night," she said in a softer tone. "He couldn't have been. He's too young."

That was true. The Ithernan could not have been much older than Reed was. But it didn't make her hate him any less.

"Did you tell the prince? What we are?"

"No, though I wanted to. He was so smug and condescending at times. And seeing the Ithernan . . . I'd have liked to call my armor and use my sword to remove his blue-painted head."

"Reed," said Aster sharply, and the initiate straightened. "Though we possess it, the Aristene are not brute force. The same advantage can be gained from a well-placed word or a sidestep to the higher ground as a head removed by a sword. You must learn to control your temper."

"I didn't actually do it. The Ithernan still walks, alive and well."

"He walks," said Aster, "but you look as if you slept in a stable. Get yourself to a stream and wash."

Reed stood and plucked what straw she could from the fabric of her tunic. Aster knocked the comb against Silco's stall door.

"And take your horse."

Reed did as her mentor ordered, never anything but a dutiful apprentice, and led Silco out into the slightly chilly morning. The city of the Docritae was almost pretty as the sun rose, and to the north tucked into the hills Reed caught sight of the sea and smoke from what must be a port. The soldiers who had come from the Salt Flats, she remembered. Like the one who had "slayed" the sea serpent. They had sailed to the Docritae and provided many of the ships the army would take to war.

Past the square, the city had started to wake: Reed saw shop-keepers at work and herds of goats and pigs being moved through the alleys. She also saw Morna loading a cart pulled by a stout black ox and raised her arm in greeting only to receive a less-friendly nod in return. No doubt the king's sister knew that Reed hadn't slept in the bed she'd offered. She could tell her she had only slept in the stable, but it was really no business of hers, so Reed simply shrugged before taking the path into the western woods. She had seen women coming off that path holding baskets of washing, so she knew she would find the river or at least a stream. When she found it, she mounted Silco and rode north along the bank to a quieter spot and used the soap in her saddlebag to wash.

"Ah," she cried out as the water hit her skin. "Bull balls, that's cold!" She tolerated as much as she could, then dried her hands and raked her fingers through her hair. She should cut it, before they sailed to Rhonassus. It was too long and formed a too-tempting handle for an enemy to grasp on to.

"Silco?" She looked around. He had gone so far in search of grass that he had mostly disappeared around a curve—all she could see was his round black rump and flashing tail.

"Are you ever not hungry?" she muttered. But she supposed that was why he was so fast and so strong. He ate more and drank more and ran more than other horses. Almost like he knew he was in training to be an Areion and was trying as hard to become a member of the order as she was. Reed stood to retrieve him and heard Hestion's voice.

"I know you," Hestion said from upstream, and Reed followed the sound around the bend. He saw her and grinned. "Of course. The horse who belongs to the mercenary."

"Be careful," Reed warned. "He's not a nice horse." She went over and tugged on his bridle. "Say a proper hello, Silco."

Hestion reached out and patted Silco's forehead. "What does his name mean?"

"Nothing. It's short for Silver and Combat."

"That must be a fine story."

"I suppose it is." Reed thought of his Ithernan companion. "I'll tell you some other time. I didn't expect you to be awake after all that drinking."

"I have not yet slept."

Reed looked at the taut lines stretched out in the water. She recalled quiet days like this in the settlement, by the river with her mother, wading through warmish currents and casting the nets. Those had been days of peace, but she knew how quickly that peace could be shattered, and as Hestion watched the river go by, she sensed that he knew it, too.

"What are you fishing for?" she asked.

"Eels." He bent toward the shallows and pulled up a submerged basket, unfastening the top to show her the long green bodies writhing inside. Her revulsion must have been plain on her face, because he laughed. "They're ugly, but they're good eating."

"The woman with you," he said. "She calls you her apprentice, but she seems . . . Is she also your mother?"

Reed snorted a little. Except for their height, she and Aster looked nothing alike. Aster's skin was three shades too fair, and her hair was straight and brown while Reed's was black and wavy.

"No, she isn't," Reed said. "And yes, she is."

Hestion nodded. He didn't ask who her mother was then or where she was. Perhaps as someone whose mother was already lost, he could sense that such questions might not be welcome.

"I hope I didn't offend you last night," he said. "With my questions. I am cautious when it comes to my brother."

"I wasn't offended. Or at least, not by that."

"Let us start again, then." He heaved up the basket of eels, letting the water run out to soak his leg and leave the poor fish—if indeed they could be called fish and not worms—inside to flop. "Do you think Silco would mind carrying this heavy basket on his back?"

"He won't as long as we don't tell him what's in it."

As it turned out, though, he did mind, and danced around, stomping his feet against the cold water that ran out of it and the strange, slithering sounds from inside.

"There," Hestion said. "We must deliver these to the feast, and then I will take you to the altar like I promised." He held out his hand. For hers, she thought, or perhaps for Silco's reins. Either way she politely declined; she needed no steadying and Silco was likely to take a good chunk out of his shoulder.

When they emerged from the trees within sight of the lodge, Hestion untied the basket from Silco's saddle. He had barely finished before four fair-haired and long-limbed, giggling young women came to take it from his arms. "My cousins," he explained when he caught Reed watching with an arched brow. "Well. One of them was my cousin."

"Hestion!" Morna waved to him. She couldn't quite tell from

such distance, but Reed thought the woman was glaring at her. "I require your help. I've already done everything in the kitchens and now I need to get out to the fields."

"What would we do without you?" Hestion called out.

"Starve and die all covered in filth," Morna replied. She wiped her brow. Hard as she worked, her hair was still braided and strung through with white ribbon, which set off her silver streaks, and underneath her apron her gown was finely spun, edged at the collar and sleeves with bright white embroidered flowers. "Now come along."

"Forgive me, Reed," Hestion said as he jogged away. "I will find you when I am finished!"

But Reed didn't see him again until that night at the feast. This feast seemed more of a social affair, with the gathering spilling into the square, where several fires had been started in iron pits. Women and children were welcomed this time, and not only there to serve the meal of roasted mutton and gold-baked eel pies. The pies pleased Aster greatly; she loved a good eel.

"In some parts of the world, Reed," Aster said as she ate, "they'll pay your day's wages in eels." She nudged Reed in the shoulder. "Where is Hestion?"

"There." She nodded toward where he sat with his companions and a few girls. The girl seated on his knee was lovely, with long braids in her brown hair. But Reed's eyes followed Sar, the Ithernan, who sat on his other side with cheeks painted blue.

"Don't try to get between them, Reed," Aster cautioned. "They have had years together. Fought together. You are a stranger."

"What if I had been unlucky," she asked, voice dull, "and the well had shown me the Ithernan's face instead?"

"Then you would have guided him, helped him, earned his trust."

She knew that. She knew that an Aristene didn't choose her hero. But just the same, she didn't know if she would have had the stomach for it.

"People like him killed my family."

"But *he* did not," Aster said.

"Mercenary."

Reed looked down as a little girl with long blond hair tugged at the end of Aster's tunic. Aster bent so the girl could fill her cup from a pitcher almost as big as she was, holding the neck with both hands, the wide part tucked beneath her arm. She kept on pouring even after Aster said enough, and both laughed when ale spilled over the edge. "You are welcome," the girl said before Aster could thank her, and then ran off still laughing.

"That child will be exhausted tonight," Aster said. "She'll curl up on her mother's lap beside some fire and be asleep the moment she shuts her eyes." She nudged Reed. "But you can't do that." She nodded toward Hestion. "Go."

Reed stood and started to make her way over, but the Ithernan was so near. And despite Aster's words she still hated him, and she was still afraid.

By his fire, Hestion saw the look on her face and gently removed his girl from his knee. He left the fire and came to Reed, so directly she wondered if she'd called him.

"There's no need for you to leave your men," she said. "Or your women."

He glanced back to the fire, where the girl sat laughing with the others in the space he had just left.

"Stina and I have been friends since we were young. She won't mind." Though Reed doubted that, judging by the suspicious glances she kept stealing at them.

"She's not your betrothed?"

"No, though she is quite . . ." Hestion paused and looked at Reed. "I think she will make a fine wife for one of my men someday. I must marry for alliances. It's not as important for me as it is for Belden—" He paused. "And it will not be until after the war with Rhonassus ends."

Hestion led her away from the fires and into the stables. There were no torches there, but enough light found its way in from the square to illuminate it as they walked to Silco and Rabbit.

"My horse again," she said. "You are quite taken with him."

"Indeed. I've not often seen his equal. And I owe him attention for carrying the eels." He scratched Silco's ears and only laughed when the mean horse swung his head around to bite. "You are fearful of Sar," Hestion said quietly. "I know he looks fierce, but really he is like the cats who dwell in these barns—" he gestured up into the piles of hay and straw. "Wild and hard to catch but happy to be petted."

"What if I don't intend to pet him?" Reed asked. "Why have you brought me here? Not only to fawn over my horse."

Hestion nodded. "Are you familiar with the Port of Lacos?"

"I am. It is host to a great race."

"Yes," said Hestion. "And this year they host one for the war. My brother is to ride in it with three of his soldiers, and the prize for winning is leadership of the joined armies of Cerille and Glaucia."

"I've heard it can be dangerous," said Reed.

Hestion regarded her quietly. "I thought to ask you for the use of Silco. With a mount like this, my brother could win—I would pay you—"

"Silco's use is not for sale," Reed said. "Though I could be convinced, to lend him to *you*."

Hestion looked away and quietly stroked the horse's nose. "I won't be there to ride."

"What do you mean?"

"My father seeks to abdicate to Belden. It's been known to his advisers for many years, but the time has never been right. This war will show Glaucia what a leader my brother can be. That he will be a good king. So I have elected to stay behind."

"Stay behind," Reed said numbly. "You can't stay behind—"

"My personal guard will be disappointed," he went on as if he hadn't heard. "Sar has ached for battle. But there will be others."

But not for Reed. If Hestion didn't fight in the war, she would fail her trial. She would be thrown out of the Summer Camp, out of the order. She would never again see Atropa or Aster or Lyonene, not unless she took the vows of an acolyte and lived out her days as a servant.

Kleia Gloria, why have you done this? she thought. *Why have you granted me a hero who doesn't want to fight?*

"No," she whispered. She pressed her hands to the sides of her head; when he reached out to steady her, she took him by the wrists. "You must change your mind. You must sail.

"I thought only to become your companion," she said, half to herself. "To find a way onto his ship. To attach myself like a burr to his side, not to Belden—"

"To Belden? What are you muttering, mercenary? What plans did you have for my brother?"

Reed stepped back in the dark as Hestion called for his guard. They came quickly, none faster than the Ithernan, flooding into the stable like ants. When the Ithernan grabbed her by the arms, she nearly screamed; it was only Aster's words of warning that kept her armor in the aether.

"Take her out the back," Hestion ordered. "Quietly. Take her to my quarters and send for my brother. So we may question her away from her master."

Reed struggled to untangle her thoughts as she was dragged through the empty halls of the royal household. It was difficult, with the Ithernan so near, muddling her wits with fear. Hestion thought she plotted against his brother. He wouldn't believe her now, when she said he had misunderstood and that she'd misspoken.

They shoved her through a door and pushed her onto the floor. Someone lit a candle and the room brightened: she saw Hestion's bed covered in furs and a low wooden table; spears and a quiver of arrows rested against the wall.

"Sar, get her up," Hestion ordered. "The rest of you go and find my brother." The warrior moved to do as he was told, and Reed glared at him.

"Touch me again, Ithernan," she warned, "and you will find your mouth free of teeth." He stopped, and she got to her feet. When Hestion gave him a look, he turned up his palms and said, "What? I like my teeth."

"I don't know why," Reed muttered. "They're horribly orange and crooked."

"Silence, mercenary," said Hestion. "Tell me. Who paid you to get close to my brother?"

Reed squared her shoulders. With her back straight she was just as tall as Hestion, if not slightly taller. "Well, which do you want? Do you want me to be silent, or do you want me to tell you?"

Hestion's jaw tightened. He made a fist and Reed eyed it warily. He couldn't hit her. Kleia Gloria had bound them together, but if he struck her, he was no kind of hero.

"Tell me," he said slowly, and relaxed his hand. "Speak truly, and no harm will come to you or your companion. You have my word."

There was no choice now. Aster did say she would know when it was time.

"I will speak," she said. "But to you alone." She looked at Sar. "Go, Sar."

"Are you sure? She is still dangerous."

"Wait outside. Bring my brother to me when he arrives."

Reed waited for Sar to leave and for her and Hestion to be alone before she took a deep breath. "I was not sent to Belden," she said. "I was sent to you."

"To me?" he asked. "For what purpose?"

"For the purpose of your glory." Reed spoke through gritted teeth as Hestion squinted at her in curious disgust, as if he thought she was afflicted with some kind of madness.

"When you saw me throw the knife in your father's hall," she said, "when you found me in the woods, or when I found you beside the river. Did you not feel the thread that stretched between us?"

"You are a girl," he replied, eyes narrowed. "You interested me."

"It is more than that," she said. "And I am more than a mercenary. The aid that I bring you is not only a sword, and it is greater even than victory."

Reed reached into the aether and saw the light reflected in his eyes as her armor settled upon her shoulders. Hestion's lips parted as he looked at her. This was how she had imagined it.

"What are you?" he whispered. But it was Belden who answered, his voice full of wonder as he stood in the door with the Ithernan at his side.

"She is an Aristene," he said.

21.

A RELUCTANT HERO

"Don't worry, Reed," Aster said. "They know of us. That will make things easier." It was the morning, and she and Reed had been summoned before the throne of King Arik. He and Prince Belden awaited their presence in the lodge.

The Glaucans knew of them, though how much they knew was uncertain. The night before, when Belden had released her, he'd said only that they were legends. Myths. But he had apologized for any ill treatment and he'd let her go, so that was a good sign.

As they walked through the square, men and women stared openly. It seemed that the whole city knew of them, too, or at least knew of them now: a few sketched hasty bent-kneed bows, and a few others cowered and hurried away like they were monsters.

"Most of them do not really believe," Aster said. "They won't, until they see our armor or until they see us fight. They'll try to get you to prove it"—she eyed Reed with a raised brow—"and you must resist the temptation."

"I don't have enough magic to show them anything," said Reed.

"You have enough. Kleia Gloria is with you when you need her."

"How can you be sure?"

"Can you not call your armor? Do you not feel her when you are garbed in silver and white?"

"That's only your magic," said Reed. "Borrowed."

"Her or me." Aster shrugged. "There is really no difference." The broad doors of the hall opened before them, pulled by two blushing, bowing girls, and the warm smells of roasted meat and smoke drifted into the square.

"They think that our being here means the Docritae will win the war," Reed murmured.

"Let them think so. They may be right. Great personal glories are often accompanied by victory. And with you and Lyonene both maneuvering heroes against Rhonassus . . ."

"You think we're fated to win?"

"I think that fate is not worth guessing about. It is only worth making. You'll make your own fate, Reed, and Hestion's along with yours."

They stepped into the hall, where King Arik sat upon his throne, which was outfitted in the black-and-gray fur of wolves. Belden stood by his side as expected, but Reed was surprised to see Hestion. He'd not said a word to her from the moment he discovered what she was.

"Aristene!"

King Arik beckoned them forward. That was another thing. "Aristene" was all they were called now. As if they had no names at all. They reached the king and bowed.

"Had we known who you were when you arrived, we'd have done more to make you welcome."

"There's been no shortage of welcome, King," Aster replied. "Your hall is warm and plentiful."

"And you have come to it," said King Arik with a look at Hestion, "to drag my son to war."

"Don't misunderstand," added Belden with his easy smile. "We are glad. I've been trying to convince him to come out and fight for months."

"You speak as though it is decided," Hestion said quietly. "When it is not."

"But you must sail," Aster said. Her voice was low and strange, and Reed looked at her mentor and saw Aster's eyes lit as if by a reflected flame. "If Hestion does not sail to war with his brother, then he will not sail at all." Then Aster relaxed, and the burning circles in her eyes disappeared.

Hestion looked shaken, but his jaw was tight when he looked at Reed. "There is no 'must.' There is only what I will do. My apologies if you thought to arrive and find me a willing dog for your leash."

"Hestion!" the king snapped, but the younger prince bowed to them and left.

"Forgive him," said King Arik. "He has been this way since . . ."

"Birth," Belden supplied. "But he will come around. He will sail, you will see. He is the only man here I would readily follow, into storm or into war. He's sulking because your coming has robbed him of a season of chasing girls. But he will get over the loss."

"Your goddess," King Arik said with a pious nod of his head, "she sees glory for us, then? Victory?"

"Glory," Aster replied. "As for victory, you will have to do that on your own."

"Good," Belden said, and Reed found herself liking him. "I never seek to depend on anyone for too much. Not even a goddess."

"Nor do I," Reed said, "so I had better go find the prince."

"You will likely find him in the altar of the prophet. He would pray there upon his decision."

Reed and Aster bowed again, but before they left the lodge, Aster asked, "How is it you have come to know of the Aristene here in Glaucia?"

"Your kind were here in the time of my father's father. Some thought you were only legend . . . ," King Arik replied, and Aster turned to go.

"Such are our ways," she said, her voice like a shrug. No doubt she had done this many times, sung this same song, danced this same dance, but for Reed having the magic and the knowledge in the open was the very first taste. They left the king's hall, and as she walked across the square to find her hero, she felt like the string of a bow drawn back.

"Aster," Reed said. "What was that magic that let you see, just now?"

"That magic was yours. I saw through the blood I drank at the Granting Ceremony. Your blood carries his destiny, even though you aren't yet an Aristene. Go on. I will await you in the stable when you have secured his attendance."

Reed made her way quickly down the forest path. She found Hestion inside the temple, just like Belden said. He was seated on the stone bench and had lit many candles. Perhaps one for each of his men. Perhaps one for the memory of his mother. Perhaps he had stomped one into the dirt, for Reed.

"Your brother was right about where to find you."

"Strange he didn't also say that in our lands, when we pray, we pray alone," he said without turning. But Reed couldn't heed his words. It was her task to guide him down the right path.

She walked farther inside, studying the altar and its hundreds of candles. White and pale blue, grays, and yellows. Each burning candle stuck into the melted wax of the ones that came before so the wax itself had begun to seem part of the temple's design. She looked above at the carving in the stone, the vine-wrapped pillars, the intricate sculpting of the ledges, and the archways that looked out upon the woods in all directions. "Your mother truly was a great talent."

"Don't praise my mother."

"Your prophet, then. He must have been pleased by this place."

"He was. And now he's dead, because the king of Rhonassus would have kept him for his own."

"What have you heard," Reed asked, "about your prophet's murder?"

Hestion's voice lowered. "That King Oreas has gone mad. That he keeps the prophet's rotting head at the side of his throne, holding it up to his ear as if it can still whisper his fortune."

"There is so much anger in your voice," said Reed. "Yet you would really not sail to war?"

He curled his lip. "Anger will not manipulate me into battle. The murder of the prophet is used by kings as an excuse to sack the capital. Because it's easier to call men to war for vengeance than to summon them for the gain of coin. But the coin will flow. Straight into Cerille's coffers."

"You think Cerille dishonorable. But if the prophet was the Prophet of All, you are not the only country whose righteous anger is genuine."

Hestion said nothing.

"Will we struggle for the entire war?" Reed asked. "You were kind to me when I arrived—"

"I was kind to a mercenary girl. But that was only a disguise." He gestured to her tunic, her stitched leggings. "All of this is a disguise. Your order is an order of secrets, yet you show yourselves and expect blind faith. My companions earn my trust."

"I am happy to earn my place," she said, and felt the borrowed magic waking. "And if I am to earn your trust then you should know: I am not an Aristene yet. I am only an initiate."

"An initiate?" He turned. "What does that mean? How many victories have you won?"

Her silence answered for her, and he laughed.

"Yet I am supposed to trust your counsel? You are no immortal warrior, and you are younger than I am!"

"Your extra years would prove of no use were we to cross swords." Reed clenched her fists. "I should have known you would be this way. I should have known by the look in your eyes when I glimpsed you so long ago."

"What do you mean? I have never met you before."

"You have not met me. But I have met you. When I was a child, just after Aster found me, I was taken to the city of the Aristene. I touched the water of the sacred well, and it was your face that I saw when I broke the surface."

Hestion's frown lessened. "How did Aster find you?"

"What?"

"You said she found you. How?"

"I don't know. She says it was because I was marked by the goddess when my family was killed. I have a dead mother, too," she said, eyes low. "Murdered. By an Ithernan raider, like your friend Sar."

Hestion glanced to one side, at one of the lit candles. Perhaps the one he had lit for the Ithernan.

"Is that why you look at him the way you do?"

"I know he wasn't among them," said Reed. "But he looks like they looked. And I carry the memory of that night and those days. After they sacked my settlement, they took me with them. That's where I met Silco."

"They took you both for sacrifices," Hestion said. "Silver and Combat—"

"Is how we were saved. Aster and another Aristene fought and paid for us."

"Fought *and* paid?"

"I suppose they didn't need to pay. But it was the polite thing to do."

He snorted.

"I'm sorry you don't want to fight," she said. "I'm sorry that I must ask you to. But it is your destiny, Hestion. Your destiny to rise alongside your brother."

"What will happen to you?" he asked. "If I don't?"

"You are my first hero," she said simply. "If you don't, I lose my place within the order. I will be cast out."

Hestion looked down into the candles. "I shouldn't care," he said. "But somehow I do. Perhaps it is true what you say and I sensed the thread between us even before. I was drawn to you, Reed. Asking for the use of your horse was not the only reason I brought you into the stable."

It took her a moment to understand what he meant. When she did, her surprise came out as laughter.

"Most girls don't laugh when I tell them such things," Hestion said. "Or if they do it is laughter of a different kind and more pleasant-sounding."

"I'm sorry," Reed said, still smiling. "I mean no offense. But I am your Aristene; there can be none of that between us."

"More's the pity." Hestion sighed. "So you will be my Aristene. And you will advise me."

"And fight by your side. I will use my gifts, and the gifts of my order, to make of you a legend."

He scoffed, like all was a joke, but she wasn't fooled. The intrigue in his eyes was plain. No man truly wished to escape his destiny. And all men desired to be legends.

22.

FLAGSHIPS IN THE HARBOR

In the morning, Reed was buoyant as she readied their horses for the sea voyage. They would sail for war. Well. First they would sail to Lacos for the race, and to meet Lyonene with the prince of Cerille.

"She'll not be able to gloat," Reed said to Silco as she brushed his coat. "Her rich prince can't be any finer than Hestion." Cerille's army would be larger, though. And with the power of more coin. Only the superiority of the Glaucan fighters and the cavalry horses she and Silco would win in the race would tip the scales. But even if Lyonene did gloat, it would be good to see her. She stroked Silco's soft neck. "I miss her. And I wish—"

She wished Gretchen would be there. To be reunited at Lacos, with their heroes at their sides, what a time that would have been. Instead, Gretchen was far away on the road to Centra, a chill country to the north where rains kept you inside during the winter months and the only thing to do was huddle near a fire and spin thread.

"I hope she doesn't regret it," she whispered to her horse. "Because it's too late now."

"Too late for what?" Aster walked into the stable with a bit of bread and cheese. Reed took it and stuffed it into her mouth. "Not too much," her mentor cautioned. "An empty stomach may serve you well once you get upon the waves." Reed frowned. She'd spent much of her youth in a port city but only on land. And for all she knew, Silco had never seen a ship.

"Control your fears." Aster took the brush from Reed's hand. "Or you will groom him bald."

"I'm not afraid. Rabbit will look after him down in the cargo hold. And you can—"

"We'll not be on the same ship as you, Reed."

Reed paused. "What?"

"I am sailing on another ship. I will see you safe in Lacos, and then we will part ways."

"You're leaving me?"

Aster looked at her and chuckled at Reed's struck expression. "Only as I was always meant to! The trial has begun, Reed, and you must be on your own. Already I've been too near, too active; you can be sure that in Cerille Lyonene has been by herself since the very beginning—Sabil probably didn't even travel into the capital. She tends to make camp in the wilds nearby and spend her days hunting and fishing."

"Is that what you'll do? Go to the wilds near Roshanak and wait?"

"I don't know. I may return to Atropa. We are bound by the magic in the blood we shared. I'll know if you're in need of me."

All the way to Atropa. All the way through the Veil. And she, left on her own in the middle of a war. *Listen to yourself,* Reed thought. *Panicking because she won't be right behind you. What kind of a trial would it be if Aster was always there to catch a fall?*

"But I am your foundling!" Reed cried.

"And I have always coddled you, like the other mentors said."

Aster laughed, and after a moment, so did Reed.

Aster placed her hand on the top of Reed's head, still slightly shorter than her own. Reed had only until the end of the trial to catch up; if she succeeded and became an Aristene, she would be frozen in time, no more growth, no more change. She didn't know why Lyonene called her "Ox" when Aster was still taller and when there were giant Aristenes like black-haired Aethiel walking around.

"Many of our order have come to us with tragedy in their pasts," Aster said. "Many with broken hearts or spirits. That doesn't afford them favored treatment. You can be no different."

"Aster, what if I don't succeed?"

Aster pulled her near and gently folded her in an embrace.

"Mothers do not love their children only in success," she whispered. "But you will succeed, Reed. I know it."

Reed gazed out across the bright blue water. More than a dozen ships lay anchored throughout the harbor, long and large, with holds for horses and weapons and one broad sail. She saw ships with oars for thirty and others for more than a hundred. Those had been moored farther out, and smaller crafts went back and forth from the docks and the shore, loading them with cargo and soldiers.

Reed and Silco were to travel on Hestion's flagship. It was smaller than his brother's but still well-equipped, and awaited them grounded on the beach, the dark belly of the cargo hold open, visible above the gangplank. Men of the Docritae jogged back and forth across gangplanks, carrying sacks of grain over their shoulders. They rolled barrels of water and wine, and Silco watched with suspicion, blowing air hard out of flared nostrils. It wasn't going to be easy to get him on the ship. It would have gone easier had Rabbit been there to go first and show him the way. But somewhere across the sand, Rabbit was already docilely loaded in a ship manned by the soldiers of the Salt Flats.

While Reed was distracted, someone tried to take Silco's reins. The horse reared up and kicked them in the shoulder.

"I only meant to take him on board!" the boy said, cheeks coloring as he scrambled away.

"I'm sorry!" Reed called after him. "He is . . . a horse of war!" She caught the flying reins and tugged Silco gently down. Horse of war. A spoiled brat is what he was. She stepped confidently toward the gangplank, listening to his tail lashing. Just before the dark square of the cargo door, he reared, and thrashed so violently that it was a wonder they both didn't fall off the gangplank and into the water.

"Easy, boy." Reed patted his neck as he pawed the wood. "It's all right." She tried again and he went high on his hind legs. "Silco." He hunched and leaned his weight back to shore, where people had gathered to watch the commotion.

"Silco," she said as sweetly as she could through her teeth. "Come ahead." She tugged gently, and he snorted. "Come ahead, my love, or I will leave you here, I swear to the goddess."

"Keep him still," she heard a voice from the rear of the gangplank, and the Ithernan, Sar, appeared behind Silco's haunches. Before she could warn him about flying hooves, he had slipped defly around and drawn a length of fabric across the horse's eyes. "I'll hold the blindfold," he said.

Reed clicked her tongue and tugged the reins lightly. Silco's forehoof raised and hovered as he decided whether to take a step or start to paw.

"Encourage him with your voice," said Sar. "Let him know you are safe and right in front of him."

"I know how to comfort a horse," Reed snapped. But she whispered to Silco, and after a few halting strides he followed her onto the ship, docile as an old dog.

Sar held the blindfold in place until they had him securely in his stall. Then he slowly slid it off and patted the horse's wet black neck.

"He's never been on a ship before?"

Reed shook her head.

"He'll be all right," the Ithernan said. "He will adjust to the darkness and the movement. And Hestion ordered plenty of dried fruit on board." He reached into a pouch at his belt and Silco nearly bit his fingers off in his haste to get at the treat. Sar grinned. "Maybe I should have tried the fruit before the blindfold."

They weren't alone in the hold. Soldiers and workers moved constantly past. But Reed felt frozen just the same. The Ithernan was smaller than she was, with a wiry quickness to his movements. The blue upon his cheeks had mostly faded and flaked away, but the black kohl around his eyes gave him a look of menace. She heard the voices of the raiders reach across her memory like cold fingers and smelled the smoke and the burning bodies despite the cool breeze off the sea.

The Ithernan put out his hand. When she didn't shake it, he let it fall. "I've been meaning to thank you, and to apologize for—" He mimed the struggle of dragging her into Hestion's bedchamber.

"Thank me for what?" Reed asked.

"For coming to serve the prince. For getting us into this fight."

"You like to fight?"

"I love a fight." He showed her his arm and its lines of small scars for every victory. He showed her his calf, where a shorter line of scars marked every defeat. "My name is Sar."

"I know."

"It is not much of a name here, but in my tongue it means, 'beloved son.'"

"'Beloved son'? Yet you were given to live with an enemy? Is that what your people do with their 'beloved sons'?" She braced herself, ready to reach for the knife at her waist. But the Ithernan seemed not offended in the slightest.

"An enemy-turned-ally," he said. "I've never been in any danger here, not from the Docritae." He smiled at her, and his teeth were actually just fine. "We know of your people, too, in Itherna. The Aristene. It is a great honor that you are here."

Reed studied him, trying to look past what she knew of his country and what she remembered of the raiders. He wasn't one of the men who murdered her family. And he was of the Docritae now. But he could still not be trusted.

"Thank you," she said quietly, and Sar nodded and went above.

She looked around the hold. On all sides of Silco's stall were tied-down stacks of crates, goods to be traded for supplies, as well as sacks of feed to sustain the horse during their journey and beyond. The sail to Lacos would be short; they could be glad of that at least.

The men on the shore removed the gangplank and shut them inside, and Silco shifted nervously. The only light that remained was from the open hatch that led to the upper deck. Not long after the door was closed, Reed's stomach lurched as the ship launched and the oars were put to water. She pressed her forehead to Silco's neck and took deep breaths, and after some initial unease, her stomach unclenched. Silco, too, seemed perfectly well, snuffling around her tunic for more dried fruit.

"Is this where you will pass the journey?" Hestion asked, half-down the ladder. "Should I have bedding brought for you to sleep upon the crates?"

"Silco was frightened," she lied. "But yes. This is where I should like to sleep. Though I don't require any bedding."

Hestion came to them, winding through the stacks of supplies. The sea must have been calm and the winds fair because he didn't knock up against the crates. He reached Silco and offered him a handful of fruit before running his hands over the horse's haunches and down his legs, like Reed had done that morning in the stable. He glanced at Reed sidelong, still wary. At least he liked her horse.

Hestion straightened. "You're alone now. Your master has left on another ship. I suppose there's no more need of playacting master and apprentice."

In the dark of the hold she couldn't see his face or gauge how serious he was. "You know if you didn't have the fruit in your hand he'd bite you," she said, and to her relief, Hestion snorted.

"Then he is a fitting horse for you."

"In the order we don't say 'master and apprentice,'" Reed said. "We say 'mentor and initiate.' But Aster is still my mentor. We'll see her again in Lacos. It won't be until we sail for Roshanak that I am truly on my own."

Hestion gave Silco one last pat and tossed a few handfuls of grain into his shallow trough. "Come above."

As Reed emerged from the cargo hatch, the sunlight and the strength of the breeze were a welcome surprise. Hestion walked her past the lines of men rowing with impressive precision and past the main sail, flagging as it tried to catch the wind.

"Argon! The rope!" Hestion called to one of his men and pointed to a failing knot. The soldier, Argon, unwound it and pulled the rope taut. He shouted to the two men manning the sail and in a moment the wind filled the cloth and the ship surged forward. The sailors rowing cheered as the oars were called up, and Argon grinned. When the soldier's gaze slid onto Reed, it became notably less friendly.

"Argon," Hestion said to Reed as they walked. "One of my finest. His shield bash will throw a man three lengths." Reed already knew his name—she knew many of the soldiers by name; she had been listening during the nights of feasting. Argon seemed older to her, though like most of the Glaucan men he kept his face shorn smooth. She didn't doubt what he could do with a shield; his arms and shoulders bulged beneath his brown tunic.

"He doesn't like me," she said, eyes on the waves. "None of them do." They scowled and squinted at her; they flexed their fists and wrapped lengths of rope around them, squeezing them like a threat.

"They don't trust you," said Hestion. "They didn't before, when you were a woman and a mercenary. Now you are a woman, a mercenary, and an Aristene. And two of those things they do not understand."

They reached the rail and Reed looked out across the water, invigorated by the wind across her cheeks. Ahead the world was vast and blue, and full of glorious futures. She wished that Silco could come above and enjoy it. But not even an Areion would have been allowed on deck.

"When Aster and Veridian found me, they thought my people might have come from Sirta and been of the sea."

"So perhaps sailing is in your blood." Hestion tipped his chin toward a few of the deckhands, boys of twelve or fourteen years, seated together with their backs to the rail and their faces slightly green. "Not everyone is so lucky." He turned his attention to the horizon and pointed at the nearest ship: larger than the rest, with a bright red sail painted with the stag of the Docritae. "My brother's flagship," he said. "But not even Belden is in the lead—look."

Reed squinted. In the distance, much farther ahead, were ten ships with black sails, white stripes running down them like dried tears.

"The men of the Salt Flats," Hestion said. "They may beat us to Lacos by most of a day."

"My mentor is aboard one of those ships," said Reed.

"A good choice. Did her Aristene magic tell her which to take?"

"One doesn't need magic to know that the men of the Salt Flats are the finest sailors," said Reed. "They never stop boasting of it."

Hestion laughed.

Reed watched the ships of the Salt Flats grow smaller across the water. Soon Aster would be out of sight, and Reed would feel even more untethered than she did already. Lyonene would be so disappointed in her lack of independence. She turned from the rail. Three soldiers leered at her as they passed.

"They won't hurt you," Hestion said quietly.

"They couldn't," Reed said, but really, she didn't know. How much Aristene strength had she been lent? Enough to fight three men? Five? Certainly not a whole ship, if they decided they'd rather not have her company.

"Normally I would order that you sleep with me—in my quarters," he added when she gave him a look. "But you are not to be touched, by Belden's orders. And by my father's."

Reed studied the soldiers' faces, deferential enough when Hestion was watching. But when he turned away their eyes were not shy. They didn't hide what they thought of her. Or what they'd like to do to her.

It won't be like that forever, she thought. *When they see the help I bring they'll change their minds. When we've spoken and they know me.*

"They are tightly wound," Hestion said. He looked back at the sea. "Some of these men will never return to Glaucia. Even great warriors like Sar may fall." Reed had seen him go past, carrying a piece of pottery. It seemed like he'd been speaking to it.

"What was that he carried just now?" Reed asked. "The pot."

Hestion grinned. "That is Sar's funerary jar. The Ithernan believe that the eyes hold the soul, so if he is killed, I may leave his body but not his eyes. The pots are placed in family tombs and painted with the great deeds of the fallen. Sar makes me bring that jar wherever we go. Even on a hunt."

Sar walked by again, the pot tucked into the crook of his arm, and Reed tried to imagine it, painted and pretty, in a tomb full of other small pots of eyes.

"They are a strange people," she said.

"Warlike," said Hestion.

"Murderers."

"To some. But to others the Ithernan are heroes. What do the

Aristene do with their dead? Some say you are immortal, that your horses are immortal, and that you can shape-shift."

Reed laughed. Then she thought of the mysterious Outfitter, dwelling far below the Citadel, and wondered if it was really so far-fetched. "The Aristene die rarely," she replied.

"So you are hard to kill?"

"I am not hard to kill at all. I am only an initiate."

Hestion frowned. "A pity. I was eager to have one companion I didn't have to fear losing. Leading men into battle is a heavy thing."

"You lead them well. Bravely, so that if they fall they may do so without shame. With the glory of the charge."

"Those are words we say to the young ones." He nodded toward the deckhands still sitting with eyes clenched shut. "The ones who've not yet seen real death. Or smelled it. Who've never seen a man try to put himself back together after a sword has taken him apart. If you fight only for glory, I will tell you now: the glory isn't worth it."

"I think you'll come to change your mind," Reed said. Hestion raised his brows and looked at the men and boys whose fates he carried on the deck of his ship. She felt her magic rise warmly and laid her hand over his on the railing. "You ask nothing of them that you don't ask of yourself."

"Perhaps." He looked down at their joined hands.

"Tell me more about the horse race of Lacos," said Reed. "They say the finest riders come from each surrounding territory. They bring their finest horses, and there is feasting and music."

"The beauty of the women is nearly as legendary as the horses," Hestion said. "But this is a special race, only between Glaucia and Cerille. The celebrations will be less grand."

"Yes, no doubt the women and the horses will be nags," Reed

joked. But Hestion didn't smile.

"You will let Belden ride your horse?"

"If you want to assure a victory, I should ride him. I assume that you and I will be among his chosen companions."

"Such decisions are left to my brother."

He sounded a little cross, but Belden seemed wise; he would know what the right choice was. And if he didn't, well, the Aristene had their ways.

23.

THE PORT OF LACOS

The good winds and fair weather stayed with them and the Glaucan fleet reached Lacos after sailing only nine days. But they were not the first to arrive. The port was already filled to bursting with their Cerillian allies.

The ship was beached and the cargo hold opened, and at the first sliver of light Silco nearly took Reed's arm off, he charged so fast toward freedom. As soon as his hooves hit the gangplank, Reed vaulted onto his back. The shore at Lacos was not the same as the shore in Glaucia, and the end of the gangplank fell short of dry land. But Silco leaped gamely into the shallows, prancing and pawing, splashing in the cool water. He even whinnied, calling out his relief to any horses close enough to hear. Reed let him play for a few moments and then turned him toward the sand and the city.

The Port of Lacos. It had been many years since she'd been beside the sea and she was surprised how much its nearness affected her—the softness of the sand and the sound of the waves, even the smell of the washed-up seaweed and empty shells. This was her other life, the part she remembered best, before the settlement. Salt air and scores of people from many different lands, merchants and silk tents. Piles of colorful spices and children chasing each other through streets of stone.

She waited for Hestion at the edge of the marketplace. The air was fragrant with roasting nuts and meat, perfumed oils and the tang of new leather. The Port of Lacos teemed with people and animals, moving carts—a child in a graying cloak darted past Silco's legs; he was chased or followed by two more. Perhaps at play or perhaps at work. Ferrying messages between merchants was something that Reed remembered well. There was so much activity and finery on display—if this was less than the city did for a normal race she couldn't imagine what it was like when they did more. The port would have burst through its boundaries into the bay.

"Aristene!"

Reed turned and saw Hestion approaching on foot with Sar and Argon. The gold and silver crests on Hestion's chest earned them a respectable berth as they moved through the throng. She dismounted, and together they walked up the hill toward other Glaucan tunics. They found Belden beside a stack of bird crates and baskets of many-colored eggs. He had a few in his hand and tossed them each one: small and green with speckled black. Reed cracked the shell and popped the egg into her mouth. It had been baked or boiled, but the yolk was still pleasantly soft.

"Will the race be held through these streets?" Reed asked as she picked at another eggshell.

"No," Belden replied. "The chosen riders must travel up into the hills."

"Who will you choose?" she asked innocently. But she'd caught a glimpse of the stallion Belden had brought: a great beast of a horse built for carrying heavy armor. He would need Silco's speed if he hoped to have any chance at all.

"Both Cerille and Glaucia will select four riders. The messenger from Lacos has already come for the names. I said you would be one of them." Belden looked at her. "I hope you don't mind."

"I do not mind at all," she said, and smiled triumphantly at Hestion. "Who are the others?"

"Myself, of course. And Hestion. And Sar."

Reed glanced at the Ithernan, who bent his head and grinned. Were the Ithernans good riders? She couldn't imagine so if they were willing to cut the throat of a fine colt like Silco.

"The riders from Cerille will be fast but not bold," Belden said. "The course will be long. We may hope to outlast them. Or to pull them from their saddles."

"Have you seen the princeling yet?" Hestion asked.

"The princeling?" Reed wondered.

"Alsander of Cerille. We have met. When we were much younger, he and his father traveled to Glaucia with a royal convoy. I killed a boar in front of him during a hunting party and some of the blood splashed onto his face. I thought he was going to cry."

Belden chuckled and nibbled an egg. "The prince was not more than ten. He's sure to have grown tougher."

"You don't think much of him," Reed said. "But he will be a great hero."

"And how do you know that?" Belden glanced at his younger brother. "Is Hestion not the only prince to receive the Aristene blessing?"

"Is that so?" Hestion asked, with an air of competition. "And who is it that he has with him?"

Belden lifted his chin and nodded farther into the marketplace.

"There is the prince now. The one with the gold shining off his helmet."

Reed turned. The helmet was under his arm, but still, the crown prince of Cerille was hard to miss. He was handsome, with calm eyes and short-cropped black hair. His blue tunic was edged in gold embroidery, and over his shoulder was a cape fashioned from the pelt of a spotted animal.

"That is quite a beauty by his side," Belden remarked, and Reed's face brightened.

"Lyonene!" Lyonene turned as Reed waved her arms and shoved through the crowd, dragging Silco along so people made way. She burst into the Cerillian party and collided with her friend, who half buckled under the sudden weight.

"Reed!" She didn't sound pleased about the greeting. "Forgive her, my prince," she said to Alsander, and pushed Reed away. "This is my Aristene sister Reed, and she has always been . . . ebullient. And large. Which is why we call her the ox."

"You are the only one who calls me that," Reed said, and Lyonene tried but did not quite manage to hide a smile. She had a sword across her back and the jeweled dagger from the Outfitter in a belt at her waist. But aside from her weaponry she looked more a lady than a warrior, in a long gown in cloth of silver and her hair braided against the back of her head. Reed turned to Alsander, but after his initial expression of surprise his attention had shifted to Hestion, who had followed in her wake.

"Another Aristene," Alsander said. "For Prince Hestion?"

"You can't have thought to have all the advantages." Hestion bowed to Lyonene, and neither Reed nor Alsander missed the way

his eyes wandered over her shape. Then he greeted the other prince
with a grin and a firmly gripped wrist.

"I did not," Alsander replied. He put out an arm and Lyonene
stepped close to coil her own around it. "Though I expected she
would have been granted to Belden."

Granted to Belden. Reed bristled at the phrase. Heroes were
granted to them, not the other way around.

"Belden or me." Hestion shrugged. "There is no difference. We
have the same goals, the same aims. As do Glaucia and Cerille,
lest we forget in the heat of the race."

Alsander smiled, and his eyes turned to Silco. "The race will be
good sport. Don't be too disappointed when I come away with the
win." He looked at Reed. "It seems you have already been awarded
the most hardy Aristene. Though I wouldn't seek to trade." He held
Lyonene possessively and slid his fingers down the length of her
throat, making Hestion raise his eyebrows and cough.

"Indeed you wouldn't," Lyonene agreed. "And besides, looks can
be deceiving—Reed has never bested me in a fight. Have you, Ox?"

"Those fights weren't real," Reed said, narrowing her eyes. But
before she could become truly annoyed, Lyonene laughed and let
go of Alsander to kiss her.

"Come away," she whispered, taking Reed a few steps into the
crowd. "And let the men talk for a few moments. Let *us* talk for
a few moments." She held Reed at arm's length. "I missed you. I
didn't think I would. There's been so much to do—I want to tell
you everything about the Cerillian court and the vipers that make
their nests there—" She cast a quick look to the princes. "They are
insufferable. The kind of people who believe women should be seen

and silent. Alsander is my only ally and only because I am *his*, and he likes that." She sighed. "You're lucky to go to one like Hestion and to Glaucia, where they will accept women as mercenaries."

"They still needed some convincing," Reed said, thinking of her thrown dagger.

"The Cerillians don't even believe that I can fight! And I couldn't bring myself to show them, in that court full of snakes. If I'd flashed my silver armor, Reed, I think they would have cut off my head."

"Lyonene!" Reed grasped her shoulders. "You must not go back there. Not until we're both members of the order and can return together to burn that court to the ground."

For a moment her friend stared at her in surprise. "Reed, your face looks like a storm cloud! You speak as though we are conquerors!" She grinned and squeezed Reed's fingers before removing them from her shoulders. She seemed better, as if the show of Reed's anger and her promise of protection were all she'd really needed. "Don't worry about me. You know how I am with obstinate people; I won't stop until I have bent them like . . . well, like reeds. By the time I'm finished with that court, I will practically rule it." She breathed deep, and looked around the marketplace and onto the bay, full of the ships of war. "Isn't this all you've ever imagined?" she asked. "The only thing I regret is that Gretchen isn't here to go with us."

"I've been thinking of her, too. And of you. So much has happened, Lyonene. I wish we were back at the tavern over a pitcher of ale, so I could tell you."

"Tell me tonight," Lyonene said. "There is a feast, hosted by Laconian nobility to honor the riders of the race. Make sure Hestion brings you and we will have plenty of time to talk. I want to know everything. I think your Hestion liked the look of me."

"Everyone likes the look of you," Reed teased, and pushed her. "And of course we'll be there. We are two of the riders."

"As are Alsander and I. But I think you ought to save Silco. . . . He seems tired, from the sea voyage."

Reed looked over the crowd to Hestion as he tried to keep Silco calm within the crowd. "You would like that, but he's actually very well. And even if I did save him, I could still outride you. On any horse, on any day."

"It is the only thing you can beat me at, Reed, so I will let you have it."

Reed smiled. She looked again at Silco, and something caught her eye near the edge of the market. She craned her neck. It was Aster, and Rabbit. And with them, standing beside a tall red horse, was Veridian.

"Do you see that?"

"See what?" Lyonene asked.

Reed pushed back through the people and grabbed Silco's reins, jumping onto his back. She raced quickly through the paved streets, her eyes on her mentor and the woman with the wild blond hair, as if they would disappear if she blinked.

"Veridian!" Reed shouted as she and Silco barged through people passing in the street to slide to a stop before the two Aristene and their Areion mounts. "Veridian! It *is* you."

"No," Veridian said in disbelief as she looked at Reed. Then she looked at Aster and back again. "This cannot be the two skinny colts. You've grown." She put her hands on her hips. "Big." Silco shoved his nose past her to sniff at Everfall, Veridian's red gelding. The two horses blew air into each other's noses, eyes bright and necks stretched. "Ever remembers you," Veridian said to Silco. "Do you remember him?"

Reed wasn't sure until Silco drew his lips back and clacked his teeth together high in the air, the way baby horses do when they meet a new adult.

Veridian laughed. "That's right. You knew him when you were a baby." Reed tugged his head back.

"Enough of that," she whispered. "You are too old now for foal snapping." Reed looked quietly between the two women. She'd been so surprised to see Veridian that she'd run up without pausing to wonder if she would be interrupting them.

"Silver-and-Combat," Veridian said. "And are you still called Reed?"

Reed nodded.

"I supposed so. They wouldn't give you a different name until your Joining. After you had proven yourself worthy." She nudged Aster. "Aster still calls you 'the foundling.'"

Reed grinned. It was strange to see Veridian. It had been so long, and Reed had changed so much when Veridian had not changed at all. She was still serious and direct, her face still unlined, her eyes still sharp. Her blond hair hung between her shoulder blades.

"What are you . . . ?" Reed turned to Aster, who had yet to speak. "What is she doing at Lacos?"

"What everyone is doing at Lacos," Veridian answered. "Shivering in the shadow of a coming war." She looked upon the passing crowds. Did the blood of an outcast prickle whenever a soldier walked by? Did she still feel the glory there waiting to be unleashed?

But she is not an outcast, Reed reminded herself. *She is a deserter.*

"None of these people seem like they're shivering to me," said Aster.

"Well, of course they're not now. Now it is all boasting and coin. Later it will be blood, and starvation. And women toiling in their fields with no more husbands or sons."

"Do not sing these songs to me," Aster said, the tone of her voice suggesting that Veridian had sung them many times before. "We do not make these wars. We merely win them."

"You do not always win," Veridian whispered. Aster gave her a look of caution, and Veridian's countenance shifted back to jovial. "But I must admit, these winds look good. Two Aristene initiates guiding heroes for the same side? And a third supporting them upon the sea?"

"A third?" Reed asked.

"Aethiel. She is out there somewhere, sailing with a hero in the fleet from Cerille." Veridian waved her hand. "You may not see her; she may not again come ashore. You know Aethiel. With her it is all water and waves and swinging about from masts.

"But," Veridian said, "it's not only the war—I came to see the two of you. I guessed that the time of your Hero's Trial was near, and this would be the only place; every Aristene in the world has their eye cast toward Rhonassus. Even derelict apostates, like me."

"Then . . . are you accompanying us?"

"No," said Aster. "Veridian is no longer of the order—"

"And so the order cannot tell me where to go or not go," said Veridian.

"There is a feast tonight," Reed said. "Hosted by the nobility of Lacos."

"Then I will go to that," Veridian declared. Aster narrowed her eyes at Reed. "We will go together and see what our little colt has grown into."

She smiled innocently, and Aster sighed.

"Very well," she said to Reed. "We will see you there."

24.

FUTURE KINGS

That night, Reed and Hestion readied themselves for the night's feasting in the cargo hold. It was not exactly the most princely place to prepare, but privacy was hard to come by on the warship, where men slept communally on deck, lashed loosely to the rail. The cargo hold and Silco's stall were some of the best accommodations on board.

Reed paced back and forth, trying not to listen as Hestion changed his tunic behind a stack of supplies.

"Stop pacing," he called, and she glimpsed a bit of fabric going over his head. "Your steps are so heavy they rock the ship."

"They are not," she said, and stopped. He had his back to her, and she couldn't help but notice the flex of his bare shoulders. *He is athletic*, Reed thought, and turned away. *Those arms are good for throwing spears and lifting shields. He would probably be terrible in bed, always picking people up and tossing them about.* Not that she would know anything about that. From Lyonene's tales she gathered it was sometimes nice to be tossed.

"You seem nervous," he said.

"I'm not nervous."

"Oh," he said, brow arched as he affixed his belt. "Perhaps Aristene initiates do not become nervous."

Reed gritted her teeth. She wasn't nervous, exactly, but the feast would be the most formal she had ever attended. She looked down at herself, in a fresh tunic and leggings, with a dagger tucked into her belt of blue cord. She lacked the gowns and the breeding for events such as this. And she regretted what she'd done in the marketplace, bounding up to Lyonene like a great, happy dog.

Hestion came out from behind the crate. His formal tunic was dyed a deep crimson and the silver stag of Glaucia was pinned at his shoulder. His dark gold hair had been washed in the sea, his skin tanned by the sun of their sail.

"Your belt is crooked." Reed went to him and tugged it straight.

"Are you not going to—?" He gestured to the air around her. "You may not be a true Aristene yet, but you may as well look the part."

"We do not wear our armor like a jeweled pin," Reed said. She was tempted, though, to call it up. To shine with power and dazzle him so his eyes would move over her like they had over Lyonene. But even still it wouldn't have been for the same reason. In her armor, Reed could command wonder but not desire. Certainly not desire in someone like Hestion, who could have his choice of beauties.

"Do you wish you could trade?" she asked suddenly. "Me for some other, perhaps one more like my friend?"

Hestion looked up in surprise.

"No," he said. His eyes took on a mischievous gleam. "Though I would like to put you in a gown like hers."

"Then you would have to wrestle me and win."

"Another good reason." He stepped close and she gasped as he tugged her belt straight as she had tugged his. He looked her over. She was not the proper escort for a prince; she looked like neither a beautiful lady nor an elite guard. Were she not traveling in Hestion's shadow, the Laconian nobility wouldn't have let her through the door.

"I do wish I was taller," Hestion remarked.

"We are the same height."

"Exactly," he said, and led her down the dock and onto the beach.

The feast was held in a large villa around the bay on the northern shore. Near where the Cerillian flagship was docked.

"Alsander wanted to hold it on his ship," Belden said as they walked across the sand and the wave-smoothed pebbles. "Can you imagine the boldness? The insult to our Laconian host?"

"I have heard he is the sort of man who enjoys staking his claim," said Reed quietly.

"Are you in danger, brother?" Hestion asked. They'd seen the Cerillian guard, outfitted in full regalia, in armor of gold plate and carrying long spears.

"No." Belden laughed. "Taking Rhonassus would cost Alsander far more without us. And he is no fool, to want a war at his back as well as his front. Besides, you remember how he was. Only a pup."

A pup. But pups grew into dogs. Some grew into wolves.

"Our host tonight is Lady Elisabetta Rilke," Belden told them. "She is the eldest daughter of the family and oversees the keep of the legendary herd."

"Why exactly is the herd so legendary?" Reed asked.

"By accident. The Rilke bloodline is not Lacos-born. After the port was conquered by a marauding king, the king enslaved the people and left the Rilkes behind to rule in his stead as he continued his conquests. It didn't take long for them to realize that the people would not be enslaved, so instead a pact was made: the folk would have their arid hills and trade freely within the port, so long as they paid their tax and tribute. The tax was small, and agreeable, but the tribute was meant to remove their hearts: each year the people had to surrender their two finest horses. But they did it, to keep the peace, and thus the legendary herd was born. Or at least," Belden said, shelling a nut and popping it into his mouth, "that is the way I hear it."

They reached the villa, surrounded by Laconian guard, and went inside. The moment they entered, a serving girl dressed in a thin red gown twirled before them.

"You are a rider?" she asked, and when Belden said yes, placed a garland of berries upon his head.

"As am I," said Hestion, and bent down.

Reed held out her hand and said, "Me as well."

"Where is the other?" the girl asked.

"Still sick from the sea," Hestion said, though really, Sar had elected to remain with the men. The Ithernan had no use for formality either.

"I would rather be sick from the sea," Reed said, balancing the garland awkwardly in her hair, "than put up with this foolishness."

"Do you not have feasts and fancy in the cities of the Aristene?" Belden asked, and Reed recalled her ceremonial tunic, and the painful waxed bun. She supposed it was better a crown of berries than that.

The villa was full of guests and loud with laughter and music. It was constructed to let in the breeze off the sea, and at the center of the villa was an open garden, lush with green plants and a fountain adorned with colorful tiles. Golden roasted birds, breads, and spiced meat pastes sat upon carved wooden platters beside flowers and fruit that Reed had never seen before and didn't know how to eat. She took a bite from a red orb and came away with a mouthful of seeds she had to spit into her hand.

"There is our hostess," Belden said. "Come and say hello." He turned toward a young woman in a fine gown of gold and white, her chestnut hair curling down her back, partially covered by a thin, golden veil.

"Soon, brother," Hestion said.

"Are you sure? She is a great beauty."

"Then I shouldn't wish to fight you for her."

Belden chuckled as he ambled away, and Hestion nudged Reed in the ribs. "There they are. Alsander and your friend. The berries may be foolish but they make them easy to spot."

And Lyonene managed to make them fetching. She had changed into a gown of deep red, and gold bangles glittered at her wrists.

"Can you really not outfight her?" Hestion asked. "She is so . . ."

"Don't be fooled. Lyonene is deadly."

"But you can outride her?"

"Can you outride Alsander?"

Hestion snorted. "Alsander of Cerille could not outride me were I on a mule and he on a winged dragon." They walked together across the room and heads turned as people wondered who Reed was, this plain-clothed girl who accompanied a prince. Some of the ladies looked down their noses or laughed behind their hands. Reed glanced at Hestion. He ignored it, but she knew that he heard.

I am embarrassing him, she thought. She should have listened to him and worn her armor. By the time they greeted Lyonene and Alsander, Reed's shoulders were hunched beneath the weight of the guests' judgment, and as she bent forward to bow, her garland of berries slipped from her head and fell to the floor.

"It seems your Aristene cannot bear finery," Alsander said above the snorts and hushed whispers.

Reed leaned down to pick up the garland. But Hestion reached it first and tossed it onto a nearby table.

"My Aristene needs no adornment." He took two cups of wine from a table and handed one to her. "To say nothing against yours, who is indeed very beautiful."

Reed accepted the cup gratefully.

"Are you prepared for the race tomorrow?" Hestion asked.

"For the race, and to lead our joined armies," Alsander replied. "I hope you won't mind taking orders from a Cerillian."

"As long as you can get my brother to issue them." He took a drink.

Alsander's smile was a grimace, and Reed glanced at Lyonene. Lyonene slipped a hand up Alsander's chest.

"Men," she said teasingly, a pretty pout upon her lips. "Ever wasting time boasting before the deeds are done. Tomorrow the race will be over, and we will know. So for tonight let us be equals, and friends."

"Well-spoken," said Hestion. "After all, you and Reed have been friends for a long time."

"Since we were girls," Lyonene replied. "Only girls, with no power and no magic, before we stood at the arms of heroes and could catch the scent of crowns upon the air."

Crowns upon the air. Reed smelled only meat and flowers, but the Aristene magic worked differently for them all. Veridian could see the beats of a past battle; Aster could not. Aster could see the mark of the Aristene dancing upon Reed; Veridian could not. Perhaps Lyonene could sense the opportunity for a crown. Perhaps after her initiation they would call her the Kingmaker. From the way Alsander was looking at her, he was already counting on it.

"Can you sense that as well?" he asked Reed with a grin. "Do you sense a crown floating above Prince Hestion's head?"

"The only crown above a Glaucan prince's head hangs above my brother's," Hestion said as a chime of bells rang out. Dancers with jangling coins hung from their belts. As Alsander and Lyonene watched them, her lips brushed against his ear and Alsander's hand slid down her back.

"I think you lied to me, Reed," Hestion said into his cup. "When you said there could be nothing between us."

"I spoke only for myself, not for Lyonene."

"So the Aristene do take lovers."

"Many," she asserted. "Constantly."

Hestion laughed, his voice low. "Constantly?"

The dance ended and the dancers turned, coins chiming, arms out to herald someone's entrance into the courtyard. Reed craned her neck to see what approached, what showpiece was being brought out. It was one of the most beautiful horses Reed had ever seen.

"This is my horse, Phaeton," Lady Elisabetta said as her groom led him into the courtyard. "In the old language it means, 'sun god,' and I trust you see why that is so." The horse's coat was gold. Pure gold, as if he'd been painted with it. "I wanted to give you an example of the prizes you may win tomorrow. You may not win Phaeton, of course. He is not part of the herd. But if you want the victory you will have to catch him."

"Catch him?" Reed wondered aloud.

"In tomorrow's race, each rider's hands will be marked with dyed powder. And each rider may place their hands upon whatever horses they reach, whom they wish to keep. But the race does not end until one rider catches me and Phaeton. You do not have to beat us. Just get close enough to place a mark upon his golden coat."

"And what if no rider is able?" asked Belden, looking over the stallion with awe.

Elisabetta shrugged. "Then there are other years to race and other horses to be purchased in the market."

Reed swore under her breath. A horse like that was fast as the wind and bred for the desert terrain. No horse from Glaucia, or from Cerille for that matter, was going to catch a beast like that.

"Can you beat him?" Hestion asked quietly. "Can Silco beat him?"

"Of course he can," she replied. But really, she had no idea.

From somewhere behind them came the sound of something crashing to the floor, and Elisabetta quickly motioned for the groom to take Phaeton back to the safety of his stable.

Across the room, the sound of laughter burst out. Laughter familiar to Reed from a lifetime ago.

"Oh no." Reed made her way through the villa with Hestion, Lyonene, and Alsander trailing curiously behind, and found Veridian on her back, after falling across a table and onto the rug.

Aster stood to one side, stomping out embers from an upturned brazier that Veridian had knocked over when she fell.

"There she is," Veridian said, and held her arms out to Reed. "Our initiate! What?" she asked when Aster made a sound. "The goddess led me to her as much as you!"

"What is happening here?" Alsander asked.

"Nothing. I stumbled." Veridian winced as she rolled over a coal and got to her feet.

"Lyonene." Alsander of Cerille nodded. "See to her."

"She is not mine," Lyonene replied, and crossed her arms as the guests began to whisper.

"Forgive us," Aster said in a tone that left no choice. She nodded in apology to Lady Elisabetta. "The warrior Veridian has always been wild. And tonight she has had too much to drink."

"It's her fault," Veridian snickered, "for having such fine wine. I have drunk a barrel. Aster, have I dyed myself purple?"

Aster reached out, and Reed was surprised to see a soft smile on her lips.

"Come away," she said gently. "But first give me the coin to pay for these rugs you have burnt. You might have burnt us all alive."

"Look at the open air. You can't burn alive inside this villa!" Veridian gestured through the room, her eyes pausing on every man, every soldier who sought to make merry before he sailed away to war. "And besides, what does it matter if I burn them now or they burn themselves later?"

"Veridian," Aster said quietly. "That is enough."

"It's never enough. Three hundred years and it's never enough. You know that." She straightened, suddenly steady as if anger had outweighed the wine. "Go and be farmers," she said, and pointed to Belden, to Hestion, to Alsander. "Be merchants. Have families.

Do not serve Kleia Gloria. Don't let that bitch drag you onto the end of a sword."

Reed stiffened. Even Lyonene, who wore her masks of calm so well, gasped softly.

"Lady," said Alsander. "You disgrace yourself."

"You don't know what disgrace is, boy."

Alsander drew a dagger from his belt and Aster stepped quickly between them. He would have advanced but Lyonene held him back with a hand to his chest.

"She is an outcast. An apostate. She does not speak for our order."

Veridian bared her teeth like she might argue, but instead she looked at Reed, her green eyes so glazed by the drink that Reed couldn't be sure if Veridian could even really see her.

"Glory is a lie," she whispered. "You should have come with me that day—I would have taken you to the port, put you on a ship. You should have listened."

"Let's go, Veridian," Aster said. She placed a hand on Veridian's shoulder, and the apostate threw up her hands. She left with them still raised in the air, assuring the guards of no more trouble.

"But Reed," she said as she passed, "if the elders offer you blood, do not drink it."

"Go!" Aster shoved her through the open door.

Lyonene moved close to Reed. "What did that mean? Blood of the elders . . ."

"I don't know," Reed replied. "But it's too late. I already drank it."

25.

THE HEART SCAR

Reed and Lyonene remained at the feast with their heroes, but after what Veridian had said and the spectacle she'd made, neither could enjoy the festivities.

"She damages us all," Lyonene said angrily. "She undercuts our influence. How are we to guide these soldiers when the Aristene look like fools? I will be lucky if Alsander doesn't cast me off tonight!"

"You said he was reasonable, even kind."

"He is, sometimes. When we're alone he is even sweet. But crown princes in Cerille cannot be soft. His father is a cruel old goat who takes every opportunity to threaten his crown." Lyonene looked at Alsander, and Reed was surprised by the soft sympathy on her face. "He will ride to glory not for me but for him. To prove to the old goat that he's worthy."

"Maybe we should bring his father into the order."

"It's not funny, Ox." But her lips twisted. "Well. Maybe just as far as the Granting Ceremony. I would like to scrub his skin off and wax his hair." Lyonene sighed. "I have to win the race tomorrow, Reed. I must win his respect, or he will ride into battle without me. He'll get himself killed before I can help him to rise. I know I can't beat you," she said, and looked at Reed. "Not unless you let me."

Reed looked away, toward Hestion. The initiates had sought a quiet corner, leaving the princes to boast and tell stories. They were laughing, and anyone who didn't know them might have thought them old friends.

"Lyonene," Reed said.

"Never mind. I was a fool to ask." She lowered her eyes to her wine cup. It was strange to see her that way. Lyonene was never shaken. She was so clever and calculating that Reed never knew whether to comfort her or shove her and demand to know what she was up to.

"What did Veridian mean about the blood?" Lyonene asked, looking back up at Reed. "What did you mean when you said you already drank it?"

"I don't know. Ferreh offered it and told me to drink. She told me to trust her."

"And of course you did. Foundling." Lyonene's eyes flashed.

"Don't sound like that," Reed said. "If Veridian spoke true then the blood was nothing to covet. And I didn't ask for it."

"No, indeed, you never ask for anything." Lyonene crossed her arms. Her eyes seemed far away. "This makes me worry for you, Reed. It makes me worry for us. Sabil may be an old stick in the mud but she was right: if every Aristene in the world can sense this war then why send us?"

"Ferreh said—" Reed hesitated. "She said that something was coming that could threaten the order. She said we were being sent into the world for more than just our Hero's Trials."

"And you kept this from me?"

"She told me not to speak of it!" Except she hadn't. The secrecy had been implied but never ordered.

Lyonene's eye twitched.

"I think we need to go and find Veridian."

Reed nodded toward the dueling princes. "Should we peel them away from each other first?" The initiates turned to look at their heroes, who seemed to be trying to not only outboast but outdrink each other.

"Perhaps a headache tomorrow will make him easier to manage." Lyonene led Reed to the door. "Besides," she said, her voice low, "it is you who will win the race anyway."

They left the loud interior of the villa and tread quickly across the sand. Reed didn't know where Aster and Veridian would have gone, but she sensed it was not a tavern or an inn. She led Lyonene along the beach where it wrapped around the bay and turned toward the cliffs. Tucked into a crevice was an orange, flickering glow.

Reed hoped to step around the cliffside and find her mentor seated in the sand, with Veridian's sobering head lying upon her lap. But there was only Veridian on a large log of driftwood with a cup in one hand. As the initiates approached, she prodded the embers of her campfire with a long stick, sending up sparks.

"Aster is not here, initiates. And neither is Sabil." Veridian gestured with the stick. "She has gone up to camp the other way."

"Where did Aster go? Did you quarrel?" Reed asked.

"You saw us quarrel with your own eyes. But we'll be all right. We are always all right. She wouldn't want you here, though. With me."

"Aster is my mentor, not my keeper." Reed searched the sand and found another log; she dragged it to the fire across from Veridian for her and Lyonene to sit upon. "Why did you say what you did tonight?"

"I had too much to drink." She leaned forward to stir the coals again. She wobbled and Reed tensed, ready to catch her if she fell into the flames.

"This is the great Veridian," Lyonene said, unimpressed. "You are legendary, you know, within the order. There is not an Aristene alive who does not have some tale of you to tell, some daring feat. Every shot made with an arrow is compared to what your shot would have been. Strange, when now it seems you couldn't even hit the target. You would be seeing two of them."

Veridian reached down. She plucked a knife from the sand and held it, wavering before her eyes. Then her gaze sharpened and Reed barely had time to shout, "Lyonene!" before the apostate had thrown it, sinking the blade deep into the tiny gap of driftwood between them.

"If I see two targets I shoot two arrows," Veridian said, and laughed as she drank. "Who is teaching you initiates these days?"

Reed and Lyonene traded a glance as Lyonene gripped the handle of the knife and wrenched it loose. It had been no easy throw. The blade had sunk in deep.

"You remind me of Aster," Veridian murmured to Reed. "Maybe I am wrong, and you will *be* just like Aster and you will be fine."

"Why didn't you want me to go with her, all those years ago? Did you see some ill omen for me, even back then?"

"My magic doesn't touch you, Colt," Veridian said. "But not a colt anymore. What did you call her?"

"Ox," Lyonene replied.

"Ox. That is good. My magic doesn't touch you, Ox. It never has."

Reed pursed her lips. "I would rather that only Lyonene called me that."

"Hmpf." Veridian stoked the flames and stuck the stick into the sand so she could refill her cup from a pitcher at her knee. "Don't take offense. If you are an ox, you are the prettiest ox I have ever seen. And it's plain enough that your Lyonene is very fond of you. She is even a little jealous."

"Jealous?" Lyonene straightened and looked at Reed. "She must be drunk, indeed."

"Of course you are jealous," Veridian said. "You've seen her hero."

"And she has seen mine," said Lyonene.

"Alsander of Cerille." Veridian blew air out through her lips. "But Hestion of Glaucia—the light of glory shines off him even in the dark. He shines like Aster said you did when we found you: like sunlight through a moving stream." She glanced again at Lyonene. "They would have given you a hero, but they would have given *her* a great one. And that is why you're jealous."

"Alsander of Cerille will be great, when I am done with him."

"Reed." Veridian leaned toward her. "Why does Hestion fight?"

"He would rather not, in truth," she said.

"But when he does?"

She remembered how he had hauled her into his quarters when he thought her a plotting mercenary. How he tried to convince her that the Ithernan was no more to fear than a barn cat.

"For his brother," she said. "And for his friends."

"He fights for love," Veridian said. "For ambition and for stature, for glory and for gains, but the greatest of all fight with heart at their core. They do it not thinking of their mortality but of what that mortality may achieve. What it secures. What it protects. Alsander of Cerille fights"—Veridian narrowed her eyes at Lyonene, as if winnowing out a secret—"from the length of his father's shadow.

To prove something. And that is why both may be glorious, but only one will be great.

"Not to mention he is kind on the eyes," the apostate said. "There is only Aster for me, but . . ." She took another drink and whistled, a poor, hollow whistle that made Reed chuckle behind her hand. Veridian was only teasing now, but Lyonene remained unamused.

"This war," Lyonene said. "Two initiates sent into it and the third Aristene is Aethiel, who will remain at sea. Why? What is different about it?"

"Why do you think I would know?" Veridian replied. "I've been away from the order now for longer than you have been alive!"

"But what did you mean about the blood? The blood of the elders that Reed shouldn't drink?"

Veridian sobered and shook her head. She stared into the fire, and soon, Lyonene couldn't bear the silence.

"Well, you are too late! She has already drunk it!"

Reed's brow furrowed. As much as she wanted to know what it meant, she wished Lyonene hadn't said it that way.

"You foolish girls," Veridian whispered.

Reed looked at Lyonene, and Lyonene frowned. The apostate was too drunk. She motioned for Reed to go. They would get no answers from her.

"Wait." Veridian leaned back from the fire, and the initiates sat quietly as she stabbed her fire stick into the sand again and set her wine cup into a crook of the driftwood. Then she hooked her fingers into her tunic and tugged it low, baring her breastbone. There was a large scar upon it. Thick and flat and slightly shiny in the light. "Do you know what this is?"

"Many warriors have scars," said Lyonene.

"But I have seen the same one. On Aster," said Reed. The very same scar in the very same place. The only scar she had been too afraid to ask her about.

"And you will have it, too," said Veridian. "Both of you, if you succeed."

"What is it, then?" Lyonene asked. "A brand?"

"No. This scar was made by a sword."

Lyonene scoffed. "For a scar like that to be made by a sword the wound would have had to kill you."

Veridian watched them in silence, and Reed stared at the heart scar. She had been right to fear it. It was indeed the wound that had ended Aster's life.

"Did you never ask how it was done? What it costs, to become a member of the order?" The apostate readjusted her tunic and went back to stirring the fire. "The final price, they call it. Even though it isn't."

"We give up our lives," Reed said, watching the orange flames dance in Veridian's green eyes. The apostate looked a little like Lyonene, she realized. In another world, the two could have been sisters. "We give up our lives, and they give us a new one. We knew that." They just hadn't realized what it meant. Ferreh would do it to her, Reed guessed. And that would be all right. That she could bear. "I suppose Tiern will do it for you," she said to Lyonene, and Veridian laughed.

"The elders can't do it for you," she said. "You must do it to yourself."

Reed felt Lyonene tense. She wanted to reach for her hand,

worried suddenly that even brave Lyonene would choose another life, like Gretchen had, one that didn't require such macabre sacrifice.

"You think we won't," Reed said quietly. "You think we're cowards."

"I do not think that," Veridian replied. "Though you will be afraid. Only a fool is not afraid to drive a sword through their own chest. But I think you should know that this is what the order asks. What it will ask of you, again and again. To become an Aristene is not to thrust one sword into your heart. It is to thrust the same sword into your heart, over and over, until the end of time."

26.

THE LEGENDARY HERD

The riders in the race were transported to the starting line in carts pulled by sure-footed mules and decorated with green ribbon and pearl-hued shells. Sar and Belden waved to the people gathered alongside the street, people of the port who came out of their shops to wish them well. Belden had to toss them some coin, too, lest Glaucia be outshone by Cerille already; when Alsander's cart passed, he'd thrown sacks and sacks of silver so that when Belden's cart came people were still picking pieces up off the pavement.

Reed and Hestion were not in the cart. They chose to ride their horses instead. Silco's stride beneath Reed was bouncy and full of energy, and she felt the same—her young legs ached for something to do, and the sword across her back hung heavy and unused. She hadn't had a good fight since leaving the Summer Camp.

"You're distracted," Hestion said to her from astride his brown mare. "Were you not happy with what you found when you left me last night?"

"I had to find my mentor," Reed said, only half lying. "I needed her counsel. Besides, you make it sound as if I abandoned you—you were with your brother and at a noble gathering. I'm sure you found a fine bed to fall into at the end of the night."

"But whose bed was it? One of those dancing girls? Or Lady

Elisabetta's, perhaps. That is what I should have done; she could have whispered secrets into my ear about the course."

Reed frowned, though she didn't know why. She didn't care who he bedded. "Elisabetta would have been an advantageous conquest." She craned her neck up toward the adorned cart of Cerille flanked by armed Cerillian guard and trailing four long-legged horses—the mounts they had chosen for the race.

"Are you even listening to me, Reed?"

"Of course. I'm just looking for Lyonene." She'd caught only glimpses of Lyonene's pale arm tossing coins from beneath the covering. Reed hadn't wanted to part from her last night, afraid of the effect of Veridian's words. She didn't think that Lyonene would waver. She was too focused, too ambitious. Of course she hadn't thought that Gretchen would either.

"Was that true what she said last night," Hestion asked, "about seeing crowns?"

"It could be. The magic of the order works differently for all of us."

"I'm glad it doesn't work that way for you."

Reed stared into the back of Alsander's cart. She should perhaps let Lyonene win. She needed the victory more.

"It may not matter," Reed said off-handedly. "You may be a king whether I see it or not. Someone must rule Rhonassus after the city is sacked, and who better than a second-born son who won't have to sail home?" She kept on riding. It took her a few moments to realize Hestion had gone silent. "What?"

"I've accepted you as my Aristene to please my father and brother," he said, eyes serious. "But do not try to put a crown on my head. I've no wish to be a king." He took a breath. "And I have been thinking; you throw a fine knife, Reed, but you have said yourself that you are not immortal. When we reach Rhonassus you must keep to the back of the fighting."

"Keep to the back of the fighting?" She involuntarily jerked Silco's reins so the horse snorted, an echo of her own feelings. "You insult me."

"It is an insult that I wish you safe?"

"Yes," she hissed, and kicked Silco around to the front of the cart. *I am sorry, Lyonene*, she thought. *But I can't let you win. It seems my hero must learn the same lesson as yours.*

Reed rode ahead of the Glaucan cart, angry as the road led them out of the port and into the desert, up a mountain road through to the valleys where the horses ran. Below her, Silco danced happily as the sounds of his hooves and the rolling cart wheels rang loudly off the rocks. It was beautiful country, the hills soft and the rolling mounds of pale sand threaded through with dark silt—but it was also hard and sparse; the vegetation brushy or waxy-leaved, the paths littered with shale. The horses who roamed these hills would be tough and clever. They'd have to be if they wanted to survive.

Reed kept her eye on every ridge, her ears tilted around every bend. On instinct, she reached down and drew the Aristene magic over her skin in an invisible shroud, so she might feel the warning pinpricks of approaching arrows. The high country held many places to hide, and any band of thieves would welcome the chance to rob the royal carts. Cerille had brought only a guard of ten and Belden a personal guard of five. Hestion had brought only Sar and Argon.

"Here we are."

The driver of the cart gestured to the end of the road, where riders on horses waited alongside a fine covered carriage. The legendary herd was there as well, nearly a hundred horses gathered in an immense pen, and Reed tightened her hold on Silco's reins. The horse tied to the covered carriage was Phaeton, and his gold ass was so bright it was nearly as blinding as the Citadel. *I had better get used to it*, Reed thought. *I'll be following it for the whole of the race.*

The door of the carriage opened, and Elisabetta stepped out, along with a tall man dressed in robes of gray. "This is Xanthos," she said to the princes once they had stepped down from their carts. "My horsemaster."

Reed looked at him. She could tell he was a horseman; he had a quiet way about him, and soft, slow hands. When he saw Silco, he gave a short nod of appreciation.

"You will have a few moments with the horses," said Elisabetta. "Before we mark your hands and start the race." She swung her arm wide, an invitation to approach the corral.

"This is where we begin?" asked Belden. He looked around at the small gathering. "It seems a poor send-off for such an occasion."

"The celebrations await us at the finish line," Elisabetta promised. "You will hear the peoples' cheers long before you see them, when I cross it first."

Belden chuckled, and the princes walked to the corral. Reed dismounted, but before she followed she checked the horses. Belden had brought his heavy black stallion, and Hestion and Sar were to ride mares hastily purchased from the port market. They looked fast, but the fastest wouldn't have been found already for sale; Lady Elisabetta would have made sure of that.

Reed looked at the Cerillian mounts. Lyonene was with them,

checking over their legs. One looked familiar.

Reed stepped closer and narrowed her eyes at the dark brown horse with two white socks. As she stared at it, it turned back to look at her, too. And cocked its head. The horse was an Areion. His name was Wonder, and he was the immortal mount of Lyonene's mentor, Sabil.

"Lyonene!" She stomped over to her friend. "That is cheating!"

"There's no such thing as cheating in a Hero's Trial, Ox," Lyonene said smugly. "And I had no choice. I knew you wouldn't give me this victory, though I needed it more. I should have known better than to even ask, after seeing what you did to poor Gretchen before the elders."

Reed stopped, stung. "I didn't mean . . . I didn't want to make you angry with me."

"I'm not angry with you, Reed. I just know you. Now don't be angry with me just because I thought to ask my mentor for her Areion and you didn't." She walked ahead and Reed stalked along behind her. It was far too late to get a message to Aster—even if Rabbit galloped to them at top speed, she wouldn't make it in time.

They reached the corral and ducked inside, where the princes were already assessing horses. It took Reed no more than a glance to see that this was a collection of the finest animals she had ever seen. Finer even than the mares they kept at the Summer Camp. And they were sweet-tempered—when Reed slipped her hand under the belly of a dark gray mare, the horse raised her head and placed her muzzle on Reed's shoulder.

"This girl is very nice," she said to Hestion, her tone still clipped from his insult on the road.

But Hestion was barely listening. His eyes were fixed elsewhere. Reed turned to see what he was looking at, sure she would find the bust of Lady Elisabetta. But instead she found him gazing at something worse: a huge white stallion.

"I want that one." He threaded his way through the herd to its side.

"No." Reed ran her hands over the stallion's haunches and he picked up his foot to kick.

"I don't mind a bad temper, Reed," Hestion said. "He will remind me of you."

Reed gritted her teeth but almost smiled. The stallion was a fine horse, scarred from fighting with the other stallions but still sound. "The problem isn't his mood; it's his color. He's so white that he glows. A walking target."

Hestion considered her words, stroking the stallion's nose.

"I still want him."

"Take him, then. To ride around on at home. Take him to be Belden's mount when he's king."

Hestion frowned, pouting. Well, at least the horse would be easy to mark. Easy to spot in the rush of muscle and pounding feet. Reed looked at the herd nervously. It was mad, a race like this. To weave in and out of so many horses. It would be easy to be clipped by a flying hoof, and any wrong step, any fall, meant death.

"Reed. Are you frightened?"

"Why? Would you like me to keep to the back and out of danger?"

"No," Hestion replied, uncowed. "Because you are our only hope of winning."

Reed sighed. She looked out of the corral, at the Cerillian horses, where Wonder the Areion stood. As she watched him, he yawned, and reached his hind hoof around to scratch his ear like a dog.

"There is no hope of winning," she said dismally.

The horsemaster, Xanthos, called them out of the pen, and the princes and their companions went to mount their horses. Elisabetta Rilke took her place at the head of the herd, riding her golden Phaeton.

Phaeton. Sun god, she said it meant, but Reed could think of other names. Treasure. Coins. Gilding. Alsander of Cerille seemed to be thinking the same thing. She could practically see him counting in his mind how much he could spare to purchase the horse. But that horse would never be for sale.

Before Elisabetta mounted, she unfastened a pin at her waist and removed her skirt to reveal a very clever pair of leggings and high leather boots.

"It just . . . comes off like that," Sar said from behind them, and he and Hestion shared a muffled laugh. Reed looked back at them as Belden lumbered up on his large black stallion and Argon nodded to them from his place beside the cart. He would see them at the finish line.

Xanthos approached the riders with a cloth sack. Belden and Hestion reached their hands inside and came away dyed with red chalk. Reed and Sar did the same, though to Reed there seemed to be little point. She looked grimly at Alsander and Lyonene, their hands powdered in blue. The chalk sprinkled onto their tunics and stained their reins.

I can still outride the rest, Reed thought. *Perhaps even Elisabetta and her monster of gold.*

She tightened her knees upon Silco's sides. The Aristene would finish first and second. And Lyonene would have no doubt as to who would've won had she not cheated.

Elisabetta trotted Phaeton to the gate of the corral. When she whistled, a hundred heads rose with ears pricked. "Xanthos, go!" she cried, and the gate swung open.

The herd bolted so hard that they shook the ground, and Silco reared up on his hind legs. Reed clung to his neck until his forefeet hit the dirt and then leaned forward in her saddle. She twisted her fingers deep into Silco's mane. He would break just as hard as the herd, and she didn't want to be left behind sitting in midair.

"Go! Go!" Belden shouted, and the riders sprang off to give chase.

Silco was ahead of the others in two fast leaps, beating even Wonder. But their lead didn't hold. Lyonene breezed first past Hestion and then past her.

"You'll have to ride faster than that, Ox!" she called, and tucked her head down beside Wonder's neck. The cheat. She wouldn't even need to steer or to control him. The Areion would know what to do.

"Where did she get that horse?" Hestion shouted, drawing even with Reed and Silco.

"From us!" Reed shouted back. "It's an Areion: an immortal mount of the order!"

"Why didn't you think of that?"

Reed scowled. Why hadn't she? Because she hadn't wanted to be a cheat! Because she had been too confident in Silco and was blinded by her love of him.

"Reed!" Hestion yelled, and she fought to regain her focus. She had to get Lyonene out of her head. They were gaining on the stallions, who kept to the rear of the herd, driving the mares and guiding them with nips to the haunches. Reed stole a glance back, where Sar had taken on the task of sidelining one of the Cerillian riders. The Ithernan rode like a madman, laughing and whooping, pushing the Cerillian horse wider and wider until the frustrated soldier gave up and pulled up short.

Reed bent low as the valley raced by, long and flat, the mouths of canyons opened up on either side. Elisabetta rode at the head, and was still six horse lengths beyond Wonder.

"Reed!"

Hestion pointed. Alsander's hand was extended toward the white stallion's rump.

"Let him have him, you fool!" she screamed, but she could see by the grimace on his face that he wouldn't. Reed growled and pushed Silco faster, her black colt racing gamely despite his fear. Silco was inexperienced and unused to running with so many. His ears flickered back and forth, listening to their pounding hooves and listening to Reed.

"It's all right, Silco," she said softly. "But we must catch that ridiculous white horse. Up the middle!" Reed shouted. She tapped her heels to Silco's sides and he put on more speed, driving past Alsander and helping by nipping at his horse, rude as usual. "Good boy," Reed whispered as she let her red-chalked hand rise and fall on the white stallion's back, leaving a bright handprint. She patted Silco's neck and prepared to wheel him away after Elisabetta.

"Look out!" Hestion cried.

Reed heard too late, and the white stallion's teeth caught her in the leg. He hadn't liked the strange black colt coming up so fast, and rider or no rider he was looking to fight. He struck at Reed with his forehooves and she slowed, the rest of the herd thundering away as the stallion plunged after her.

Poor Silco tried to defend himself, but he was young, and he had Reed upon his back. Reed clung to the saddle. If she was thrown, the white stallion would stomp her to death in the dirt.

"Reed!" Hestion and his chestnut gelding charged the horse and knocked into his hindquarters. For a moment the stallion seemed to want to stand and fight, but in a case of two against one, he chose to go after his mares instead and galloped away.

"Are you all right?" Hestion asked.

"Stop worrying about me!" She wheeled Silco around and galloped away. But there was no chance of beating Elisabetta now. They were too far behind and Silco was shaken and afraid, the heart taken out of him by the older horse's bullying.

Reed's heart sank as Elisabetta turned the herd down a canyon. They must be close to the finish. And Reed wouldn't end the race in the top two but near the bottom, with her and Hestion ahead of only Belden and his plodding black warhorse.

They rode into the canyon, and Reed slowed. The canyon Elisabetta had led them down didn't lead to the finish line. It led to a dead end. The herd and all of the riders had stopped, milling in a circle, and Lyonene had ridden close to Alsander, with her eyes on the hills.

"Kleia Gloria," Reed said, her heart pounding. "It's an ambush."

27.

MERCENARIES

Armed soldiers emerged from where they hid upon the hillsides, aiming blades and crossbows down upon Crown Prince Alsander of Cerille. Upon Sar, and Lyonene, as Reed and Hestion sat frozen on their horses. Elisabetta Rilke had led them into a trap.

"Reed," Hestion said. "Ride out of here."

His whole body was tensed and ready to fight. But their enemies had the high ground and outnumbered them five to one.

"You don't even have a shield," Reed said. "And even if you did you would never survive the charge up the hill." She studied the landscape as Belden cantered up behind them. There were no trails and little cover. But the slope to her right was gradual enough that Silco might be able to mount it.

"If we charge that slope we may be able to take our attackers from the side, on even ground," said Belden.

"Not we," said Reed. "I will take it."

In the center of the herd, Alsander faced Elisabetta and shouted, "You are making a mistake." And though his voice was unsure, he was right. Elisabetta didn't have them as outnumbered as she thought. Not with Reed and Lyonene there.

"Reed," Hestion said. "Mercenary or not, you must flee."

Reed reached into the aether. The silver armor and white cape exploded through the Veil and settled onto her body. "I am no mercenary," she said. "Princes. Ride for the center and scatter the herd!"

Belden nodded and Hestion was through arguing. He looked at the enemy soldiers. "Get a few of them down to me if you can. So I can borrow one of their shields."

Reed drew the sword from her back and held it low, parallel to the ground as the Aristene magic rose like smoke. On the other side of the canyon, Lyonene leaned close to Alsander's ear. He drew his dagger and slipped from the saddle to disappear within the horses.

"Go!" Reed shouted, and the princes and her horse leaped forward, Silco driving for the slope of the hill. In the corner of her eye she saw the garb of the Aristene burst forth from Lyonene as she and Wonder charged up the canyon trail opposite. Arrows rained down, but the Areion needed only three long bounds to reach the attacking soldiers and met them with flying hooves and the force of a charging bull.

Reed wouldn't be as fast. A crossbow bolt flew past her ear. Another aimed for Silco's shoulder and she knocked it away with her sword. When she collided with their enemies, the first one fell to Reed's blade so quickly, he didn't even have a chance to cry out. She had never killed before. But there was no time to think about it. She had to kill still more.

Reed leaped from Silco's back and cut down another in two fast strikes. She dipped low to strip his shield and placed it on her arm. Five ran at her and she breathed in deep—the shield held, and she called up every ounce of magic she had and shoved. Bodies flew and rolled down the incline to Hestion, who leaped from his horse and drove his dagger down for a quick kill. When he stole a shield, he grinned up at her, and she felt a curious surge in her pulse and a strange shimmer in the air around him.

Glory, she thought, breath quickening. That was glory, the promise of it, food to Kleia Gloria and gold as honey. Hestion continued to fight in the canyon as Belden provided cover, scattering the herd with his huge black stallion. Soon Sar had joined Hestion on the ground, his sword already bloody, and Reed glimpsed Sar's bright-eyed bay mare lost to a flurry of arrows and lying in a heap.

"Where is my guard?" Alsander screamed within the herd. Surrounded by panicked horses, he couldn't see that both of the other Cerillian riders had already fallen to crossbow bolts.

Reed ducked a blade and cut her attacker across the belly, and as Lyonene's battle cry rang through the air, the enemy soldiers began to scatter. They'd thought to find princes trapped in a canyon, and though they were armed, they were unprepared for a real fight. Hurriedly aimed arrows flew wide. What men fled up the hill, Lyonene and Reed cut down. Those who turned and ran into the canyon were met by the hacking swords of Hestion and Belden and Sar.

"Not the horses! Do not fire upon the horses!" Elisabetta shouted. But the attackers were too shaken to listen.

The horse beside Alsander dropped dead to the ground. He was surrounded, and the prince burst out from behind the fallen animal with a sword in one hand and a dagger in the other.

"Lyonene!" Reed shouted.

Lyonene saw, but she was under attack. She couldn't turn from the fight. "Reed! Help him!"

Reed whistled for Silco and mounted quickly, racing down the incline. She held her breath as he bashed into attacking soldiers and jumped off as soon as she could to draw their swords away. Her own blade felt so steady in her hand, a part of her all the way from the hilt to the tip. The Aristene magic imbued her with strength and sharpened her senses. She saw the battle clearly and all at once: the sounds of weapons clashing, the movement of wind across her cheek. She sensed the path of a crossbow bolt as if it was pulled on a string, and she reached out to snatch it from the air, a moment before it would have sunk into Sar's forehead.

He stared at her in awe as she snapped it in her fist.

"Get to Alsander," Hestion ordered them, and swung his shield, bashing aside enemies and frightened horses alike, carving a path to the crown prince. He veered off just before they reached Alsander, who was on his knees with an enemy soldier gripping him around the shoulders and a sword held to his neck.

"Back!" the soldier shouted. "Back, beasts!" He was up against the rock face of the canyon, breathless and bleeding. Under the armor he was barely more than a child.

"Beasts?" Lyonene growled. She'd finished the last of the soldiers on the hill. But she didn't attack. Not even a full Aristene would have been fast enough to stop the blade from cutting Alsander's throat.

"He doesn't mean beasts," Reed said. The boy's accent was thick and he said only "back, back" as if he didn't know much of the common tongue.

"You are alone, fool," Alsander said, his voice surprisingly bold, considering. "Drop your sword and keep your life."

"I don't think he understands." Reed sheathed her sword. She let her borrowed magic fall and was herself again, her tunic stained with dust and blood like she had worn it through the fight.

"He understands," Belden said. He dismounted from his stallion and also sheathed his sword. "He's just too afraid to make up his mind."

"Perhaps this will help him." Hestion had disappeared as they'd fought their way to Alsander. Now he reappeared to shove Elisabetta Rilke down before them. "Call them off." But she didn't need to. At the sight of her on the ground, the last of the fight went out of the boy, and he lowered his sword. All across the canyon, blades dropped to the dirt.

Alsander jerked loose and brushed the dust from his shoulders and chest.

"We don't need to ask who pays for our heads," he said. "But I do wonder where these men have come from. They are not of the Laconian guard and not of the house of Rilke."

Elisabetta sat on the ground. There were tears upon her cheeks, and Alsander reached down and took the lady's hand to help her rise.

"King Oreas sent them," Elisabetta said, her shoulders square. "We were assured they were well-trained."

The young soldier stiffened against her insult.

"We are well-trained," he said. "We come from the Bay of Pearls. King Oreas pays us well."

"Mercenaries," Lyonene said thoughtfully. She looked at Reed. Though her words were soft, her cheeks were flushed, and her eyes sparkling. She had felt it, too, with every crash of shields, in every strike of her sword. Their deeds in the canyon had honored Kleia Gloria, and even though the regalia of the Aristene was gone, Reed's heart had not stopped pounding. The heroes around her seemed brighter in her sight. Hestion shone like a jewel. Even Sar had a glow.

"What are you going to do with me?" Elisabetta asked.

The men turned to each other.

"You may have her," Hestion said to Alsander, "since it was almost your life that she took. And in return, I will take the legendary herd for Glaucia."

"One treacherous noblewoman in exchange for a hundred head of fine warhorses?" Alsander asked.

"The Rilkes are rich. Ransom her." Hestion shrugged. "Glaucia has saved your life, Prince. Without me and my companions, you would be dead."

"I was in the lead when the race ended," Alsander said. "So I will command the joined armies in Rhonassus."

"I don't think so," Hestion replied, and the princes drew their swords. Belden was fast to intervene.

"Brothers," he said to them both, "we will not draw against one another when we've only just escaped with our necks!" He put himself between Alsander and Hestion with one easy step. Belden was the older prince by a number of years, and he was also the larger man. Beside them, he already looked like a king.

"There has been no victor between the two of us," he said to Alsander. "For Cerille and Glaucia are both victorious. If there is one thing this betrayal has shown, it is that we have no need to unite under one leader. We can unite behind two."

The crown prince of Cerille didn't like that. But as he stood before Belden, his words seemed to stick in his teeth.

"Perhaps something to sweeten the pot." Hestion looked back

at the herd, and at the gold coat of Elisabetta's horse.

"No!" Elisabetta cried. "Do not take Phaeton! Please! I will pay you in gold!"

"Unless you mean to pay his weight in it, you forfeited your horse when you betrayed the good faith of your buyers," said Hestion.

Reed frowned as Elisabetta wept. She couldn't imagine having Silco taken away.

"Argon!" Sar shouted.

Argon, who had been left behind at the starting line, rode toward them on one of the unhitched cart horses. His nose was bloodied but he was otherwise unhurt, and when he saw them safe, he laughed.

"You forgot about me, you bastards!"

Sar laughed, too, as he dragged Argon down and embraced him. They had forgotten about him. They'd had more than enough to keep themselves busy.

"They jumped us the moment you were out of sight," Argon said. "Between the Cerillians and I, we killed four. And I had to kill the horsemaster, Xanthos. The rest are tied to the cart with the Cerillians standing guard. I came to look for you. I thought you were probably dead."

Sar laughed and glanced at Reed. "I nearly was."

That was true. She'd had the chance to let the Ithernan perish, and instead she'd saved him.

"I didn't want to have to harvest your eyes," she muttered, and turned away. "A disgusting custom."

Reed left the men to the last of their negotiations and found Silco standing apart from the herd. He was wet with sweat and streaked with white foam. But there was not a scratch on him. She spotted

Wonder and noted some blood leaking from his withers—not a dangerous injury but Sabil would not like to see it. Reed leaned her forehead against Silco's hot coat. She could still feel the magic of the battle coursing through her. She watched Hestion as he spoke with Sar, his eyes slightly squinted, the shoulder of his sword arm shining in the sun. She found herself wishing he would come and speak to her. She found herself wishing that they were alone.

"Reed."

Reed jumped as Lyonene appeared.

"There's no need to be jumpy. The battle is over."

"Yes," Reed said, and chuckled. "But it doesn't quite feel over."

Lyonene nodded.

"This is what it is," she whispered. "This is how it feels. And yet there was no victory. I didn't win the race, even with an Areion."

"At least they can no longer doubt we can fight. Alsander will respect that more than if you'd simply crossed a finish line. Everything will be fine, Lyonene. The goddess is with us."

"Well, at least she is with you." Lyonene pushed her cape away to show blood leaking from a hole in her arm, made by a crossbow bolt. "I pulled it out before the heat of the fighting could cool. Now it hurts."

"Lyonene!" Reed grabbed her by the shoulder.

"It's fine. I still have more of the salve from the Outfitter."

"Will that work for such a wound?"

"It can't hurt. Except for the itching." Lyonene looked at Silco. "You were lucky he wasn't injured. Too great a wound, Reed, and they would—"

"I know. You're right. When we reach Rhonassus I'll stable him far away from the fighting." He would still be there if she needed him. But he would be safe.

"Good. Not all of us can rely upon the foundling's extra protection. Unless Ferreh also gave him a dish of blood to drink?"

"Ha ha," Reed said, and Lyonene squeezed her hand.

"Gloria Thea Matris, sister."

"Gloria Thea Matris," Reed whispered as Lyonene let go and walked away.

She swung back into Silco's saddle and watched as Alsander mounted Phaeton. Atop the golden stallion he looked like a statue.

Hestion, Sar, and Argon rode near the head of the herd, where the surviving mercenaries were bound and set to march back to Lacos. Lady Elisabetta rode beside Alsander on a bay mare, her hands tied and the reins secured to Phaeton's saddle.

When they passed the horsemaster, Xanthos, lying face down in the dirt, Reed's chest tightened. But perhaps it was a mercy that he didn't have to watch his horses paraded past and his corral left empty.

28.

THE SPOILS OF LACOS

There were a great many cheers when they returned to the port with the horses, and with Lady Elisabetta in ropes. But only from the allied soldiers. From the rest of the port their welcome was an uneasy quiet.

"All of Lacos is wondering whether they will now be conquered," Aster said later to Reed as they walked along the docks. "It would not be a bad idea to leave the port quickly and put them at ease. People left too long in suspense make hasty decisions."

"We sail today," said Reed. And Aster wouldn't be going with them. It didn't make Reed sad; she was ready to be on her own. But she was always a little afraid when Aster went away. That might never stop, no matter how old she grew—that fear had been imprinted into her in the settlement, during that long night of fire and mud and dead eyes in the moonlight.

"You fought well, Reed. I felt it through our shared blood. When the glory from the battle rose, even Veridian's nose began to twitch."

"Will you stay here with her?" Reed asked. "I'm happy that you're not angry with her anymore. She was only drunk."

"I wasn't angry at her because of that. But because of what she said. Words like that sow doubt, and doubt could get you killed."

Reed glanced at Aster's chest, where the tunic covered her heart scar.

"Besides," Aster said. "They're only Veridian's personal grudges."

"Are you sure?"

"I think so. But who knows? Veridian is a private person. Some things she keeps even from me."

Veridian kept things from her, but should Reed as well? Was an initiate to have secrets from her mentor? She wouldn't have thought so, but Ferreh had asked Aster to leave that day when she gave Reed the blood.

They paused at the end of the dock, the salt air cool in the high heat of afternoon.

"You know Lyonene borrowed Wonder for the race."

Aster chuckled. "I will have to ask Sabil about that. She's not the kind to interfere. Not like me." She reached up and tucked Reed's hair behind her ear.

"She was right to. Alsander is . . ." She looked at Aster guiltily. "I don't think I like him."

Aster smiled. "You might like him better if he were yours."

"I don't think so. He's not like Hestion. But then, I have always cared for Hestion, ever since the first time I saw him in the well." Aster grew quiet, and Reed turned. "Did I say something wrong?"

"No," Aster said. But her eyes were sad. "It is right to care for them, Reed. And even if it was wrong it would be unavoidable. But so is this." She took Reed gently by the shoulders. "You are an Aristene. You will go on. Your heroes won't. Their hard chests of muscle will soften. Their straight, proud backs will bend with age. Time marches over all mortals. Even those as formidable as

Hestion will lessen and die, and there is nothing to be done about it except to make of their memory a legend."

Aster's words rang through Reed's ears as she brushed Silco down in the belly of the warship. The warning wasn't new; Reed had always known that she would guide many heroes. But the boy reflected in the water had been with her as long as the order. As long as Silco. Part of her had felt that he always would be.

"It doesn't matter anyway," she said to Silco. "His years will be many. His life long. I'll be sick of him by the time—"

"Sick of who by the time?" Hestion asked. He'd managed to creep down into the hold without making a sound. No small feat on a creaky ship. He came to her and gave Silco a bit of dried fruit.

"I need a name for my white stallion."

"I already have a name for him," Reed said as she brushed Silco's shining black hindquarters. "Target."

Hestion laughed, and Silco shifted and lashed her with his tail, unhappy being back in the cargo hold.

"He's not looking forward to sailing," Reed explained.

"Then I have good news for him: he's to come with me to drive the legendary herd for transport. Alsander knows of a trader who can do it. He's already made the arrangements."

Silco was no Areion yet, but his ears flickered like he'd understood.

"Just the two of us to drive the whole herd?" Reed asked.

"Only those we couldn't find room for in the fleet."

"The other ships will beat us to Rhonassus."

"We won't be behind them by more than a day. Belden and Alsander won't charge without us."

"You don't know that," Reed said. "Minds are lost in the excitement of battle."

He moved around her and pulled her away from her horse. "I remember," he said. His voice was so low it was barely a murmur. "You saved Sar. You caught that arrow in flight."

He stepped closer and slipped his hand into the back of her hair.

"I thought the Aristene were only legends. Old tales, like King Docran and the hunt of the First Stag. I never knew that they were real. That you are real." His gaze swept over her face, and her lips. His arm tightened around the curve of her back, and she didn't know what to do besides stand still.

"You are beautiful when you fight, Reed."

"But I'm not fighting now," she whispered, and misunderstanding, Hestion leaned in and kissed her.

For a moment Reed was too surprised to even close her eyes. His lips were so soft and slow. He didn't push her against the crates or lift her onto his hips like she'd seen other men do. Instead she was the one reaching, grasping his back and pulling him closer.

Hestion's hands moved to her hips. He tilted his head as the kiss deepened, and they knocked up against Silco.

"Here," Hestion said. He moved them away to lean against a stack of barrels. "Reed," he whispered. "What do you want?"

Her fingers slid beneath the chest of his tunic. She didn't know. She only knew she wanted more. His mouth on her skin. His breath in her ear. Her lips opened against Hestion's as his hand brushed against her bare leg.

"I want . . ." She wanted everything. She wanted what Gretchen and Lyonene teased her about in the tavern. She wanted whatever it was that made her pulse pound and made her breathe like she'd been in a chase. And she'd wanted to do it since those moments after the battle. Had they been alone, she might have taken him then and dragged him to the ground.

Hestion continued to kiss her softly, though his hands didn't feel soft, and through the pleasure and the wanting, Reed started to think.

"I want to stop." She regretted the words the moment he reluctantly stepped away. She had to clench her fists tight to keep from pulling him back.

"But it's not forbidden," he said. He was still so close. She needed only to push off the barrels and she could be in his arms again. She could ignore the words inside her head and listen to the ones inside her body, and even in her heart.

"Alsander told me he has already bedded your friend."

Reed stiffened. "Did it occur to you that he may have lied?"

"I only meant—"

"And I am not Lyonene." She wanted to push him away but did not trust her hands to touch him. So instead she ducked around him, unable to stay against him for another second.

"This is not that," Hestion said. "I shouldn't have said that. I only meant that it seemed we could . . ." He looked away. "I have ruined this. I didn't mean— You have nothing to fear from me, Reed."

"I know," she said. But what they'd done had frightened her. She'd almost given in to it. One kiss and she was ready to lie down with him on the floor of a cargo hold. *I am not Lyonene*, she'd said. And she certainly wasn't. Lyonene knew her heart and acted with a clear head. Lyonene would never be lost.

"I'm sorry," Reed said, regaining her composure. "But you are my first hero, Hestion, and you are too important. Try to understand." She moved past him and untied Silco to bring him back to shore. "Let us forget about this," she said. "We have a war to win. And horses to get there."

29.

HORSES TO WAR

Even though they were smaller in number, keeping the herd on course with only the two of them was difficult. Many times Reed and Silco had to gallop fast to get around the herd and keep them on the road or keep them moving through a particularly grassy field. But Reed was glad for the distraction. The work was hard for both horse and rider, but at least it kept her away from Hestion. She could barely look at him without remembering the cargo hold and the way he'd touched her.

"Reed! The roan mare is at it again!"

Reed groaned. The roan mare had turned back no fewer than ten times since they'd departed from Lacos. Hestion rode close and handed her a rope.

"Tie her to the saddle," he said. "It's not her fault; I think one of the yearlings we returned to the Laconians was hers and not long weaned."

Reed nodded and sent Silco cantering after the mare. She gently tossed the rope around her neck and reached down to stroke her mane. Soon enough, the colt she'd left behind would forget all about the mother who had left it. The mare, too, would forget, a little more with every step she took in the other direction. It seemed sad to Reed, yet also kind, that they should not have to miss each other forever. Already she felt the tug of Aster's absence, when they had been parted less than a day.

"We are still bound," Aster said before they left. "And the elders and I will be watching, from the white city. If you need me, it will only take one ride through the Veil."

But one ride through the Veil felt far to Reed. Lyonene would say she was being a child. Lyonene had never once complained of missing her mother. But then, Reed supposed, Lyonene had not already lost one.

The port that Reed and Hestion traveled to had no name. In Lacos it was known only as the livestock port, and Alsander had many dealings with the man who owned the horse transports, using him to import rare sheep to breed into the famous stock of Cerille.

It wasn't far, and by dusk the cove and the small port were visible in the distance. They reached the shore just as torches were lit, and found their captain on the dock, the doors of the transport yawning open.

"You were told that we were coming," Hestion said, dismounting from his white stallion—who he had indeed named Target.

"We were," the captain said. "And we were told to expect payment."

Hestion dropped a pouch of coins into the man's hand. The captain weighed it in his palm and shook it against his ear. Then he waved his arm and men onshore moved behind the herd, clapping and whistling.

"You work fast," Reed said to the captain.

"Don't worry," he replied. "My men and I know the waters

well. The times we have sailed to the port of Roshanak are beyond counting."

The entire herd was loaded and settled before dark. Reed stood on deck with Silco and listened to them moving beneath her feet. Muffled whinnies and stomping rose to her ears through the wood. They were good horses. They would pull the fastest chariots and carry warriors over the enemy in great leaps. A line of them could outflank any army in the world.

She heard footsteps and saw Hestion coming with food held in scraps of thick cloth.

He handed one to her: a small red fish that had been cooked in coals. The meat was soft and slightly sweet, and the skin pleasantly crispy from the oil it had been brushed with.

"Thank you," she said. "I'm so hungry I could eat an eel."

"When we return to Glaucia, I will see that you eat an entire basket of them."

They lurched against the rail as the cargo ship cast off, and Silco tossed his head. The hold below was full, so he and the white stallion would travel abovedeck, along with five of the mares.

"Take your ease," the captain called as the crew rowed out of the cove and prepared to set the sail. "You look ready to sleep where you stand."

"How long until we reach Roshanak?" Reed asked.

"Before tomorrow night if the winds are good. Or in the dark if they are not."

A short sail. That suited Reed just fine. She and Hestion finished their meals and found their way to the foredeck, where Hestion spied a few folded blankets for them to lie upon. He spread them out and she eyed him with suspicion.

"Do you wish me to sleep at one end of the ship and you at the other? We are not alone here—" He gestured to the crew.

Reed lay down beside him and looked up at the stars. She felt Hestion shift, careful not to touch her, though she wouldn't have minded the warm press of his shoulder.

"Reed," Hestion said.

"Hm?" The smooth movements of the ship and the sounds of the waves had lulled her eyes closed.

"Nothing."

One of her eyes snapped open, and she turned her head.

"Nothing. It's foolish. Only . . ." Hestion bent his arms behind his head and stared at the night sky. "It's hard to understand. I've always been a warrior, but I never thought to make a legend of myself. I still don't know if it is what I want."

"You'll know soon enough," Reed said. "The way you fight, it's as if you were born for it."

"Shouldn't I decide what I was born for?"

"Not in my experience." Reed put her own arms behind her head. Hestion spoke no more, but the air between them felt heavy. "There is something you want to say, so say it."

"It will sound foolish."

"Say it anyway. I'm your Aristene; you can tell me anything."

"Anything?"

"Yes, and then let me sleep."

He took a deep breath.

"You will think it stupid, but I always imagined that if a story was told about me, it would be about my pursuit of a beautiful woman. Like in the tales my mother and my aunt Morna told. Some beautiful, unattainable woman in need of rescue, or in need of winning."

"In need of winning?" Reed asked. "Women have many needs: food, shelter, a good horse—but I have never known one to be in need of winning."

He grinned. "Anyway, it was just imagining. It wasn't real."

"Well. If it will make you feel better, I'll keep my eyes out for a beautiful, unattainable woman in Rhonassus. But you'd better let me pick her out."

"Why?" he asked.

"After that debacle with the white stallion . . . you can't choose horses, and you can't choose women; that would be my guess." Reed didn't need to turn to be able to see Target tied to the rail and glowing brighter than the moon.

Hestion laughed. "Target will prove himself. Wait and see."

"You are an idiot," she said sleepily, and he laughed again.

"What a way to speak to your hero," he said, and then they fell asleep.

When Reed woke, she was curled into Hestion's ribs. He had thrown one arm around her and waking was pleasant—in the hollow of his shoulder, Reed felt small, and Reed never felt small. It was so comforting that it took her far too long to realize that the ship was no longer moving.

She sat up. It was not quite dawn, and the light cast across the deck was hazy and blue, but it was plain to see there was not a person left aboard. The oars were drawn up, and the sails tied. No crew stood at the helm, and none were asleep on deck.

"Hestion. Where is everyone?"

He came awake slowly and pushed onto his elbows.

"Where is everyone?" he asked, and Reed squinted at him and shot to her feet. Silco, Target, and the mares were dozing beside the rail, perfectly happy about the lack of movement. And beneath the wood she heard the occasional shift and snort of the herd. But the captain and the crew were gone.

Reed looked toward shore. The ship had been anchored inside a small cove, and in the growing light she could see the beach and the shadowy shapes of trees. The shore looked rocky, full of crags and stone formations; the sea sprayed white as it cast itself against them. There was no sign of a city, or a dock.

Hestion walked quietly along the rail, looking down the sides.

"They must be here somewhere," he said.

But somehow Reed knew that they weren't.

"Let's go down and check on the horses."

She went first into the cargo hold and stepped off the ladder into water up to her knees. A few of the horses neighed in the darkness.

"Did we take damage?" Hestion asked, looking down. "Is that why they abandoned the ship?"

"Without bothering to wake us?" Reed waded farther into the hold. She felt things brush against her legs—clumps of hay and probably manure kicked up by the horses' hooves and the current. The ship was taking on water, but it didn't feel fast. Still, fear crept up the back of her neck. "We have to set a gangway, get them above. Can we get the ship to shore?"

"With no wind and two of us on the oars?" Hestion called. "We'll have to wait for the ship to go down. And swim for it."

She didn't like that, but there was nothing to be done. Together, Hestion and Reed worked quickly but calmly, dragging the heavy plank to the hold. Then they went one after another and led the horses up.

Even slow it was dangerous work. If the horses panicked, they could both be trampled or drowned in the dark. There were thirty horses below. By the time she'd released ten, the water had reached her waist.

"Stay above and pull them when they make the gangway," Hestion said when she went up with another. "I'm going to loose them all."

"No, wait!" Reed shouted. But of course he didn't listen. She pulled up the first mare that came, taking the short rope that hung from her halter to guide her away from the hatch. As soon as she was clear, another horse head appeared, its eyes wide and frightened. Then another and another, and the opening began to crowd. And the water continued to rise.

Reed pulled horse after horse, slapping their haunches once they were on deck to get them out of the way.

"Hestion!"

She got no reply and was about to plunge back in when he appeared, sputtering, in the wake of the roan mare.

"She was the last," he said, and coughed. He held out his hand and Reed pulled him up.

The deck was nothing but horses. Nervous, stomping, loose horses. The ship tilted beneath their feet and Reed saw a brown mare leap over the rail to splash into the sea.

Hestion held her by the arm. "Can you make the swim?"

She nodded. Even without the magic in her blood, Reed had

always felt at home in the water. Not that this was how she preferred to go into it. The sinking ship would tug at them, and she
didn't know the cove's currents. Not to mention the sea would be
full of kicking hooves.

"Get to your white stallion," she said. "He can pull you along
and his bright ass can serve as a beacon to follow."

"He's still tied to the rail," Hestion said. In their rush to save
the other horses from drowning, they'd forgotten about their own.

"Silco." Reed pulled out of Hestion's grasp and ran headlong
into the herd.

"Reed, wait!"

But she couldn't. She shoved through horses, and the weight of
their bodies pressed the air from her lungs. There were so many,
and they were frightened, spinning around and stomping their feet.
Reed dropped to her knees as one made the leap over the side. She
didn't get low enough. The horse's hind hooves clipped her head,
and the impact sent her sprawling.

Reed dragged herself up beside the rail. Horses fell into her as
the ship lurched and she reached for her armor on instinct. The
borrowed strength surged into her and she swung onto the nearest
horse, drawing her knife as she urged the terrified animal across
the deck.

One of the mares tied beside Silco had fallen and Reed cut her
free first, then sliced through the other ropes. She threw herself
from horse to horse onto Silco's back and grabbed the white stallion.

By the time Hestion jumped onto Target, the water on the deck
had reached to the horses' pasterns. There was no time to waste. He
whirled the stallion around and charged the rail, the horse sailing
over the side like a great white bird. The rest of the herd moved

to follow and Reed went with them, knees clinging to Silco as he tensed to spring, her stomach dropping through her feet as they fell to the water and the sea crashed over her head.

It was bitingly cold. Reed gasped for breath before bobbing under again, the waves blotting out the sounds of thrashing and neighs. She held tight to Silco as he started to swim, wiping salt from her eyes as he towed her toward shore.

Dawn was breaking as they neared the beach, the light turning from orange to yellow, and Reed breathed a sigh of relief when she saw the white stallion spring from the surf with Hestion on his back.

As soon as his hooves could reach the sand, Silco snorted and broke into a leaping, jolting gallop. He hauled Reed from the waves and then abruptly shook her off. She was so happy they were safe that she didn't even mind being dumped in a heap.

"Reed!" Hestion helped her up. He took her face in his hands and kissed her.

"You're unhurt?" she asked. She ran her hands over his shoulders, down his ribs.

"I'm unhurt," he said, and she was so relieved that she kissed him back. Up and down the sand, horses trotted from the water. They had saved them all.

Out in the cove they heard a great cracking and turned to watch the cargo ship break up and go under.

"There's no doubt that Alsander planned this," Hestion said. "I knew he was angry about the herd and the loss of sole command. But I'd hoped he'd grown up."

"He could have killed us," Reed growled. "And for what? Horses and pride?"

"Never discount what a man will do for pride. Especially a princeling like that one."

Reed hugged herself, angry and shivering. The sun hadn't had time to heat the air and the golden light on the beach was still cold. The horses rolled in the sand, trying to dry their coats.

"Stay close to me," Hestion said, and held her, his breath warm against her neck.

She nodded, but as the feeling returned to her body, she became very aware of his nearness and the press of his arms around her. She frowned. Every time she looked at him, her thoughts were muddled. And the way he had kissed her just now and she had kissed him back—

I care for him too much, she realized. It wasn't only the trial and the heat of battle. It was years of carrying him in her mind, years spent dreaming and imagining who he might be.

"I wish you were more like Alsander," she said. "I wish you were awful." Kleia Gloria had made a mistake, giving him to her. Like Reed had made a mistake when she'd broken the surface of the well. She should have been given wild Sar, who she could never care for. Or handsome Prince Belden, who she was fond of but couldn't have wound his way into her heart.

Hestion pulled her closer. Her armor had rippled back into the aether and left only a thin wet tunic between them. She felt no cold at all now pressed against the firm muscle of his chest.

"I will be as awful as you tell me to be," he said. "If you will let me keep you warm." Hestion lowered his lips to Reed's neck. She might have said yes, had she not seen Silco walking along the beach.

Only he wasn't walking. He was limping.

30.

THE AREION

"He's hurt!" Reed pushed away from Hestion and ran across the sand.

Her chest flooded with panic. But it couldn't be that bad; he'd swum all the way to shore. He'd galloped out of the water.

Reed slowed and held her hands out as she approached the colt. Silco's eyes rolled in pain. He held his hoof aloft like he wanted to show it to her, and Reed's stomach went cold when she saw the blood. She got down on one knee and cradled his hoof in her hands, rubbing away the blood and sand. A deep, wide crack ran from his coronet to his toe. When she pressed on it, Silco pulled his leg away and whined.

"He must have hurt it during the swim," Reed said numbly.

"Coral," said Hestion. "Or rocks." He stroked Silco's side gently. "Reed. An injury like this . . ."

She knew what he was going to say. An injury like this would never heal. An injury like this was the end of a horse.

Reed heard Hestion unsheath his knife.

"You stay away from him!" she shouted. "Don't touch him!"

"I'm not going to hurt him. I'm going to find some leaves. Something to dress the wound."

Reed stood and wiped wetness from her cheeks. "I'll go with you. Tell me what you need."

"Stay with him. Keep him still." He turned for the trees.

"Hestion!" Reed cried out. "He will be all right. Won't he?"

"Perhaps," Hestion replied. "Like you he seems simply too mean to die."

She kissed Silco's muzzle as he hung his head. "Too mean, he says," Reed whispered. "Yet such a baby. Pouting over one cracked hoof." She couldn't bring herself to look at it again. She couldn't turn off the voice inside her head that kept repeating what it really meant.

Reed stood quietly while Hestion washed the hoof with seawater and tore his tunic to use as the first layer of bandage. He covered the hoof in thick, waxy leaves and secured the wrapping with fibers of rope he'd taken from another horse's halter. After he was finished they lit a fire and tied Silco near it to rest.

"I saved him," Reed said, watching the colt raise his sore foot in the air. "The goddess gave him to me and I saved him from being sacrificed. Only to lose him to a piece of coral!"

Hestion slipped his arm around her and tugged her close.

"He'll be all right, Reed. He'll always have a limp, but he'll be happy enough in an Aristene pasture."

"But not with me. They won't let him be an Areion now. Not with a limp. Not with a foot like that."

Hestion was silent as she stared across the fire.

"He was supposed to be mine," Reed whispered. "Like you were supposed to be mine." And like Aster had been meant to find her. For so long she'd believed that Kleia Gloria had given Silco to her for a purpose. The horse had been woven into the fabric of her every hope, a part of every daydream. She had no words for how it felt to see those dreams dissolve and to wonder, that if this one was false, then what did it say for the rest?

"I didn't know," Hestion said quietly. "I thought the Areion were another breed. That perhaps a herd of them roamed free on a mountain somewhere and one day you would go and claim one."

"No. They begin as mortal colts, just as we are mortal girls. Silco was given to me when I had nothing. And that giving set me on the path to the order as much as any mark. Without him . . ."

"Without him you will not fail, Reed. I won't let you." He kissed her temple and wiped a tear from her cheek with his thumb. "I will fight like the god of death is at my back. I'll win so much glory that they'll have to take you and him as well."

"They won't," she said. She looked at her sad, wounded horse. He was mean and spoiled, and he was her friend. One day she'd hoped to hear him speak.

An Areion may die, she thought. *Like the Aristene, they may be killed. But I never would have let you.*

"Without him, Hestion, I don't even know if I want it."

"Don't say that. I have not known you long, but I know that you don't mean it." He wrapped his arms around her tighter, like he could shield her from any pain. "What if I bring him home after the war is over? He may live out his life in our herd at the seat of the Docritae, and I'll surround him with beautiful mares."

Reed snorted. "You would look after a lame horse for so long? With that kind of pampering he could live for thirty years, out of spite."

"It would be my honor to have him," he said. "And it would give you cause to come to Glaucia. For after this trial is over"—he touched her face—"you will go."

She would go. Back to Atropa and then on to other heroes. "It may be years before we would see each other again. I might return to find you gray-haired, with a wife and children."

"Yes," he said without humor. "You've promised to find me this wife. This beautiful, unattainable woman of legend. But first let us get to Rhonassus. And let me make Alsander of Cerille pay for what he has done."

"I will make him pay myself," Reed said, looking at Silco. "And I will make him pay in blood."

"The initiates near the coast."

"Finally."

The elders of the order stood within the dome, Ferreh beside the sacred well. She lay one hand upon the rough, sparkling stone while Tiern paced like a big cat, slowly, around the silver circle of the World's Gate.

"Patience, sister. This will be a war, not one battle." Ferreh looked down into the dark, still water and saw only the reflection of Kleia Gloria's mural. No more omens and no guidance. No clues for what lay ahead.

"Patience indeed," said Tiern. "For we know that even this war is only the first fight of many." She stopped pacing. "It is a mistake to rely on the initiates."

"Lyonene is the finest I have seen in generations," Ferreh replied. "And as for Reed, we will rely on her for much more than this, if she is successful."

Tiern touched a toe to the gate, and the ancient etchings across the silver. "We should have stomped out these priests ourselves, before they could ever find these magics."

Ferreh sighed. They should have stomped them out. But that was an easy enough thing to say now, when it was too late. When the priests had taken the Prophet of All and turned and twisted him into a weapon against the gods he once spoke for.

"Priests," Tiern said, and spat. They had risen in secret and gave themselves no names, hiding behind the cover of drab, gray robes. Ferreh didn't know what grudge they held against the order, what slight or mistake had caused it. Perhaps there had been none. Some men did not need a reason to hate the women who steered them. Some, like the priests, thought that for a woman to wield influence at all was cause for death, no matter how worthy the woman was, nor how wise her counsel. Ferreh didn't understand it, but she could recognize it like smoke on the wind.

She peered again into the well and resisted the urge to break its still, black surface. Few threats rose high enough to challenge the Aristene. Long ago were the days when they'd been forced to flee and seek the protection of the Veil. But these priests were different. These priests could hurt them.

"But it wasn't only the priests. It was the world. The world that turned away from glory and began to find other virtues more valuable. The changing world that thinned their blood and stemmed the flow of glory to a drip."

"We should send more of us into the war," said Tiern. "We cannot depend only on your foundling."

"The foundling will save us, Tiern. She has to."

Tiern turned, her strange red-and-gold-and-black hair tumbling down her back. "What awaits these initiates on the shores of Rhonassus? What did you see when you peered into the well?"

"A monster," Ferreh replied, eyes fixed above the water as if afraid to look down and see it again. "Only a monster."

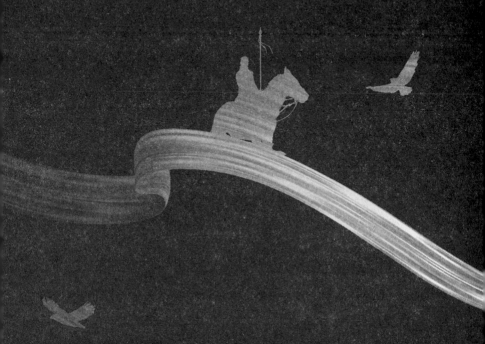

FOUR

THE WAR

31.

THE STRONGHOLD OF ROSHANAK

When Reed and Hestion reached Roshanak, the capital city of Rhonassus, their allies had already taken the port. All across the southern shore, men of the joined armies wandered the docks as leisurely as if they had been born there. Men of the Salt Flats gathered in the shade of a canopy to play a game of rolled marbles, and small landing boats sat tied to the docks. The rest of the fleet lay anchored in the harbor, dotting the vibrant blue of the bay.

"They stormed it without us," Hestion said, sounding surprised and disappointed.

"I told you," said Reed. Though it didn't seem like it had been much of a fight. Aside from a few burned-out food stalls, she could hardly tell there had been an attack. Perhaps there hadn't been, and King Oreas had ordered the port be emptied, and the people and goods brought inside the city before they arrived. "Strange that they would give it up; with an army like that of Rhonassus you'd think Oreas would have tried to scare us off. Burn up some ships in the bay." Instead the city was eerily quiet. It made Reed feel as though something was listening.

The men on the docks gave a great cheer at the sight of Hestion and the horses. Reed was riding the roan mare, who seemed to miss her colt less with someone on her back. Silco limped slowly beside them, his head low over a rope attached to her saddle. Hestion looked at Reed.

"Go ahead," she said.

He drove the herd into the port to a chorus of joyful shouts, and a glimmer of magic danced across Reed's skin. Hestion glowed even brighter than his ridiculous white horse. The sinking transport, their mad swim through a horse-filled sea: these tales were the beginnings of his legend, the deeds that would weave together to become his story, and in Reed's mind she heard Ferreh's words echo across the years.

We are shadows to the greatest warriors, at hand for the greatest of quests. We place kings and queens upon their thrones. Kleia Gloria sends her heroes to the worlds of men, and it is up to us to help them to find their ways back to her.

Beyond Hestion sat the stronghold of Roshanak, a city of stone washed gold by the sun. Through her magic Reed could sense the thread that ran between Hestion and the city gates, between Hestion and the maze of streets, floating loose like the silk of a spider's web all the way to King Oreas. She could sense that path so strongly she was sure that if she tilted her head she would see it there, glistening.

A clamor rose as Belden came, riding through the port on his great black stallion. The young king leaped from the saddle and dragged Hestion off Target's back.

"My brother returns!" he shouted. "And a day too late! What kept you?"

"Ask the men," Hestion said, and grinned.

"Don't tell me you have tired of telling your tale already? I am thinking we will hear it again, many times, and each time it will grow longer." Belden grinned, but his mirth faded when he saw Reed approaching with her limping horse.

"Perhaps we would rather hear how you've taken the port without us," she said.

"It wasn't me," Belden replied. "Cerille attacked the moment they made the bay." He gestured to one of the docks, broken off into the sea where Alsander's ships had rammed into it. "The princeling wanted to make a statement, but the port was already bare. There was nothing even to loot, and for all the damage he took to his fleet, he won only a few barrels of wine. Though he did get the first pick of the villas—" Belden pointed up the hill to the east, where the lordliest of the port merchants resided.

Belden reached up to help Reed from the mare, but she shook her head.

"The horse has been injured, brother," said Hestion. "Will you see him to a stable? Reed and I have business with Alsander."

Belden glanced between his brother and his Aristene. "Do not make another enemy."

"I'm not making one," Reed said, angrily turning her little mare up the road. "I am keeping one."

The villa Alsander had chosen for his temporary palace was built high on the hill, overlooking the bay and the rest of the port.

Hestion dismounted and nodded to the balcony. "There is your friend."

Reed looked up and saw Lyonene gazing down upon the city like a leopard in a tree.

"Lyonene!"

"Reed!"

She might have said more, but Reed didn't wait. She and Hestion shouldered through the Cerillian guard set at the doors, knocking aside their crossed spears. More than one dove out of Reed's way as she took the steps by two.

"There you are, Ox," Lyonene said when Reed and Hestion burst into the room. "We expected you days ago."

"Though we did not," Alsander added, rising from a chair, "expect you to storm into my bedchamber."

The sight of Alsander filled Reed with rage. He was an empty hero, with all of the look but none of the heart. He was petty and weak; his only strength came from coin and the size of his army. As she'd made her way through the villa, she'd noted the finery left behind with no signs of struggle—woven rugs unstained by blood, ornate shelves hurriedly cleared of valuables—as the previous inhabitants gathered their things and fled. Alsander had claimed it and thrown the blue and gold of Cerille over the top like a flag. As if he had won it when, really, he'd crawled inside like a crab into a newer, fancier shell.

Reed drew her sword. Its edge was against his neck so quickly she almost didn't realize she'd done it.

"Reed!" Lyonene cried.

Reed bared her teeth. She would have liked to knock his head against the stone. But Alsander couldn't die. Lyonene still needed him. Reed pushed herself away and reared back from the flash of Lyonene's sword.

She and Lyonene had crossed swords before. Sometimes even in anger, in the Summer Camp during tense days of training, when arguments had broken out. But it had never been real.

"Reed!" Lyonene shouted. "What has come over you?"

Reed didn't reply. She swung her sword and swung it again, every impact driving Lyonene back. Alsander shouted, and Hestion put a dagger to his neck. . . .

"Call your guards and we'll kill them all," Hestion growled.

"Enough, Reed!" Lyonene sidestepped and ducked, always the quicker, and knocked the butt of her sword hard between Reed's shoulders. She'd been wearing the red gown, but when Reed turned, Lyonene was in her armor. They crossed swords again and Lyonene's arms no longer trembled. It took no time at all for her to have Reed back on her heels.

"Why are you doing this? What has happened?" she asked when Reed dropped to one knee.

"The ship Alsander provided sank. After the crew sabotaged the hull and abandoned us."

"Did you lose the horses?" Alsander asked.

Hestion pressed the dagger harder to his throat. "Not a one."

"Then why are you so angry?" Lyonene asked. "It was just a jest."

Reed studied Lyonene carefully. She hadn't been sure that Lyonene had known. But she was sure now.

"Why did you let him do that?" Reed asked. "We could have drowned."

"But I knew you wouldn't. The elders wouldn't allow it. Despite my superior skills it is you they watch! Ferreh dotes on you as if you became an Aristene the moment you were found!" She glared at Reed. "You're only reacting this way because you're not used to being tested. So you behave like a brat over one small challenge that cost you nothing."

"It cost me Silco!" Reed screamed.

Reed leaped to her feet. The elder's blood sat heavy in her belly as she rained down blows, barely hearing Lyonene's cries as she weakly tried to defend.

"Stop her!" Alsander shouted, and Hestion grabbed Reed around her middle and hauled her away. As her vision cleared, she saw Alsander go to Lyonene and tug her into his arms.

"Stay away from me, Lyonene," she snarled. "And do not forget! It was you who started this. I would never have pitted my hero against yours! I would never have pushed if you hadn't pushed first."

Reed fled Alsander's villa with Hestion trailing behind and didn't stop until she had reached the peak of a hill. Across sat the palace of King Oreas, surrounded by gardens and an ornate hedge maze in sprawling green. Below that stretched the city and the city wall, and the land between it and the sea that would become their battleground.

"You would have killed her," Hestion said quietly.

"No." Reed turned to him. "But I might have hurt her, and I didn't want to do even that. So thank you for stopping me."

"I thought we only went to give the princeling a bloodied lip. Which I did."

Reed exhaled. She'd thought that, too. But Alsander's treachery had only made her angry. Lyonene's had hurt.

"Will you forgive her?"

"I don't know," Reed replied. She knew that Lyonene was sorry. That was the only reason she'd been able to win the fight. Even with Reed's advantage of the elder's blood, Lyonene was still the far better fighter. She could have turned Reed back anytime she wanted. "We must get our minds off this. There is a battle to fight tomorrow."

"I will give you a moment," Hestion said, and retreated down the hill.

Reed listened to his footsteps fade and looked again down to the battlefield. The land past the gates lay broad and flat, and the beach hardened to form wide roads leading from the port and into the city. It was good, solid ground, that would favor the chariots of Cerille. But nearer the gates, on either side of the road, the surface changed. It was hard to see, and had she not been looking just right, she might have missed it.

The ground on either side of the road was falsely smooth. As if it had been tended with rakes.

A current of magic rippled through her.

King Oreas had been preparing for their coming. That was why the port was empty and why he didn't send his own soldiers through to the beach. He had been preparing, perhaps since the moment he removed the prophet's head.

Reed moved down the hill and waited for the shadows of evening before leaving the cover of trees. She couldn't go close enough to touch the strange earth—the area was open and well within the range of the night archers—but she knew a trap when she saw one. The ground had been treated or softened. Made to look like innocent sand. But if a hoof or a chariot wheel tried to cross, it would find itself sunk and foundering. In order to reach the city walls their army would have to filter through the narrow passage of the road, where they would be easy picking for the archers on the city gate. Dozens, perhaps hundreds, would fall.

Eventually we could just jump across the tops of Alsander's lost chariots, Reed thought, and smiled meanly in the dark. But no. The Docritae would simply make another way across.

She looked to the top of the walls at the soldiers there, wishing she could approach and sink her hand into the sand. Was it simply loose to slow them down? Or was it something worse? She'd heard of sands that shifted like water, deep enough to submerge a man to his head. Or perhaps it was thickened liquid, dusted over. One well-thrown rock would show the difference. But she couldn't chance it. Some of the men on patrol had the helpful eyes of hawks perched on their shoulders. It was a wonder she hadn't been spotted already.

Silently, she retreated the way she came. Once she was back in the port she hurried to the stable, where she found Hestion changing the bandage on Silco's foot.

"Where have you been?" he asked, the expressions on the faces of man and horse so similar that it took a moment to be sure which had spoken. "Belden means to take the city gates and seize control of the wall tomorrow. Perhaps even push the Rhonassans back to the market annex." He made a snorting sound.

"You don't think they can," said Reed.

"I think they are overconfident. Belden is hoping for looting. Supplies. But Roshanak has a reputation as a stronghold for a reason."

"We will breach it," Reed said. "We will make the wall and breach the gate."

Hestion set down Silco's hoof.

"You sound certain."

"I snuck onto the battlefield. King Oreas has laid a trap. A trench that runs along the wall."

"Our scouts saw nothing."

"It's been disguised. But I know it's there."

"We'll need planks to get across," he said, thinking quickly. "We will have to break down one of the ships. We should tell Alsander."

She shifted her weight, and Hestion looked at her in surprise.

"Reed, I know you are angry at your friend, but—"

"Of course we have to tell them," she said. "But we'll tell them tomorrow, before the attack."

"When they'll have no choice but to go along with the plan?"

"And when they can't ruin it. The pup of Cerille would have troops up all night breaking down ships and cutting plank. He would give us away. Our best chance is to use him as the main force and keep the Rhonassan archers focused on the road, while a small force of Docritae moves across." If it didn't work, the losses to the Docritae could be heavy. But if it did, the glory of them taking the wall—just the thought of it made her blood race.

Hestion watched her quietly for a long time.

"Very well," he said. "I will trust you."

"Reed?"

Reed and Hestion turned. Lyonene stood in the doorway of the stable, wrapped in a hooded cloak of crimson, but before Reed could speak, she rushed past them to kneel before Silco and unwrap his hoof.

"What are you doing?" Reed demanded.

"I'm trying to help." From inside her cloak she produced a small silver pot, and hope bloomed in Reed's chest as Lyonene dipped her fingers into the glowing ointment. But the moment it touched the horse, the glow faded. Even though Lyonene applied more and more, all she had left, it did no good.

Lyonene bent her head and began to cry.

"I will leave you alone," Hestion said.

"Stop crying," Reed said after he'd gone. "You don't get to cry when it was your fault."

"I didn't know."

"You are not stupid, Lyonene."

"Yes, I am." She pressed her forehead against Silco's shoulder. "It never occurred to me that anything would happen. Not to you. And not to Silco, the horse picked for you by the goddess." Lyonene wiped her nose. "I thought you would be annoyed by the sinking of the transport. I wanted to slow you down because Hestion—"

"Is a better hero than Alsander?"

"He is not better. But he is . . . more natural. He doesn't need so much from you—" She wiped her eyes. "I'm making foolish mistakes!"

"Am I supposed to feel bad for you? After this?" Reed asked, and Lyonene shook her head. She kept one hand on Silco's shoulder, stroking and stroking like an apology. And after a moment, Reed did feel bad for her. Alsander of Cerille was a princeling, just like Hestion said he was. A hero like that would need to be led by the nose, and the trick of it would be making him believe that he was not being led.

"I'm sorry your first hero is such a petty ass," Reed said.

"He is not an ass." Lyonene set Silco's foot down. She'd been waiting, hoping that the ointment would regain its glow. "Alsander is a good person. Better than his father. And brave because he forces himself to be, not because he was born to it."

"He is petty and childish."

Lyonene chuckled.

"Yes. But many kings never grow out of that." She stroked Silco's nose, and he pushed his muzzle into her hand.

"What did Alsander do with Lady Elisabetta?" Reed asked. "I expected to see her lashed to the prow of his flagship."

"He ransomed her life for a small fortune. Then he sent her to Cerille to be imprisoned in a castle. After the fight has gone out of her, he'll marry her off to some Cerillian noble, so more of the Rilke fortune will come to him through her bride price."

"Was that your idea?"

"Not all of it." She looked at Reed, eyes large in the low light. "I am so sorry, Reed. I know what Silco meant to you. All that you had planned."

"Plans change," she said softly.

"Let me take him to Atropa," Lyonene said suddenly. "Let me take him there tonight. They can care for him better there."

Reed put her hand on Silco's forehead. He was so calm and quiet that he was hardly the same horse. The pain took all the life out of him. "In my every imagining Silco has been there," Reed whispered. "He has been an Areion for so long in my heart that I don't know how to let it go." She looked at Lyonene. "What about you? Can you make it back in time for the charge tomorrow?"

"I'll see him settled and then return. It will be hours, only." But she would be tired for the fighting. Tired from the Veil. It would cost her. "Have you looked upon the city, Reed? Upon the palace?

Do you sense something emanating from inside?"

"What kind of something? Glory?"

But Lyonene didn't answer. "The trial wasn't meant to be easy. But we haven't come so far to fail. Have we?"

"Of course not," Reed said. "What's come over you?" Lyonene was the one who never faltered. Reed took half a step back when the smaller initiate wrapped her in an embrace.

"I am sorry, sister."

Lyonene let go and slipped a lead over Silco's head. When she led him out of the stable, his limp made his shoulder drop with every step. They would save him in Atropa. Aster would save him. But he would always have a limp.

I will choose no Areion until you have passed, she promised in her mind, and Silco looked back like he'd heard.

As night marched on toward dawn and the impending attack, the mood in the conquered port shifted from one of ease and boasts to nervous rest and finally to resolve. Reed saw it all because she herself found no rest and spent the night alone, walking the beach.

Hestion had gone to the villa that Belden had taken over. The Glaucans had transformed it into a temporary hall, and for a time Reed could hear the songs rising from its open doors in the hills. A few fires burned there still, and a few survived beside the tents on the beach, flickering in the breeze or burned down to coals that pulsed like bright eggs in a nest. And somewhere down the beach lay the wreckage of a ship, the wood from the decks and hull to be refashioned into planks for crossing the sand trap. She had helped the soldiers make them, instructing them on the width and length, tearing the boards loose with her borrowed Aristene strength. Come dawn, every Glaucan raiding party would carry one, and each was broad enough for three men to charge across shoulder to shoulder.

"Reed."

Reed gasped at the sound of her name and turned to see the dark shape of a woman leap into the shallows from a small beached boat. The woman waded toward her in big strides, black hair loose to her elbows and wavy from the salt spray.

"Aethiel?"

The big Aristene grinned, her teeth flashing white in the shadows. "Yes, it is me."

"I'd heard you were near—I didn't think you meant to come ashore." Reed went forward to greet her and found she didn't know what to do. How was an initiate supposed to greet a member of the order outside of Atropa? A bow? A drop to one knee? In the end she simply inclined her head, and said, "Gloria Thea Matris."

"Gloria Thea Matris, little sister," said Aethiel. "And you are right; I don't intend to come ashore. My hero's glory will be found in the bashing of ships and the cutting of sails. The screams of foes abruptly cut off as they sink beneath the waves." Aethiel took a deep breath. She was so strange, this Aristene. Even in the dark she reminded Reed of a wolf savoring the smell of a rabbit.

"Then why are you here?"

"To bring you this." She reached over her shoulder and unhooked the shield that rested on her back. When she turned it beneath the stars, the edges shone bright silver. It was fine and engraved and heavy, and Reed knew instantly what use it would be when they attacked the wall. She could cover herself and Hestion easily with that shield, and most of Sar besides.

"This is Ferreh's shield," Aethiel said as Reed touched it. "Taken from its case within the Citadel. It will be the first time it's been blooded in many, many years. And I am sure that by now the old girl is thirsty."

"Ferreh's shield." Reed withdrew her hands. "Why would she give me this?"

"I didn't think to ask. Perhaps Aster asked for its use. As a favor. Do you mean to refuse it?"

"No," Reed said quickly. She took it and felt the heft as Aethiel released it into her care. Without the borrowed magic, she would have had a hard time simply raising it over her shoulder. She should be proud to carry it into battle. But she couldn't help thinking of what Lyonene had said. The shield was another advantage that Reed hadn't earned. Another show of her favored status.

No one thinks you can do it on your own.

But she wasn't the only initiate to be shown favor. Aethiel stood right before her, a queen allowed to join the order, and rumor had it, mentored by Tiern herself.

"Is it true that you were mentored by an elder?" Reed asked.

"Yes. Tiern. And it was only right. I came with a crown etched into my head—" Aethiel traced the black band that marked the skin above her brow. "And I was born a warrior. Glory worked through me long before I had ever heard of an Aristene. Though, not even I was lent a weapon like that. So do not be jealous, little Reed."

"I'm not jealous," Reed said. "I wouldn't like to be mentored by an elder. And Tiern is . . . terrifying."

Aethiel laughed. "Then she and I were well matched." She shrugged. "It does not matter much what we like or don't like. All is the whim of one goddess or another. Aster is your mentor. As she was meant to be. And anyone can see that she was certainly meant to be."

Reed squeezed the shield. Yes. Aster loved her. Aster brought out everything that was good in her underneath the anger.

"Thank you for this great gift, Aristene," Reed said, and Aethiel grinned.

"You are welcome. And you are ready for battle?"

"I am now," Reed said, and Aethiel pushed her boat out of the shallows and back into the bay.

32.

THE SHIELD OF FERREH

Reed and Hestion met Lyonene and Alsander in the darkness of predawn as the army assembled. It was a tactic of intimidation; when the sun rose the enemy would look upon line after line of armed soldiers on the beach, so many that they blacked out the sand.

"I'm surprised that you agreed to meet us," Hestion said. He put his arm out and Alsander gripped him by the wrist.

"It was only at her insistence." The crown prince glanced at Lyonene. Reed was glad she'd made it back. And she didn't look too much the worse for it. A little tired around the eyes, perhaps. A little pale. She listened quietly as Hestion explained the sand trap they'd discovered and their means of getting across it.

"And a force of the Docritae will rush the trap," Alsander asked. "To attack the archers and the wall?"

"Yes," said Hestion.

"We've supplied planks for you as well," Reed added. "For a similar force of Cerillians to attack the east end. In case we're not successful."

They waited. Reed expected that Alsander would be suspicious. Ungrateful. That he would whine about not being the sole commander of the army.

"I will put my best fighters to the cause," he said. A fine response.

But she wouldn't mind if he disobeyed and sank his chariot right into the sand trap. They parted ways to return to their respective armies, and Lyonene saw the shield strapped to Reed's back.

"Where did you get that?" she asked. But of course she knew. She'd seen it for herself in the case within the Citadel. "Another favor," she said, and only the memory of what happened to Silco kept her from saying more. "It won't matter, you know. I'm still going to win our bet."

Reed snorted and followed Hestion back to the Docritae.

"What bet do you speak of?" he asked. "Do you play with us like toys? Is that what the Aristene mean to do?" His voice was low, his temper hotter with the nearness of battle. "Was that why you arranged for us to charge the wall?"

"I arranged nothing. I presented a way across the trap and you agreed."

"Listen to me. These are not only soldiers to be lost. They are lives. If you steer them toward danger for your own aims—"

"I ask nothing of them that I won't do myself. And if you disagreed with the plan you had time to come up with a better one." She reached for his shoulder and he stopped. "I wouldn't put them in danger. I wouldn't put you in danger unless I thought it was the way."

Hestion nodded. He looked across the vast army of men and weapons. "I thought my men were safe from this war."

"But not Belden. Your brother was always going to be here, and now we're here to look after him."

Hestion turned. He took her by the arm and she felt his fingers tighten. "Stay with me when the fighting begins." A shiver passed through her, from his touch or perhaps from the rush of the coming attack.

"You still doubt me?" she asked with a grin. "Do you not see the size of the shield upon my back?"

They rejoined the lines, and the sun rose to show them the assembled Rhonassan spearmen standing before the wall. They must have been terrified, facing the vastness of the joined armies, and Reed wondered if they knew they had been placed there as bait—to fight first and die first, all to lure them into the sand trap and the range of the archers.

"Where is King Oreas?" asked Argon, standing to Reed's left. "Does the coward mean to hide inside his palace?"

"He is an old king," Hestion replied. "He wouldn't lead the charges anymore. It will be Ostar or Oren. His sons."

"And what kind of men are they?" Sar asked, to his right.

"Good ones, when last we met. Ostar is skilled at warcraft and can throw a javelin as well as any among the Docritae." Hestion looked at Sar and Argon and the rest of his men. "So be sharp."

He stared at the long stretch of stone wall, and the scant rows of armored soldiers. "King Oreas is showing us what he thinks of us."

"I think he is showing us what he thinks of his wall, and his sand trap," said Reed. "And he'll be disappointed by the performance of both."

She craned her neck toward the center of the army. Their leaders, Belden and Alsander, were hard to miss, Alsander on his shining gold horse and Belden in his shining helmet. She didn't see Lyonene. She would be with the Cerillians going over the sand trap.

Reed took a breath. She felt the attack coming, a steady, growing buzz as if from insect wings. The magic swelled in her blood, making Ferreh's shield lighter, and the potential for glory crackled overhead like thunder. The sensation came from all sides: it whirled through the ranks of Cerille and rose in a cloud around the Glaucans. It glimmered atop the wall of Roshanak.

She listened to the chatter of the men as she waited for the charge, craving the sound of arrows pinging off Ferreh's shield. The silver armor and white cape of the Aristene hovered just inside the aether.

Ahead, the city gates creaked open to allow two horses and two riders. The princes: Ostar and Oren, their armor gold, the hair peeking out from beneath their helmets curling and dark. They rode to meet the army on well-matched black horses, and Belden and Alsander kicked their mounts forward to wait in the middle of the road.

"Nothing they can say will make us leave their shores," Hestion said. "No coin they can offer, no trade. No earthly currency will pay for the life of our prophet."

And he was right. The negotiation lasted only a few moments before the princes separated, and Ostar and Oren cantered back through the city gates. When the Rhonassan princes closed the gate behind them, they ordered their spearmen into ready positions, and the spearmen stepped back and thrust their weapons forward with a collective grunt.

"A meager display!" Sar shouted, and laughter rippled through the lines. Reed slipped Ferreh's shield down onto her arm as Belden and Alsander ordered the charge, and the screams of men filled her ears.

The lines sprang forward, bolting like horses, and Reed felt herself swept up by the storm. She sensed Hestion to her right and heard Sar's wild laugh above even the deafening roar. To the men protecting the wall, watching the coming soldiers must have been like staring down a wave from the sea. They waited tensely for them to hit the sand trap and sink, to crash into a pile and be forced to funnel onto the road. When the army stopped short instead, the men waiting on the other side were unprepared to react. A hail of thrown spears skewered the Rhonassan ranks.

"Lower the planks!"

The planks went down, and Reed lifted Ferreh's shield and ran across. She felt the ground give way under the sturdy wood and looked down to see the surface rippling and shifting like water. When they reached the end of the plank, she, Hestion, and Sar gave a great leap just to make sure they were well clear.

"Get to the wall!" Hestion shouted. "The battering ram!"

The ram made its way slowly across the trap, the men who pushed it protected by shields. Yet still men fell from lucky or well-placed arrows. On the road so many had fallen that they were beginning to form a blockade, and soldiers were forced to leap over their dead and dying friends, or shove them aside and let the bodies sink into the sand. Reed surveyed the battle. There were too many soldiers and too little land. The planks to cross the trap were working, but the men who made it across were felled by arrows. Those who reached the gate were cut down by swords or pierced through by spears.

"Attack the flank," Hestion ordered. "Draw them away from the road!"

"We have to get the ram to the gate!" Reed shouted.

"And besides," Sar added, "I want to take the wall!"

They fought ahead, and Reed heard a familiar cry. Lyonene had made the crossing to attack the Rhonassans on the opposite side.

Reed braced as a storm of arrows struck her shield. She was taking more fire than anyone else—Ferreh's shield drew the archers' eyes.

But Reed barely felt it. It seemed that she could hold the shield aloft forever, that her sword arm would never tire as glory infused her from head to foot. The Rhonassan soldiers she faced were no cowards; they didn't turn and bang on the city gate. They fought, and as each died she felt a jolt—glory to the goddess running through her body.

"The ram!"

The ram had reached the gate, and Lyonene grinned at her, blood-streaked across the mass of fighting. Wordless, they lent their strength to the battering ram and in two strikes the gate cracked and buckled, and their men began to pour through.

"It's not a victory!" Reed shouted when they cheered. "There are more inside!"

"It is not a victory *yet*!" Lyonene shouted back, and leaped into the cart of a Cerillian chariot as it raced past.

Reed clambered over the top of the discarded battering ram as fighting began inside the wall. At the first sword clash she heard Sar cry, "I want the wall!" and turned to see him leap up the stairs, hacking his sword recklessly against descending soldiers.

"Argon!" Reed threw the shield of Ferreh to him with a great heave. "Help Sar!"

Argon gave a mighty roar and bashed attackers with the shield. He cleared the stairs so Reed, Hestion, and Sar could race to the top.

As Hestion leaped to cut a man down, an archer took a knee

and drew an arrow aimed for Sar's throat—Reed swung her sword and sliced it out of the air.

"That's the second time I've kept your eye-jar empty," she said, but the Ithernan just laughed.

They fought along the top of the wall, pushing the archers back to a barricade of barrels.

"Halt!" Hestion called. "Here! Set the blockade here!"

Below in the city similar orders rang out, for troops to retreat and for barriers and boundaries to be placed. In the street at the end of the marketplace, the Rhonassans had constructed a makeshift fence and set it ablaze as Belden and Alsander cantered triumphantly behind it with bloodied swords high in the air.

Reed lowered her weapons. How long had they fought? How long had it taken to push the Rhonassans into their own city, to conquer a length of Roshanak's wall? Around her men stood panting, covered in dirt and sweat, in blood that was theirs and not theirs. Yet they smiled. They cheered.

Reed looked at Hestion and saw the glow upon him, glorious gold rising up to Kleia Gloria.

"Have we done it?" he asked, breathless. "Are you an Aristene?"

"Not yet." She felt the glory they had won, filling her as wine in a cup. "But we will." He stepped closer to her and he felt her arms, making sure she was unhurt.

"Now I see the true benefit of an Aristene," one of the men called as they stood pressed together, and Hestion and even Reed smiled. Such was the way of soldiers.

She pulled loose.

"Where are you going?" Hestion asked as she walked down the wall.

"To survey the rest," she said. "Stay with your men."

Reed trudged through the aftermath of the fight, past scenes of celebration side by side with the grim treatment of wounds and the recognition of fallen friends. The army had fought all the way through the lower marketplace and over a broad stone bridge that crossed a river before stopping in the face of the flaming blockades. To the west they'd stopped in the face of something different: huddled refugees from the port. The Rhonassan merchants and their families who had been ordered inside lived in temporary tents that were not much more than canopies.

"Aristene!"

Belden walked toward her and grasped her shoulder in greeting. He had taken a cut on his arm and another below his knee. But most of the blood on his tunic and cape belonged to others.

"Where is Hestion?" he asked.

"He's with his men, securing the wall," Reed replied.

"And he fought well? Though perhaps not so well as I. Your goddess truly has chosen the wrong champion for you."

Reed smiled slightly. She nodded to the frightened merchants. "What are you going to do with these people?" But Belden had no time to answer before Alsander rode toward them on his golden stallion. The first of the merchants fell to his knees in the dirt in a wordless ask for mercy.

Up and down the gathered line, more dropped to their knees. Their wives, too, knelt, and tugged their children down with them.

Belden nodded to them. "Rise."

The men rose timidly. They were older men only and well-dressed. Nobles, whose elder sons served in the Rhonassan army and may have fought and died, perhaps at the ends of the swords of the princes to whom they now bowed.

"You've been made to stay here?" Reed asked.

"Some of us found shelter with friends within the city," one of the merchants replied, a tall man with narrow shoulders and kind wrinkles at the corners of green eyes. "But not many."

"We're living like animals! Look at our things, ruined in the mud! Stolen when our backs are turned." The woman who shouted gestured to piles of goods protected by a sheet of fabric and tied with ropes.

"We have no things, Sara," the merchant said to her. "We have only our lives, so long as it is the will of these kings that we keep them."

"I've no use for your lives, old father," Alsander said. "You know why we have come. You know what crime your king has committed."

The merchant lowered his head. Reed wished that Lyonene was there to keep the princeling from doing something stupid.

"Gather your belongings," Alsander said. "Return to your homes in the port. You will have to share your hearths with soldiers, but you will not be harmed. And you will not be robbed. What service you provide to us we will pay you for, with good coin."

"Fair coin?" Sara asked.

"Fair coin. King Oreas will fall, but Roshanak will not. You have my word."

"That was well done," Belden said to the younger prince as the merchants backed away and began to uncover their stacks of ceramic pots and wooden crates. "You will make a good king in Cerille."

Alsander looked at him in surprise. "It is easy to be a good king when you have the means."

"No easier than it is to serve greed. Don't discount your acts." Belden clapped him on the arm. "These people will remember it. And so shall we."

Alsander's cheeks flushed as he returned to his horse.

"He doesn't know how to take a compliment," Reed said.

"I am thinking that's because he has not had many," said Belden. "His father is unkind. He's raised Alsander to be proud, but a little recognition will soften him."

"You know how to make an ally. You will be a good king, too, Belden."

"But not of Roshanak, for you intend to give that crown to my brother." Belden smiled. "Is that not what you said?"

"It was only a thought."

"Well, it didn't amuse him. But I wish you luck. You may make a king of Hestion yet." He looked at her carefully. "Perhaps the two of you will rule here together."

Reed blinked, unable to hide her own blush. "I'm afraid that an Aristene can wear no crown. I will be leaving you as soon as the war is over."

"A pity. Then we will take of your company what we can. Let us go and celebrate this first victory."

33.

THE BLUSH OF VICTORY

The capture of the marketplace and Alsander's restoration of the merchant class made all the difference in the celebration of victory that followed. As word of his mercy spread, cautious Rhonassans crept back to their food stalls and shops, and by nightfall the port and the southern shore were filled with workers and soldiers, Glaucans and Cerillians, the air loud with boasting and tales, as well as barters and the exchange of coin. Warriors gathered around fires with newly purchased jugs of Rhonassan wine, still wearing armor coated in drying Rhonassan blood.

Reed listened to them shout their victory to the gods as she walked across the sand. She listened to them shout the loss of their friends into the sky. They screamed in triumph and in defiance of death. But death would stalk their steps for longer than just one battle.

As she passed, they raised their cups and called her Aristene. One soldier gave her a piece of fish skewered and roasted over his fire. Another gave her the boiled claw of a crab brought up in a trap. "The goddess of glory smiles upon us," they said, and they were right, at least for that day. Kleia Gloria had fed well. Wherever gods reside, Reed imagined she must be sated and happy.

She found Hestion at a fire with Sar and Argon and a few of the other soldiers.

"Aristene!" Sar cried when he saw her. "She saved my life again today from another flying arrow!"

Reed sat down beside him. He was still an Ithernan. But he was difficult to dislike.

"When I die, the jar of my eyes belongs to you," Sar pledged. "Along with my heart!"

"And your manhood!" one of the men shouted, and grabbed himself.

"Then she will need a bigger jar," Sar replied, and the men laughed so hard they spilled their wine.

"Enough of that," Hestion said.

"Yes," said Sar. "Before you make our prince jealous." He turned to Reed, and she steeled herself for more of his wild, ridiculous laughter. Instead he held out his hand for her to shake. "The battlefield is no place to give proper thanks. But I thank you now. And I meant what I said about the jar."

"I hadn't thought to save you so many times," Reed blurted. "To be honest I hadn't thought to save you even once."

The Ithernan's brow knit. Hestion hadn't told him about what his people had done to Reed and her family. She was surprised to find that she was glad—if Sar had known, he might feel odd about the streaks of blue upon his cheeks.

"He has always been this way," Hestion said. "Chasing the afterlife as the afterlife chases him, two dogs after the same tail. But always the gods have smiled upon him." He squeezed his friend's shoulder and Sar grinned. As Hestion and Reed walked away from the fire, the men traded elbows and sly glances.

"I think it means that they like you," Hestion said.

"I think it means they're pigs."

Hestion snorted. He tried to slip an arm around her and she stepped away.

"Look around." She gestured to the beach, to the port, where young women from Rhonassus and the surrounding villages had come to feast and celebrate with the soldiers. There were many pretty girls around many of the fires, getting sand into the folds of their best gowns. "There's no shortage of loveliness to choose from. And I'm sure at least one would be interested in you."

Hestion looked as they walked, and many of the women's gazes floated from their fires to stare at him as they passed. He was undoubtedly handsome—his hair dark gold and wild, the strength plain in his shoulders and chest. *But it is his smile,* Reed thought. *His smile and his confidence that draw the eye.*

"I'm sure some of the men will find loves here," Hestion said. He turned his face away from the women, though Reed noticed he seemed to have a hard time keeping it turned. "Some will even find Rhonassan brides. Or Rhonassan mistresses, and will return to find their Glaucan women very cross." He walked closer. "You wanted to kiss me today, atop the wall. You would have had we been alone."

She would have. She could still remember what it felt like, that fire, that need that he seemed able to inspire with only a look. *It was only the thrill of the fighting. I would have felt the same about any finely formed soldier.* Except that since the moment she'd seen him in the well, there had been only him.

"Perhaps it's time I made good on my promise," she said, and his brows raised hopefully. "Not that. When did I ever promise that?

I mean to find you your bride. Even if you refuse to be king here, a high-ranking Rhonassan lady would be an advantageous match."

Hestion sighed. "I don't think you'll find any high-ranking Rhonassan ladies on this beach."

"You don't know who may have snuck out of the city beneath the cover of a cloak. And I can spot her through my Aristene gifts. We can see glory through marriage, not only through battle." Reed surveyed the beach. She saw no ladies in disguise but plenty of worthy others. She pointed to a beauty with a long smooth neck and hair a brighter gold.

"How about that one? The two of you would have lovely, golden-headed children."

He shook his head. "I like dark hair."

So she nodded to a dark-haired young woman with curving hips and pretty eyes.

"No," he said. "She's too short."

"Her, then." Reed gestured to another with chestnut hair and deep brown skin, nearly as beautiful as Lyonene.

"She is not bad," Hestion remarked. "But she is not an immortal warrior."

Reed crossed her arms.

"I was right. You can't choose horses, and you can't choose women."

"I think, Reed, that your goddess has chosen for us both."

Reed's smile faded. All the teasing had gone out of his voice.

"We cannot have that," she whispered.

"Someone ought to tell them, then."

Across the sand, in the streets of the port, Alsander carried

Lyonene on his hips, her legs wrapped around his back as he spun her around to the cheers of his men.

"You would prefer this?" Reed asked, gesturing to them. "To use me as an ornament to gain the respect of soldiers?"

"Not to gain the respect of soldiers, but I would prefer that, yes." Hestion raised his cup. "Alsander!"

Alsander set Lyonene down. As the pairs walked toward each other, his gait was loose and pleased, like a cat strolling through piles of pulled bird's feathers.

"Prince Hestion. A great victory we won today," he said, and both princes poured wine into the dirt for their gods. "I hope your Aristene celebrates your prowess as heartily as does mine."

"There is little chance of that," said Lyonene, her fingers walking across Alsander's chest. "Every Aristene is different. Reed has talents that I do not, and I have talents"—she nibbled Alsander's ear—"that are all my own."

"I can't even say that you never tried to teach me," Reed said, and snorted. At that, both Alsander and Hestion perked their ears.

"Is that so?" Alsander asked. "I would very much like to hear about it."

"And me as well," Hestion added.

Lyonene rolled her eyes, and Reed laughed. Over Lyonene's shoulder, she thought she caught a glimpse of a figure in a cloak, but when she looked again, there were only shadows.

"Our mentors must be proud tonight," Lyonene said to Reed as Hestion and Alsander conversed, burying the bad blood between them in the sweeter dust of victory. "I imagine Sabil is somewhere in the hills as drunk as old Veridian."

"I imagine Aster is as well." She thought of her mentor, beyond the Veil. "Only, proud. Not drunk." She had rarely seen Aster drunk.

Reed and Lyonene walked together through the celebrations in the port, their heroes trailing behind them. Relief flooded through them both—though they would have denied it, they'd feared that first charge. Secretly, they had feared that one would fall or one would fail. But now—

Lyonene breathed deep of the salt air.

"I want inside that city," she said. "I want to know what waits for us inside the palace walls." Reed looked toward the hills of Rhonassus, past the great hedge maze and into the palace lit with torches. It was the only part of Roshanak that seemed to still be awake and alive. "Do you feel it there, too?" Lyonene asked. "Coiled like a snake about to strike?"

But to Reed it was only a palace.

"How much wine have you had?" Reed asked. She threw her arm around her friend and again her eye caught movement—something in the shadows, following alongside them. She glanced at Lyonene. Normally her friend's senses were sharper, but they'd been dulled by drink and by victory and, unaccountably, by Alsander's charms. Reed tugged Lyonene close. "Do not react. Someone is following us. I need you to make a distraction with Hestion and Alsander so I can slip away and catch them."

Lyonene nodded. Then she grinned wide and kissed her on the cheek, a great smacking kiss, and called to Alsander. "Come and dance with me! And Hestion as well since his Aristene will not!"

Reed fell back as Lyonene brought both princes close. She was a natural at commanding attention and used to being at the center of it. Reed was used to shadows and to hiding the bulk of herself in plain sight.

She slipped behind the food stalls, listening to the cheers and whistles of the soldiers as they watched whatever show Lyonene had chosen to put on. Reed's eyes adjusted to the darkness and quickly glimpsed the hooded shape that moved just beyond the light of the torches. When she caught them, she shoved them over a crate and lifted them up by the back of the neck.

It was only a boy. A boy with deep tan skin and dark hair braided to the nape in the Rhonassan fashion. He was small and wiry but well-fed. In another life he might have been Reed's brother, but in this one he pulled a dagger and tried to put it into her throat.

"No," she said, as if scolding a puppy. She twisted his wrist and the blade fell to the sand. "I won't hurt you. Why were you following us?"

"I was not following you," the boy spat in the common tongue. "I was following them."

Reed turned. Lyonene had rejoined her, with Alsander and Hestion.

"I thought I saw an assassin in the shadows," she explained. "But it was only this boy."

Hestion looked the boy up and down, from his fine plaits and gold barrettes to the gold-threaded tunic beneath his cloak. "That's no boy," he said in surprise. "That's Prince Oren."

They took the Rhonassan prince to Belden in his villa. When they dropped him before the hearth, Belden, too, knew who he was. He had just seen him during the negotiations on the battlefield.

But the boy in that saddle, gleaming in golden armor and a black cape, had seemed a grown man. The armor must have been several times too large to pull off such an illusion. Kneeling on the floor, his head bowed and his teeth bared, Prince Oren couldn't have been more than ten or eleven.

"Do not be afraid, Prince." Belden stood. "We're not in the business of killing messengers. And certainly not royal ones."

"I am not afraid," Oren snarled. "This is what I intended." He rose to stand before Belden and tipped his head back to look up into the older prince's eyes. Perhaps a meeting with him was Oren's aim. But it was plain to see that now that he was here, he was afraid.

"And what was your intention in meeting me?" Belden asked.

Oren glanced at Alsander, who stepped nearer, as if to remind those in attendance that he was also a crown prince. "I come to seek your help."

Reed and Lyonene traded a glance.

"Do you betray your father?" Belden asked.

Prince Oren swallowed. His whole form trembled and he took a great breath, as if steeling his resolve. He dropped to the floor in a pose of bent supplication.

"I come to beg you to go."

"Get up, Prince Oren," Alsander said. "This is no way for a royal to behave." But the boy remained motionless, his hands stretched out palms down, his bow so low that his nose touched the ground. Alsander looked at Belden and Hestion. "We cannot just leave!"

"My brother and I will smuggle you gold. Gold and treasures to fill your ships. If you take your army and sail tonight."

"I have gold," said Alsander. "I want this city. I want this port!"

Hestion looked at Belden. He shook his head.

"We cannot just go," Belden said to the boy gently. "Your father has committed a grave wrong. And he must pay for it." He drew the boy up off the floor.

"We will pay for it," Oren insisted. "In gold!" But Belden only sighed.

"Take him away." Alsander gestured to the soldiers.

"He's a messenger who comes in good faith," said Hestion. "He should be escorted safely back to his city."

"And give up a prince who brought himself to us? Are you mad?" Alsander turned to Lyonene for agreement, but she said nothing. "What about you, then, Aristene Reed?" Alsander asked, and Reed looked at him in surprise. "Should we return this gift that was freely given?"

Reed regarded the little prince, who had refused to look at her or at Lyonene since he'd been captured. He had the pride of royalty, but he was still only a child. And he'd come to them for help.

She knew what Hestion thought, but it was Belden who would have the final word. He respected the order, and she knew that whatever she said would carry weight. She looked at the little prince again. As much as she hated to agree with Alsander, the boy was valuable.

"The prince should not be harmed," she said. "But nor should he be hastily returned." Hestion exhaled through his nose, and turned away, disappointed.

"Prince Oren will remain with us for a time," Belden announced. "As our guest. He will remain here with me in my villa, looked after by my personal guard."

"You are making a mistake," Oren cried, his eyes wild as Belden's men came to take him by the arms. "You must let me go!"

They listened to his protestations fade as he was walked away down the hall.

"That was ugly business," Reed said to Lyonene, watching Hestion speak with his brother. "Did you see how frightened he was?"

"He was frightened," Lyonene agreed. "But not of us."

34.

EMPTY STALL

In the morning, the Rhonassans fought to regain the wall. They attacked the barricades before dawn, sending arrows flying in the dark to kill men as they slept. They pushed the occupying force back nearly to the stairs before Belden or Hestion or any of the leaders could reach them, but when they arrived, they turned the tide. Docritae warriors bashed their way through attacking soldiers. They knelt behind their shields and Hestion jumped off their backs and into the nest of the enemy, in one hand his drawn sword and in the other a torch. He lit men ablaze and made bright targets of them for Glaucan arrows.

Through it all Reed haunted his shadow and guarded his flank. She sliced crossbow bolts out of the air and sent men rolling with the shield of Ferreh. Hestion's charge gave the men courage, and when the Rhonassans called a retreat, they had not given back one stone's length of the wall.

Reed rode back to the encampment with Hestion on a horse that wasn't Silco, and despite their fine showing, she found herself unsettled. Maybe it was the early hour or her empty stomach. Maybe it was the strangeness of the horse's gait. But she knew it was none of those things.

"I can't stop thinking about Prince Oren."

"Then maybe you should have listened to me and let him go."

"A gift prince is too useful to simply be let go," she said. "And your brother will treat him well. What bothers me is how afraid he seemed." She recalled Lyonene's words. "And not of us. You said Prince Ostar is a good man?"

"A very good man and honorable. I shouldn't like to kill him, though I will if it comes to that."

"And King Oreas—he's old and mad?" She recalled what he'd told her in Glaucia, the whispers that the old king kept the prophet's severed head and pressed it to his ear as if it could still tell his fortune.

"Older than my father by a good number of years," Hestion replied. "What are you thinking, Reed? What do you sense?"

They rode through the port and toward the stable. Reed looked back toward Roshanak. It was still beautiful: gold baked brick and white walls, the buildings growing in height toward the palace on the hill. But when the war was over, it would be changed. Blackened in places. Bearing its scars. It would not be so proud and unconquerable, and that made Reed sad, despite knowing what King Oreas had done.

Do the people fear their king? she wondered. *Are they disgusted by his murder of the prophet?*

Does it even matter? she heard a voice say in her head that sounded like Aster and also oddly like Veridian. *It is not for the Aristene to pass judgment or take sides.*

They put their horses into the stable and placed Target into the stall beside the one that used to be Silco's. That one Reed kept empty, but on the other side she had placed the little roan mare who had lost her colt. Hestion grabbed a blanket and laid it down upon the clean straw of Silco's empty stall.

"What are you doing?"

"We won't attack again until the heat of midday breaks—unless the Rhonassans attack us first. I'm going to take a nap."

"In a stable? Why not return to your brother's villa? Or one of the tents on the beach?"

"Too many men there wanting stories. With too much ale." He lay down on his back and closed his eyes. Then he patted the straw beside him.

"I thought you said you wanted to rest."

"Why, Reed," he said. "What are you suggesting?"

She snorted and lay down beside him. She hadn't gotten enough sleep the night before either, with the predawn attack. Yet the moment their shoulders touched and she felt the warm length of him stretched along her side, she was no longer weary.

"Did I perform well today?" he asked.

"You know that you did; you were there."

"But not too well, I hope."

"What do you mean?"

"Not so well that your goddess is completely sated." Hestion rolled onto his side and rested his head on his hand, looking down at her. "Not so well that your Hero's Trial is complete?"

Reed smiled. "No. Not so well as that."

"How will you know?" he asked. "When it's enough?"

"I don't know." She shifted, the blanket beneath them crunching against the dry straw. "Perhaps it will be so much that I'll pass out." Hestion chuckled. "No one has really told us. They say only that we'll know when it happens."

"I hope it isn't too soon." He rolled over again and shut his eyes. "For when your trial is over, we will be parted, and I will no longer have your sword and your shield at my back. I will no longer have your company. And Sar will die."

Reed laughed. "What if I promise to stay even after my trial ends?"

"You could do that?"

"I think so, at least until the war is over."

Hestion smiled. But his smile didn't last.

"How will I do without you now?" he asked.

"You'll do as you have done before we met."

"That's just it," he said. "It no longer feels like there was a time before. It feels like you have always been there."

"I suppose part of me always has been," she whispered, and even though she knew she shouldn't, she leaned down to kiss him.

At first he moved slowly, tentatively, as if he didn't want to go too far and frighten her into stopping. But that changed when she slid her leg over him. He rolled on top of her, and then it felt like being devoured, like she'd imagined it would feel had she done what she'd wanted on top of the wall.

Hestion lifted himself slightly, his breath fast like he'd come from a fight.

"Reed," he said.

"This is only a distraction," she whispered, and slipped her hands up his back, pushing off the straw to kiss him again. "Only that and nothing more."

"I will want more. I already want more," he said, and Reed realized with an ache that she did, too.

Footsteps raced through the door of the stable and stopped short when they caught a glimpse of what was happening in the stall.

"Prince Hestion."

Hestion groaned against Reed's neck.

"What?"

"Forgive me, my lord, but Prince Ostar has attacked. And your brother is fighting him."

Hestion rolled back and he and Reed burst up from the straw.

"Where?" she demanded.

"On the road into the port. Prince Ostar and his soldiers charged the villa in hopes of freeing Oren, but Lord Belden was ready—he and his guard drove the prince back and now they duel in the street."

Hestion grabbed Reed by the wrist.

"You will never reach him, my lord," said the young messenger.

Reed looked at Hestion.

"The rooftops," she said.

35.

A DUEL OF YOUNG KINGS

Reed led Hestion from the stable and together they raced through the alleys. She'd mapped the port in her mind almost the moment they arrived, identifying vantage points and vulnerabilities to the camp. So she knew just where to go as she mounted the steps at the rear of the white stone temple.

"Jump!" she ordered, and Hestion jumped with her onto the low-pitched roof. They ran quickly, crouching atop the uncertain footing of clay tiles, and when they reached the edge they leaped again, to the next building and then the next after that, following the sound of the crowd and the faint ringing of metal against metal. It didn't take long for the duel to come into view, but when the rooftop path dead-ended she drew up short. They were still too far away to jump down and join the fray.

"You can't make that leap," Reed said, and grabbed Hestion by the arm. She could have, with her borrowed magic. But she didn't want to leave him.

Belden and Prince Oreas traded blows in the middle of the street. Each one landed with a brutal clang. The testing swings and feints were past. Both men fought with their full strength.

Reed looked down, watching every spin, every duck. Every cross of swords and every shove that skidded a young king backward in the dirt. She didn't see any blood, and the way they were fighting, she didn't expect to; when blood finally showed, the fight would be over, and the man bleeding would fall down to die.

"Don't bare your offside, Belden, damn you," Hestion hissed. He paced back and forth like a cat, studying every turn of the duel without blinking.

Belden was strong. Tall and athletic. But the longer the fight went on, the more nervous Reed became. He should have ended it by now, and the fact that he hadn't meant that Ostar was as good a fighter as his reputation suggested.

In the street, soldiers from both sides had gathered around the duel. The path of retreat was held by the Rhonassans, where soldiers waited with Prince Ostar's black horse at the ready. If Belden fell, they would throw his body across the horse's hindquarters, and Ostar would parade it through the city. There would be offerings of mourning on both sides, Prince Oren would be given back, and Belden's body would be returned to the Glaucans to be burnt on a pyre beside the sea. That would be it. His loss would end the entire war.

Reed's fingers twitched toward her dagger. She saw Lyonene at the front of the crowd beside Alsander and knew she was thinking the same thing: that Belden could not fall. But to interfere would be a violation of the code of battle. If Reed's Joining was already complete and she had the fullness of her magic, she might be able to see the beats of the duel, like Veridian could. She might know in which way the scales had tipped—if victory shone upon Belden like the sun or if death marked him like a shadow. But borrowed magic was limited. With every rise and fall of a sword she saw nothing but her own dread.

On and on the duel went, and still both princes' sword arms remained quick. Belden fought in the Glaucan fashion—forward, forward, forward—while Ostar had more flourish. Both fought with sword in one hand and shield in the other. And both spoke, sometimes to taunt and other times seemingly to simply make conversation.

"Your brother is a fine dinner guest," Belden shouted. "I will be happy to host him throughout the war!"

"Keep him and feed him and clothe him if you like!" Ostar shouted back. "But I will take your little brother in kind."

Hestion's eyes narrowed. But Belden refused to be baited.

"It is only fair," he said, and bashed Ostar with his shield.

"He's tiring," Hestion said quietly, and from the shake in his voice Reed knew he meant Belden. She stepped to his shoulder and held it tight, watching as Belden pushed his way ahead, so far that the Rhonassans had to back up several steps along the road. It looked like progress, until Ostar forced his shield up and out and sent Belden wheeling away.

"Don't!" Hestion jerked forward. Don't bare your back. Don't leave it open to your opponent's weapon. It was close, but Belden caught Ostar's blow with the end of his sword; the blade sang upward and sliced into the Rhonassan's forearm.

Ostar wasn't injured; he had taken most of the hit to his armored bracer. Still, it seemed to have given him pause.

"You fight well, prince of the Glaucans," he said.

"As well as you," Belden replied.

"Today perhaps. But not tomorrow."

Belden smiled. "We'll see."

They stood tall and put away their swords. They did not bow, but Belden allowed it when Ostar turned and walked to his horse.

"Will you take gold for my brother in trade?" Ostar asked after he had mounted.

"I will take your father for your brother in trade," Belden replied, and the other prince laughed.

"Then I will see you again, on the battlefield."

The princes nodded to each other, and the Rhonassans rode away.

"I've never seen him so well-matched," Hestion said. "I've never seen anyone stand against Belden."

He frowned, but when Belden saw them atop the roof, he grinned and raised both arms.

"He didn't lose," Reed said. "And that is what matters."

36.

THE CAPTIVE PRINCE

That night, the soldiers gathered in Belden's villa to celebrate the duel, and to feast with Oren, the captive prince. When Belden saw Reed arrive with Hestion, he rose from his seat to greet them and embraced Reed fondly.

"You fought well today, brother," said Hestion.

"As ever," Belden replied. He wrapped an arm around Reed's shoulders. He seemed a little drunk, as if the fight with Ostar had shaken him more than he cared to admit. "And after such a performance it is only right that I have the honor of the Aristene's company. Leave her to me tonight and go and drink with the men."

Hestion glanced at Reed before nodding and walked outside to the fires.

Belden's villa was low on the hill, shabbier than Alsander's, and sprawling; the western rooms that housed the soldiers had been haphazardly added on and didn't match the original structure. But it was open and inviting, easy for men to stumble in and out of.

The main hearth had become as the lodge of the Docritae: a close room of mirth and drink, food and tales, with a long table set in the center. Belden sat at the head and placed Reed to his right. He poured them cups of the straw-colored ale of the Rhonassan port, filled nearly to the brim.

"Don't worry," he whispered into her ear. "Their ale is as water compared to ours—I could drink two barrels and still ride out to fight." He poured a splash to their gods and grinned at her. Reed grinned back. It was infectious. Belden's smile had the same ease as Hestion's, and he had the same indomitable confidence.

Around the table sat mostly Glaucan soldiers, though at the farther fires she saw a few Cerillians. None yet seemed tired, though a few had bloodstained wrappings on their arms or shoulders. Belden called for meat to be piled onto a scrap of bread and placed before her.

The captive prince sat on Belden's opposite side, and Reed watched him from the corner of her eye as she ate. The boy's back was straight, his chin raised high above the table. The food in front of him went untouched, and he sneered down at the clean tunic he'd been dressed in.

"What will you do with him?" Reed asked, and gestured to Oren.

Beside Belden, the Rhonassan prince seemed even younger, his shoulders narrower. "Oren is our guest until the business of war is concluded. We will treat him with courtesy, so long as he does the same." He filled the boy's cup. "So eat, Prince. Drink. Better with your own hands than for my men to do it for you."

"I will not eat at this filthy table," the boy said. "As you eat with your filthy hands." He glared at the Glaucans, and his lip curled with disgust at the rivers of ale that dropped from their lips and chins. "I will not eat your burnt, bland meat."

"It is your meat," Belden said, and took another bite. "We stole it from you. So take it back, and the ale besides. We have no fine plate here, no perfumed water. . . ."

"And we have none at home either!" a soldier shouted, and the men laughed.

"The meal is not fit for hosting princes," Belden went on. "But it is what we have. So eat."

Oren swallowed. His hair was still adorned with gold pins and fastenings, but Reed got the feeling that those would be pulled out soon enough if the prince didn't cooperate. When Oren again refused, one of the Glaucans grabbed him by the shoulders, but Belden shook his head. He sighed and turned to Reed.

"Tell me the tale of how you discovered the trap before the wall."

"Have you not already heard that tale from Hestion?"

"I have. He couldn't wait to boast of you. But I would hear it from your own lips. Somehow I think you will tell it without embellishments."

"But it's the kind of tale that requires embellishment—I recognized the trap by chance. That's all there is to it."

"It saved us many men and horses. We will owe the Aristene much in gold and tribute by the time this war is over, I am thinking."

Reed smiled. *We will take whatever portion of the spoils you feel that we have earned.* Isn't that what Aster said? Reed touched her cup to Belden's just as Prince Oren overturned his and spilled it across Belden's forearm.

"You dress women as soldiers," Oren hissed. "You sit them at your table and take their counsel. You are too weak to face my father."

"Your father would take the counsel of this one as well," said Belden, shaking his arm dry. He nodded to one of his soldiers. "Take him to his quarters." The soldier hauled the prince up by the elbows and the boy scowled into Belden's back.

"Forgive his disrespect," Belden said to Reed.

"He's young. And those are the Rhonassan ways."

"The Rhonassan way is not rudeness. His brother, Prince Ostar, would not think much of his behavior."

"Are you glad you didn't kill him today?" Reed asked.

"No. For if I had we would be closer to victory. But I wouldn't have relished it. He is a good man and would have made a good king. His father's crimes are not his crimes." He cocked his head. "But you would rather my brother be the one to do the prince-killing. He's told me you are in a hurry for him to prove himself."

Reed watched Hestion as he sat with Sar and Argon around the fire outside.

"What else does Hestion say?" she asked.

"He says many things." Belden grinned. "But I would not betray him. I know he has hopes."

Outside the villa, Hestion drank and laughed—girls had come to soothe the soldiers and a pretty one sat on his lap and leaned into him. The sight of it gave Reed an unpleasant feeling in her belly. But when the girl raised her lips to his, Hestion gently removed her arm and set her to one side.

"Since the moment he came of age, I have never seen my brother turn down a beauty like that," Belden said. "Not once. In fact, he has been known to accept the challenge of five—"

"Five?"

"I don't know why I said that." Belden peered into his cup. "Perhaps this Rhonassan ale is strong after all."

"And what of you, Belden?" Reed asked, eager to steer the conversation away. "Have you loved many?"

"Many," he said, and for a moment he looked upon Reed with a different eye, as if he suddenly remembered that he, too, was young and handsome and unattached. Then he looked again into his ale cup. "I have loved many. But I have loved them like a king: as I love my country. I've never loved one above the rest."

"You are saving your heart for your queen," said Reed, and Belden grinned.

"Yes. As my father saved his for my mother. As Hestion has for you." He blinked. "This ale loosens the tongue!" he said, and threw his cup away. Then he leaned close to Reed, his eyes at once sober and serious. "You will not hold his past against him? What I said about five—that was a boast; it was four. And all young men have dalliances . . ."

Reed put her hand on Belden's arm.

"You must speak to him," she said. "You must tell him it's not possible."

"Why?"

She looked at Hestion beside the fire. She knew he watched her when she wasn't looking, the same way that she watched him. Sometimes when she looked at him, he was hardly her hero at all, but only a young man full of heart and possibility. And in those moments she was only a young woman, not an initiate with a long destiny already unfurled before her feet.

"Because I care for him," she said. "And I wouldn't have him hope when it cannot be."

"Why do you not speak to him yourself?"

"I can't."

"Why?"

"Because I also hope," she said.

Reed excused herself from Belden's table. She didn't know why she had admitted her feelings. It couldn't have been the Rhonassan ale; she'd had no more than a cup. Maybe it was because Belden had had enough to make him safe to confess to.

Lies, she thought. She had wanted to tell him.

"Nothing can turn me from my course," she whispered. Over and over in her head she said it, that heroes were not for keeping. That only the order was forever. But no matter how many times she said it, it didn't seem to matter.

As she passed the door of the captive prince, she heard him call out to her.

"You," he said. "The woman who fights. Who they allow to dress as a soldier and speak as a general. But how many generals climbed on top of you for the privilege?"

Reed stopped. She was weary and in no mood to fight with a little boy. But since he'd started it . . . "Not so many," she said. "Certainly less than could fit on one ship. I saw your brother fight today."

"You saw him," Oren said. "And was he not a spectacle? Was he not near to the gods?"

"Near," Reed agreed. "He was one of the finest fighters I have ever seen. Though he didn't win and you're still here, so perhaps he is near to the gods only tangentially."

The prince's face twisted with fury. "I will bear no insult from a woman! When I am free and my sword is restored, I will cut out your tongue." One of the guards beside the door took a step, but Reed shook her head. "You are not men, to take orders from her," he said to them. "Women are to be protected. They are to be treasured, not to be obeyed."

"Women are to be protected yet you would cut out my tongue?"

"You would survive it," he muttered, and a short bark of laughter escaped Reed's throat. He was an ill-tempered thing, but his wit was sharp.

"Is the princeling throwing insults at you?"

She turned. Sar had left the fire outside.

"A few," she said as she walked to him, leaving Prince Oren's doorway behind.

"Don't take it personally. The nobles he treats with respect, but he tosses insults to the soldiers like coins at a peasant. And I do not think the Rhonassans know of your order." Sar waved a dismissive hand. "But it is nice that he thinks well of his brother! So often with royal sons it is all stabs in the ribs and cups full of poison. I think it would have been that way with my own brother. Had I not come to the Docritae, one of our jars would be painted and sitting in the family crypt by now." He jutted his chin toward the prince's room. "Oren will settle. Out of the necessity of keeping the peace once his father is dead. Or from becoming a foster, should the Docritae need to keep him."

"Like you," Reed said.

"Like me and like you," Sar said, and his eyes brightened. "Many people leave their homes and find new ones. But not all find new people to call their kin. We are lucky."

"We are," said Reed quietly as he walked away.

37.

SIEGECRAFT

The Aristene initiates knew before anyone else that something was wrong. The Glaucan and Cerillian army had assembled on the beach, so large that the last of the men bled into the sea and waited in water to their thighs. They allowed Prince Ostar and his soldiers room before the wall, space for one last negotiation. But no Rhonassan army greeted them. Again, only a small group of a dozen spearmen were posted before the city gate.

Reed stood between Hestion and Sar with a gnawing feeling in her gut. There was no current in the air. And again, the great city had fallen eerily silent, like it had during the first days of their arrival. Reed tried to sense what was happening inside, calling up her borrowed magic and casting it over and over toward Roshanak. But it simply slithered back to curl up in her blood like a cat in the sun.

"They're not coming."

"What do you mean they are not coming?" Hestion asked.

"Do you hear an army? Do you see one, besides our own?"

They had heard them, though, all through the night. Roshanak had been loud with preparations, and it sent such a chill of warning through Reed that she'd barely slept. Lookouts had watched from the balconies of hillside villas and scouts had returned with reports of movement. But as the Glaucans and Cerillians formed ranks upon the beach, the Rhonassan army had dissolved. They had pulled themselves back, like ants into a hill.

Reed and Hestion slipped through the lines of soldiers, giving rise to startled murmurs like so many dust trails in their wake. What was happening? When would they attack? Had the Aristene spotted another trap?

She wished she had. But as she shouldered her way through to Belden she already knew that there would be no attack today. The carefully buckled armor on the soldiers and their freshly sharpened blades were all for nothing.

"Reed!" Lyonene's face was a storm cloud. Her tall black mare looked like a drop of ink next to Alsander's Phaeton and his shining coat of gold.

"I know," Reed said. "There is nothing here."

"Nothing?" Alsander asked. "How? Where have they gone?"

"They will be here," said Belden. "Prince Ostar said he would fight." But his face beneath his helmet was unsure.

Lyonene nudged a step closer to Alsander.

"Give Reed your horse," she said.

"What?" he asked, but after a moment he slid down from Phaeton's back. Reed vaulted into the saddle.

"I should go with you," said Hestion. "It may be a trap."

"It is no trap."

She and Lyonene rode toward the small waiting force of spearmen that stood before the city gate.

"Let's get them out of our way," said Lyonene, and the silver armor and white cape burst onto her through the aether. Reed called up the magic and felt her own armor settle upon her, light and coolly shining. At the sight of them the Rhonassans called a retreat. Though they might have done it anyway. It was clear they were following orders.

Reed and Lyonene walked their horses through the silent city and into the empty marketplace. It was completely bare. Stripped of anything that could be of use.

"They've drawn even farther into their stronghold," Lyonene said.

"But why give us this part of the city?" Reed asked.

"Stop." Lyonene put out her arm. They were approaching the fortress of the palace and the archers set atop the towers. No need to give them an easy shot.

"Kleia Gloria," Lyonene muttered under her breath, looking upon the fortress. "They've dug a moat."

It was fresh and could not have been that deep, but it ran around the wall of the palace, even cutting through the main road. Just enough to slow attacking soldiers and to make the Rhonassan position clear: King Oreas meant to wait them out.

"The city sprawls out behind the palace all the way to the valley," Lyonene said. "Alsander says tunnels were constructed five hundred years ago to protect the supply lines." Reed's jaw tightened. The capital would have food and fortifications to last for months, and even without ousting their immigrants and their peasant classes. Lyonene glanced up at the palace and gripped Reed's arm. "Do you feel that?"

Reed followed Lyonene's eyes. She felt something. A gaze sliding over her armor and down her back. It felt like an unwelcome hand upon her and she fought the urge to brush it off.

"What is that?"

"I don't know." Lyonene turned her black horse in a tight circle and spat on the ground as if the feeling left a bad taste. "But it doesn't matter. Now we will have to fight a siege. Let's go back before the archers find their nerve."

A siege, Reed thought, her blood bubbling with frustration. Sieges were grueling campaigns. Piercing the barrier of the stronghold would be slow and grinding. They would lose men to boiling oil dumped on them from atop the walls of the palace. They would lose more to arrows and dropped stones. And the odds of winning favored the city.

As she and Lyonene rode back to the army, Reed stared up at Roshanak.

You think you're safe, she thought. *You think you have beaten us. You don't know that you already lie in piles of rubble and smoke.*

After the initiates returned, scouts were sent to verify what they'd found. The army disbanded with shoulders slumped. Reed and Hestion followed Belden back to his villa. The young king had spoken few words, and his mood was black. He stood listlessly beside his hearth before walking to his table and overturning it with one great heave.

"Brother," Hestion said as Belden stormed through the halls. He and Reed hurried after him. He was headed for Oren.

Reed had never seen Belden angry. She'd wondered if he even possessed the emotion. Now she understood why he buried it, as he shoved a guard to the floor and broke through the captive prince's door.

"What ways are there through to the city's interior?" Belden demanded in a bellow. Oren scrambled backward, caught off-guard.

For a moment he looked terrified, eyes flicking right and left for a way to run. It was only when Reed and Hestion arrived that he regained his composure.

"There are no ways," he replied.

"Tell me!" He stepped to the prince and shouted into his face. "We will take our armies around the mountains—we will attack your flanks! How do we get into the tunnels?"

"You can't."

Belden raised his fist, and Hestion stepped closer. But as angry as Belden was, it was all a bluff. They could never take their army around the mountains; they hadn't the means or the supplies for such travel.

"Your father is a coward," Belden growled. "He is no king."

"My father fears nothing," said Oren quietly. "And if you are a good king, you will take your soldiers and sail away."

As the siege set in, it became clear that King Oreas was not truly content to remain behind his palace walls. Day after day Prince Ostar rode out to raid and harass the allied lines inside the narrow streets of the city. He attacked before dawn, when the lookouts were blind; he led forces up through tunnels and seemed to appear out of nowhere. And he disappeared just as quickly.

"Kleia Gloria should have bound one of us to Ostar," Lyonene muttered in frustration, after she and Reed had once again arrived too late to an ambush. "Already his legend circulates: 'Ostar, the ghost prince, who travels in the morning mist and vanishes in the first light of dawn.' If he was ours we would be back in Atropa by now, celebrating."

Reed couldn't say she was wrong. Hestion continued to fight where he could, and so did Alsander, who surprised many with his daring—his assault on the river gained them control of a small fleet of barges and brought fresh supplies of grain and wine. But it wasn't progress. It was exhaustion. King Oreas and Prince Ostar were simply biding their time, letting the Glaucans and Cerillians use up their weapons and food stores, as well as their strength and patience.

"It is a distraction," Alsander declared one night at Belden's hearth. He had taken to drinking too much of the wine he had won, and when he spoke his cheeks were rosy. "Prince Ostar attacks always from the same two entrances—he is drawing us away from the weakness of the others. We must attack at night. Use the rams. Send men to scale the walls at the weak points."

It was worth a try. Alsander commanded an assault on the eastern drawbridge under cover of darkness. He ordered men beneath shields to construct a bridge across the moat. And while the Rhonassans were occupied with that, he sent other soldiers to quieter parts of the wall to find a way to climb over. He even sent Lyonene.

But it didn't work. Lyonene returned with an arrow deep in her shoulder, and Alsander lost so many men at the moat that he nearly succeeded at constructing his bridge—but only out of his own soldiers' bodies.

"We must find a way inside the city and into the palace," Alsander said when they gathered before Belden's hearth. He sat with a jug of wine in one fist and his head drooping. A Cerillian handmaiden knelt at his knee and washed his skin and armor free of blood. He didn't look like a princeling anymore. War had made him rougher.

Beneath his armor his tanned skin flexed with springy, wiry muscle.

"The only way we're getting into the palace is by invitation," said Hestion. "I am sorry, brothers. But Roshanak is everything we have heard. There is a reason it hasn't been sacked in a thousand years."

"We can't stop now," Lyonene said. "Not after all this."

"If we leave," Belden said, "we leave with enough supplies to complete our journey home. If we wait and no progress is made, we will have lost still more. We will have to sail dangerously bare and hope to resupply along the route."

"Or we could sail home with all the riches of Roshanak," Alsander objected.

"It is hard to see the shine of riches, Prince Alsander, when we are covered in dust and there is less and less bread in our mens' mouths."

As the princes talk dissolved into infighting, their Aristenes were forced to intervene, pulling their armor through the aether to scold their heroes like children. But not even that was enough to stop them. What stopped them, finally, was the sound of Prince Oren's laughter.

The young prince sat at Belden's long table with his hands tied, picking at a piece of dried fruit.

"I think you are in no position to laugh at us, little lord," Belden cautioned. "Be silent, or you will find me a less than gracious host."

"You are not my host," Oren replied. "I am yours. I have always been yours."

"Get him out of here. Take him to his room."

The guards took Oren by his thin arms and the boy sneered at Reed and Lyonene in their silver and white.

"My father would like you," he said as he passed. "He likes things that are of the gods. That is why he decided to keep the prophet."

As Reed watched him be taken away, a curious voice came into her head, one that sounded like Aster's, and like her mother's, half-remembered.

To lay siege to a city is to pry open a clamshell. You will slip and strike against it. You will use up your strength with scraping and pulling. Until you find the point of a knife. Then it will crack apart with a turn of your wrist.

38.
CHOICES

In the morning, Reed crept out of the camp to hunt in the hills. During the long weeks of the siege, hunting had become her escape, and though for her it served as mainly distraction, her pastime was welcomed by the soldiers, who ate well when she returned with a fine doe or a wild goat slung over her horse's back. She took her longbow and a quiver of arrows, and from the stable she took not the dark gray gelding she rode into battle but the roan mare. The mother who had mourned her colt on the road from Lacos had been set to pulling carts, and though the work was hard, Reed was glad that it kept her from the worst of the fighting. It was silly, but she felt a kinship to the stubborn little horse. They had experienced a loss at the same time. And the mare had been sweet and slow with Silco when he had been tied to her saddle.

Still, no matter how many times she carried Reed into the hills, or how many times Reed brushed and scratched her, Reed refused to call her anything besides Roan Mare. To give her a name was to claim her, and Reed couldn't do that. Not when Silco was still alive.

They traveled into the foothills, picking their way across streams that were too narrow and shallow to fish. To the east, the sun peeked over the mountains, turning the cool shadows of the western hills the early gold of morning, and Reed dismounted in a sloping meadow where she had seen many deer. At first the takings had been easy; it seemed the Rhonassans didn't hunt there, and the deer were bold and fearless. Shooting them felt a little like shooting the stupid, tufted grouse that Aster had brought to the Summer Camp, the ones she called Orillian noblebirds. But, after a few weeks of being shot at and catching the scent of blood in the air, the game had turned cautious. Hunting took skill now, and Reed eagerly slipped into her hunter's guise, letting her mind go sharp and empty, so she was nothing but eyes and ears and arrows in the grass. The peace took her far away from the clang of metal and the pressures of the Hero's Trial. Away from the deaths of allies and enemies. There was only her, and the deer. And the watering of her mouth when she allowed herself to remember how tasty those noblebirds became in Aster's frying pan.

Across the meadow, a dark brown head emerged from the trees. The young stag flicked his large ears back and forth. He raised his black eyes above the grass and took several deep, careful sniffs. They were different deer than Reed was used to hunting—larger and rangier, their antlers fat and rounded at the tips. This one looked to be several seasons old, with strong haunches and a muscular neck. She had to drop him with one arrow. If she only wounded him, she would be chasing him through the hills all day.

Reed carefully raised her bow. Sensing nothing, the stag now felt at ease, and walked into the early-morning sunshine to search for soft shoots of plants to eat. His meat would bring soldiers and port merchants alike to Belden's hearth fire, and his fur was so glossy and full that his pelt could be kept for a rug. Reed drew the arrow back.

A snapped twig behind her was all it took. The stag erupted from the meadow, sending birds flying out of the trees around him. He was gone in three fast leaps.

"You line up for too long," Hestion said. "And now look—" He clucked his tongue. "A fine deer lost."

"It was you who lost it," Reed grumbled. "You rode up and scared him with your enormous white horse."

She glanced toward Target, who nibbled the neck of her roan mare.

"May I join you?" Hestion knelt down and took his bow from his shoulder.

"If you join me, we'll only hunt each other and the soldiers will go hungry."

"I promise." He held up his hands. "Not until we've shot a deer."

He settled into the grass and they fell silent to wait. The sun hadn't even fully risen in the sky before Hestion sighed and snapped, "Where in the gods are these deer?"

Reed laughed. But the light mood was fleeting. "There aren't enough deer in these hills to feed our army. Not if we were to shoot them all. We're running out of time."

Hestion pulled a sprig of grass and tore it between his fingers. "I didn't think we would sail across the sea to lose this way. Humiliated by a king who doesn't even acknowledge our presence. Why did the goddess of glory give you to me if this is what we were fated to do?"

"It's not over," Reed said. "And you've already done much."

"You have done much. You spotted the trap; you devised a plan to breach the wall."

"In the eyes of the gods and the army, I am you. I am your Aristene."

"Is it so?" he said softly.

"It is."

"But you'll not be my Aristene for much longer," Hestion said, and stared quietly across the meadow.

"Will you marry me, Reed?" he asked.

Reed breathed slowly. Her head and chest felt starry, and numb.

"The Aristene cannot marry."

"I know," he said. "And I know that is the life you planned. But I'm asking because maybe the Aristene were never a choice—you were orphaned when they found you and alone. But you don't have to be that, Reed. I could be your family. I want you. And not only for a night."

Reed sat in the silence.

"But you would make me eat eels," she said, and Hestion smiled.

It was another life that he offered, something Reed had never allowed herself to imagine. Since the moment she'd walked into the dome of the Citadel, her future had been set. Yet sitting in the grass of the meadow with Hestion she could see a different future: a good, long life, without goddesses or an ancient warrior's magic. A good, long life of peace.

"Reed?" he asked.

"I will consider it," she said. But she said so very quietly, afraid that in the white city, Aster would overhear.

Reed found Lyonene after she and Hestion had returned from hunting. Or rather, Reed happened across Lyonene, where she sat atop a slanted rooftop, her long tanned legs stretched out and crossed at the ankles with a jug of wine upon her lap.

"Where's the feast tonight?" Lyonene called down. "I saw you come back into camp with two horses loaded down with stags and strings of grouse and rabbits hanging around their necks like furry, feathery garlands."

"Some will go to the men on the beach and some to Belden's villa."

"None to Alsander? Do you want me to waste away, chewing on boiled saddle leather?"

"I don't think you're down to that just yet," said Reed, and Lyonene patted the space beside her. Reed went inside the empty building and up the stairs to the balcony, where a stack of crates made for an easy jump to the roof. "What are you doing up here, Lyonene?"

"What were you doing out there, *Reed*?" Lyonene countered. She cocked her eyebrow. Then she sighed. "You look so well. Is that the elder's blood that you drank?"

"Maybe it's only the wine that I did *not* drink."

Lyonene snorted. "You know during the bloodletting at the Granting Ceremony I drank every drop of Sabil that she would give. And then I licked her arm."

"You didn't."

Lyonene shook her head. "But maybe I should have. And maybe I should have squeezed more out of her. Maybe they should have given me the elder's blood, too. And Ferreh's sword to match that shield. Then we wouldn't be locked outside these walls." She raised her jug toward the palace on top of the hill and mimed throwing it, as if she could throw that far. She touched the healing arrow wound in her shoulder and grimaced.

"You shouldn't have used all your ointment on Silco."

"Yes, I should have. Besides, I hardly feel it when I'm in my armor." She held her jug out so Reed could take a drink.

"Truthfully, Lyonene, I don't know what the elder blood has done for me. I'm still not that much stronger than you and still not a better fighter—"

"Indeed not."

"—and I cannot seem to fly, so . . ."

"So what does it do, then?" Lyonene asked.

"I don't know. Ferreh said we were sent into the world with a purpose beyond our trials." She looked up at the palace and frowned. "Now it seems we will not even pass those." Lyonene offered the jug again, and Reed shook her head. "Lyonene," she said as her friend leaned back on one arm. "Do you . . . ?"

"Do I what?"

"What will you do when you have to leave Alsander?"

Lyonene's brow furrowed. "What do you mean? I will leave him when I have to leave him."

"So easily? There's nothing about him you'll miss?"

"I'll miss many things. I'll miss his bed; he is quite . . ." she raised her eyebrows. "I may return to that a few times, after my Joining Ceremony is over." She lowered the jug. "Why are you asking this?"

"I don't know."

"Yes, you do. To leave them is the Aristene way, Reed. The way of the order." She looked into Reed's eyes and all traces of drunkness and joking disappeared. "Kleia Gloria, I would have expected this from Gretchen. But never of you."

"I don't know what you're talking about."

"You say no, but I can see. How he dotes upon you. How your eyes follow each other. But he is a man, Reed, and not even a man. A prince. Spoiled and used to getting what he wants, and the fact that he can't have you has piqued his interest—"

She reached for Reed's arm and Reed shrugged her off.

"But once you have given in, that interest will fade."

"You think that his feelings aren't real. That he doesn't really care for me."

"I am saying it doesn't matter! Real or false, it is the way of princes, and eventually Hestion would put you aside for some royal. Some girl with shinier hair, or a more flexible back. Even if he kept you for a year—for five years—you would age and be left, and what then?"

"You don't know him." Hestion didn't ask for one night or one year. He asked her to marry him. "You don't know any of this."

"I know that my sister Reed wished to be an Aristene more than anything in the world," said Lyonene. "And I know that I won't let one whelp of a hero take you from us."

"I am not going anywhere," Reed said, but she jerked away angrily.

"No marriages," Lyonene said. "No crowns. No oaths to anyone, save the goddess."

Reed snatched the jug of wine. "The order is where I belong. The completion of the Hero's Trial, driving a blade through my heart—these tasks are as steps I have already taken. And you're the one who—"

"Wait." Lyonene sat upright. "Do you hear that?"

Reed listened as sounds of an argument rose from the direction of Belden's villa.

"Come," Lyonene said, and slapped Reed's thigh as she scrambled to her feet. "They are up to something."

The initiates leaped down from the balcony and ran through the port to the villa on the hill, where the argument continued, and the firelight cast orange shadows of wildly gesturing arms. They burst inside and found Alsander, Belden, and Hestion before the hearth, speaking loudly before a small gathering of soldiers.

"So you would turn your tails and return home in defeat?" Alsander cried. "When there is a way to draw King Oreas out and it is sitting in a room inside this very villa?" Alsander looked at Belden. For weeks he had been pressing on the Glaucans to use their prisoner, to blacken Prince Oren's eyes and scar his face and post him atop the wall for King Oreas and Ostar to see.

"He is only a boy," Hestion said quietly.

"He is not only a boy. He is a prince. As we are. And as such he is a piece within the great game of war."

"There is no guarantee it would work," said Hestion. "No matter how badly we beat that child. King Oreas has devoted much to this siege. He will not give it up for one younger son."

"But Prince Ostar might."

Reed and Hestion turned at the sound of Belden's voice. As the siege had drawn out, his words had become measured and few.

"Prince Ostar might be moved," he said. "If it was not a beating that we threatened but an execution."

"You can't be serious." Hestion looked at Reed, as if she might speak. But she was not the leader of the army. The lives of many soldiers had already been lost. A prince's life ought have no more value than theirs, even though the prince was young.

Belden called for a messenger.

"Ride on a mule to the palace gate. Tell Prince Ostar that if he doesn't march his army out, tomorrow his brother will die upon the wall. Give him this—" He removed the pin from his cape, the silver stag, the emblem of the Docritae. "So he will know it was me who sent you. And so he will know that I am true."

39.

THE MAZE

They were going to kill the little prince.

They didn't want to do it. Some of the guards had even come to like him. Belden liked him, on those rare occasions when Oren forgot to be haughty and shared a joke with them over a cup of wine. But like him or not, Belden was a king. And kings would do what they felt they must.

It should have been good news for the initiates: they would finally have the great battle they needed, and Hestion and Alsander would achieve their victories. Prince Oren's death would be the Aristenes' hope.

He is a bratty thing anyway, Reed thought as she crept through the halls of the sleeping villa. *Always with his insults and sneering down his nose. I will be glad he's dead*, she added as she cracked her knuckles and readied herself to knock out the guards set outside his door.

Except when she arrived, there were no guards. She went inside and found Hestion standing beside the prince. The two Glaucan guards lay unconscious on the floor.

Hestion quickly drew his knife. When he saw it was Reed, he lowered it and sighed.

"We had the same thought," he whispered, and Reed gestured

for silence. She gestured for it from Oren as well and pulled Hestion out into the hall.

"We had the same thought but not quite," she said, her tone hushed. "You mean to set him free. But I mean to go with him back into the palace."

"For what purpose?" Hestion asked, and Reed shrugged.

"To return him to his home. And then to tie him up in a corner while I sneak through that home to open the gate from the inside."

"Reed," Hestion whispered. "That is madness."

"Do you have a better plan? We are down to this or executing a child."

Hestion glanced around the villa. He knew, too, that Belden would make good on his word. His brother had no choice. "How do you expect him to get you beyond the gates?"

"How did you expect him to do it himself?" she asked.

"I was going to take him into the hills and let him go there. Let him find his own way overland."

"Leave him to stumble around in the wilderness. Good, that's what he deserves. But I was thinking that he might know another way. He had to get to us somehow, that first night when he crept through the marketplace like a ghost. If there are secret routes through Roshanak, he will know them."

Hestion considered it. After a moment, he nodded, and he and Reed went back inside to Oren. They found him searching the sleeping guards for weapons, and he came up with a dagger, pointed at Hestion's chest.

"Stop that," Hestion said, and knocked it away. "We're here to free you."

"Why?" the prince asked. He looked at Reed knowingly. "Oh. Because you are a woman and do not wish to see me killed. Because you are a woman and in your heart you are weak."

"You're going a long way toward changing my mind."

"Do not be insulted," he said, and sniffed. "That is the first compliment I have paid you."

"Prince Oren," Reed growled, and grabbed him by the tunic. "Quiet now. There is no time to beat you." She shoved him at Hestion. "Throw a cloak over him and let's go."

Outside the villa they found the streets deserted, but they wouldn't be so lucky all the way to the palace. Near the gate, in particular, there was hardly a shadow to duck into.

"You should let me go here," Oren said.

"We're going with you," said Reed. "You'll never make it to the palace on your own. So tell me where to go—unless you want to collapse before the city gate with a dozen arrows in your chest."

The Rhonassan prince looked at her, then out at the port—his port but full of foreign soldiers—and balanced his mistrust of one against his fear of the other.

"What do you want in return for your help?" the boy asked.

"An audience with the king," she said. "For myself and Prince Hestion." To ask for nothing would have been suspicious, and she couldn't tell him that once she was inside she would find a way to lower the central drawbridge so their army could storm the palace. She couldn't tell him that her hero and his companions would cut down the rest of his family, right before his very eyes.

"Give me your knife," Oren ordered. "And your bow. I would have your oath you would not take up arms against my brother."

"We'll give up our weapons when we are inside," Hestion said. "You can't be seen walking through the port with a dagger. And there will be no more creeping. We walk, with you ahead and us behind, as if you are being escorted somewhere on my brother's orders."

Oren nodded, and together they walked down the street, past the garden with the altar of the gods, past the empty stall of the fishmonger. They held no blades to his back, for they wouldn't have needed to with such a young, unarmed charge.

"Lift your chin," Reed said quietly. "Don't look so shifty."

"I do not look 'shifty,'" Oren snapped.

"That's better," Hestion whispered. "Be yourself. Resent our presence; it shouldn't be hard."

"*Her* presence is below my resentment," the prince muttered. But he did as he was told. Despite his words, he was afraid, and Reed could tell that he appreciated having directions to follow. They passed a group of soldiers—Cerillians, and Reed was briefly worried they would raise an alarm to Alsander. But they were drunk, and only nodded as they passed, happy to do nothing and move on to whatever hearth fire had good roasting meat.

As they left the safety of the port and made their way to the city gate, Oren let out a heavy sigh and looked over his shoulder at Reed with a grin.

"When we get inside, you must stay behind me," he said. "No harm will come to you, you have my word. You will be rewarded. Welcomed."

She doubted that would have been true. But Oren looked so excited to be going home that Reed nearly stopped and turned back. He was their enemy, but he was only a boy. And he had done nothing to them except sling a few ineffectual insults.

Perhaps his brother will be spared, she thought. *Perhaps Ostar and Oren will be left here, to rule as nobles, after King Oreas is defeated.*

But those thoughts were no more than lies. Stories told to children to get them to sleep at night.

Hestion nodded to the guards set atop the wall and to the Glaucan soldiers burning fires in the old lower marketplace. The outskirts of the great city had been reduced to a wasteland: the colorful cloth of the merchants' stalls torn down, stained and scorched, the barrels of fruits and spices gone dry and empty.

"This city has never seemed so large," Hestion said tensely. He nudged Oren. "Now will you tell us where we are going?"

"You do not need to know where we are going if you are following right behind me."

He had a point. Still, it would have been nice to know.

"It is beneath the dignity of a prince to help me escape," Oren said to Hestion, lip curled. "Are all men of Glaucia so delicately stomached?"

"I have never wanted to see you executed, Prince Oren," Hestion replied. "Yet I am always wanting to see you beaten."

Reed snorted.

Ahead, the barricades loomed larger, manned by Alsander's soldiers. If she and Hestion were seen trying to help Oren escape, Glaucia would also be at war with Cerille by morning.

"We have to get out of sight," Hestion said. "And quickly."

"Quiet," Oren ordered. "There is a secret passage into the palace from the middle of the maze."

The maze. Reed tried to imagine it, leafy walls in the dark.

"None of our soldiers have found any passage," Hestion said. And it wasn't for lack of trying. In their boredom, the soldiers became as children, getting drunk and losing their way through the tall pillars of stone and taller hedges.

"That is why they call it a secret," Oren said, and pressed his lips together. "Have any of your oaf soldiers even discovered the way to the maze's center?"

"Of course they have," said Reed. But she wasn't sure. The maze that lay between the city and the palace walls was no toy but a true puzzle, another component of the stronghold. Lyonene had tried to master it twice to no avail, and the second time she cheated, using her Aristene strength to leap atop the stone pillars and map her way ahead. Yet still she returned looking surly and muttering, "The cursed thing shifts when you're not looking."

Hestion frowned. They weren't far from the opening.

"If we are caught," he said, "act drunk and say we demanded he show us the maze's secret."

They slipped quietly through the dark streets, skirting the patrols of soldiers. So close to the maze, the guise of an evening's stroll was dropped, and they slid from shadow to shadow.

"There it is," Oren whispered as they huddled against the adjoining wall, their backs pressed flat to the golden stone.

"Why is everything in this city so light-colored and hard to blend into?" Reed asked.

"Silence," said Oren, apparently giving the orders now. "Stay low. Wait for that soldier ahead to . . . Go!"

Reed and Hestion darted for the opening of the maze on soft feet—Prince Oren didn't know how to keep his steps from slapping, so Hestion scooped him up and didn't drop him until they were hidden inside the hedge.

They took a breath and looked around. The opening of the maze was wide and inviting, a safe, sweet introduction to the choking web that awaited. It was difficult to see much in the dark, but in front of them was the statue of a hawk—guardian of the maze or perhaps just a hint that it was impossible to reach the center without a pair of wings.

They followed Oren as he took off, hurrying through the tall corridors of leaves. He ignored one path for another and another after that, and Reed knew that without him she would have been lost even in the daylight. There were no markers to show him the way, no telltale sculptures or cuts in the hedge.

"How do you know where you're going?" she asked.

"Memory," he said. "I have been playing in this maze since I was able to walk."

"It doesn't seem so difficult," said Hestion as the path narrowed and crushed them together until they had to go at first single file and then sideways, the leaves brushing their backs and the tips of their noses. They had entered what felt like an endless spiral that squeezed them tighter and tighter until it seemed impossible that it would open onto anything but a dead end. Yet just when Reed was certain Oren would confess he'd gone the wrong way, the path twisted once more and revealed a thin plank, nearly buried in the hedge. They walked carefully across the plank single file as it rose high as a bridge, until their heads and shoulders peeked above the maze, and Reed and Hestion had to duck to keep from being seen. In the starlight Reed could barely make out the many turns they had taken to get there and the spiral that had seemed to go to nowhere but eventually had curled right underneath the thin, pale bridge.

She turned her head and craned her neck toward the maze's center; it didn't look much farther—she could see the fountain that marked it. But though the hawk could have flown to it in moments, there might be turns and turns in the path before they found the right one to lead them there on foot.

"I wonder how Lyonene was unable to get to the middle," she said. She saw the stone pillars Lyonene must have stood upon, and her eyes traced fast paths. She was no pathfinder, like Aster, but by the third try she seemed to have mapped the way.

"Sometimes the hedges are moved," said Oren. "Some closed while others opened. There isn't even always a way to the middle. It depends upon the day."

"Then how do you know there is a way on this day?" Hestion asked, and the boy turned and grinned. It wasn't a mean grin, only the impish expression of a child with something to show. But the sight of it on Oren's face made Reed's stomach tighten.

At the height of the plank bridge, Oren stopped short.

"Keep going," she said.

"No. Not that way. That way lies nothing but corners."

"Then where?" Hestion asked. "There is no other path."

"Wait for me to call to you before you jump," said Oren. "Or you will crush me with your bloated, Glaucan ass."

"That's not the language of a prince," Reed said. But Oren was not a royal just then—he was all boy. She watched as he scanned the hedge beside the slender plank bridge with balance as good as any alley cat—Reed had to call a little of the Aristene magic just to keep from teetering off the edge.

Suddenly, Oren jumped. Tucking his arms in tight, he dropped into the hedge with a soft rustle of leaves and disappeared.

There was a concealed hole in the hedge.

They couldn't see where it led, but they heard Oren roll out onto the gravel path.

"Jump now. You will have to crawl and roll forward when you reach the ground."

"But—" Hestion protested. Reed shrugged and jumped. After all, the brittle prince had lived. She only hoped that she chose the right place, and crossed her arms over her chest, eyes closed and expecting to feel the stab of the hedges' unforgiving branches. Instead she fell through the false top and landed on a leather sling that slid her easily to the ground. She crawled on her hands and knees, feeling ahead in the dark. Then she dragged herself out beside Oren's waiting legs.

"Not bad for a girl your size," he said.

"Stop being constantly terrible," she grumbled, and he smiled and helped her up. Hestion followed through the hedge a moment later, somewhat less gracefully. He emerged with several scratches on his arms and shoulders.

"You played in this when you were a child?" Hestion asked.

"Perhaps the children of Glaucia are not so vigorous as the sons of Rhonassus," Oren replied, and smirked. "Hurry. It is not far now."

Reed and Hestion jogged behind the prince as he touched his hand to the wall of the hedge and tracked it past dead-end turns.

"Oren," Hestion called softly, "not so far ahead!"

The boy's pace had increased to an all-out sprint. It was a struggle to catch up as he darted around one turn only to disappear around the next, and Reed regretted not bringing rope to tie around one of his ankles. If they let him get away, they would be trapped in the maze for who knew how long. The way they'd come was no way back—they couldn't climb up through the hedge and jump onto the plank—and even if they could, they had taken far too many turns for either of them to remember.

"Oren! No games!"

"What is the point of a maze if it is not to make of it a game?" Oren called softly back.

"You know, in the legends of mazes that I have heard," said Hestion, "there is always some great beast residing at its center."

"You would say that now," said Reed.

They dashed around a turn, chasing a glimpse of Oren's flying foot, and nearly skidded into him. They had reached it. The fountain, and the heart of the maze.

Reed looked up, glad to see more of the sky. The night was clear, the sky dark and full of sparkles. An obliging half-moon cast some light into the small courtyard. It was slightly overgrown, unkempt during the siege. But the grass beneath her feet was soft, and even in the dark she could see the formations of wood trellises, wound around with flowering vines, the blooms perhaps white or pink or lavender, impossible to tell exactly which in the moonlight. Stone benches sat on each edge of the space, and to their right was a covered seating area and a gilded table for tea.

The way from the palace must be easier, Reed thought. *Because no one is jumping into a hole in the hedge without spilling a tea service.*

She looked in the direction of the palace. The hedge was high and there were rows and rows of pathways that lay between the center of the maze and the palace gate. But the palace of King

Oreas loomed over them. Blossom-filled vines slithered up the southern-facing side but gave up and turned back before the first balcony, where ornamental arrowslits had been cut into the shapes of flowers. Ornamental but still functional, and Reed edged Hestion into the cover of the shadows.

"All right, Prince," she said. "Where is the passage?"

"Don't be in such a hurry. I've brought you this far." Oren wandered around the fountain and ran his hand along the stone edge, looking up at the fountain's cap of golden horses as if he was counting them. He climbed up onto the edge of the fountain.

"Now what?" Hestion asked.

Too late Reed saw the glimmer of Aristene magic sprinkle across Hestion's shoulders. Too late she felt the tingle of archers at the top of the palace wall. She reached for Ferreh's shield and remembered she'd left it behind. She had only her sword to cut arrows from the sky, and there would be far too many.

Oren raised his arms and waved them in the air.

"Don't fire!" he shouted. "It is me, Prince Oren!"

The first of the arrows fell like rain. Reed pulled Hestion close and tracked their paths, slashing them from the air as they came too close. But she couldn't get them all. One grazed her leg. Another sank deep into Hestion's shoulder.

"Follow me!" Oren shouted. He jumped into the fountain and ducked beneath the water.

Reed and Hestion dove for the side of the fountain and dropped to the ground, their backs to the cool stone.

"What is the little brat thinking?" Hestion growled. "He cannot hold his breath forever!"

"I don't think he means to." Reed chanced a glance over the

edge. The water of the fountain was deep and dark—too dark to see Oren floating anywhere in it. But even if the sun had been out, she didn't think she would have been able to spot him. Because somehow she knew he wasn't there anymore.

The water in the fountain began to swirl at the far end. Oren hadn't lied about the passage into the palace. There was a door at the fountain's bottom. And their only chance of escaping the arrows was to get through it with the boy, before it closed behind him.

"There's a trapdoor in the bottom of the fountain," Reed hissed. "We have to go through it. Now!" She scrambled up over the edge and dove into the water, swimming in the dark, her hands feeling frantically for the opening. Splashing and gurgles reached her ears and she hoped it was Hestion; she stilled her panic and felt for the current, then moved with it until she felt it start to pull her down—right through the open trapdoor. The fall dumped her in a heap with water crashing all around—she barely had time to roll out of the way before Hestion landed in the same spot, and both crawled, coughing, from underneath the fall of the drain.

"Where is Oren?" Hestion wiped water from his eyes. "He has probably run all the way to his father's throne room, the brat."

But Oren hadn't run. The wet, dark chamber was suddenly filled with the warm light of torches. Torches that were held by the Rhonassan royal guard.

40.

THE RULE OF KING OREAS

"They are mine!" Oren leaped before the points of the spears and threw his arms out between Reed and Hestion and the guards. He spoke some words to them in Rhonassan and turned back. "My hostages."

"Hostages?" Hestion growled, and one of the guards struck him in the stomach with the blunt end of a spear, hard enough to double him over.

"Do not harm them!" Oren ordered. "I mean they are my guests." He grinned at Reed. "Guests as I was once their guest."

"So, hostages," Reed said, and gritted her teeth. She could call up her cape and armor. She could strip these royal footmen of their weapons, and she and Hestion could skewer them before the brat princeling's surprised eyes. But she didn't. Hostages or not, it didn't change her plans. Get inside the palace. Fight her way to a drawbridge. Open it and let the Glaucan and Cerillian armies flood inside. And she felt much less guilty about it now.

"I will present you to my brother," said Oren as he led them toward an underground gate. "You will be safe, you have my word. And we will get the woman a fine woman's gown." Oren grinned. He looked pleased with himself, like a boy bringing home a pair of fine deer trussed and ready for the cooking fire. Reed glanced at Hestion. The glimmer of glory upon him had faded, and she worried for the arrow in his shoulder. But he could still fight. She and Hestion would break the palace open like an egg. They would fight through men as twin storms upon the sea. He would kill the king, and her Hero's Trial would be over.

And then what? she thought, and looked at him again. *What about the life we dreamed of in the hills?*

She didn't know. So she pushed the question away.

They were escorted through a gate and up a short set of stairs into the interior of the palace. Reed looked around. It wasn't as fine as she'd expected. The walls were bare, and straw and mud and bits of filth dirtied the floor and piled in the corners. It was a lower level, but the palace of Roshanak was such a jewel—she thought every bit of it would be covered in tapestry and gilded.

"This way. Hurry." Oren walked quickly out of the dark corridor. He led them up stairways and past storerooms, and the farther inside they went, the more the palace became as Reed thought it should be. She spotted long tables of shining wood and intricately carved chairs covered in soft, woven cushions. The walls lost their plainness in favor of painted murals, and embroidered hangings hung large as horses. Some of them even featured horses in life-size, and she was reminded of the mural of the Areion painted inside the dome of the Citadel.

They rounded a corner and the scents of floral oils and spices rose to Reed's nose. Pleasant smells but heavily applied. And still not enough to cover the scent of rot underneath. She reached out and discreetly brushed Hestion's hand with the tips of her fingers.

"Brother!" Oren called. He raced into the throne room, and

Prince Ostar stopped pacing and ran to lift the boy in a massive hug. There was such a difference in size and age. Ostar was a young man, well-muscled and strong. How had they managed to look so similar when the two had ridden out as the generals of Rhonassus?

"Oren," he said into the boy's ratty, falling-out braids. He whispered to him in Rhonassan, and Reed thought she heard the words for "small" and "treasure." But where was the king? As before, when she had stood below in the city with Lyonene, Reed felt his gaze before she spotted him slouched upon the great throne, which was set upon a block of metal-veined marble. Marble stairs stretched out before it to bleed into the larger marble of the throne room floor.

"You see," King Oreas said. "I told you he would return."

"By the gods," Hestion whispered.

Reed had seen the king once, depicted in the book Sabil had showed them after their Granting Ceremony. The ink and paint had rendered a handsome man in a bright green cape. But that man was nowhere to be found. In the flesh, King Oreas was hunched, diminished by the years. He wore a large ill-fitting robe of black and gold. Gold rings adorned each of his fingers. And each of those fingers tapped against the rotting head of the prophet.

But not rotting anymore, Reed thought. What skin was left upon the skull was shriveled and dry, and the eye sockets were empty. Perhaps some spoilage still dripped from the neck or drained from the ear, and that was what accounted for the smell. Or at least that's what she thought until she saw the table and the shape draped in black cloth. It was encircled by candles warming dishes of scented oil, and a censer of smoke swung from a pendulum fixed above. It could only be the rest of the prophet's corpse.

"Why did you leave it to rot?" Reed blurted. "Could you not decide what to do with it?"

King Oreas shrugged.

"Not every part of my friend is useful," he said. "But all parts are holy and worthy of preservation."

"That is not preservation," Hestion said, his voice low and angry. "That is offense, and an invitation for disease."

The king looked at Hestion with eyes like dull stones, and fear crept up Reed's back. This was no king who respected the rules of war, who would ransom an enemy prince or hold him captive. Oreas would order a spear through Hestion's chest on a whim.

"Father," Prince Oren said. He stepped forward and bowed his head. "Please. They intended to return me unharmed."

The king didn't look at his sons, but both Oren and Ostar seemed afraid to move. Did they fear him because he had gone mad? Or had they always? Reed suspected it was both. The princes were too close, and there was too much protectiveness in that closeness. Even now Ostar was poised to jump to his brother's rescue if he had to.

"Unharmed, you say?" King Oreas asked. He hooked his fingers into the prophet's jaw. His gaze slipped back onto Reed, and she struggled not to squirm.

Inside the palace all was quiet—no revelry, no music, not even the soothing twang of the long-necked string instrument that someone in the city always seemed to be playing. They'd seen few servants and only a handful of soldiers posted in doorways. The throne room was vast and open, the wall to the south a stone railing and columns, to allow in air from the sea.

"They escorted me past their own guards so I would not be

harmed," Oren explained. He looked at Reed. "I know she is but a woman—"

"This creature is more than a woman," said King Oreas.

Creature, Reed thought. Was that better or worse than a woman in his estimation? She couldn't be sure. Nor did she care. She'd had enough of the mad king and his severed prophet's head. It was time to go. Discreetly, she called her Aristene magic and sent it out in a thread to show her the way.

The teeth of the prophet clacked in King Oreas's lap, and the thread snapped like it had been bitten through.

She looked at the skull. She looked at the king. Both appeared to be looking at her. And both appeared to be grinning.

"Now," the king said.

At the word, guards flooded into the throne room. Twenty, at first. Then fifty. She didn't know where they had come from, where had they been waiting, with blades and armor glinting in the torchlights.

Reed and Hestion backed away from the advancing spears, only to feel sharp points digging into their shoulders as more guards cut off their path of retreat. But retreat to what? Through the columns to the south and over the side to fall to their deaths? The drop was too far for even a full member of the order to survive.

"Stay with me," Hestion said. He reached up and jerked the arrow free from his shoulder. Reed felt her silver armor and white cape burst through the aether.

"I am with you," she said. She ripped a spear from a guard's hands and stabbed backward, past Hestion. Hestion gripped the handle of the weapon as the guard fell, but the point of a spear pierced his leg. Another sank into his wounded shoulder.

Reed stabbed and struck, fighting guard after guard. But there was always another. She could do nothing but watch as Hestion was beaten to the floor. She swung her spear to gain them space and it closed up again before she could take a step.

"Hestion!" she shouted as a shield bashed into her. Pommels of swords hit the back and sides of her head, so she dropped the spear and stole one, swinging wildly—blood sprayed across her face and the white of her cape. She fought in a panicked rage and saw glory gleam upon the Rhonassans as they valiantly charged her, so many impaling themselves on the blade of her sword that she was forced to drop it.

So Reed stole another. She lowered her shoulder and charged like the ox Lyonene said she was. She barely felt the cuts or the tips of spears that sank into her shoulder and hip. But there were too many to fight.

The magic inside her ebbed. Hestion screamed her name. But the last thing she saw before she closed her eyes was the face of King Oreas and how much he had enjoyed watching her fall.

41.

INSIDE THE THRONE ROOM

Reed came to because someone was prodding at her wounds. She opened her aching, swollen eyes and jerked slightly; the girl kneeling beside her paused.

"You are awake," she said.

Reed looked down. The spear wound in her shoulder wasn't being prodded at but sewn closed, by a girl with bright red and gold paint upon her eyelids.

"I know someone who would like those eyes," Reed said, thinking of Sar and the Ithernan girls Hestion had told her about, who affixed bright feathers to their lashes.

"My king likes my eyes," the girl replied, and Reed remembered where she was.

She was in the palace of Roshanak. On the floor of the throne room. Bound in chains.

"Stop that." She shoved the girl gently away, wincing when the thread she'd been using to sew the wound snapped off in her skin. "Where is Hestion? What have you done with him?"

"Reed," he whispered.

She rolled over and regretted it immediately; everything hurt—but there he was: seated upright and chained to the same wall, some distance away. Her relief at seeing him alive lasted only as long

as it took her to see his injuries. His handsome face was covered
in dried blood. The wounds in his shoulder and thigh had been
wrapped with bandages but were still bleeding.

"Tend to him." Reed pushed herself up and nudged the girl.
The handmaiden was pretty, with long loose brown hair, her skin
a shade or two lighter than Reed's and soft and well-cared for. She
wore as much jewelry as a queen. The daughter of a high-ranking
merchant family, perhaps. Or a low-ranking relative of the royal
family.

"I was sent to tend to *you*," the girl said.

"Please." Reed heard the panic in her voice and felt sharp prick-
ing at the backs of her eyes. The chains at her wrists and ankles
weighed her down and she wanted to claw out of them. She would
strip the skin from her hands like gloves if only she could get them
off and go to Hestion. "Please, tend to him," she said slowly. "Or
I will make it impossible for you to tend to me."

The girl sighed. "Heseba!" she called through the archway of
the throne room, and another handmaiden in a crimson tunic and
embroidered skirt came through the doorway. The first girl spoke
to her in Rhonassan and pointed to Hestion. Reed's Rhonassan
was rough, but she knew enough to know what the girl said: *Help
me with this brute.* Hestion must have known the word as well,
judging from the way he curled his lip.

"Brute," said Reed. "A strange thing to call a man who is chained
to a wall and covered with wounds. A strange thing to say at all in
the court of a king who severs the heads of those he calls friends."

"Do not speak against my king," said the girl. "He keeps us well.
Well-fed, well-paid. He keeps us safe."

"He's brought an army to your shores, in case you hadn't noticed."

The handmaids looked at each other and shrugged. They knelt beside Hestion and quickly went to work, one washing his wounds and the other threading the needles to sew them shut.

"We do not fear that army. Our king is of the gods. None in the world is mightier." It was the first handmaiden again who spoke. Reed wondered if the other girl, Heseba, didn't speak the common tongue or if she simply couldn't be bothered with them.

"Don't waste your words," said Hestion. "They will not be swayed." Then he smiled. "And don't make them angry, when their needles are in my leg."

Reed smiled softly. Then she used the length of her chains to drag herself back against the wall, where she reclined with a grunt.

"You should have let her tend you first," Hestion said.

"I can tend to myself. Magic." She tried to make a fluttery gesture with her fingers and winced.

"I doubt your initiate magic will be closing up those gouges in your shoulders."

Reed leaned her head back, wondering what the mad king intended to do. Order Prince Ostar to execute them atop the wall, perhaps. Except she didn't think so. That seemed too easy.

As the handmaidens sewed Hestion's wounds closed and rebandaged them, Reed looked around the throne room. The high domed ceiling was painted in gold and accented by silver stars. The tapestries that hung behind the throne depicted the sea in vibrant blues and rusts, full of crustaceans and curving shells as well as sea serpents and many-legged octopuses. There were hangings of horses and of the king or his ancestors, showing them crowned and haloed in yellow. Heroic, and far saner than the crown's current occupant.

Reed stiffened as people came through the arched doorway, but they were only servants. They set out beautifully painted pitchers of water and wine and freshened the flowers around the corpse of the prophet, bending to refill the bowls of scented oil. And they prayed. Each and every one knelt before the corpse and touched their fingers to their hearts.

She and Hestion were chained past the table that held the body, to the last of the eastern wall. The room was half of an oval, and the throne sat empty with its back against the center of it, the king's black-and-gold robe puddled in the seat like so much shed snakeskin. Or at least Reed had thought it was empty. When she looked closer into the folds, she saw the black sockets of the prophet staring back at her.

"Do you feel as though we're being watched?" Reed asked, and Hestion chuckled.

"It is no funny thing to see the body of my friend desecrated," he said. "But at least I know now that my friend is gone. That head is not him. It has become something else."

Something that chewed through Aristene magic.

"I'm surprised he left it." Reed eyed the head, waiting for it to move, for its jaw to open and shut and its teeth to clack together. Maybe for it to topple from the throne and roll greedily toward her across the floor—*I would kick it*, she thought. *Send the cursed thing flying*. Or she might only scream.

"The Prophet of All is my king's eyes and ears," the handmaiden said as she moved from the wound on Hestion's leg to the arrow puncture in his shoulder. "To be watched by the prophet is to be seen by the king himself."

"The skull is just a skull," said Hestion. "And your king is mad."

"Then how did he know to expect you?" the girl asked, and washed his wound a little too harshly. "To have the guards waiting by the fountain's trapdoor?"

"Even paranoia has its benefits."

But it was more than that. When Reed looked at the skull, she felt her magic coil and tuck its nose beneath its tail. The head of the prophet saw too much, and the Aristene didn't like to be seen when they didn't mean to be.

When the handmaidens finished with Hestion, Reed submitted to her turn being washed and sewn and bandaged. It hurt, but it wasn't the pain that made her eyes tear and the breath catch in her throat. It was humiliation, that she'd failed.

"No one could have fought better," Hestion said softly. "For a moment I thought you really would break free and bring my brother and our army to save me."

"I tried," she said. "I should have tried harder. Lyonene would have—"

"No one would have," he said. "I'm only glad you lived. If you hadn't, I—"

"Don't worry about that," she whispered. "Don't think of it."

"I'll never let anyone harm you. That seems a foolish thing to say to a warrior such as you. But I swear it."

Reed leaned against the wall. She wanted to touch him, to rest her head on his shoulder. The distance between them seemed particularly cruel.

"Don't be afraid," Hestion said. "Belden will realize what's happened. He'll find a way to bash through these walls."

"He hasn't managed to bash through them yet," said Reed.

"That was before Oreas had his beloved little brother." Hestion tried to grin but winced instead. "Or perhaps he'll purchase our return. Or hold Alsander at sword point and force him to purchase it."

"They may not do anything. They may find us gone, and Prince Oren gone, and think that we set him free and ran away together. That is practically what we tried to do."

"We weren't running away. We won't need to run away to be married," Hestion said, confident even when he was patched together by stitches and chained to a wall. She didn't know if that made him stupid or just very endearing. She supposed it would depend on whether he was right and they lived.

He was wrong about one thing, though. He said that no one would have been enough to keep them from being captured. But that wasn't true.

Aster, Reed thought desperately. *Aster, I need your help.*

Through the heat of the afternoon, Reed and Hestion waited for King Oreas to declare their fates. It was infuriating, to watch the guards change and the servants come and go, to listen to the sounds of the palace and of their own army outside the walls in the port. Reed thought she heard a commotion there not long after their wounds were tended and wondered if they had discovered Prince Oren's empty room. Or perhaps she was only hearing things. It was difficult to tell from that distance, especially with her magic curled up and hiding from the empty-socketed gaze of the prophet.

"Guard!" Hestion shouted. "I need to be taken out," he explained.

"Unless they wish me to mess their lovely marble floor."

"I do as well." Reed pushed onto her knees and rattled her chains. "Guard!"

It wasn't long before they heard the slapping of sandaled footsteps. But it wasn't a guard who came into the throne room. It was Prince Oren.

"I could not ask for a more fitting escort," Hestion declared.

Oren reached them and held out his arms. "What? What do you want?"

"We need to be unchained. Taken out. Unless"—Hestion turned in the direction of the prophet's draped, scented corpse—"you would rather I piss all over that."

Oren frowned. "Do not make yourself difficult. It will only be worse."

"What will be worse?" Reed asked.

"Not the smell," said Hestion. "In fact, the smell of piss might be an improvement. You should get more oils for that corpse. Stuff it with scented petals."

Oren shook with frustration so the whole of his small frame appeared to tremble. He was a prince again, his skin cleaned, his dark hair glossy and braided against his nape, secured with clips of gold. And his tunic was a royal tunic, bearing the gold emblem of his family: the flowered shield and crossed spears.

"I didn't intend for this," he said. "And I will convince my father—"

"To reward and release us?" Reed snorted. "If you please, princeling, send in attendants to take us to relieve ourselves. I may wet myself in the time it takes you to indulge in that fantasy."

Oren scowled and snapped his fingers. Two guards came to unchain Hestion and lead him out of the throne room. Four came for Reed, along with two handmaidens.

"Four guards," she said as they helped her to stand, every muscle in her body tight and creaking. "Twice the number as Hestion but still not enough to flatter me."

"Move." One of the guards prodded her in the back with the tip of his spear. Reed walked ahead, docile, her eyes on the palace corridors. Outside the throne room the guards led Hestion one way and Reed another, to a small closed area with a pit toilet, the opening far too small to escape through and besides, she had no wish to jump down there. The handmaidens helped with her clothes and held the weight of her chains while she did what she needed to do and then led her back to the guards without a word exchanged between them.

Four guards, with more posted along the hall. Too many to fight through? She called her Aristene magic up as a test and found it ready away from the prophet's skull. At her sides the guards were tensed, despite her chains. And she may have to worry about the servants as well. The ones who had removed the bodies of the guards she'd killed looked like they might be all too eager to stick a broom handle into her path.

"You will not put her in that."

Hestion's voice rang from inside the throne room. Of course he was already finished and back inside. She only hoped he wasn't already chained to the wall.

I may have to leave him, she thought. *Leave him and come back for him later.*

But she couldn't do that. She let the guards prod and push her through the doorway, where she saw two things: first, King Oreas seated upon the throne, hunched and robed and cradling the prophet's head; and second, a small gold cage set upon the middle of the floor.

"He's right," Reed said. "You will not put me in that."

It looked like it had been built to house a goat. And not even a large goat from the mountains, but one of the smaller bouncing goats that the merchants milked in the port market. "Are your eye sockets as empty as that skull's? Can you not see my size?"

King Oreas didn't look at her. His gaze was upon the cage, as if he were imagining her already in it.

"Behave," he said, "and you will earn a larger one." He pointed a long finger, and Reed felt herself pushed from behind.

"No," she said in disbelief. The cage wasn't big enough to stand up in. She would be curled on her side or on her back. She would be on all fours. They couldn't keep her in that. She would be powerless.

"No." She dug her heels in but there was no grip against the marble. As she pushed and panicked, the world tilted, her skills and her magic forgotten. She heard Hestion's voice as if from far away and couldn't make out what he said. She only knew she did not want to be pressed into that cage.

When the door swung closed, the room spun so fast she could barely see. She turned on her side and kicked; the impact made the whole cage ring. Reed squeezed her eyes shut and reached out to feel the cold metal. There was cold metal against her hip.

"The cage could be hung, my king," someone said. "Suspended, from the ceiling. Or simply placed upon a table."

"Keep her on the floor," said Oreas. He leaned forward on his throne. "Show me your armor."

"No," she replied through clenched teeth.

The king narrowed his eyes, and his fingers curled around the rotten neck of the prophet. He nodded, and guards came with feet and spears to kick her through the cage and strike her with the blunt ends of their weapons. Hestion growled and jerked to the ends of his chains as they bloodied her nose and tore open the injuries that the handmaidens had sewn shut that morning. Beside the throne, Prince Oren stood with his fists clenched, his face a child's frightened grimace.

"Father," he cried softly. "Father, stop!"

But King Oreas wouldn't give that order. The guards would keep at her through the bars until she gave him what he wanted, so she reached down deep and tore the Aristene magic from her gut, screaming as her armor emerged through the aether. The kicking stopped. She lay, breathless in her white cape, her fingers gripping the bars.

"There," Oreas said, and smiled. "Beautiful."

42.

THE DUTY OF A MENTOR

By the time the sun began to set Reed's panic at being locked in the cage had been dampened by the simple, pure pain of being inside. She could straighten her arms through the bars but not her legs. She could turn from one side to another, but the turning hurt. Against the hard metal all of her skin was sore as a bruise, and her reopened wounds ached. The only thing that would have alleviated the discomfort was to rest on her hands and knees, but she would not be on her hands and knees before King Oreas. Not in the Aristene armor. And every time she let the armor recede, he sent in guards to beat it back onto her.

"Reed," Hestion whispered as servants moved through the room, cleaning up and setting tables for the night's feast. "Reed, I'm here."

"It would be better if you weren't," Reed whispered, and shut her eyes.

She didn't open them again until the nobles of Rhonassus arrived, their slippered and sandaled feet passing by the bars, the skin soft and perfumed. The kind of feet that had never seen a day's labor and certainly never a step of battle. They whispered about her, and one or two dropped down to get a better look. Their heads cocked and their eyes stared, and as Reed stared back she saw no feeling in any of them. No pity. Only an expectation of amusement, like they were waiting for her to perform a trick. When she didn't, they moved on, to pause before Hestion and snicker at him behind their hands.

The guests took their seats around the long tables. Soon the room was full, though notably the princes, Ostar and Oren, were not there. Perhaps young Oren couldn't bear to watch more of his father's cruelty. Or perhaps he had returned to his saddle and armor and was harassing the Glaucan soldiers from atop the palace wall.

Dishes were brought in, disguising the scent of the decaying corpse with the smells of roasted meat and spices, and the noise in the throne room rose with the feast. Musicians blew flutes and strummed soft notes on long-necked instruments. And the temperature, which had been cooling after dark, once again rose from the crush of bodies and enough torches and candles to light the space like day. Chatter, gossip, and laughter flowed freely, and wine flowed freely, and as the revelers grew drunk their curiosity turned back to Reed.

"Does it sing?" someone asked loudly. "Does it dance?"

"What kind of dance could she do inside such a small cage?" someone else shouted, and the room erupted in laughter. A young woman came and tried to teach Reed how, miming a jaunty step before the bars. It earned her claps and smiles, and then she shrugged and returned to her seat, deciding that the girl in the cage was hopeless.

"But what does it do?" a man's voice inquired. "Please, great king, you must reveal the secret behind such a riddle! Who is she, to earn such a place before your throne?"

Reed peered up. The man asking was dressed in a tunic of light green edged in gold thread. He had a youthful, clean-shaven face, and his brown hair was secured with gold rings in a style similar to the king's. When he saw her looking, he took a strip of meat from his plate and tossed it at her through the bars. "Does it eat, at least?" he asked, and the room again pealed with laughter.

"Don't hate them," Hestion said loudly, and the noise diminished. "They're only playing their parts. I saw their faces when the feasting began. The frozen smiles. The way they forced the food between their teeth. It's only the wine now that lets them pretend." He turned to the king. "They hate him as much as we do."

Reed looked around the throne room, at the sudden fear upon their faces. But after a few tense heartbeats they began to laugh, and threw their food to smear across Hestion's cheeks. They stopped only when the king raised his hand.

"She does not dance," Oreas said. "She does not sing."

"Then what does she do?" asked a woman, her long golden neck draped in long golden necklaces. "How has she earned such a lovely gilded cage?"

"She is a great warrior," Oreas replied. "She is an Aristene. A warrior of the gods. A daughter of the goddess of glory." Reed's head jerked to Oreas and the decapitated head that he cradled. Had he known all along, she wondered, or had the head whispered her identity into his ear?

"With her in this cage, our city will never fall," Oreas bellowed. "With her in my power, victory will always be ours!"

Reed couldn't help but snort as the people clapped and cheered. Many thought that the alliance of the Aristene meant victory. She'd never been so happy to have someone get that wrong.

"Another great achievement for our king!" The man in green stood and raised his hands in fists, and voices joined his own, more cries from every table, praises for King Oreas, godly King Oreas. A few even joined Reed on the floor, lowering their foreheads to the marble.

"What . . . a pile . . . of shit."

Reed froze at the sound of that voice. Throughout the throne room, the laughter and cheering died as Veridian walked out from behind the shrouded body of the prophet.

"I don't know what smells worse," she said, passing her wrist through the rising plumes of scented smoke. "This rotting corpse or the spew coming out of the mouths of your nobles." In the frozen moment, the confused palace guards nearest the prophet's alcove tensed, like they might rush her. Veridian stopped them with a look and walked farther in, brushing her shoulders as she left the offending body behind, like she was brushing off the stench.

"Who are you?" King Oreas demanded. "How have you come to be here?"

"Your guards are not very good." Veridian leaned over a noble woman, who shrank away, and sampled the sauce on her plate with a fingertip. Except for the swagger no one would guess what Veridian was; she was dressed as a vagabond, in worn leather and rags, her blond hair a tangle down her back. "And this wall is completely open—" She gestured to the south and the empty air between the columns. "Any lizard or bird or spider is free to come right in. And I have been called all of those things during my long life." She stole another bite off another noble's plate and shifted her cloak. Unease rustled through the room at the sight of her sword and the daggers strapped to her hip.

King Oreas studied Veridian silently. He stroked the rotten head in his lap and turned it this way and that, massaging the withered jaw as if willing it to move and whisper a secret, or to clack down hard on the Aristene magic. But Veridian was an apostate. Divided from the sight of the goddess. Her magic had changed its habits, the way a wolf who leaves the pack must change its hunt. Severed from Kleia Gloria, Veridian's magic was as a ghost.

"I want the girl in the cage," she said.

Reed wrapped her fingers around the gold bars as Veridian leaned against one of the long tables, stealing food and chewing.

"This girl?" King Oreas asked, and gestured to Reed.

"And the boy on the wall," Hestion added in a low whisper.

For a long beat, the room was quiet. Then the king began to laugh. The entire court laughed and laughed, as the same guards who had filled the throne room the night before filled it again, spilling into every empty space, clogging the wide arched doorway that led from the throne room into the broad hall and the antechamber.

Reed tried to call to Veridian through the noise, but if she heard she pretended not to. She appeared to be ignoring everything, including the growing number of soldiers with spears pointed at her throat. Instead, she threw her head back brazenly and shouted, "Shut up!"

And they did. To a man.

"We wouldn't have interfered," Veridian said. "We shouldn't be interfering. When some small pup"—she leveled her gaze at Reed—"gets itself caught in a trap, it is up to that same pup to figure its way out." She sighed. "But my lady insisted."

"Your lady?" King Oreas asked. "The goddess of glory?"

But before she could answer, Aster dropped from a rope onto the railing of the southern balcony, white cape and silver armor shining.

"No," she said. "Her lady is me."

Aster and Veridian attacked too fast for Oreas to give an order, too fast for the guards to react. They plucked spears from the hands of soldiers like plucking flowers from a field and swung the weapons wide. Reed pulled herself closer to the bars of the cage. Aster's magic was a thing to behold. It created space where there was none, throwing men into each other and casting them away, tossing them over tables to land in plates of food. The noble guests abandoned their dignity in favor of screaming and crawling across the floor. The throne room had erupted in chaos, yet the weight of Aethiel could still be heard when she too landed upon the balcony.

"And who are you?" Oreas bellowed as the big Aristene straightened her shoulders and lowered her brow with its crown of black ink.

"*I* am just a friend." With a heave, she threw a curved blade into the crowd—it sliced through the midsections of two palace guards before embedding itself in the fleeing back of the nobleman in the green-and-gold tunic. Aethiel jumped easily to the floor, and grinned as she drew her sword.

"Aethiel! Here!" Reed stuck her arms through the bars and waved for her to come, and the Aristene shouldered and elbowed her way through the fight, stepping on the hands and limbs of nobles cowering on the marble. When a guard moved between her and Reed's cage, she snorted at him and ran him through, lifting him high on her blade before throwing him aside to strike the wall and slide down.

"I should have tossed him over." Aethiel gestured to the open air to the south. "It is already becoming crowded with the fallen. I have been on the ship too long; I am too eager."

"Aethiel!" Reed grasped the Aristene's tunic and shook her to regain her focus.

"This cage is too small," Aethiel declared with surprise.

"I know," Reed growled.

"Where is the key?"

"With the king." But when Aethiel moved, Reed dragged her back down. "Hestion is chained to the wall. Please! Help him! Get him free!"

The black band on Aethiel's forehead wrinkled. "Aster said we were to save you."

"What good am I without him?" Reed asked. "What good is an initiate if her hero is dead?"

Aethiel glanced at Hestion, who watched them with great interest, flinching from flying weapons and kicking when panicked noblemen clung to his ankles for help.

"I suppose he cannot die in chains," Aethiel said. She stood to her full height, and Reed took a breath of relief. Hestion would be all right. Aethiel would have no problem brawling her way to him and breaking him loose. Now she could worry about herself.

Aster and Veridian were making short work of the palace guards. But neither had come close to the king. Oreas hadn't even risen from his throne; he still sat, half in and half out of it, his mouth an ugly grimace of bared teeth and curled lip, his left hand shaking around the head of the prophet. He appeared distracted, but the head did not: it turned and twitched in Oreas's grasp, tracking Aster's movements.

Reed turned toward the sound of running feet; a guard raced

toward her, his spear pointed low. His eyes were frenzied, panicked. He meant to kill something, even if that meant skewering his king's prize while it was confined to a cage. Reed felt her magic reach out and find the path of the spear—she twisted as it thrust through the bars and narrowly missed her ribs. She grasped the handle and jerked it from the guard's hands, then poked the blunt end hard into his stomach before swinging it up under his chin. He fell to the marble floor with a soft grunt.

She pulled the weapon back inside the cage. Now she had a spear, but so what? She was fighting from her knees. Frustrated, she snapped the spear in two and heaved the short bladed end into the fight—it struck a guard advancing on Aster and he dropped to the ground with its broken handle protruding from between his shoulder blades. Aster caught Reed's eye and smiled.

"Aster! The king! The king has the key!"

It was affixed to his hip, twinkling in the same gold that the cage was made of. With one quick jump Aster was beside the throne, and with one snap of her wrist she had relieved Oreas of the key and held it in her fist.

The jaw of the prophet yawned wide and snapped shut.

Aster stepped back, instantly dazed.

"Veridian!" Reed screamed. She didn't know what the head had done. She didn't know what it could do. Aster was a full member of the order; her magic was not borrowed, and it was no initiate trifle. But when the jaws had snapped shut, it had sapped her, Reed could see it.

King Oreas saw it, too. With his right hand he threw off his robe to reveal a tunic of black and gold. He got up from his throne and drew the sword Reed hadn't even known was resting beside him.

When the king rose, the chaos in the room calmed. Aster stumbled back, down the marble steps as he towered over her. He had seemed so old beneath the robe and curled around the skull of the prophet. He'd seemed bent and wizened and even weak. But King Oreas was none of those things. King Oreas was a monster.

"Veridian, get her out of that cage," Aster said. She threw the key to Veridian, and Veridian hurried to Reed while Reed watched the first clash of Oreas's and Aster's swords.

"Hurry, Veridian, hurry," Reed whispered as the apostate fumbled with the lock.

"I am trying!" But she was watching the fight as well.

Aster spun from beneath a strike that would have cleaved her in two and leaped onto a table to regain the higher ground. She had no sooner regained her footing than Oreas roared, and with one arm, flipped the table out from under her to crash across the room.

Aethiel approached the cage while helping a limping Hestion as Veridian finally made sense of the lock and swung the door open. Reed slid out. When she straightened she nearly wept from the sharp pain and the sharper relief, but the sensation lasted only a moment. She needed a weapon. Aster needed help.

"That is not the Oreas who came to my father's shores," Hestion said.

"It is that thing he has." Aethiel mimed holding a ball. "That dead trinket."

"Then let's take it," said Veridian.

"We can't." Reed grabbed her shoulder. "It does something to us. It eats our magic."

Veridian looked between Reed and the head as if she were mad. But before she could ignore the warning, Aster shouted, "Veridian, get her out!"

Veridian growled deep in her throat and took Reed by the arm. There were few standing in the way of their escape; what guards still survived had positioned themselves behind the king, and the nobility had slipped out the door—those who hadn't been able to huddled against walls or cowered beneath the table of the decaying prophet.

The sounds of Aster's and Oreas's clashing swords were nearly the only sounds in the room, along with those of Aster's boots landing as she jumped from table to railing and back again. She was buying time. She hadn't the strength to beat him.

"Let's go," Veridian said. "She will get out on her own."

"No." Reed struggled but there was no arguing with Veridian, and Reed found herself dragged toward the hall. Until Aster screamed.

Oreas held Aster aloft, impaled through the gut on the end of his sword.

Reed didn't know who shouted the louder, who moved the faster. She and Veridian bolted—Veridian raised her own sword and drew a long dagger with her off hand; Reed scooped a spear from the marble floor. They charged the king, and he tossed Aster away. When Reed raised her weapon, the first of his blows rattled the bones in her stiff, weakened arms, but Veridian struck like a snake, cutting and cutting, fighting not for the kill but for pain and for vengeance. But even as Oreas bled, he laughed, and knocked them back like he was not fighting at all but playing a game with children.

"Reed," Hestion said as he helped her up. Despite his wounds he, too, held a spear. "Are you all right?"

Her only answer was a grimace. In the center of the room the king fought one-handed, with the skull curled in his left wrist, opening and closing its mouth, chewing up Reed's borrowed magic and searching for the thread of Veridian's. If it found that thread, they were all dead. She was the only one who could meet Oreas sword to sword.

"Veridian!" Aethiel called to them from across the room, where she had gathered Aster in her arms. "We have to go now!"

Veridian looked back. The sight of Aster sparked one last fury and she swung her sword hard. Oreas caught it and broke off the blade, but as he leaned down, she reared back and kicked him, a clean blow that sent him crashing onto the table of the decomposing prophet.

"*Now* we run."

King Oreas's bellows chased them through the palace as they fled, his angry echoes ringing off the walls so loudly that at any moment Reed feared they would hear his monstrous footsteps crashing down the halls behind them. But as the sounds of his rage faded, a new problem arose: they had no idea where they were going. They ran quickly from large room to large room, through antechambers and down hallways and staircases, and somehow seemed to get no closer to the open air.

"Do you know which way to go?" Hestion asked. He waved his hand at a cloud of flour as they passed through a room of ovens and startled several servants at their bread-making.

"Not exactly," said Aethiel. She shifted Aster in her arms. "Aster is our pathfinder, and she is . . . lessened."

"Pathfinder?" Hestion asked. "You mean her Aristene magic allows her to—"

"Of course," Veridian snapped as they ran. "How do you think we found our way into this fortress?"

They raced past several more servants and members of the merchant class going about their business. They passed no guards, as all of those had been dispatched to the throne room.

"There!" Veridian pointed through a vast ballroom that opened in a wall of pillars. "Outside!"

"Wait, where is the army?" Reed asked. "And the princes? Where are Prince Ostar and Oren?"

They ran through the pillars and skidded to a stop. Across the courtyard, the army waited, guarding the gates. Prince Ostar rode at the head of it seated on his tall black horse.

"Reed," Veridian said, "you must learn to stop talking."

"Back around the outside of the palace," Aster whispered, her head resting against Aethiel. "To the east. There is a door. Tunnels."

Reed reached out and squeezed her hand. They broke for the tunnels just as Prince Ostar gave the order to charge, and found their way to the wide wooden door. Once inside there was nothing to barricade it, but the army couldn't follow in great numbers. They would have to go single file, and face them hand-to-hand, and Prince Ostar seemed in no hurry to give chase.

"Where now, my love?" Veridian asked, and Aster flicked a finger. The tunnel they found themselves in was dark, not lit by torches as the tunnel beneath the maze had been. After carefully making their way down the steps blind, Reed heard Veridian feeling along the wall and then heard something scrape and strike. A moment later orange light bathed the space as her torch caught.

They looked at each other, panting and covered in blood. Aethiel studied the ruin of her white cape.

"I like the red," she said. "In my family we were always forced to wear black, and the blood never showed." She lowered gently to her knees, and Reed and Veridian came near to Aster. The wound in her side bled freely. She was wet darkness from her hip to the tip of her right toe, and her skin was far too pale and glistened with sweat.

"I told you I would come," she whispered to Reed, and Reed pressed her forehead to her mentor's shoulder. Aster reached for Veridian. "I am sorry. You know I had to."

"I know," Veridian said. "I know, you idiot."

"We have to get her to the healers," said Aethiel. She glanced up at the low ceiling as though studying the stars. "There is still time. We go now, through the Veil."

Hope fluttered in Reed's chest. They would go through the Veil. To the healers in Atropa and the seat of the Aristene magic. Aster might recover. She might survive.

"Yes." Veridian kissed Aster hard, and quickly. "Take her. Go."

"You must come," Aster whispered. "You will not make it out of these tunnels without me."

"You know I can't return to Atropa. And what of him?" She gestured to Hestion. "Heroes are forbidden."

Reed looked from Veridian to Hestion. An apostate and a mortal hero, but what choice did they have?

"I will bear the consequences," Reed said. "Please, Veridian. Please come."

Veridian looked at Aster and lowered her head. "I will bear my own consequences."

They stood together as Aethiel rose and used her magic to open the Veil.

"I will bear none of the consequences," the big Aristene said. "Just so we are clear."

In the dark, the Veil crept close on soft feet; it stood open before them in a blink, and Reed felt the vast space of it swallow the tunnel ahead.

"What is that?" asked Hestion. "Where is the tunnel?"

"The tunnel is gone," Reed said softly. She reached out for his hand. "Hold on to me. Don't let go. No matter how long the journey seems."

43.

UNWELCOME GUESTS

The journey through the Veil was never easy, but that one felt particularly grueling. Even with Aethiel holding the path, the Veil seemed poised to pull away from them. Veridian's chant was barely a whisper, and Reed's was quickly exhausted as her magic slackened and she began to feel every injury. She also felt Hestion's fearful wonder, and his stumbling footsteps were a weight constantly dragging her back to the tunnels. But though the Veil seemed endless, it was not, and eventually they stumbled out of it into the bright, white light of Atropa.

"Aster, there's Rabbit," Reed said as the gray mare cantered to them. "Aster, do you see her?"

"I am still here, Reed," Aster said gently. "I see her."

"Good," said Aethiel. "We will take her to the Citadel. No need to bow, mare," she said when the horse moved to lower herself. Aethiel leaped into the saddle with Aster in her arms and Rabbit galloped for the city.

Veridian stared after them, her mouth closed. She wouldn't pray. Perhaps out of spite for the order, and the goddess. Or perhaps out of fear that here in Kleia Gloria's city her prayers would be heard and turned away.

"I thought it would be easier," she muttered, speaking of the journey through the Veil. "I thought at least that she might be hurried along, since one of her own was so near to dying."

Reed had thought so, too, but she didn't say so. "Maybe we ruined that," she said, and Veridian shrugged.

"An Aristene returning through the Veil from a rescue attempt she never should have undertaken, with an apostate and a forbidden hero? I suppose you're right."

"I didn't mean to imply that the Kleia Gloria was petty."

"But she is," Veridian said. "She is every bit that petty."

Veridian's eyes slid dispassionately over the city. But Reed could see where her gaze lingered: on the white stone of the Citadel, and the light blue and gray canopies in the central market. All those familiar places in Atropa that she had once called home.

"Where are we?" Hestion asked. He stood dazedly in the grass. "The journey was long, but the sun had just set. . . ."

"This is Atropa," Reed said. "The city of the Aristene. Time here isn't the same." She peered down into the streets, trying to track the path of Rabbit, Aster, and Aethiel, but the fast gray mare had already disappeared. Soon they would arrive at the steps of the Citadel. They would be met by attendants and Aster would be hurried to the healers.

She will be safe now, Reed told herself. *Surrounded by the magic of her goddess and her sisters.*

Reed looked at Hestion, and despite everything, the awe on his face made her smile.

"This is where you come from?" he asked. "This place?"

"No," she said. "I come from a land across a sea. I come from a port. And from a destroyed settlement in Orillia. But this is my home."

His eyes roamed every inch, the look in them hungry, like a dreamer determined to remember every moment upon waking.

"This is where I first saw you," she said, and gestured to the Citadel. "Up there. In that dome. Your reflection rippling in the well."

"Will you show me?" he asked softly.

"She will not."

Veridian paced the slope of the hill, irritably swatting at innocent bees when she interrupted them at their flowers. She looked untethered, alone without Aster and without even her Areion. And Reed realized something else: Veridian's armor had not appeared when they emerged upon the hill. Reed, Aster, and Aethiel had already been wearing theirs so she hadn't noticed—but an Aristene returning home always found themselves in their armor.

"Where is Everfall?" Reed asked.

"I left him with your allies. With Lyonene—" Veridian pointed at Hestion. "And with that one's brother. With orders that he not be touched. I don't need Lyonene lending out my Areion for her hero to use. Ever will stomp any prince into the ground who dares to try."

"Belden will see your wishes respected," Hestion said. "He will look after him."

"But who will look after us?" Veridian muttered. "Reed may go into the city but you and I?" She shook her head. "We may find ourselves at the unfriendly ends of Aristene swords. Oh look," She turned at the sound of hoofbeats. Two Aristene riders approached on their immortal mounts. "Here they are now."

The riders slowed at the crest of the hill. Both had swords upon their back and one a small crossbow hanging from her hip.

"Did she reach you in time?" Reed blurted. "Is Aster safe?"

The nearest Aristene looked down at her, though not down far; even from the back of an Areion it was hard to look down upon Reed.

"Gloria Thea Matris, Initiate Reed," she said.

Reed bowed her head, admonished. They were in the city now, not gathered around one of Belden's hearth fires.

"Gloria Thea Matris," she said, and when she looked up again the rider's expression had softened. She wore a headband of silver and had long reddish-brown hair the same shade as Gretchen's. She was no one that Reed knew.

"You were not to bring him here," the Aristene said.

"I had no choice. I will bear the consequences."

"Initiates do not decide who bears the consequences," the rider replied, and Reed's eyes flashed at her a moment before she lowered them. "The initiate and her hero are to come with us to the Citadel. As are you, apostate."

"No," said Veridian.

"You will disobey?" the Aristene in the silver headband asked, and Reed saw the rider with the crossbow slip her finger into the trigger. Veridian saw it, too.

"Do you wish to cross swords with me, Ellora?" she asked, her tone tired and a little disdainful. "After I rode to your aid when your hero's reinforcements drank themselves unconscious on poisoned wine?" The rider removed her finger from the trigger. "And you, Mol. Stop calling me 'apostate.' We all have names and we all know them. Now tell me: how is Aster? Who is tending her?"

"Veridian," Mol said as a warning. Veridian drew a dagger and in a blink it was slid up against Mol's ribs.

"Who is tending her?!"

"Mia," said Ellora, the Aristene with the crossbow. "Mia is tending her."

"Mia." Veridian lowered her dagger. "Good. Mia is the best of healers," she told Reed. "She will stop the bleeding. She will pack the wound and sew it so well it will not even make a new scar." The Aristene were hard to scar. But a sword through the middle of the gut was still likely to leave one.

"Yes," said Ellora. "So come. Come to the elders. Tell them what's happened."

Veridian turned. "Reed can go to the elders. She can tell them what's happened."

"Veridian, sister—"

"I will wait!" Veridian said loudly, and plonked herself down in the grass. "Right here, until I know that Aster is well. Then I will tumble back through the Veil and be an apostate again, wherever it is that she wants to spit me."

Mol sighed, but eventually she nodded to Reed, and Reed climbed up into the saddle behind her. Ellora called for Hestion and he climbed up awkwardly, the stitches pulling in his leg. The horses turned back toward the city, and Reed looked one more time at Veridian on the hill.

"You won't go before I return?" she asked.

Veridian looked up from under one eyebrow. She said nothing, but she nodded.

"Perhaps I will get to see that sacred well after all," Hestion whispered to Reed, and Mol chuckled.

"Perhaps you will both be drowned in it," she said.

"Is that a joke?" Hestion looked at Reed as the horses broke into a trot and then a canter. But Reed didn't know the punishment for an initiate who broke a sacred law. It seemed like it must be a joke, for Mol to say it so casually. But perhaps not. After all, it wasn't as if Reed and Hestion could escape.

He won't be harmed, Reed told herself as the Areion carried them swiftly through the quiet streets. *Heroes are sacred to the order. And it wasn't his fault.*

But a hero who wandered where he shouldn't may forfeit his sacred status. And fault may not matter, to the elders.

Her mind raced ahead, thinking quickly of what she would say, how she would convince Ferreh and Tiern that Hestion shouldn't be held responsible. That nor should Aster be or Veridian, for saving her from her blunder. But when the horses stopped in the square, at the foot of the massive steps that led up to the gold-capped fortress, her stomach wobbled in her gut, and she forgot every word she had silently rehearsed.

"The hero stays here," said Mol, after Reed and Hestion had slid from the Areion's backs.

Hestion turned to Reed. "You will be all right?"

"Of course," she said. "These are my sisters." But she made no move to start up the steps.

"You are welcome to accompany her, I suppose," said Mol. She drew her dagger. "I would just need to blind you first."

Reed stepped away from Hestion and he turned to Mol.

"I never know if you're joking," he said.

"She is joking," said Ellora, and slapped Mol across the shoulder. "And this is no time for jokes. Go, initiate. And good luck."

Reed placed her foot on the first stair. Then she looked back at Ellora. "He's a friend to my horse," she said. "In case he needed someplace to wait. Silco, the black colt—"

"We know him," said Ellora, and to Reed's relief she smiled a little. "We'll take your hero there while your fates are decided."

She wished Ellora hadn't said that last part. *We'll take your hero there*—that would have been a fine enough point to end on. Reed took a breath and started up, keeping her eyes front. When she looked down, her head swam, and when she looked up, it swam as well, as the city fell farther and farther below.

It wasn't long before her legs began to wobble. Upon the back of the Areion her wounds had begun to bleed again; they striped her white cape with red and dotted the marble stair with fat dark droplets. In Atropa, the Aristene magic was everywhere, and she felt it in her veins, stemming the flow. But even so, when she took the last step and walked into the hall of warriors, she had to lean against the statue of an ancient Aristene whose mount was a great stag. One of the Citadel acolytes came to her with a cup of cool water.

"Thank you. Those stairs were easier when I was eight."

The acolyte glanced at Reed's blood. "You are welcome, initiate. The elders are waiting." She gestured through the hall, and Reed mounted the marble staircase and walked to the first level, past the walls and walls of books, past comfortable-looking reading chairs piled with soft cushions. *Torture*, she thought, *passive torture*, and then she heard Tiern.

Even when Tiern's voice wasn't raised it always sounded to Reed like scolding, but it was strange to see Tiern scolding Aethiel, who was so strong and appeared so much older, physically. Aethiel didn't seem to be taking it well; instead of shrinking beneath Tiern's words she grew taller, looking more and more like the queen she once was, her white cape and armor streaked with Aster's blood.

I shouldn't interrupt, Reed thought. *I should wait outside.*

Her eyes blurred, and her body tumbled face down into the room. She briefly came to when she was rolled over, and saw Ferreh's face, her eyes worried but not warm. The elder's lips moved, and Reed heard Tiern issuing orders like a bark.

"It wasn't their fault," she said, or she thought she said, and then her eyes went dark.

44.

OF GLORIOUS DEATH

Reed awoke in a bed draped in crimson. So much crimson that for a moment she thought she hadn't opened her eyes and was staring at the backs of her eyelids in the morning light. But the light that came in through the cutout windows and the open balcony was the Atropan light of midday. And the bed she lay in was large, piled with pillows embroidered with red and orange flowers.

Reed sat up and pushed aside the drape to see murals upon the walls: bold suns and bright flames, seas of boiling blood. Some seemed half finished. Others had been partially painted over with something new.

"Where am I?"

"You are in my chamber." Ferreh sat at a desk of dark wood. She had been writing or drawing and set her instrument to one side—it looked like a thin length of shaped charcoal.

"Did you paint these?"

"Yes." Ferreh chuckled. "I crave color in this city of white. These are the colors that Atropa lacks. And they make me feel warm. Sometimes the city is too temperate."

Reed gazed through the open window. The breeze felt just about perfect to her. Soft on her skin. Skin that, she realized, no longer hurt. She touched the wounds upon her shoulders and found them nearly closed. The wounds in her legs and at her hips were the same. It felt so good that at first, she grinned. Then she sat bolt upright, half out of the bed before Ferreh could hold her palms up to stop her.

"How long has it been?" Reed demanded.

"Not long. Not more than hours."

"Hours?" She touched the wound in her shoulder and felt the deep itch. She wanted to scratch her entire body, to drag herself across the bed like an animal. "The Outfitter. Has she been to Aster as well?"

Ferreh shook her head. "But she has seen to your hero."

"What does that mean? What about Aster? Where is she?"

"Aster's fate lies with the healers. But I believe she will live."

Reed slipped a leg out of the bed. Her silver armor and white cape had receded as she slept and they had dressed her in one of the initiate tunics, the shoulder folded and knotted tightly, the silver-embroidered edge sparkling even in the shadows. Ferreh, too, was no longer in her armor but in a simple gown of undyed linen with a thick gold belt.

"Can I go and see her?" Reed asked.

"Soon."

"Where is Hestion?"

"In the stable where you said to bring him. Perhaps taking a nap with my Amondal and your black colt." Ferreh's eyes wrinkled at the corners. But Reed remembered the look in those eyes when she had fallen to the floor.

"What will our punishment be?" Reed asked.

"What your punishment *should* be," Ferreh said, "is to be ridden through the Veil to have your throats cut. And be buried where you fall, returned to the earth so you may be reborn to try again. But what should be is not what will be."

"It wasn't their fault," said Reed. "Not Aster's, not Veridian's. Not Aethiel's. And Hestion we gave no choice at all."

Ferreh sighed. She stood and came to sit on the foot of the bed. She ran her hand over Reed's dark hair. "The hero does as he is advised. He trusts you. And he loves you, if I am not mistaken."

"Is that wrong?" Reed asked. "Is it forbidden?"

Ferreh chuckled. Silly initiate. Silly, still-mortal girl. "No feeling is forbidden," she said. "As long as you do your duty to the goddess."

"What about Aster? Will she be punished for interfering?"

"To join the order, an initiate must earn her own way." Ferreh looked down. "But Aster's grief for her lost initiate still clouds her judgment. She should have come to us instead of going to an apostate, even if that apostate was Veridian. She should not have involved Aethiel without our permission. And Aethiel should not have helped her. But Aethiel, too, is a special case." Ferreh sighed. "An immortal order of warriors soon finds itself filled with special cases." She touched Reed's hair again, as if implying that she, too, was one.

"What makes Aethiel special?" Reed asked.

"Aethiel is special because she was once a queen. And being a queen is difficult to forget. She also comes from a place where royal sisters are forced to kill one another in order to ascend the throne. So it is only to be expected that she be protective of sisters whom she doesn't have to kill. Anything Aster asked, Aethiel was never going to refuse. We know this about her, and we knew it when she joined us."

Reed looked out across the city. Ferreh's chamber faced north, and the balcony showed the sides of distant, green hills and the sparkling sea, the northern marketplace with its bright canopies and quiet merchants, and pens full of well-behaved goats and sheep.

"Have I failed?" she said. "Is it over?"

"And if it was?"

Reed looked down. If it was over she would take Silco out of the stable. She would take Hestion and return with him to Glaucia to be a wife there in the wild green forests of the Docritae. She would be a mother. She would be happy.

She looked at Ferreh.

"It can't be over."

Ferreh held out her hand.

"It is time for you to know. Come with me into the dome."

Inside the dome they found Tiern already waiting.

"I was wondering how long she would sleep," Tiern said. She looked at Reed. She didn't seem angry. Rather she seemed impressed that she was there, perhaps that she was alive.

Reed fidgeted under the strange elder's gaze. She'd never felt the connection to Tiern that she had to Ferreh. Ferreh, who had presided over her Granting Ceremony, who had sent Reed her shield. It left Reed with a feeling of mistrust for Tiern that was unfair.

Reed glanced up. Above, the painted face of Kleia Gloria blazed upon the ceiling. As a child in the dome, she'd thought the goddess had looked like Aster and like her mother and not like either of them at all. Now it seemed that the painting looked very much like her mother, but only, she realized, because she had begun to forget what her mother had actually looked like. The image had become a jumble of sensation and recalled moments, an impression of dark hair and fierce stances. Though she could still see the precise movements of her mother's final fight: the angle of her shoulders when she charged the raider, the white of her teeth as she snarled at him.

Reed would have preferred to keep a different memory. But what was kept and what was lost was not up to her.

Mortal lives are short, she thought. *We are made to forget and be forgotten.*

But did that change for an Aristene? Aster and Ferreh did not seem to forget much.

"Why did you send your shield to me?" Reed asked. She skirted the flat silver of the World's Gate and followed the elders to the sacred well. Ferreh removed the heavy slab and leaned down, her hands resting atop two different stones, one pale and rough, the other dark and smooth and veined through with white. Different stones from different places, stacked together to their waists. As she drew nearer Reed could smell the water, cool and mineral.

"Why did you send both of your initiates to the war in Rhonassus?"

The elders traded a glance.

"It was because of King Oreas, wasn't it. Because of the head of the Scylloi Prophet. You were aiming heroes at that head."

"Of course we were," Tiern said. "And we thought that the magic of initiates might fare better against its attack."

"I thought the order didn't take sides," said Reed as Tiern walked around the well, her gait easy and swinging, her strange hair of blond and brown and silver and red tied behind her head with a strip of leather.

"The order doesn't take sides," Tiern replied. "But Kleia Gloria does when she is threatened."

"A force is rising, Reed, against the order and the goddess." Ferreh reached into the well and swirled the water with the tip of her finger. Her face, once in shadow, filled with the rippling light of reflected images. She beckoned for Reed to come.

In the well Reed saw Aristene warriors, covered in blood. She saw their bodies burning upon pyres. She saw Atropa abandoned, the Citadel a crumbling ruin, the great gold dome tarnished and dull. She saw the end of the order.

Reed looked at Ferreh. "King Oreas . . . he will do this?"

Ferreh waited for the water in the well to grow still and for the flickering light to disappear.

"I do not know. But he is the start of it."

"That's not possible." The order was too strong and too protected. It could never be toppled. But the mere thought that someone would try filled Reed with rage. Her anger must have shown on her face, because Tiern looked at Ferreh and nodded.

"Do you remember what I said to you here, the day that Aster brought you to us?" Ferreh asked. "I brought you here, to the center of the Citadel, and we looked up together." She raised her chin and Reed's eyes followed, up to the mural of the goddess.

"I told you that she wanted you just a little bit more than she wanted the others."

Reed's brow furrowed. Much of that night had been blurred by the distance of years. "I don't remember that," she whispered. But part of her did. The sound of Ferreh's voice was a vague, warm whisper at the back of her mind, and it would explain why she had loved Kleia Gloria so much and with such easy, childhood speed. Because the goddess had loved her first.

"That was just something you said to convince me to train," Reed said.

"Perhaps," said Ferreh. "But it was also true."

"Why?" Reed asked.

"Because glory is glory"—Tiern walked around the side of the well—"but not all glory is equal. The glory of a hero who raises her family into royalty by surviving court politics and seducing a crown? That is good. The glory of a hero who hunts nightmare forests and returns with the head of a monster—that is better. But the most celebrated is the glory of the hero who slays their monster . . . and perishes in the attempt."

"You have heard it said that some Aristene have special purpose," said Ferreh. "No doubt you have heard me referred to as the mind of the order and Tiern as the teeth. I would have been the one called to guide that hero through the court and into her crown."

"And I would have guided the one who returned with the head," said Tiern.

"But you, Reed," Ferreh said, "are to guide those heroes who do not return. You are an Aristene of Glorious Death."

"What?" Reed asked.

"Few are strong enough for such a calling," said Ferreh. "But I saw the potential within you from that first night. When you came to us, a child shrouded in blood. That is why I chose you. That is why I gifted it to you, in the blood I shared at your Granting Ceremony.

My blood, given in secret. I have imbued you with glorious death."

"Every hero you are called to," said Tiern, "every quest. No glory burns brighter. No legend endures longer than those of heroes who give their lives in pursuit of their greatness."

Reed couldn't breathe. She must have misunderstood. Every hero she was called to, every single one, was fated to die?

"But not Hestion," she said. She glanced at Tiern, and the elder's smile chilled her to the bone.

"Yes, Hestion," Ferreh replied. "It was Hestion who made me sure. That night when you broke the surface of the well—for a child so young to be called to one whose glory was destruction—that's how I knew that you possessed the will to carry this burden. It was as if the goddess herself had said so."

"No," whispered Reed. "It's a mistake."

"It is no mistake." Tiern's hand shot out and grasped Reed by the wrist. In two fast motions she pulled Reed to the mouth of the well and used her dagger to slice a shallow cut in the bottom of Reed's arm. "Look," she said. "See."

Reed's blood dripped into the water and the well ate it up, ripples becoming waves that splashed against the deep stone sides, and the waves became a whirlpool to peer down into. The well showed her the inside of Oreas's palace. She saw herself and Hestion rush forward as the reflection of Oreas rose like a monster. She saw Hestion dive for the head of the prophet and saw Oreas's hand grip the back of Hestion's skull.

Reed twisted loose, gasping. She hugged her bleeding arm against her chest.

"The Aristene need you, Reed," Ferreh said. "We need the

strength your gift will give us if we are to weather the storm that's coming."

"No!"

"Yes," said Tiern. "You are one of us. You are ours. We will give you a new name and you will be beloved of the goddess above even Ferreh and me. You will be a legend, even within the order."

"I am none of those things." Reed backed away from the well. "I will be none of those things." She turned and fled from the dome, down the steps and through the Citadel, running until she could no longer hear the elders calling after.

45.

DESTINIES

Reed raced through the Citadel with her stomach in her throat. She barely felt her legs as she stumbled down the staircase. When she finally stopped, the Citadel steps wavered before her eyes as if they were baked by the sun.

Aster, she thought. Aster was the only safe thing she could run to.

She turned back into the Citadel and grasped the arm of the first acolyte she passed.

"The wounded Aristene who was brought here today—where did they take her?"

The acolyte girl looked at Reed's initiate tunic. "I—"

"Tell me!" Reed shook her once, hard, and the girl pointed toward the eastern wing.

"Down that hall, to the Healer's Quarter."

Reed let go and ran, ignoring the gasps of the acolytes, even as she collided with one and left her groaning on the floor. The Citadel was vast but the Healer's Quarter small—how often was an Aristene so badly injured as to require a healer?—and it didn't take long to find her mentor lying on a bed beneath a thin linen sheet. Reed crept through the doorway, afraid to see Aster's eyes closed and her cheeks swollen. But when Reed stepped inside, Aster was awake. She lay propped against a wall, with her hands folded atop her stomach. And tucked into a chair beside her bed was Veridian.

"I thought you refused to set foot inside the city," Reed said breathlessly, and Veridian jumped up.

"You didn't really think she could keep herself from me," said Aster.

"Apparently neither of us can." Veridian jutted her chin at Reed, and the thin stream of blood that marked her arm from being cut above the well. "Aren't you supposed to be in the dome, with Ferreh and Tiern?"

Reed swallowed. She wanted to tell them everything, but the words refused to take shape. Aster held out an arm and Reed rushed to her bed and knelt to tuck her head against Aster's shoulder.

"What's wrong?" Aster asked. "It cannot be only me in this bed."

"I didn't know," Reed whispered. "I didn't know how much joining the order would cost." She felt Aster's arm tense and her mentor's head turn toward Veridian.

"You told her."

"She saw the scar that night in Lacos. I wasn't going to lie." The heart scar. The scar an Aristene gained when she drove the blade through her own chest. That's what they thought she meant, and Reed squeezed her eyes closed.

An Aristene with a long black braid walked into the room, wearing the brown-and-white robes of a healer, and Reed got to her feet. Initiates did not huddle in the crooks of their mentor's arms. Mentors did not whisper to their initiates and stroke their initiate's hair.

"Reed, this is the healer, the Aristene Mia."

"Gloria Thea Matris, Aristene," Reed said, and wiped at her eyes.

"Gloria Thea Matris, Reed," Mia replied. She had a kind face, her eyes dark and angular, her skin golden. "Aster has told me much about you." But the healer's expression seemed to say something more, and Reed wondered what else she had heard, beyond Aster's telling.

"I shouldn't be here." Reed backed up a step.

"Nor should I," said Veridian.

"You will be all right, Reed?" Aster asked.

"She will be fine." Veridian clamped a hand on to the nape of Reed's neck. "Get some rest. You'll see her again soon."

Veridian walked her out of the Citadel to the long steps, Reed's legs still weak and watery. The light of the city seemed too bright. It hurt her eyes. And the unnatural quiet grated on her nerves—she would have welcomed a bustling port full of shouting merchants to lose herself in.

"I gather that they told you," Veridian said.

"You know?"

The apostate nodded. She reached into the pouch of the bag she wore over her shoulder and brought out an apple and a knife to cut it with.

"How do you know?" Reed asked.

"I know because they tried to do it to me. It's why I left the order."

"I thought you left the order because of what happened to your initiate."

"No." Veridian bit a slice of apple off the edge of her knife. "What happened to Selene broke our hearts. But that was only sorrow. Sorrow I could have lived with. Sorrow I expected. But what the order wanted . . ." She shook her head.

"And now they want it from me." To protect Atropa. Their place of peace, Aster sometimes called it. A sanctuary outside of the world, afforded to them through the magic of their goddess. "Veridian," Reed asked. "Have you ever thought that Atropa could fall?"

The older warrior looked out across the still city. "Atropa is a mean old bitch," she said, but her voice was fond. "To take her down and the Aristene besides would take more than an army. But I know that the elders fear it. And that fear has made wise women do foolish things. Accepting initiates they shouldn't have accepted, like Aethiel. Turning me into an apostate." She cut another slice of apple. "Giving an initiate the blood of glorious death even before her Joining."

The blood of glorious death. Reed could still taste it on the back of her tongue.

"Did Aster know?" Reed asked.

"No. Aster would never have allowed it."

"Why did they choose me for this? Why not someone older and stronger? Why not Aethiel, who seems like she might like it?"

"I think that was their aim. But there was already magic in Aethiel's veins, and it made even the Joining difficult. Besides, Aethiel will still have her part to play."

"But why do they need it?" Reed whispered. "I've felt glory running through me. With every Aristene in the order—"

"It's not enough." Veridian walked slowly down the steps and Reed followed, half a step behind her on numb legs. "The world changes, and strong as we are, as each of us is, the order grows weak. That sweating, slogging, struggle through the Veil; it was not always like that. It used to be like passing through a shadow.

Now it's like the Veil is trying to bite through the border . . . to crack Atropa off and set it adrift. Perhaps to swallow it whole.

"These are the things they're too afraid to speak of." They reached the bottom and Veridian handed her apple core off to a passing goat.

"So it's real," said Reed. "It's true."

"It's true." Veridian sighed. "If you do not do this, the order may fall."

"And if I do?" Reed asked, her voice hollow.

"Then Hestion will die. And his death will be the first of many. *Or*," the apostate added, putting away her knife, "you can take him away through the Veil with Silco. Just because they lay this burden upon you doesn't mean it's yours to carry. It wasn't mine."

But if not hers then whose? Beyond the square, Atropa no longer swam before her eyes but nor did it sparkle. Since she was a child she had gone to sleep every night dreaming of the city. Imagining the day when it would be hers.

"I love the order, Veridian."

"As did I," Veridian replied. "As I do, still."

They stood together a moment as the afternoon grew later, and the shadows of the Citadel began to stretch.

"What are you going to do?" Veridian asked.

"I don't know."

Reed walked through the stable and into the rear pasture, her thoughts muddled as she followed the fences around the Citadel where they stretched toward the mountains and the sea. She found Silco and Hestion by themselves as the sun was tilting behind the

western peaks, turning the warm air soft and pink. Hestion had
his arms across Silco's back, his chin resting on the horse's withers
as Silco stuffed himself with rich, green grass.

When Reed approached Silco lifted his head and whinnied.
He slipped out from beneath Hestion's arms, and as he trotted
over, she didn't need to look to know that the Aristene grooms
had done their jobs—his hoof was healed. But the limp remained.
His shoulder hitched with every step, and his head bobbed when
it should have been smooth and upright.

"You must have missed me," Reed said, "if you're willing to
leave all that grass."

The horse breathed warm air into her ear, and bit her in the
shoulder.

"Ow!" she yelped, and Hestion laughed. He came to them, and
Reed ran her hands over his shoulders. There were no bandages,
no dried or caked blood. Only new, small scars.

"That Aristene, Ellora, gave me a cup of wine and I fell asleep
in the stable. When I woke, I was healed. This place is filled with
magic."

Reed nodded. Aristene healing lent to a hero. Another rule
broken. But they needed him whole if they wanted him to destroy
the skull of the Scylloi Prophet. And if they wanted to keep their
glorious death.

"What happened?" he asked. "Are you forgiven?"

"For now," she said, and kissed him. He was surprised but
happily so, and Reed slipped her arms around his back and held
him tight. Hestion didn't deserve his fate, for his life to be ended
so soon when there were other glories he might have, other deeds

he might do. But fate came to all, deserving or not.

"Reed," he whispered, his breath heavy in her ear. She hadn't realized how she'd been kissing him, too lost in her thoughts. "We should go inside," he said, fingers curling around the edges of her tunic. "Or . . . behind that rock."

"Soon," she said, and kissed him again. But first they would have to kill a king and win a war. Because as much as Reed loved Hestion, she also loved Aster and Lyonene and vagabond Veridian, and she couldn't let them face such a danger if she could be the one to stop it. She had been found for this. Raised for it. She would save the order, and she would save Hestion, and then they would go back to Glaucia with Silco and Belden and Sar, to live as mortals. Gretchen was right. One good life was not worth less.

"The skull of the prophet," she said, her hand against his chest, "you saw what it does to our magic. A threat like that can't be allowed to remain. We have to destroy it."

Hestion reluctantly stepped back. "You're right. But how?"

"Go and wait for me in the hills where we arrived," Reed said. "I must see the elders. I have a plan."

Reed returned to the Citadel. She found a room where weapons were stored and let the elders come to her as she took fresh daggers for her belt and selected a new sword, turning it back and forth before the candlelight.

"So you have chosen," Ferreh said.

"It was not a choice," said Reed. "Or at least it wasn't much of one."

"And Hestion? You are ready to lead him to his glory?"

"No." Reed slid a blade into her belt. "My hero and I will return to the war to face Oreas. But Hestion lives."

Tiern and Ferreh looked at each other.

"If he lives, you will fail your trial."

"But I will still destroy the head of the prophet," Reed said. "And the order will be safe."

"Reed," Ferreh said gently. "We need you."

"And you would have had me. I would have served. But not like this." She looked at the elders. She had admired them, and feared them, almost as the goddess herself. "One of you must come with us. We need an Aristene strong enough to breach the gate and pull down the drawbridge. Lyonene and I can't do it."

"Aethiel has already returned to the fight," said Ferreh.

"Not even Aethiel can do it alone."

"I suppose that I will go," Tiern replied. "If I cannot help Aethiel bash through one drawbridge, then I have no business residing in this Citadel or wearing this armor." She tightened the buckles of the bracers on her forearms. "But I will be of no help to you inside the palace. The head of the prophet cannot be destroyed by one of us."

Reed nodded. That part would be up to the initiates.

"Wait." Ferreh turned away to pace and turned back, her dark eyes troubled. "This is too much interference. The order cannot deviate so far—"

"The rules of the order will not matter if there is no more order to follow them." Tiern sucked in her cheeks. "I am going. And I'm taking your horse with me. Initiate, let's go."

Together, Reed and Tiern left the Citadel and hurried down the stairs into the fading light. When they reached the stable, Tiern went inside to retrieve Amondal, the Desert Fire. Reed called for a horse, and as it was being brought, Veridian emerged from across the square.

"Reed! I saw Hestion go into the hills. What are you doing?"

"I'm going to do what I set out to do. I'm going to help my hero. And I'm going to help the order."

"So you'll let him die?"

"I'm going to save him."

"Reed," Veridian said gravely as Reed sprang into her horse's saddle. "You can't."

"I can," she said, and backed her horse away.

"What if you don't come back? What do I tell Aster?"

Reed paused as Tiern returned on Amondal and the splendid blood bay Areion reared high in his eagerness to be off.

"Veridian," Tiern said, her voice a mix of disdain and surprise. "For an apostate you have certainly entwined yourself in the order's business." Veridian set her jaw and stepped back. "Come, initiate!" Tiern ordered, and thundered away.

"Reed!" Veridian called when she moved to follow.

Reed pressed her lips together. There was nothing she could say to Aster that would have been sufficient. "Don't tell Aster anything," she said finally. "Everything we've been to each other she already knows. And Veridian!" she called over her shoulder as her horse galloped into the night. "If I don't survive this, make them build one of those statues of me in the hall."

46.

A HERO'S TRIAL

Reed, Hestion, and Tiern emerged through the Veil on the beach before Roshanak. In the light of the moon the fortress upon the hill glittered as if lit by a thousand torches, and the glow from each caught the armor of a soldier in Rhonassan gold. Inside, the Rhonassan army waited, jostling against each other with ready spears and swords. Prince Ostar and his finest fighters. Young Oren in his too-large breastplate. And nestled in the heart like a well-fed insect was the king, huddled beneath his deceiving wrinkled shroud and clutching the head that ate their magic.

"Go and find the other initiate," said Tiern. "I will find Aethiel and have her ready for the charge." The elder didn't wait for a response before turning Amondal and galloping down the beach.

"She's a fierce commander," Hestion noted, behind Reed in the saddle.

"Fierce and eager. And I don't know why she's giving orders; this was my plan."

They rode for the port, where their arrival sparked an immediate uproar. Soldiers roused themselves from sleep and poured from buildings to swarm their horse.

"Aristene," they said. "Prince Hestion! The Aristene and the prince have returned!" Men called for Belden and shouted questions about where they'd been, but she and Hestion ignored them. They simply rode until Reed saw Lyonene shouldering her way through the crowd.

Reed jumped from the horse and Lyonene threw her arms around her.

"Where have you been?" Lyonene hissed into her ear. "There has been talk that you had deserted—"

"You should know better," Reed whispered. "I would never leave you."

"I didn't say that I believed it."

Reed spoke to Hestion, who was still mounted. "There's much I need to explain to Lyonene. Go and find Alsander. Meet us in Belden's villa."

He nodded. "I'll saddle Target and have this mare ready for you in the lines."

"Not Target, damn you," Reed snapped. "Stay on this hard-to-see, dark brown horse." She reached for his arm. "And don't do anything unless I'm right beside you. Do you understand?" He didn't understand, that was plain to see. But he trusted her and nodded before he rode away.

"Reed," Lyonene said quietly. "What's happened?"

"Tiern is here." Reed grasped Lyonene's shoulder. "She's going to break down the drawbridge and get us inside the palace."

"Tiern." Lyonene's eyes quickened. "Why is there an elder here?"

Reed tugged her aside, their purposeful strides sending soldiers scattering. She told Lyonene what had happened, of their capture and their encounter with King Oreas and the head of the Scylloi Prophet as the sounds of the army rose around them with the drowsy snorts of horses and the shouted orders of men. It was all happening quickly. Soon enough, the air would no longer smell of salt and the sea but of blood.

"How did you get out of Oreas's cage?" Lyonene asked.

"Aster had to save me," Reed said. "As you'd expect. She was nearly killed doing it, but we made it to Atropa in time."

"You brought your hero to Atropa?"

"Yes," she said. "I know. My every step is a blunder worse than the last. But we're here now, and we have Tiern. And we'll need her to get inside, where you and I must destroy the skull."

"It eats our magic," Lyonene said. "How are we to fight it, then, if we won't be strong?"

"We were strong before the magic. We trained without it. And we'll be surrounded by heroes."

Lyonene humphed. "So we will be. This is it, then."

Reed nodded. She had told Lyonene everything—except for her fate, the blood she'd drunk, and what Ferreh and Tiern had conspired to turn her into.

The initiates made their way to Belden's villa. They didn't have to wait long before they were joined by the princes.

"Aristene," said Belden. He took her by the arms, pleased to see her safe. "My brother has told me of your time in the palace of King Oreas."

"And of your release of our captive," said Alsander.

"Don't be angry," said Lyonene. "If she hadn't returned Prince Oren, we would never have known what we faced."

But Alsander wasn't angry. And he was no longer a princeling. He was a hero and he looked like a king, and though Reed would never forgive him for sabotaging the horses, she swelled with pride for her friend. Lyonene's heroes would achieve great things and perform great deeds, and they would live to tell the tales of them.

"Is King Oreas really so fearsome an enemy as Hestion says?" Alsander asked.

"You think I exaggerate?" Hestion gave him a shove.

"According to your brother, you often do. And you faced this monster and yet return with not a scratch?" The princes smiled at each other, even Belden, who was usually so grounded and practical.

"Do not go into this as fools," Reed cautioned. "Don't believe the rumors of your own immortality." She looked at Belden as the older prince's eyes turned dark. "King Oreas is everything that Hestion said he was," she said. "And worse."

"Then we go," Belden said, and Hestion and Alsander quieted. "For glory and for the prophet, not only into war but to slay a monster." He turned to the initiates. "What is your plan?"

"Tiern and Aethiel will bash through the drawbridge," said Reed. "Then the army must cut through the Rhonassan forces and get inside the palace. Finding Oreas will be up to us."

"The men are ready," Alsander said. "They are tired of waiting. We will take this city tonight."

"Tiern and Aethiel will meet us at the gates," said Reed. "Whatever preparations you have to make, make them now."

Alsander and Lyonene took their leave. But before Reed and Hestion could do the same, Belden caught his brother by the arm.

"I want you to know that I never wanted to kill the boy. It was only . . ."

"A decision a king must make," Hestion said. "I know."

Reed touched the brothers' shoulders and left them to have a moment alone, wandering out of the villa into the frenzy of soldiers' preparations. The sudden order to attack had shaken the siege dust from the men's backs. They knew that something had changed. Even without magic they sensed it in the air.

"Aristene!"

Sar twisted past soldiers. "Reed. You and Hestion have returned."

"We have." Reed turned back toward the princes.

"You look at him like you expect to never see him again," the Ithernan said.

"Perhaps I won't. There are many here tonight who will not be here tomorrow." She looked at Sar. He was ready for war, armed and armored, with fresh blue paint upon his cheeks. "You must look after yourself this time, Sar."

"And who is looking after you?"

Reed smiled. "I need no looking after."

"Normally I would agree. But the Aristene are not the only ones who can spot someone hunting for glory. The Ithernan have a nose for it, too, especially when that glory is foolish."

She looked at Sar quietly. She could lie to him, she supposed. But she found that she didn't want to. How strange it was that she looked at the blue upon his cheeks and no longer felt revulsion. She saw only Sar—foolish Sar who now thought to lecture her on foolishness. Wild Sar, who had become her friend.

"If you mean to do this to protect him," said Sar, "to put yourself in harm's way . . . He would not want me to let you."

"Do you think you can stop me?" she asked, and he grinned.

"No," he said. "You and I are warriors, Reed. We were made

for bloodshed. Made to charge at the sword and see if we can spin away in time."

He held out his hand, and Reed shook it.

"Make sure you spin away in time," Reed said.

"And you, mercenary. I will see you at the gates."

Veridian paced back and forth in the square, her sandaled feet slapping rhythmically against the stones in the dark. There was no reason for her to remain in Atropa. Aster was recovering, and the initiate had gone on to meet her fate. She'd said her hellos to all she'd wished to see there and even stopped into a tavern for a taste of the good, buttered bread that she'd missed. There was nothing left to keep her. She should be gone, returned through the Veil with Aethiel the moment Aster was out of danger.

But she had one last bone to pick.

Veridian took the stairs up to the Citadel by threes and didn't stop until she reached the interior of the dome lit by moonlight.

"You're lucky no one spotted you," said Ferreh, where she leaned against the railing. "For an apostate to set foot here . . . you might have been dropped by an arrow."

"Is that supposed to frighten me?" Veridian asked. "When we all know what leniency you show to your Aristenes of Glorious Death?" She walked across the dome to the elder, ignoring the pull of the sacred well, which she still felt. She kept her head low, to keep from looking up into the eyes of the goddess she had spurned.

"Another refusal." The apostate clucked her tongue. "Two attempts and two failures. That must sting."

Ferreh crossed her arms and chuckled. "Is that why you've

invaded this holy space? To rub it in?"

"No indeed. For what fun is it to heckle you, who is always beautiful, always unflappable, even in defeat?" But it was clear that the elder was troubled. Ferreh stood in the dome in her armor, silver and white in the moonlight. She rarely did that, unless there was a ceremony to be done, or if she needed to feel the goddess close at hand. "If Tiern was here," Veridian raised her brows. "Now that would have been a worthwhile ribbing."

"If Tiern was here she'd have put out your eyes," Ferreh said, and laughed. "I have missed you, Veridian."

"Then you shouldn't have driven me off. Like you shouldn't have driven Reed off. What did you do it for, Ferreh? Did you see what she'd suffered and thought an eternity of more suffering couldn't hurt? And to give her to Aster after what happened to Selene. You have been hard at times, but you've never been cruel."

For a long time Ferreh stood still as a statue. Veridian couldn't even detect her breath. Then she inhaled and rose off the wall, and Veridian stepped back as she approached.

But Ferreh simply lifted her hand to Veridian's cheek. The elder could speak much through her eyes, and Veridian needed no words to understand: it would have all been easier had Veridian just done as she'd been asked.

"Can I change my mind now," Veridian said, "to save her?"

"You are always welcome to change your mind," Ferreh replied. "Always welcome to return to us. But it will not change who Reed is."

"*What* she is, you mean. What you've made her into."

Ferreh looked down upon the white city. Her city, for as long as anyone alive could remember it.

"No," she said. "That is not what I mean."

Ferreh walked calmly through the dome. Veridian followed after and watched as she uncapped the well with an easy, grinding of stone.

"Ferreh," she said. "Why don't you seem disappointed?"

Ferreh reached down to the still, inky water and touched it with the tip of her finger. When she drew back, the water pulled back with her, sticking to her finger like a spider's web before bouncing back and showing Reed among the ripples.

But it wasn't Reed as she was now. It was Reed as she was all those years ago when they'd found her. When she was a small skinny thing who bit Veridian's hand.

"You and Aster are not the only ones who care for her," said Ferreh. "And you are not the only ones who know her. I, too, have watched, from the waters of the well, as she grew and trained. As she failed and won, fell down and got back up again." The elder smiled. "Reed is like any who is faced with these choices and has their moment of doubt. But it will not change who she is. So no," Ferreh said, and whisked the image of Reed away with the palm of her hand. "I do not seem disappointed. Because I know in the end that Reed will not disappoint me."

Belden, Alsander, and Hestion waited, mounted on their horses upon a rise at the rear of the army. Their faces were lit by torches held by grooms, and past them, assembled on the beach, the allied forces of Glaucia and Cerille waited in the dark like an expansion of the sea, their movements rippling in waves and currents, the silver of their weapons glinting like the moon and stars off the water. Tiern and Aethiel were mounted a short distance away, with expressions like hunting hawks. Aethiel's black band stood out starkly against her forehead. Tiern had used kohl to blacken a stripe around her eyes.

Their presence made the soldiers uneasy. Anyone could see that they were not like Reed and Lyonene. In their war armor their power radiated and made them as gods upon their saddles.

"What is your plan to break down the drawbridge?" Belden asked as Reed and Lyonene rode up beside them.

"They are the plan." Reed nodded to Tiern. "She is an elder of our order. She will breach it."

Belden glanced at Tiern. "If we were able to send fifty men over the wall they would fail. I do not wish to doubt the Aristene but . . ."

As he spoke, Aethiel's black eyes burned like coals, but Tiern didn't react. Amondal simply shifted his feet and then both horse and rider rolled their eyes.

"Such doubts are tiresome," Tiern said loudly, and Reed couldn't tell whether she was speaking to her or to Aethiel or to the stallion. "But after tonight, no such words will ever escape his lips again. I require a charge," she called to the princes. "Men to appear to attack the wall, to throw their rope hooks atop it. Then to retreat and move clear. We will handle the rest."

"The Docritae will do this," said Belden. "We will land our hooks upon the wall. And we will be the first across the bridge to face the army."

Not the Docritae, Reed thought. *Not Hestion.* The losses of those first to cross would be the heaviest. But Belden was the leader. Belden would be king. And as she watched, strands of bright glory wound themselves around his and Hestion's shields like ribbons.

"Once we're inside," Reed said to Hestion, "stay with me."

"Always," he replied, and nodded.

Reed rode to Tiern and slipped Ferreh's shield from her back. "Take it."

"You'll have more need of it than I," the elder said.

"If the skull eats through my magic, I won't even be able to lift it." She thrust the shield out again. "You have her horse. She would want you to use it to look after him." Reed looked at Amondal, and the Areion's wise eyes looked back at her. He felt no fear, and he had fought in more battles than the initiate could dare to imagine. He snorted, and Tiern took the shield upon her arm.

"Go on, then, initiate," Tiern said. "Find these Docritae and order them to clear a path."

Reed nodded. Tiern smiled, and in the light of the torches her teeth appeared elongated like fangs. As Tiern began to salivate, Reed wondered how long it had been since the elder had seen a battle and began to pity the Rhonassans that waited behind the drawbridge.

Belden and Hestion summoned the Docritae to the outer gates. The entire army spilled into the city behind them, so many soldiers that Reed felt the ground give beneath their weight as they marched. Soldiers began to shout, and the Rhonassans echoed with cries of their own until it was nearly too loud to think. Reed and Hestion, Belden and Lyonene and Alsander were crushed in the throng on their horses, pressed so tightly together that their knees ground against each other's saddles.

Only the Aristene appeared to enjoy the crush of the advance.

Aethiel's laughter boomed over the noise of the men, and Tiern's grin had only grown, the hunger and menace in it so great that Reed wouldn't have been surprised to see her stab a dagger through the head of the soldier nearest to her just because she couldn't wait.

The army lined up before the drawbridge. It was cut into the high walls that surrounded the palace, broad enough that when opened twenty men could run across it shoulder to shoulder.

"Sar and I should lead the men to lay the ropes," Hestion said. He looked at Reed. "You and I will follow for the charge after your elder drops the bridge."

"No," said Reed. "I'll go with Sar. You stay here with your brother, and I'll rejoin you for the charge." She turned and Lyonene caught her arm.

"What are you doing, Ox?" She glanced at Hestion.

"We'll need him inside," Reed said as she swung down from her horse.

"We'll need you as well."

"I will be fine. I just have to look after Sar." She took the sword from her back. "He seems to attract arrows. Or maybe the blue on his cheeks simply makes him a good target."

"Reed—" Hestion dismounted and reached for her. "What's happening? Why do you keep me here?"

"You have to trust me." She pointed her sword at Belden. "Don't let him out of your sight until I return!"

"Reed!" Hestion shouted, but she ignored him and moved through soldiers until she reached Sar's side.

"I thought you said I would have to look after myself," he said with a grin.

"And yet you agree to lead the first charge."

"Hestion says to me, 'Lead a charge,' and I am supposed to refuse?" He handed Reed a coil of thick rope with a curved hook attached to one end. "How many of these does she need?"

"As many as we can land. Some are sure to be pried off and thrown back before we call the retreat."

Sar leaned away from Reed and signaled to the Docritae. He took a deep gulp of the night air, and Reed jumped ahead, surprising him so he nearly choked on it.

"Go, go!" he shouted, and the Docritae raced toward the drawbridge. Reed drew up her borrowed magic like a cloak and threw her hook without breaking stride. It sailed through the air over the heads of the attacking Docritae and overshot the top of the wall, sinking into one of the Rhonassan archers.

"You have to wait until we're closer to the moat!" Sar shouted, and Reed cut two arrows out of the air, headed for his chest and thigh.

"It will still work!" she shouted back. Her rope dangled down the side of the wall—it would only have to be yanked out of a Rhonassan soldier first.

To their right, one of the Docritae fell to an arrow and Reed took up his shield. She jumped ahead, drawing fire and providing cover for the men as they aimed their throws. She cut another arrow away from Sar just as he let his hook fly; the hook landed heavily and locked on to the top of the wall. The Docritae were gifted fighters, throwing hooks even as they took arrows to the shoulder or the gut. It wasn't long before ropes hung from the wall like banners on both sides of the drawbridge. Tiern and Aethiel would have plenty to choose from.

As Reed watched, two Rhonassan soldiers pulled a hook loose and threw it to the ground. She waved to Sar to call the retreat, and the Docritae backed off. Seeing them go, the Rhonassans raised their weapons in celebration and left the ropes alone.

Reed followed Sar back into formation. Argon stood beside him with an arrow broken off in his shield shoulder.

"Argon, you're injured."

"It did not go deep; I will pull it out later."

Reed nodded. "Look after yourself, Ithernan."

"Look after our princes," said Sar.

She slipped back through the army and mounted her horse.

"Argon and Sar?" Hestion said.

"They're safe."

"A successful attack," Belden said. "Now it is up to your elders."

Only Tiern was an elder, but it wasn't worth correcting him. Though she hadn't been in the order long, Aethiel was enough like one.

The Glaucan and Cerillian forces waited as the Rhonassans taunted them from atop the wall. The path between them and the drawbridge was clear. Only the water of the moat stood in Tiern's way, and it was not even much of a moat. From somewhere in the dark, Reed heard Amondal scream.

"Here they go."

The horses, and the Aristenes upon their backs, raced toward the drawbridge at breakneck speed. The sight of their coming brought a halt to the Rhonassan voices, and for a moment the men atop the wall stood dumbfounded, watching the two women ride them down. But ride them down to where? The only thing they raced toward was the closed drawbridge and the wall. Soon enough they would have to wheel away or fall into the water of the moat.

It should have made them laugh. But something in the charge made them draw their bows instead. They aimed their arrows down upon the horses, holding their fire until the horses began to slow. Waiting for them to turn aside and make for easier targets. But the horses galloped on.

Reed saw the first of the arrows shot, and Aethiel swatted it from the air with ease. The commander on the wall gave the order to loose, and a hail of arrows flew. Many went wide. The archers misjudged the horses' speed and arrows sank into ground they had already covered. The rest were cut from the sky or bounced off shields. As the archers reloaded, Tiern and Aethiel jumped up to crouch on the backs of their saddles.

Aethiel leaped first. She flew through the air with arms and legs wheeling and grasped on to one of the dangling ropes. Tiern took aim for the same side but in less of a hurry—she and Amondal waited out another flurry of arrows. Neither horse nor rider flinched as one sank into Tiern's arm and another into Amondal's haunches.

Just when Reed thought Tiern had truly lost her mind and intended to jump her horse straight into the wall, she sprang. The leap was so great that it carried her almost to the top—she grasped on to one of the ropes and flung herself over the wall before any of the soldiers had a chance to react.

"That horse," said Belden. "It launched her with its hindquarters."

Reed's mouth quirked. He had. And even riderless, Amondal would gallop into the city with the army. The Areion would fight with hooves and teeth and the bulk of his weight. More Rhonassans would fall to Amondal than to the soldiers armed with swords.

As chaos erupted around Tiern's arrival, Rhonassan guards scrambled to cut the rope that held Aethiel. But the Docritae had planted many, and she simply leaped from one to the next, scaling the wall like a spider before joining Tiern inside. Her bellow was terrifying as she dove upon the soldiers and Reed had no doubt that Aethiel had killed at least three just upon landing.

"They are going to do it," Alsander said with wonder. "They are truly going to do it."

Reed looked at Lyonene.

"Gloria Thea Matris," she said as the drawbridge fell.

47.

THE MONSTROUS KING

The charge across the drawbridge was a blur. A jarring, teeth-rattling, deafening blur. Reed felt the Aristene magic swell, taking it in, inhaling every clash of swords, swallowing every splatter of blood.

Her sword cleaved a Rhonassan at the shoulder as she wheeled her horse around broadside and used its hindquarters to bash men back. Hestion rode to her left, his horse injured and slowing. She sensed the frantic energy of Sar there somewhere and heard his wild shouts. But she wouldn't leave Hestion. The Ithernan was truly on his own.

Reed wiped blood from her eyes. Ahead, Tiern fought streaked in red, her sword and dagger so swift it was hard to follow their arcs. The elder controlled the flow of battle all by herself—the sight of her sent all but the bravest soldiers shoving backward in retreat.

"Where is Oreas?" Reed shouted. "Where is the king?" Dawn had begun to creep over the mountains, and the early light cast the battle in gray. Soon enough they wouldn't need the fires their army had started along the wall to see by.

"Can't you smell him?" Tiern shouted back. "Can't you smell the filth of him and the head, scurrying away?"

"Why would he flee?" Hestion called out.

"Perhaps the head told him he was going to lose." Tiern raised her dagger and brought it down between a man's neck and shoulder, then pulled it loose. The blood rose up like a fountain.

"Hestion!" Reed blocked the point of a spear as it jabbed for his sword side. The gray of the dawn was the same as the light in the vision from the well. That fate may have already been averted. But she wouldn't take any chances.

"I'm all right!" he shouted. "Look to yourself, Aristene."

The Rhonassan forces were plowed back farther when Lyonene and Alsander arrived with the second wave. The Rhonassan army hadn't really shown much heart. Perhaps it had been taken out of them by the twin scourges of Tiern and Aethiel. Or perhaps down deep, they knew their king was an abomination.

"There is the other initiate!" Tiern called. "Take her and get to the head. Do not leave until it is destroyed!"

Reed nodded. She almost asked whether Tiern and Aethiel would be all right, but that was a foolish question—a Rhonassan soldier sailed over their heads, screaming after Aethiel had thrown him.

"I don't know how she doesn't sink every ship she sails on!" Reed shouted, and Tiern laughed.

"Lyonene!" Reed waved her sword. "With me!" She turned her horse toward the palace and rode through soldiers, breaking the ranks that remained between them and the palace interior. Lyonene and Alsander followed, Alsander's bright gold stallion shining even in the dim of early morning. They leaped through the open palace archway, and Reed jumped from her saddle to crouch on the floor of the same large ballroom that she, Aethiel, Aster, Veridian, and Hestion had fled through after escaping from the throne room.

Hestion landed on the ground beside her. "Do you remember

the way back to the throne room?"

"No, she said. "You should stay with your brother."

"Belden can hold the lines."

Reed glanced over her shoulder. Inside the noise from the battle was muted, but the fighting was still fierce. The air rang with clashing swords and the screams of the dying. "Lyonene and I have to do this ourselves."

"Then why is Alsander coming?" he asked as Alsander dismounted and sent Phaeton away with a soft clap on the hindquarters. The other horses followed the stallion like a glowing beacon.

"Reed," Hestion said quietly. "What's happening?"

She looked past him, upon the waves of soldiers still flowing across the disabled drawbridge. They had breached the wall, but the Rhonassan army was larger, and its reinforcements came from both sides, flanking the advance.

"We should be losing," she whispered.

"But we won't," said Lyonene as Tiern and Aethiel cut through the lines of fresh-legged reinforcements like they were dolls filled with straw.

Alsander watched them with wide eyes.

"One day you will be that?" he asked Lyonene.

"After today I will be that," Lyonene replied with a grin. "Thanks to you."

Reed looked at Hestion. There was no convincing him to stay behind.

"Well," she said, and cocked her head at Alsander. "She may not be *that*. But she will be something. Let's go." She led them through the palace, retracing the steps they had taken from the throne room. As they neared it, she told Lyonene to bury her magic, and the initiates' armor evaporated into the aether. Lyonene adjusted her grip on her sword and glanced at Reed. The moment the magic left them, their weapons seemed to double in weight.

"Ox," Lyonene whispered. "I sense something."

Reed sensed it as well. They hadn't seen the Rhonassan princes during the attack. Both Prince Ostar and Prince Oren were sure to be lurking somewhere with a regiment of soldiers and the palace guard.

They turned into the antechamber before the throne room and listened. Silence. After a moment, Reed led the way.

"Oren!" she cried in surprise. "Prince Ostar!"

The princes were chained to the wall with the same chains that had bound Reed and Hestion, their faces swollen and eyes black. Ostar's head hung limp.

"Get him free," Reed said, and Lyonene called up her magic and swung her sword where the chain thinned. It snapped and Oren's arms dropped to his sides.

"What happened?" Reed asked. The throne room was in the same state as they had left it after King Oreas's fight with Aster, the long tables overturned and the food from the feast dried upon the floor. In the corner, the altar that had housed the body of the prophet lay empty, the candles burned out and the corpse missing. Yet the corpses of the those who had died in the battle remained. And more, it seemed—perhaps of those who had defended the princes.

"The head told our father that our hearts were no longer with him," Oren said as Reed cradled his shoulders. "No. Not ours. My heart. He said my thoughts were with our enemies. Ostar defended me. So my father beat him. . . ."

"He didn't beat him," said Alsander gravely. "He killed him."

He turned Prince Ostar's head back and forth. Oren cried out and clawed the air but Reed held him tight.

"Let him go," Hestion said, and she did. He scrambled across the floor to throw himself onto his older brother's body. Hestion's jaw clenched. "Who would do this to their sons?"

Alsander knelt and put his hand on Oren's back. "Oren. Where is your father now?" But the boy could only scream, Ostar, he killed Ostar. "Oren . . . Prince."

"No," said Hestion. "Not 'Prince' anymore. Oren, King."

His palms flat on Ostar's chest, Oren sucked back his sobs. He was the younger but he had still been raised a royal, and he knew what that responsibility meant. He looked at Reed and even with her magic buried she saw a glimmer: Oren was a pain and a brat, but he would not be conquered.

"My father did not tell us his plans," he said. "But I heard him order his guard to follow him into the tunnels, toward the mountains."

Reed stood. "I know where that is."

"Wait," said Oren. "There is a faster way: through the storage room beside the ovens."

Reed quickly led the others out, but before she left she gave one last nod to the boy. "Stay here, little king. You are the future of Rhonassus now."

Down behind the kitchens, they quickly found the passageway and went into the tunnels. Hestion and Alsander took torches from the walls. Lyonene sheathed her sword in favor of a long sharp dagger. One after the other they descended into the cool dark beneath the city.

Alsander went first, casting his torch back and forth, but even though Hestion was safe beside her, Reed fought to stay focused. He shouldn't be here. She should have made him stay above. Every step closer to King Oreas was a step nearer to the monster's hand crushing the back of Hestion's head.

"Which way?" Alsander asked when the tunnel forked. Lyonene crept ahead and looked down one path and then the other. The air around them was completely silent. There was no way of knowing which path the king had taken.

"Send your magic into both tunnels," said Reed.

"What will that do?"

"We'll go in whatever direction your magic doesn't want to go."

Lyonene looked skeptical, but she took a breath and did as Reed said. After a few moments she recoiled with a look like she had eaten something rotten. "That way," she said, and pointed left.

Reed took the lead with only her sword—her silver armor and white cape still in the aether. The head of the prophet mustn't be allowed so much as a whiff of their magic. If it began to track them, they would never be able to sneak up on the king.

The tunnel widened into a chamber lit by torches and candles, and Reed motioned for quiet. She needn't have bothered. The chamber was a dead end, and King Oreas wasn't there. Neither was the head of the prophet. The thing that Lyonene's magic had shied away from was the prophet's headless corpse, set upon a rise in the stone.

"Is it a trap?" Alsander asked, looking above and around.

"No," Reed said. "It's a misdirection. He doesn't want us. He wants Tiern."

48.

THE HEAD OF THE SCYLLOI PROPHET

Reed and Lyonene raced back to the battlefield far ahead of Hestion and Alsander, using their magic to add speed to their legs. They emerged from the tunnels beside the palace and jumped quickly atop the broken remains of a statue.

Though the battle still raged near the drawbridge, around the king the fighting had paused. Rhonassan and Glaucan soldiers alike stood frozen in a broad circle around King Oreas, who crouched over Tiern as she lay on the ground. At the sight of him, Reed forced her magic down again and grabbed Lyonene by the arm.

"We will get only one chance at this," she said when Lyonene bared her teeth and hissed. "Your Aristene strength won't last long after the head gets a taste of it."

Reluctantly, Lyonene dropped with her behind the statue to hide. They peered out and saw the king lower his face to the elder's, almost close enough to kiss. He had one hand on her chest and the other curled to his side, cradling the blackened, rotten head of the prophet.

"I have to stop him." Reed drew her sword.

"You?" Lyonene asked. She looked at Reed, and when the light came into her eyes, Reed knew that she'd begun to shine with glory. Not like an Aristene but like a hero. "Not you! Them! It must be them!"

"Lyonene. When I was in Atropa, I looked into the well. If I don't do this, Hestion will die."

"I don't care!" Lyonene grabbed her by the shoulders. "He's a hero, Reed—heroes die!"

"And you could just let Alsander die?"

Lyonene's eyes clouded. But then she blinked and looked at Reed fiercely; her fingers dug into Reed's shoulders like claws.

"Yes. I could. And I will if I must, to keep you from leaving like Gretchen!" She looked down at Reed and the shabby sword in her hand, the weak leather of her armor.

"Don't look so doubtful," said Reed, "To be an Aristene is a sacred thing, but I'm a warrior even without it."

Lyonene pressed her lips together.

"You were not supposed to be this," she whispered. "You were supposed to be ours."

Hestion and Alsander emerged from the palace and ran to them, and at the sight of Hestion Reed cursed under her breath.

"I thought you would attack without us," said Alsander. He looked down the battlefield at King Oreas and Tiern. "What is he doing to her?"

"I don't know," Lyonene replied. But every few moments, Lyonene winced, and Reed knew she could feel the teeth of the prophet open and close as it chewed on Tiern's magic. A short distance away, Aethiel lay face down, perhaps dead but certainly unconscious.

"What do we do?" Alsander asked. "Do you have a plan?"

Hestion scanned the battlefield. Near the drawbridge, Belden was still attacking, hacking through men on his black warhorse, but his progress was slow. "Spread out in the crowd and attack him. Tell the soldiers what he's done to the princes."

"To make sure no one interferes," said Alsander. Though no soldiers on either side seemed inclined to. "Where is the other Aristene?"

Lyonene nodded to where Aethiel lay face down.

"Is she dead?"

"She's not dead," Reed said with stubborn surety. "And when she wakes she's going to be angry."

Together they raised their heads above the wreckage of the statue to look upon the twisted shape of Oreas, the unnatural length of his spine and the sinewy muscle in his back and arms. It was not a man but a beast crouched there, and it had managed to vanquish the two strongest fighters any of them had ever seen.

"I've no real wish to fight that," Hestion said.

"Nor do I, if we're being honest," said Alsander.

Reed waited. Any moment and Lyonene would say something, do something to give him courage. Alsander must rise. He must fight now, and gloriously, for Lyonene to pass her trial. But Lyonene, too, looked afraid.

"Alsander," Reed said. "This is your chance. Kill the king. Claim the crown."

"Young Oren wears the crown."

Reed grinned, a wild grin like she had seen on Sar. "But he's a boy. He'll need someone to share his rule for at least a few years."

Alsander began to smile. But before they could attack they heard a great cry and turned to see Belden, leaping at Oreas with his sword raised high. It was a great leap, made from a heroic distance, a feat of bravery that made two armies stare at him in wonder.

"Belden!" Hestion shouted, and launched himself over the statue.

"No, Hestion!" Reed scrambled after him. This wasn't the plan but she had no choice. Oreas had already absorbed the brunt of Belden's assault, and the two squared off.

"I thought you would have run," the king said.

"The Docritae do not run!" Belden cried, and around him it seemed that the men remembered. The fighting between the armies began anew, roaring and grunting and the clashing of swords. Reed heard a wild, ululating battle cry and knew that, somewhere, Sar the Ithernan still lived.

Belden jumped again, so high Reed didn't know how he'd done it; he must have leaped off a soldier's back. Oreas caught him in mid-leap, and Hestion sliced into the monster's forearm to break his brother free.

"Flank him," Belden ordered. They pivoted into position, and Reed slashed wildly with her sword. But Oreas's armor was strong, and he was surprisingly fast for his size. Every other blow was pushed wide.

"He killed your prince," she heard Alsander shout to the Rhonassan soldiers. "He killed your commander, Ostar! He killed his own son!" The crown prince of Cerille jumped and sank his blade deep into Oreas's shoulder. On a normal man the limb would have been shorn straight off. Oreas simply took the hit and shoved the sword back at Alsander with so much force that he almost dropped it.

This close to the king, Reed could see every grotesque, muscular bit, from his elongated arms to his massive legs, to the sandaled feet that had kicked Aster across a room. A clean hit from Oreas could break through bone. She didn't know how hard or how many times he'd had to strike Prince Ostar to kill him, but she imagined that it wasn't much.

"Alsander!" Reed cried. "Where is Lyonene?"

"I don't know!" They looked around wildly, and Reed caught a glimpse of her, a white cape passing through soldiers like smoke. She'd called her armor back, and Reed knew the precise moment that the skull of the prophet caught wind of her. King Oreas jerked upright like a wolf scenting a deer, the lower half of his face red with blood as if he'd bitten into Tiern with his teeth. He held the head of the prophet slightly aloft as Lyonene's white cape flickered behind the lines of the army, fast as a ghost and the perfect distraction.

"Now!" Reed screamed as the princes regrouped. Their assault came from all sides, cutting with swords and slicing with daggers. Oreas swatted Belden and knocked him to the ground; he kicked Alsander so hard that he flew into the battle and out of sight. Hestion covered his brother and Oreas reached for him—Reed's heart hammered in her ears as she cut hard with her sword, aiming for the unprotected flesh between his chest and shoulder. The king moved so fast that she barely felt the blow; the ground rose up to meet her, and the next thing she saw was Hestion, pulling her behind the cover of an overturned chariot.

"Reed."

"Is she all right?"

She opened her eyes. Belden crouched beside them, bloody but not badly injured.

Reed sat up and slipped her hand around the back of Hestion's head. He was safe. Her eyes widened. "Lyonene! She can't face him!"

"She's doing all right so far," said Belden, and she turned around.

Lyonene ducked and spun as Oreas leveled blows at her head. She fought like in a dance, all feints and sharpness, all calcula- tion, not with brute force like Aethiel or with careless disdain like Veridian.

"Lyonene! Get out of there!"

"Quiet, sister." Lyonene called, her green eyes burning. "You know I was always the better fighter." She flipped forward and slid beneath Oreas's sword arm. "Alsander! With me!"

Reed saw the jaws of the skull clack shut.

When the head of the prophet had cut through Aster's magic, it had simply left her dazed. But Lyonene was an initiate. She dropped immediately to the ground.

"Get to her, get to her!" Reed and Hestion and Belden raced from behind the chariot. They were going to be too late. "Lyonene!" Reed screamed, and on the ground, she saw Tiern roll.

"Get away from my initiates," the elder growled, and plunged a dagger into Oreas's foot.

Oreas roared and leaned back, and Alsander erupted through the crowd, leaping over Lyonene's body and colliding with the king. He wrapped himself around the arm that held the skull of the prophet and drove a knife into it over and over, until the king flung him away to land beside Lyonene in the dirt.

"Stupid boy," Oreas snarled, but his expression shifted from rage to fear as Alsander lifted the skull of the prophet clutched tightly in his hand.

"Alsander," Lyonene gasped, and he looked down at her. Then

he smashed the rotten head against the stones until it shattered into pieces.

The magic in Reed's blood filled to bursting. She saw the shine build upon Lyonene and Alsander until she thought she'd be blinded looking at them. "You've done it," she cried, laughing and exhausted. "You vain and gilded princeling!"

A rude thing to say, but Alsander and Lyonene didn't seem to mind. As the soldiers cheered, the shine of the goddess faded. It lasted only a moment. But all who saw it would remember.

Lyonene touched Alsander's chest. Reed wondered what it had felt like when her hero had joined her to Kleia Gloria so completely. She supposed she would never know.

Then she saw King Oreas rise up from where he had fallen.

"Look out!"

Lyonene grabbed Alsander and pulled, and Oreas's blade sparked off the gold-plated Cerillian armor instead of severing his neck.

"I thought you said it was the skull that gave him strength!" Lyonene screeched as she shoved away through the dirt.

"Am I expected to know everything?" Reed screeched back. Lyonene scowled at her as they hauled their allies back to cover. They met behind the overturned chariot and listened, wincing each time the monster bellowed.

Alsander breathed hard and spit blood upon the sand. Beside him, Hestion and Belden crouched, covered in dust.

"I've lost my sword," Belden said. "I've not even a dagger left." Reed looked at her own sword and tossed it away. Its blade had broken off somewhere, perhaps the other half still lodged in the king.

"He's just going to stroll over here and kill us," said Alsander.

"No," said Reed. "It's not the same now. Without the skull, the Aristene are back in play."

"I'll cover your shield side," Hestion said.

"No. Not you."

"You can't ask me to stay behind. Or if you do you can't expect that I'll obey."

Reed turned to him. "Listen to me. When we were in Atropa, I looked into the well. If you face Oreas you will die."

Hestion turned to Lyonene, to see if it was true, and Lyonene lowered her eyes.

"But your trial," he said.

"I know," she said, and shrugged like it meant nothing, like it didn't feel like she was about to cut her own throat. "So let me do this while I can. Let me be an Aristene one more time."

Hestion bent his head and nodded grimly.

"I must borrow your sword." Reed took it and rose to crouch on one knee beside her sister, watching the bulk of Oreas as he brandished his long daggers and waited for them.

"His weapons don't even bother me," Lyonene noted, watching the joints in his arm stretch and buckle in unnatural places as if he'd somehow grown more of them. "The weapons are the least of our problems. If he hasn't grown weaker—much weaker—even we are likely to die if we go charging in."

"You'll have to distract him, then," said Reed, and when Lyonene looked offended, added, "You've had your turn. And besides. I have a score to settle."

"Very well, Ox." Lyonene took a breath and prepared to charge left. Reed stood, and Hestion caught her hand.

"Reed." He looked at her. He couldn't seem to find his words. "Don't do anything foolish," he said, just as they heard Sar's war cry ring out across the battlefield.

"Who has time to be foolish when we have Sar?" Reed murmured, as the Ithernan came galloping toward the king, on the back of none other than Amondal.

"He's on an Areion," Lyonene said with wonder, and the Ithernan raised a long spear.

"That won't be enough." But she could help him. Reed readied herself for the charge and when Sar drew back to throw, she sprang out from behind the chariot. Sar was a better distraction than Lyonene would have been; he made so much noise when he fought, so many whoops and screams that it was like being assailed by a very large and lethal seagull. King Oreas spun away from the thrown weapon just as Reed's armor erupted through the aether. This time when their swords met, his didn't knock her down. To their mutual surprise, her arm held firm.

"You," he said to Reed, and showed his bloodstained teeth. "I see you still behind golden bars."

"Never again." She reared back to kick him in the gut and attacked. Her muscles were tight as she leaped and spun, her sword singing through the air, their blades meeting and the metal ringing so loudly that it hurt her ears. She felt no fatigue, no sluggishness as she lowered her shoulder and drove the monster back. It was one last time, one last taste of the magic and there was no better fight to have, no greater monster to vanquish than King Oreas.

Reed brought her sword down in a clean, graceful arc. In the space of a breath the king was coated in red from chest to toe. If he had still feared death, she might have won. He might have sunk to his knees and begged for mercy.

Instead, he let her sword bury itself to the bone and wrapped his enormous hand around her throat. He squeezed so tightly that despite the magic Reed's vision began to blacken, the pain in her neck so great that she feared her head would tear clean off. She dragged her blade free, grimacing, as her legs dangled weakly in the air.

"Reed!" Lyonene was there in an instant, but Oreas knocked her brutally away. Hestion and Belden and Alsander charged in her wake.

"Reed!" Hestion cried, and held out his hand. "Give me your sword!"

Reed heard the bones in her neck grind and begin to pop. With the last of her strength, she lifted her arm and threw her sword. But not to Hestion.

Reed threw her sword to Belden.

She saw the gold upon Belden's shoulders shine like the sun and felt the glory course through her like a second pulse. Before the eyes of the army Belden drove the sword deep into Oreas's chest and ascended into legend. And then the king drove his dagger through Belden's back.

"No!" Hestion screamed. Oreas fell dead but his final act had been lasting. Belden sank to the ground. "Belden!" Hestion caught him and pressed his hand against the blood.

"I had no choice," Reed whispered.

"But you did," Lyonene said. "And it's over now. And now we let them be."

Around them, the men of the Docritae dropped to one knee. Sar rode close on Amondal with tears streaked through the blue on his cheeks.

Hestion sat with Belden's body for a long time. Long after Tiern had been carried away, and after Aethiel had been roused and stumbled off after her. The Docritae placed Belden upon their shields to carry him back to the port. Reed and Lyonene and Alsander watched as they went, and though Reed said his name, Hestion walked right past her.

49.

THE NEW KINGS

The loss of Belden colored the victory with sadness. But it was still a victory, and in the port and throughout the city, soldiers celebrated. They drank to Belden's bravery and poured libations. They took what spoils they wished and cleaned the marketplaces of food. They set fires as men did who were angry and elated and full of sorrow. It was only when Oren emerged from the palace to claim his father's body that Alsander gave orders and set limits. The war was over—now came negotiations, and amends. Gifts of gold from Roshanak to Cerille. Gifts of ships and weaponry to Glaucia. And Alsander would remain in the capital for a time, and Roshanak would become an open port, to be shared between the allies.

Hestion should have been there to negotiate in Belden's stead. But since he had returned from the battle he had not left his brother's body.

Reed hid herself away, torn between fear of his anger and the desire to comfort him. But in the end her desire won out, and she went to find him inside Belden's villa.

They had wrapped the dead prince in linen. Attendants had washed his body and prepared it with oil for burning. He lay with his arms atop his chest, a silver dagger between his hands, the pale wrappings layered with herbs and the wildflowers of the Rhonassan mountains.

Hestion gave no indication that he heard her when she stepped quietly into the room. So she waited. And wished that Belden would rise. But there was no Aristene magic for returning the dead.

"I wondered when you would come," Hestion said. "I wondered if you would come at all."

"Of course I came. It was my fault. He died saving me."

"A pity," Hestion said. "A good, kind king is a poor trade for someone so deceitful as you. You've made my brother's death a waste."

It is always a waste, she wanted to say. *And I know what this pain is; I remember. But I will help you through it. I will be here, if you will let me.*

She looked upon Belden's face.

"This is not what I meant," she whispered.

"Do not lie." Hestion stood, the lines of his shoulders trembling and tense. "You had a choice. You chose him."

"Because I couldn't choose you."

"It was my fate."

"I didn't care. I don't care. Hestion, look at me."

He turned so she could see his profile, but that only made it worse. He wouldn't see what was in her eyes, and she could see the coldness in his.

"The elder told me what you are," he said softly. "The kind of Aristene you are. Of glorious death." His lip curled. "She told me she should kill me for what I'd cost them. I wanted to cut her throat. And I'm glad that you won't get what you want."

"What I want." Reed swallowed. Tears slipped from the corners of her eyes and she hated them. She hated herself. She even hated him, a little, for his rage and his lack of understanding. "I suppose it should have been me."

"I wish it had been you," he shouted. "My brother died because of you!"

"Your brother died in war!" Reed shouted back. "He died a hero—"

"If you speak to me of heroes—" Hestion spun toward her and raised his hand in a fist. "If you ever speak to me of heroes again," he said, but he lowered his fist to his side.

"I gave up everything for you," Reed whispered. "What you said to me in the hills . . ."

"What I said to you in the hills means nothing!" Hestion turned back to his brother and pressed his fists to the table he lay upon. "You have taken my brother from us. So I am a king. You have put a crown on my head after all."

She took a step toward him, and he stiffened.

"I loved you, Reed. I loved you, and now I would burn you on my brother's pyre. So go. Fall through the shadows into your white city. I never want to look upon you again."

Reed gritted her teeth. She swallowed the words she might have shouted, that she couldn't return to the white city, that she had nowhere to go. Instead she turned and walked away.

When she reached the door, she saw his head turn a fraction.

"I love you, Hestion," she said quietly. "I have loved you for as long as I have loved the Aristene."

"But not enough," he said, and this time when he turned, she knew he wouldn't turn back again.

Reed strode out of the villa with straight shoulders all the way to the stable to fetch the little roan mare. She rode fast and didn't stop until she was away from Roshanak in the hills where she had hunted. Then she fell against the horse's neck and wept.

That is where Lyonene found her, hours later, seated beside the mare's hooves before a small fire that she prodded with the end of her sword.

"There you are, Ox. Still dressed in your bloodied clothes of war." Lyonene had changed into a fine gown dyed the vibrant blue of Cerille and edged in gold thread. Even at a distance, Reed could smell the perfumed oil she had touched to her temples and wrists.

"Have you brought me something to eat?" Reed asked.

"I thought you would have hunted for your own, by now," said Lyonene. But she held up a small parcel. She tossed it to Reed and Reed opened it to find roasted meat and fresh berries. A wedge of cheese.

"Thank you." She stuffed her mouth full, and as Lyonene watched she snapped. "Stop looking at me like that. And if you're going to gloat about passing your Hero's Trial, you can do it somewhere else."

"We saved each other's lives today," Lyonene said, "and you think I've come to gloat."

"Then why did you come?"

She looked at Lyonene's lovely face, and Lyonene smiled sadly.

"Because you're my sister," she said, and shrugged.

"But I'm not," Reed said, around a mouthful of berries. "Not anymore."

"I don't understand. Why did you do it, Reed? For him? For one mortal hero?"

"I didn't do it only for him," Reed said. "I did it for myself. Because I didn't like the price." *Of glorious death.* Yet it had cost her anyway. And even now she was beginning to forget why she had resisted in the first place. Having lost everything, such a calling no longer seemed like so much to pay. She eyed Lyonene with envy, her beautiful face, her shiny tawny hair. Lyonene, who would be a full member of the order.

"What's done is done," Reed said, and threw the scrap of cloth from her food into the fire. "Where do you go, now?"

"To Atropa." She looked at Reed gravely and nodded in the direction of the port. "They won't burn Belden here. They are taking him home, to be burnt on a pyre by his father. Alsander will sail there also, to pay his respects."

"But not you?"

Lyonene shook her head. "My time with Alsander is over. But even if it weren't, Hestion has forbade the presence of any of the Aristene." Her eyes swiveled to Reed. "He will never forgive you."

"But he will live. And that is enough."

"That is enough," Lyonene repeated, like she thought it was anything but. She walked to the roan mare and picked up the strands of her mane that Reed had cried into. "You have made a mess of her."

"She doesn't mind. That mare is made for sorrow."

"Is she? She does not look so to me." She stroked the mare's nose and looked into her dark eyes. "May I have her?"

"Have her?"

"I have to choose a horse to become my Areion, don't I?"

The roan mare shook her head, her coat pretty in the firelight.

Though she was of the legendary herd, she was not fine enough for Lyonene. Not tall enough, not swift enough. But she was good, and true. She was brave.

"I thought you would make your choice from the Aristene herd," Reed said.

"I meant to. But I like it better to choose one who was here. Who was here with us, during the trial. I suppose you think that's silly."

"Not silly," said Reed. "Only surprisingly sentimental."

"I will return and find you, Ox," Lyonene said as she led the mare away. "Or Aster will."

Aster, Reed thought, and closed her eyes. Aster would know, by now.

"What for?" she heard herself ask.

"Someone will have to return Silco to you," Lyonene replied. Then she faced into the shadows and whispered. The Veil yawned open and Lyonene looked back at Reed one last time before she and the roan mare walked into it and disappeared.

50.
GLORIA THEA MATRIS

Reed departed from Roshanak not long after the armies sailed for home. She hid in the port and watched as they loaded their spoils, and as Hestion loaded Belden's body onto his flagship. She didn't think he looked for her. Of all the Docritae, only Sar seemed to be searching when his eyes, darkened with charcoal in mourning, swept across the beach and up toward the villas.

Reed left the city with a pack of meager supplies and a mule, purchased in trade for one of her daggers. She said no goodbyes, but she did stop by the palace to look in on Oren.

Little King Oren. When he saw her he smiled wanly, and waved his attendants away so they could have a moment to themselves, out on the fine open balcony of the throne room.

"You are leaving," he said with a glance at her pack.

"And you are a king," she said.

Oren shrugged. "I never meant to be one."

"Yes," Reed said. "That is going around."

They stood together with their elbows on the railing, looking over the mess of the city. The jewel of Roshanak, the stronghold of Rhonassus. Walls had toppled and drawbridges had been broken. Treasures from its storerooms had left on ships, and the chins of its people dipped in defeat. But it was still Roshanak. And it had a Rhonassan ruler. In time, it would rise again.

"I had my father's body thrown into the deepest tunnel to rot," said Oren. "The priests say it will anger the gods, but what more can the gods do? I would not have him entombed beside Ostar. He would not have that honor, to rest forever beside the son he murdered."

"It was a good decision," said Reed. "The gods won't punish you for the likes of him."

Oren grinned.

"Are you a priest now as well as a soldier?"

"Perhaps not." She snorted. "I suppose my words are not worth much."

"They have been worth something to me." The boy king turned. "You will always be welcome here, Reed. And you know that you could stay."

She had nowhere else to go. No home to return to. But she couldn't stay.

"Will you be all right?" she asked. "Ruling with Alsander at your back?"

"He seems fair," said Oren. "I think he will be fair."

"I think he will be, too. He has come a long way, from princeling to young king."

"But he will not stop at young king. He will not stop until he is the half-king of Roshanak and the High King of Cerille. I am only days into my crown and already I know that much."

Days into his crown but already savvy. Reed smiled.

"You'll be all right."

"And so will you be." He cocked his head. "Now that you are

no longer an Aristene, perhaps you can go and learn to be a proper woman." She raised her hand to slap him and he laughed.

"Goodbye, King Oren," she said. "I will return some day. To beat you."

Before she left, she turned.

"What became of the skull of the Scylloi Prophet?"

"We sent priests to collect the broken pieces so they could be laid to rest beside the body," Oren replied. "But we could not find it all. There were portions missing. Fragments. The jawbone." He looked at her, his eyes troubled, and she felt a shiver run down her back.

"I'm sure they were just lost in the fighting," she said. "Or taken for a souvenir by some eager and impious soldier."

He pressed his lips together. "Yes. I am sure you are right."

Reed left the palace, departing the city on the same road she and Hestion had taken into it. She didn't know where she was going. She supposed she would make her way back to Lacos and wait for Lyonene to find her with Silco. From there she could find work or catch a ship to almost anywhere. Perhaps to Gretchen, in Centra. Or to chase Veridian and serve as an apprentice to an apostate, if such a thing existed.

At night she camped beside a small fire and fell asleep, listening to the mule chew grass and trying not to think of Hestion. She tried not to think of his father, King Arik, and his tough aunt Morna, and how they would suffer when they learned that Belden was dead. She tried not to think of Aster, or of Lyonene and her Joining Ceremony. And then, one night, Lyonene appeared.

She stepped out of the Veil and surprised Reed so completely that she nearly rolled into the embers of her fire.

"What are you doing here?" Reed asked after she had finished clapping out the small flames on her tunic. "Where is my horse?" She peered into the darkness, but had Silco been there she would have known; he would have raced out of the night to bite her.

"Such a greeting for your oldest friend," Lyonene chided. "Do you not have anything else to say?" She stood before Reed and held out her arms. She stood in the silver armor and white cape. Reed had seen her in them many times, but this time was different. Now they were no longer borrowed. They were hers.

"Did you get taller?" Reed asked, only a little bitterly.

"Maybe. I will tell you that passage through the Veil is much easier now. So come along." She extended her hand.

"Come along where?"

"To the only place the Veil will take you from this direction," Lyonene replied as though Reed was stupid. "To Atropa."

"Why would I go to Atropa?" Reed asked. "I'm not an initiate anymore. I'm not subject to Aristene justice. Tell Tiern and Ferreh to . . . to . . ." She sighed.

"Tell them yourself. They still want you, Reed."

Reed said nothing. She thought she had misheard.

"It is like I've always said: you are the favorite."

"The favorite. Because of what I could bring to them. The death and glory that I brought to them."

"Belden's death was glorious. The strength in his charge, the thoughtless sacrifice . . . the songs that the men sing of him are honey in our ears. They reach us, all the way in the white city."

"But Belden was not my hero."

Lyonene shrugged. "Rules bent and rules broken." She smiled at

Reed, that pretty, beguiling smile. "Now, are you coming or not?"

For a moment Reed just gaped at her.

"What about my mule?" Reed looked back at it blinking at them quietly, and Lyonene made a noise between a laugh and a groan.

"Bring it with us. Good goddess, Ox. *Your mule.* I come to say you are to be welcomed into the order that you have dreamed of joining since you were a child, and you are worried about your mule. We don't even know this mule; I have never seen it before!" She whirled her fingertip, whispering into the Veil.

Reed shrugged. "He's a good mule," she said, and took him by the rope to lead him into the darkness.

The way through the Veil was perhaps easier for Lyonene, but it was no easier for Reed: she emerged into the morning of Atropa with her tunic stained from sweat and had three times nearly let her mule's rope slide through her fingers. She took a deep breath. Even though she was no longer an initiate, the invigoration of the white city remained. The magic that soothed her shaking muscles from the horror of the Veil still felt like it was hers. The city of the Aristene still felt like home.

Beside them on the hill, a horse whickered, and Reed was surprised to see the little roan mare. She didn't seem so little anymore, with the silver on her bridle and a band of silver and leather across her chest. She nickered to Lyonene, and to Reed, who she remembered. She pushed her head into Reed and looked her in the eye.

"She looks like stars and strawberries," Reed whispered, and Lyonene laughed.

"Strawberry. Good. I have been searching for a name for her.

Bloodfire seemed too grand—" The mare snorted, like she was offended. "But the only other thing that seemed to stick was 'Roan Joan.'"

Reed gave Lyonene a look.

"You're not going to name your Areion 'Roan Joan.'"

"Indeed I'm not. Strawberry it is." Lyonene nodded to the mule, who had happily discovered the Atropan grass. "Can you ride that thing?"

They mounted, Lyonene on her Areion and Reed saddleless behind her mule's packs. They rode down from the hills and through the quiet streets, making their way to the square before the gold-capped Citadel.

"I will never tire of seeing the Citadel rise like the sun," Lyonene said happily, and Reed bit her tongue. The Citadel lay to the west, so more truly it set like the sun. And it was easy for Lyonene to say that now—but even Ferreh painted and repainted her bedchamber just to have something new to look at.

Reed kept her eyes away from the gold cap. The greatness of the dome, the height of the white walls.

"Why are you so surly?" Lyonene asked. "I thought you would be happy. I'm happy—even though you cheated and needed the elders to intervene. This is what you've always wanted." Lyonene smiled at her, cautiously. "Isn't it, Reed? This is what we've worked for."

What they had worked for. And all she'd ever wanted.

"It's Hestion, isn't it," Lyonene said. "But that is over. He cared for you, but it was never going to last. It was never going to be this—" She gestured to the dome, to the mountains and the sea.

Reed looked at her friend. Lyonene's pretty face was troubled, and her fingers worked absently into the roan mare's mane. She seemed so innocent suddenly, and when had that happened? She had always been the first and the fastest, the first to love a boy, the first to fight. She'd seen more of the world and had always seemed the oldest and the wisest. But not anymore.

"It's not only Hestion." Reed smiled with closed lips. "It's the mucking of your stall. I won't do it, Lyonene—I refuse."

Lyonene laughed with relief. "You can't refuse. You agreed, and I won." She smiled impishly. "What luck that I chose Strawberry, so you'll be cleaning up after a horse that you know."

"Because knowing her is better?"

They laughed until they reached the steps of the Citadel and dismounted as acolytes came forward to claim their reins. When she handed the mule to them, Reed had a sense that she was giving him up, but that wasn't so bad; in Atropa the mule would have a life of ease. He would never be asked to carry too much. He would never be asked to hurry.

"Let's go," said Lyonene. "They're waiting."

Reed followed Lyonene up the steps. When she had come to the Citadel for the first time, all those years ago, she had tugged nervously on the edge of her dirty tunic. Now she wished she was wearing the clothes she had worn into that last battle, marked with Belden's blood.

At the top of the stairs, Aster and Veridian waited, heads bent close together and clasping each other's wrists; when they saw Reed Aster slid free and rushed to her.

"Foundling." She kissed the top of Reed's head. She wrapped her arms around her tightly and Reed clung to her mentor like she had since the moment they met.

"You're better," Reed said into her shoulder. "You're healed."

"Forgive me, Reed. I didn't know what we were sending you into. I didn't know anything."

"I know."

"All right, Aster, let her breathe." Veridian tapped their arms, and they drew apart. But even the apostate's eyes had a shine to them, though happy tears or sad, it was impossible to tell.

"What am I doing here?" Reed asked. "Lyonene says the elders wish to receive me into the order. But that can't be right." She smiled lopsidedly. "I thought they might be luring me back to kill me."

"Let them try," said Veridian. "We'll fight our way out. Then it will be the three of us on the run, or perhaps four—" She glanced at Lyonene. "And I can't think of anything better."

"You think we could war against the elders and win?"

"I don't know. But more important, neither do they."

An acolyte appeared in the hall, and Aster placed a hand on Reed's shoulder. "It's time. I'll go with you."

"We'll wait here." Veridian stepped beside Lyonene. "Unless we hear you scream."

"Don't mess this up, Ox," Lyonene called.

"Don't boss me around," Reed said back, and heard Lyonene chuckle.

Aster led her not to the dome but to another room on the lower floor, meant less for ceremony than for lounging. The elders awaited them inside—Tiern seated before the game board of black and white stones, a black stone in her fingers, and Ferreh at the cut window with her hand on the sill, feeding bread crumbs to a bird.

"A quaint scene," Reed said as they entered.

Tiern set down the game piece and stood to greet them, or to greet them as much as she ever did, by walking toward them a few paces and crossing her arms.

"You look much better than the last time I saw you," said Reed. "What about Aethiel? Is she all right?"

"Of course," Tiern replied. "Recovered and already gone, searching for her next hero upon a ship." But Reed noted that the elder wasn't completely healed: she wore a soft gown of white and gold and black instead of her silver armor.

"What am I doing here, Ferreh?"

"You are here, child, to make the same choice as the night you first came." Ferreh moved from the window. "To go, or to stay. The same choice again, with Aster to keep you or Veridian to take you away."

"You barely tolerate one apostate. Now you'd allow two?"

"You wouldn't be an apostate," said Tiern. "You would be nothing. You'd be an apostate's groom."

Reed couldn't argue with that. Already the borrowed magic faded in her blood. Each day she woke and felt less. She couldn't even call up her armor anymore.

"Why do I get to make the choice?" Reed asked. "I failed my Hero's Trial."

"You know why," Ferreh said.

"Of glorious death," said Reed.

"And you didn't fail. Not completely."

Reed's brow furrowed, and Ferreh came closer, her long-fingered brown hands folded elegantly before her.

"You saw a hero and delivered him. Glorious death."

Reed opened her mouth to say, *I didn't mean to*, but the words died in her throat. That wasn't true. She knew. It would be one or the other of them, and she chose Belden.

"He was not the right one, perhaps, but Belden's legend spreads. Young men gather around fires in the countryside to hear his story, and to hope that they may grow to be as brave as he was."

"More to the slaughter," Reed said.

"Not all heroes, die, Reed," Aster said softly. "Some are saved, through our aid. Some families, some cities, are spared through our protection."

"And we are not the ones who kill them," said Ferreh. "They know the costs and they accept them, for such a good death."

"I don't judge the order," Reed said. "I only weigh my role within it. Not all heroes die. Only all of mine."

"It is hard," Ferreh began, but Tiern walked back to the game board and flipped it from the table, sending the board and the stones clattering to the floor.

"What are we trying to cajole her for? She knows what she will do." The elder stood tall, fearsome even without armor or weaponry. "She wants to be this. She wants to be strong. Strong enough to keep those she loves safe, and strong enough to prevent anyone from ever again taking them away." Tiern walked to her, and Reed flinched when she reached out to touch her hair with surprising gentleness. "And she is ambitious. To gain this strength she will do many things. What she has to do. Even if that means humiliating her dearest friend or betraying a boy who offered her the world.

"Ferreh was right to choose you." She placed her hands on

Reed's shoulders. "I see that now. So stop fighting, my fierce girl. And come home."

"You don't have to do this, Reed," Aster said, still beside her. "Whatever you choose, you will not lose me. Or Veridian. Or Lyonene. We would be with you, wherever you would go."

Reed looked at Ferreh. At Aster and Tiern, and past them to the white city of Atropa, the home and the order she had set herself for like an arrow into a bow. So many steps she had taken and none of them easy. And none would she trade.

Except for Hestion, she thought. *Except for that.*

But Lyonene was right. That was over.

"Of glorious death," Reed said. "It must be very valuable."

Ferreh smiled, and Tiern laughed aloud before holding out her palm.

"Very well, foundling," she said. "What more would you have of us?"

"I want my horse."

"An Areion. Of course. You will have the finest—"

"No. Not the finest. Mine. I want Silco."

"Silco," Tiern said. "Silco cannot be an Areion. He will always be lame." She looked at Aster. "Tell her."

"Just because he's lost the full use of one foot doesn't make him unworthy," Reed said. "You will have us both, or you will have neither."

The elders looked at each other, and Ferreh nodded.

"Very well. We will have Silco brought to the chamber."

The chamber where the Joining was performed was not in the Citadel. It was in the mountains, in a cave that lay at the end of a softly winding trail. Lyonene escorted her there as Reed led Silco slowly up the path. She saw her glance at every uneven step the black colt took, but she said nothing. Her only criticism was for Reed's dirty clothes.

"You were supposed to be ceremonially washed," Lyonene said.

"I remember that ceremonial washing," Reed said. The harsh scrubbing that had pulled out fistfuls of her hair and turned even her tan skin a shade of deep pink. "No thank you."

"So you will go before the goddess looking like a vagabond."

"I let them anoint my hands with oil," said Reed. "Here, smell."

Lyonene swatted her away with a laugh. "You have changed, Reed. I used to think you would serve the order and the goddess with so much piety you would be boring. Now I don't know what kind of Aristene you will be." She looked ahead, up the path, where the dark mouth of the cave lay open. "But maybe that's fitting. After all, when you emerge from the chamber, you will be changed again. You will have your magic and a new life. A new name."

"A new name," Reed mused. "But you didn't get a new name."

"That's because Lyonene is already a name for a warrior. There cannot be an 'Aristene Reed.' Perhaps Kleia Gloria would have even given a new one to Gretchen."

"'Aristene Gretchen' doesn't sound so bad to me."

"If only it had sounded better to her," Lyonene said, and sighed. "But your name won't matter to me anyway. To me, you will always be Ox." She looked at Silco and scratched his neck. "And he will always be stubborn as a mule. You will be the Ox and the Mule of the order."

Reed snorted. "You're happy."

"I am. And I wish that you were."

"I will be. It will just take time."

"Well, time we have," Lyonene said as they slowed the horses. "After you emerge from in there, time is nothing."

They reached the end of the path and stopped before the opening of the cave chamber. There were no attendants. No Aster. Only lit torches, and from inside the scents of minerals and water and oils that smelled like roses.

"After all the ritual around the Granting Ceremony, I expected to find a table with golden chalices and jeweled daggers. Acolytes swinging censers of smoke, and maybe Tiern to bite my neck."

"Hmpf," said Lyonene. "If any elder had come to bite your neck, you know it would've been Ferreh. You are ever her favorite." She nodded into the darkness.

"Everything you need you already have," she said. "This we must do alone. And there will be plenty of ritual and celebration when you rejoin us at the Citadel."

Reed turned to her friend. She reached out and gently tugged down the edge of Lyonene's armor, down just low enough to see the tip of Lyonene's new, silvery pink scar.

"Have they told me true?" Reed asked. "Or is this their punishment for disobedience? Will I drive my sword into my chest and never wake?"

"I think," Lyonene said, "that is a question that every Aristene has asked inside this chamber."

Reed turned and took Silco by the rope. Stepping into the darkness of the cave couldn't be any more terrifying than stepping into the Veil. She squared her shoulders.

"Reed, wait!"

"What?" she asked, jumping back.

"Here." Lyonene tossed her something through the air and Reed caught it. "Your silver bracelet," she said. The one that had belonged to Lyonene's mother. The one they had wagered for as they waited beside the Outfitter's chamber. "But I lost."

"I wanted you to have it anyway." Lyonene shrugged. "I love you, Reed. And it will look nice on your wrist when you're shoveling Strawberry's manure." She grinned and lifted her chin. "Go on."

"An eternity with you," Reed called over her shoulder as she slipped the bracelet on. "I am making a mistake!"

She smiled in the dark. The last thing she heard as she stepped into the chamber was Lyonene's soft laughter.

The mouth of the cave was long, but inside the blackness wasn't total. As her eyes adjusted it was easy enough to see the rocky ground and follow the glow from the torches. As the light grew stronger, she saw faded images both carved and painted, images of hunts and heroes, of Aristene and Areion. And somewhere inside, she knew she would again face the eyes of Kleia Gloria.

She stepped into the belly of the cave and listened to the last echoes of Silco's hoofbeats.

There was nothing inside. No grand altar or fine cloth drape. No gilded throne to bow before. Only the stone and the torches. And the sword, lying on the ground.

This was it. The place where everything ended, and everything began.

Reed ran her hand down Silco's shoulder, and his bent leg that favored his broken hoof. It seemed another lifetime ago that she'd looked down at it and seen Hestion there, kneeling in the sand, trying to save him. It seemed like a long time since he'd looked up at her and told her it would be all right.

"I shouldn't do this with those thoughts in my head," she said to the horse. "Lest Kleia Gloria hear them and decide I'm better off dead."

She hadn't thought she would come to the order with a broken heart. But perhaps that would make it easier.

From the corridor came the sound of grinding as Lyonene rolled the heavy slab of rock across the opening, trapping Reed and Silco inside. If they didn't emerge from the cave, perhaps she would open it again in a day or two. But the implication was clear: no mortal had the strength to roll the stone on their own. Within the chamber one ascended to the order or within the chamber one would stay.

Silco sniffed the air and snorted; he pawed the ground with his bad hoof.

Reed looked into her black colt's eyes. He'd not been a colt for a very long time. But that was always how she would think of him.

Reed picked up the sword from the ground, and let her eyes wander the walls until she found the gaze of the goddess, flickering with torchlight.

"Are you ready, Silco?" she asked.

She turned the point of the blade to her chest and plunged it through her heart.

Epilogue
THE ARISTENE

The Aristene and the black horse looked down upon the city of Atropa for one last time. The days of celebrations were over. Veridian was already gone, disappeared through the Veil the moment that Reed and Silco had emerged from the cave chamber. Reed had spent time with Aster and with Lyonene. She had not yet gotten used to being called by her new name.

"Machianthe," she said out loud, and Silco snorted. "What? It is a good name." Good but not yet hers. She was still Reed, inside. Reed and Ox, and farther away, the name given to her by her parents that she had long forgotten. She and Silco had come to the hills to open the Veil. To learn what her unique Aristene magic could do.

The elders had wanted her to find her next hero right away, but not even Tiern could argue when Reed said there was plenty of time. For now, Reed just wanted to wander.

Aster had laughed at that. She said that Reed was becoming more and more like Veridian.

"There's plenty of time for heroes," Reed said to the Areion, and her mind turned for a moment to one hero in particular, who was perhaps a king now and ruling in a country where she was no longer welcome. For just a moment, she thought she felt something. A tug, as from a golden thread, tied to her heart. Perhaps he was thinking of her, too. Or perhaps he could feel it when she did and the tug was him again turning away. Or perhaps it was nothing, and the link between them remained only in her mind.

After a moment, Silco dipped his head and bit her in the arm.

"Ow!" She rubbed the bite mark. "It's a good thing being an Areion hasn't taught you any manners." But had it taught him how to talk?

"You know, not even Amondal will speak to Ferreh. If you were to speak to me, it would make you technically the greater." She studied him from the corner of her eye, and Silco eyed her right back. She sighed and turned, casting her fingers in a slow circle and opening the Veil. "Where should we go? Tell me and we will go wherever you want. Or I can take us to somewhere very unpleasant. With hardly any grass." She jangled his reins as the passage yawned open. "Silco, say something. I know you want to."

The horse turned to look at her. His lips quivered. What would his voice be like? Would he speak and speak and never stop so she wished she had never asked to begin with?

Silco showed her his front teeth. Then he bit her and darted into the void, pulling Reed into the darkness beside him.

Acknowledgments

It's not my intention to turn these acknowledgments into an Afterword, but if you'll indulge me, a quick note on the dedication. I've never dedicated a book to anyone before, except for one time when a jokester at a school visit asked me to, but here we are with *Champion of Fate* and a dedication to not one but two individuals. Mia Togle and my horse, Lassie. Let's address Mia first.

At some point during the hell year that was 2020, I received a message from someone I didn't know. I think it might have even been filtered into a spam folder, and I found it just by luck. This person had been a close friend of Mia Togle's and took the time to write to me to let me know about Mia's passing. She informed me that Mia had been fighting a chronic illness, and the complications from the pandemic—the delays and limited access to previously routine treatments—had resulted in setbacks. And Mia passed away. The person who wrote me told me that she'd reached out because I was Mia's favorite author and because Mia had forced her and many of their friends to read my books. She said that once, very early in my career, Mia and I had exchanged a few emails. She doubted if I remembered that, but she wanted to tell me about Mia because she thought Mia would have wanted me to know.

I did remember Mia; actually, I'd saved her emails. I have them to this day, along with some of her artwork, squirreled away in a folder I'd labeled "Sentimental Saved Mail." It came as an unexpected blow, the loss of this person whom I'd never met, and with whom I hadn't corresponded in close to a decade. Rereading her emails, I became reacquainted with a kind, bubbly soul, a voracious reader, and I realized that the Mia who'd written to me had still been in high school. She was so young. In 2020, she was still so young. Far too young to be gone.

So I created Mia the Aristene—a healer and a warrior who would ride in the hills of Atropa forever. It was a small thing. It was all I could do. I could name a character, and I could remember.

Later that year, my horse Lassie also passed away, but much less sadly. My Lassie girl was old. I'd had her since she was born, and she couldn't have asked for a better life. Silco is very much like her. And though some readers will say it was unrealistic when Silco hurt his foot and held it up to Reed for her to look at, I can swear to you that Lassie did the same thing when she got into a fight with another horse and kicked a fence post. She held up her foot and screamed, "Mom! Come look at my foot!" I have witnesses.

I'd already been writing Silco when Lassie died. I hadn't figured on dedicating the book to her, but I figured she'd be pissed if I didn't and return to bite me from beyond the horse grave.

So that's it. A note on the dedications. Apologies, I guess it wasn't that quick.

On to the real acknowledgments: Alexandra Cooper, my goodness you are the loveliest editor around! Brilliant, kind, a cool person, a cheerleader, and a champion. Also, I just enjoy chatting with you, but you're very busy and I don't want to take up much of your time.

Adriann Zurhellen is the best agent. I don't know what I would do without you, where my career would be, but I'm pretty sure it would be a big old mess. If any aspiring author is out there wondering if you should sign with Adriann, let these acknowledgments serve as a blanket yes.

Thank you to the entire team at Quill Tree: Rosemary Brosnan, Jon Howard, Michael D'Angelo in marketing (do you guys know Michael? Because you should, he's talented and a delight and a STAR), Lisa Calcasola (also a marketing magic-maker), Katie Boni in publicity (a thousand thank-yous and high fives, Katie!), Allison Weintraub (who is an incredible assistant editor and a consistently awesome person), David Curtis in design and the artist Tomasz Majewski (I have heard nothing but raves about this cover, holy cats), Patty Rosati, Mimi Rankin, and the rest of the amazing school and library marketing team! Thank you for all the love you show to students and librarians. I know those librarians can get a little wild, haha 😊. Also, shout-out to teachers and librarians for that wildness. Thank you to Robin Roy for another meticulous (and patient) copy edit, and thank you to so many other people who I know are working magic but who I rarely get to meet: sales reps! How are you all doing?

Thank you also to the lovely publicity team at BookSparks: Crystal Patriarche, Hanna Lindsley, and Rylee Warner. You are excellent.

Thank you to the usual suspects of Seattle/Tacoma writers, who keep me in good spirits and on track with their camaraderie: Marissa Meyer, Lish McBride, Arnée Flores, Tara Goedjen, Nova McBee, Rori Shay, Margaret Owen, Martha Brockenbrough, and Allison Kimble. Our numbers continue to grow; if you're not here, I'll tag you next time.

And thank you to my personal circle for not minding when I'm totally losing it: Susan Murray, Ryan VanderVenter, and my children: Tyrion Cattister, Agent Scully, and Armpit McGee, with an honorable mention for my mom's dog, Gracie Lou Freebush, and our new stray-cat-who-adopted-us, Tom Bezos-Daytona. Thanks also to my dad, for constant support, and my mom, who I lost not long before this book was finished but was certain it was good without having to read it. Miss you, Mom. I'll dedicate one of the next ones to you—don't come back and bite me from beyond the mom grave.

And thanks to Dylan Zoerb, for luck.